ADVANCE PRAISE FOR
PIERCING THE VEIL

I fought with the Soviet Army against the Afghans and their supporters during the 1980s as a member of Spetznaz and vowed that I would seek an alternate path when I returned to the mother land. Your book is a painful reminder that both paths have their perils.

—FATHER DIMITRI DOMOTROV,
PATRIARCHATE OF MOSCOW

I found more truths and insights in Wentz' book about the personalities that create problems and solutions in the world than in all the factoids posing as journalism.

—RALPH D. (USN, RETIRED)

Wentz is at once funny, satiric, challenging, frightening and highly entertaining. His book is also beautifully written. It is a most unusual blend of politics, history, romance, and even anthropology.

The imagery of Wentz' style combines with nuanced and layered story telling in ways that I found compelling. I was riveted from the very beginning. He poses questions that compel answers even when we must grope in the dark for them.

—CHRISTINA WU, ANALYST, (DEPT. OF STATE, RETIRED)

This is a most captivating adventure story. It is as much an exaltation of the ancestors of humanity who compelled us to strive for greater purpose in our lives as it is about dangers of ignoring the evils of society. Wentz lifts the veil on forgotten stories, forgotten legacies, and forgotten perils. He demonstrates that the past is a constant presence that prods the good to do their duty.

—TOMAS DARIUS, FORMERLY OF BRITISH CONSULATE, DUBAI

Wentz' book should make certain people feel uncomfortable while making the rest of us glad we are not one of his targets.

Wentz takes his pen, dips it in poison, and stabs with it repeatedly. As a retired soldier and author of several books myself, I am reminded that some people construe sharp pens for the pointy end of a spear. Lord have mercy!

—ANONYMOUS

The breadth of knowledge in a variety of fields that it took to write this book is staggering. Wentz is obviously an experienced professional, quite possibly, in several fields.

Sparkling, funny, and exquisitely entertaining. This is a great book for those who enjoy intrigue and the beauty of the written word.

This is a book for people who like to read.

—M. HAGUE, DEPT. OF ENGLISH, AMERICAN UNIVERSITY

PIERCING THE VEIL

A NOVEL BY

ERIC WENTZ

iUniverse, Inc.
New York Bloomington

Jordan —

Your insights & your everyday expression of what can only be a genuine love of literature is well appreciated. You will be missed!

Eric J. Wentz

May 19, 2009

iUniverse books may be ordered through booksellers or by contacting:

iUniverse
1663 Liberty Drive
Bloomington, IN 47403
www.iuniverse.com
1-800-Authors (1-800-288-4677)

Because of the dynamic nature of the Internet, any Web addresses or links contained in this book may have changed since publication and may no longer be valid. The views expressed in this work are solely those of the author and do not necessarily reflect the views of the publisher, and the publisher hereby disclaims any responsibility for them.

ISBN: 978-0-595-53238-4 (sc)
ISBN: 978-1-4401-2905-6 (dj)
ISBN: 978-0-595-63301-2 (ebook)

Library of Congress Control Number: 2009925856

Printed in the United States of America

iUniverse rev. date: 04/09/2009

To my wife, by whom I am blessed,
To my children, by whom I am remembered, and
To my parents, by whom I am.

A narrarvi quella verro, la quale udita, forse piu caute diverrete nelle risposte all quistioni che fatte vi fossero.

—Boccaccio, *The Decameron*

Now, I shall tell you this story, and when you have heard it, perhaps you will become more cautious when you reply to questions put to you.

CONTENTS

PROLOGUE
Through a Glass Darkly 1

CHAPTER 1
The Killing Games 5

CHAPTER 2
Tight Lips and Banter...15

CHAPTER 3
The Voice of Diamonds..20

CHAPTER 4
Broken Vows 33

CHAPTER 5
Thrilling the Messenger 41

CHAPTER 6
A Shared Mystique 48

CHAPTER 7
Godless and Silent 53

CHAPTER 8
The Vanity of Human Wishes...58

CHAPTER 9
Mind the Gap 65

CHAPTER 10
A Gathering...72

CHAPTER 11
Military Bearings 80

CHAPTER 12
Ozification 82

CHAPTER 13
Guns..91

CHAPTER 14
Ancient Lore..99

CHAPTER 15
Speeding to Spean Bridge..105

CHAPTER 16
Diggers and Stuff..112

CHAPTER 17
Mothers and Mayhem...120

CHAPTER 18
A Night at the Castle..133

CHAPTER 19
The Listeners...140

CHAPTER 20
Crying Wolf...149

CHAPTER 21
A Live Grenade...159

CHAPTER 22
Rifting toward Bethlehem..163

CHAPTER 23
Loch Maree's Guest..175

CHAPTER 24
Survivor's Guilt...187

CHAPTER 25
Nothing is Sacred...190

CHAPTER 26
Knossos Revisited...197

CHAPTER 27
Gratitude..209

CHAPTER 28
Unleashed...213

CHAPTER 29
Chatter 215

CHAPTER 30
Of Blood Lines and Nordic Knights.................................223

CHAPTER 31
With Friends like These 234

CHAPTER 32
The Stuff of Dreams...237

CHAPTER 33
Preparations...242

CHAPTER 34
Shaking Hands..250

CHAPTER 35
Wedding Gifts 254

CHAPTER 36
The Scolding and the Blessing 268

CHAPTER 37
The Path Less Travelled 271

CHAPTER 38
Abduction 274

CHAPTER 39
Uninvited Visitors 281

CHAPTER 40
Dutch Treat..291

CHAPTER 41
Sirens and Shoals 296

CHAPTER 42
Wheels Within Wheels 299

CHAPTER 43
The Lion's Den 304

CHAPTER 44
Confession..308

CHAPTER 45
The Sins of the Father...313

CHAPTER 46
The Mortal Remains 317

CHAPTER 47
Shadows and Riddles 333

CHAPTER 48
Anagnorisis 344

CHAPTER 49
A Doubting Thomas..360

CHAPTER 50
The Induction...362

CHAPTER 51
Riddling Rhyme..370

EPILOGUE
Archival Dust and Smokes..376

PIERCING THE VEIL

PROLOGUE
THROUGH A GLASS DARKLY

How will the Future reckon with this man?
How answer his brute question?

—Edwin Markham, "The Man with the Hoe"

Earth could not answer.

—Edward Fitzgerald, "The Rubaiyat"

—*SCOTLAND, THE HIGHLANDS, 1941*

LIKE THE TEETH OF SOME GREAT MYTHOLOGICAL BEAST, THE SHARP peaks of the hills and mountains bit into the morning sky. Puffs of mist and fog blew about against the ominous red of the sun in the morning chill.

Cold blue eyes sparkled behind the calibrated lenses of the precision-made Steiner binoculars. Lieutenant Mark Chisolm focused upon the gradually evolving detail of the land, animating it with the starkness of his gaze. Reddish-brown hair and a complexion that still radiated the heat of summer sun enveloped a strikingly mannish face with a straight nose, intelligent brow, firm jaw line, and soft lips.

Perched upon a Munro overlooking the valley that separated him from the opposite sequence of the skeltonic teeth of the horizon, he enacted the motion of a great bird of prey. He scanned the valley below, piercing its morning mist to illuminate its hidden spaces. The binoculars, a gift from his father at the age of seventeen, four years earlier, were superior to any made in the United States or Britain, and had accompanied him on his hunting forays into the Montana wilderness and now into the military exercises across the commando training grounds.

In a disciplined survey, he glassed the foreground of the valley hundreds of feet below him, which extended for several miles in either direction. From left to right and then back again, Chisolm gradually and systematically reconnoitered the entire field, slowly and progressively moving his sights toward the distant Munros. Only one road lay within his vision, passing by an old inn that had only a year earlier been converted into a command center for high-ranking British officers.

As he spied the mountains and their various undulations and outcroppings, he noticed sheep on a distant height. This was nothing peculiar in and of itself here in the Highlands. But it was in this particular region since the Crown had forcibly removed or bought out all the land owners and sheep herders in the area. This land was now used for military training only. This had caused some resentment among the locals, who referred to this compulsory selling of their land to the Crown as a second Clearing of the Highlands, an event of the eighteenth century in which thousands of Scots had been forcibly removed from the countryside and their means of livelihood in hopes of quelling the prospect of any further rebellions against English rule.

Standing on the Munro, high up, memories of home and his father crept up on him. *Stretch the sinew and snap the brain; one you do smoothly, the other in pain.* Maybe his father was right, but he could never tell which was done smoothly and which in pain. Physical accomplishments were exacting and often done in distressingly unforgiving country, and the idea of a brain snapping into quick thinking didn't always comfort him with quiet reassurance.

Snap it like a whip, boy. The brain did not snap—too much in life required reflection. Still, his father's teachings forced him to confront the moment and respond and not duck the occasions of living forcefully and excitedly.

Having been born and reared on a cattle ranch for Black Angus at over six thousand feet, he found the training in the Highlands easier than the other soldiers. The thin air of the Highlands seemed downright fat compared to the thin air of the much higher Rockies. As he surveyed the surrounding terrain, the voice of his father, now dead, spoke to him in ways that were as demanding as they were consoling. He knew too that his father's stealth in the woods came from his own hunting days in the Highlands. He had violated Scottish law by tracking and then killing red deer in retribution for the Crown having sent an Englishman to be the local game warden. In two instances over a period of years, his father claimed to have killed deer by stalking them with his knife, since a gunshot was likely to attract unwanted attention. Moreover, even in his father's youth, guns were a rarity, except among the few with wealth enough to spare. Venison was a delight that he and his family shared and about which they could keep quiet.

Could a man really stalk a deer with a knife and bring it down? If properly camouflaged and if the wind were blowing in the right direction, it could be done. Chisolm had done it once as a sixteen-year-old, when going after mule deer. Delicate, soft feet and sensitive muscle control had put him next to a resting buck that ignored his crouched and incrementally moving body until it was too late.

As he dropped his binoculars to his side, he involuntarily tensed slightly in resentment at his father's discipline and ruggedness. He thought that his father might have been just fine had it not been for his heritage. He had come from a clan known for their rascals and the fear among family members was that father and son were still too much like their untamed ancestors. These were kin who fought nobly at the Haughs of Cromdell and ignobly at Culloden, on both the English and Scottish side. They had also thought that a distillery was for selling their whiskey, not for paying the king's taxes. It was a custom maintained by his ancestors in Appalachia and, to a lesser extent, by his father in Montana.

He snapped from this reverie and again held up his binoculars to survey the mountains of Arran, when he noticed white dots high up on Ben Nevis: three grazing sheep, stationary like painted clouds or lingering mist. His eyes went past them as he surveyed the territory to their left and then back again as he watched admiringly at their sure-footedness as they then descended to a kind of plateau that jutted out from the side of the mountain.

On a level outcropping stood the stone ruins of an ancient church. Perhaps something abandoned during the Clearing of the eighteenth century. The roof was completely gone, but the masonry of the edifice was firm, quietly reassuring in its permanence and blending with the countryside. The stones that made the walls were the color of the terrain from which they were taken: quarries chiseled into the mountainside.

He scanned the mountain again, left to right, up and down. No sheep. Where there had been three moments ago, there were now none.

Life in Montana had taught him sheep don't just fly away. And even in the mist of the Highlands, sheep don't just disappear. Everything had to be somewhere. But where were the sheep?

Unless, he thought comically to himself, these were specially trained sheep that carried weapons and fell upon unsuspecting soldiers. *What would they be called?* he wondered. *The Woolen Warriors? The Mutton Marauders? The Lamb Choppers? Or what about the Unshorn Shearers?* His mind moved whimsically as he hummed "Mary Had a Little Lamb." Maybe Mary was really a British commando and she lurked in the Highlands, falling upon those who wore wool.

✳　　✳　　✳　　✳　　✳

While he continued to scan the terrain, looking in the areas where the sheep had just been, another soldier with dark green eyes trained his binoculars on Chisolm from behind. Where he thought that Chisolm had been looking, he too focused. He watched as Chisolm climbed down into the glen and began his excursion toward the heights and to the ruins. Perhaps, he reflected, he might someday be on the next team selected in the punishing guerrilla warrior games in which Chisolm had already distinguished himself. If he were to do so, he would be Chisolm's enemy, but not necessarily just another one of the six designated by the command. Chisolm had bothered him, perhaps because he realized that he bothered Chisolm. Moreover, Chisolm's cordiality and linguistic virtuosity were a cause for envy. He got along too well with too many, and his gift of tongues elicited fires of resentment in the green eyes of this fellow soldier. Smoldering behind his binoculars, his eyes pierced Chisolm's back like steel daggers.

CHAPTER 1
THE KILLING GAMES

Animals thick as thieves
On God's rough tumbling ground

—Dylan Thomas, "The Author's Prologue"

—COMMANDO TRAINING GROUNDS, SCOTLAND

LYING ON HIS BACK IN COMPLETE DARKNESS, MARK CHISOLM GASPED in exhaustion and triumph. In the cool and lifeless granite cavern, he turned over onto his belly with his legs extended and his hard and muscular frame still tense with anticipation and exertion. His sweat glistened on his face, dark with the oily black camouflage paint, and his whole body melded its wetness into the soft woolen pants, cap, and jacket that absorbed the slight sounds of his own movements on the hard stone. The prospect of discovery left him attempting to quell his still heavy breathing from his rapid ascent to his recently found lair. He listened.

Outside his refuge, in near total darkness, came the almost imperceptible sound of something or someone in exacting caution. Chisolm moved himself deliberately, slightly impeded by his eleven-and-a-half-inch stilettolike knife that hung at his left side in a leather scabbard that scraped against the cavern wall. The prospect of his shoulder-slung Thompson machine gun's barrel inadvertently clanging against the cavern walls elicited more than the usual gentleness in his movements. The hard leather holster holding his Webley revolver scraped slightly against the ground. As his own breathing returned to normal, he moved his six-foot-two-inch frame into a crouched position near the entrance. He tucked his sofoes under him, soft-soled shoes worn

5

by stealth warriors. He cringed as he slightly scuffed his toes against the floor of his cramped quarters. His woolen cap brushed the lair's ceiling.

From outside came other sounds: footsteps, heavy with fatigue and without the cautionary delicacy that had he heard just moments earlier. Confident and almost boorish in their assertiveness, they invited detection and the prospect of assault from those who sat and waited. A minute later, more footsteps, only these were muffled movements balanced on the balls of the feet, the heels seldom touching the ground, their creator still straining to avoid detection. Catlike in their softness, they caused Chisolm to smile at their tremulous straining to minimize sound. A man marking his path with such precision and quiet suggested that he was a team leader and a man most to be avoided.

After several minutes of soft whisperings from without, the voices and quiet feet faded like a memory. Lieutenant Mark Chisolm was left alone in the stillness, the void, with the harshness of Mother Earth on which he rested. He heard his own heartbeat and the slight wheezing of his own breath as he felt the blood coursing through his temples. For the second time, he had eluded the finest trained soldiers in the British armed forces. They would not be pleased. Nor could they discount his achievement.

Moreover, he could not let the greatest challenge yet go untried. He began calculating his next move, knowing that it would take all his endurance, stealth, and ingenuity. He was tired but alert, and his body began to take on what some called the second wind; he called it being in superb physical condition.

He moved his invisible hands with the grace and dexterity of a musician in a well-rehearsed orchestration of violence. They lingered like a disembodied spirit in front of his face as he imagined them executing a garrote, snapping a neck, or suffocating an unsuspecting foe. His body tensed and relaxed, then coiled again as he sniffed at the evening's air for human heat. In complete darkness, he sucked in the cool night and gave it back to the blackness in a warm, invisible breath that hovered in the frosty air like unseen death he would become.

As he waited, he pushed his right hand against the wall to brace himself, when his fingers slipped into a two-inch-deep cut that seemed to move in a diagonal line. Like a blind man reading in Braille, he followed the cut toward the bottom, where it stopped and then moved back up in another diagonal. He followed the V-shaped cut to its top and realized it fell again in yet another diagonal and, at its bottom, into another. The V was actually a W or possibly a series of such shapes. *Interesting and curious*, he thought, *but hardly vital.*

Dropping his hand to his side, it touched something that was smooth, almost feathery or velvety, and at the same time quite familiar. It bore the same general texture of his own clothing. Chisolm felt the strands of wool torn from the side of one of the prior four-legged visitors on one of the jagged edges of the cavern's interior. As if the wool were some kind of talisman, he stuffed it into one of his pants pockets. After all, it represented the disappearing sheep whose mystery had led him to this location in the first place.

Rocking himself forward, from his haunches to his knees, toward the small and hidden opening, he moved from his lifeless womb, holding his breath to listen as he slowly and silently lifted the heavy rock that partially eclipsed his hiding place. Like one born again, he emerged on the side of the mountain. In an unearthly glide, he followed the moonless night partway down, delicately touching the ground, shallowly breathing in and out, expelling doubt and inhaling the confidence of an enemy to whom he was as invisible as he was dangerous. As if a creature from some nether world, he relished the night and slowly turned his blindness into a shadow world. In his sinewy tautness, his muscles folded one leg and then another under him and then alternately stretched out like feelers against the hard earth or the sweet and slightly slippery heather.

An unseen force of beauty, his muscular frame left only his own warmth in its path as he flicked his tongue slightly and his ears verily twitched at the sound of a fellow soldier muffled by distance. He listened.

Now the mirror image of darkness itself, he seemed to wed with it in a conjugal embrace, gathering its predatory stealth into his being until he sat by a large rock in a feral poise of anticipation. There he waited as his prey felt for his presence, walking slowly and obliviously, hoping to stumble upon Chisolm and his hiding place. In the dark of the rock's hardness and amidst the skyless night, he sensed the vibrations that came with his first victim.

Hushed and tensed, Chisolm suddenly slipped behind the soldier as he passed by and, in one motion, wrapped his arm over the man's shoulder, cupping his hand over his mouth, tripping him face down into the heather. Chisolm broke the man's fall with his own leg as he threw his other arm over the opposite shoulder and placed the blade of his Fairbairn-Sykes commando knife against the man's throat. The soldier, cowed, cupped, and controlled, and sensing the futility of resistance, held perfectly still as Chisolm whispered into his ear, "Pray be silent; you are dead."

Slightly, the man shook his head, causing his woolen cap to fall off. Chisolm then added, "Remember, dead men don't talk. Stay here until I claim your body."

As Chisolm got up, taking his full weight off of his victim, the soldier sat up and resignedly surrendered, sitting quietly and in frustration as Chisolm removed the man's Thompson, which he had dropped upon being jumped. As quickly as he had come, Chisolm disappeared. For a moment, his defeated foe, still seated where he had been "killed," wondered if it had all been a dream, until he reached for his machine gun. Dreams did not take a soldier's firearms. Chisolm had. The nighttime training maneuvers were not going as smoothly as the British commandoes had anticipated. The "dead" British soldier, in compliance with the rules of training and engagement, sat and simmered in his own juices as he thought angrily at his having been taken unawares by the fox that he his teammates hunted in the evasion exercise. He would have to wait at his kill site until the morning assessment team arrived to debrief him on his mistakes and his untimely but fanciful death.

As part of their nighttime training maneuvers, the British commandoes operated in the rugged and mountainous terrain of the Highlands in six-man teams that simulated the conditions that would be required once they moved into the German-held territory to reclaim the offensive against a foe that had sent them reeling. Here, on their home turf, they executed the textbook guerrilla movements that were expected to neutralize or kill the soldier selected for the day's training. His task was to avoid capture as part of what were known as E and E, escape and evasion training.

Their rear guard taken unaware by Chisolm, the remainder of the six-man team continued to advance along the side of the mountain and in the adjoining valley in a broad front. They telegraphed their relative position to one another in a deliberate, periodic tapping on their

Thompsons or by cocking their pistols to create a slight but readily discernible clicking sound. Like Chisolm, they were dressed entirely in black woolen pants and jackets, which were free of noisy zippers and fastened only with buttons. The shoes were soft, pliable, and silent leather, and rubber soled. The attire muffled sound and retained the body heat in the nighttime chill.

The next member of the team dropped back from his position several hundred feet up the side of the mountain and moved down toward the valley floor to relieve the supposed still advancing rear guard, to keep a constant backward counter-clockwise rotation. Chisolm advanced into the appropriate position, mimicking the movement of his adversary.

As the soldier's footfalls grew louder, Chisolm stood still until he was close enough to hear Chisolm's repeating of the clicking sound with his pistol in imitation of the other stealth warriors. The soldier approached almost nonchalantly and then stiffened. Chisolm, navigating by sound, positioned himself directly in front of his adversary. He embraced the soldier with both hands, covered his mouth, and shoved him roughly to the ground.

Struggling to sit up, the soldier felt Chisolm's forehead bump his own slightly but firmly, as if to say that more would follow if he didn't relent. The soldier stopped moving.

"Pray be silent. You are dead," Chisolm whispered. "Dead men don't move. Stay here until I claim your body."

As the soldier attempted to sit up, Chisolm grabbed the man's Thompson, pushed him back down with the gun barrel, and then slipped off.

With the two clickers now missing, the other four sensed that something might be wrong. So instead of a backward motion to relieve their dead comrades, they froze their positions. Chisolm, sensing their stillness, crawled forward and then around them until he determined that he was in advance of the lead man. An hour passed. They heard no motion; neither did he.

Then the lead man shuffled his feet slightly, still feeling his way through the darkness. Chisolm lay directly in front of him. As his foot hit him, Chisolm reached up and grabbed at the man's belt. He threw him to the ground in a loud thump. Holding his blade against the man's cheek, Chisolm whispered, "Dead! Don't talk." Without awaiting a reply,

Chisolm moved away into the dark with yet another piece of weaponry as the remainder of the team converged cautiously toward the sound.

Two hours later, as the first glimmer of sun arose in the east, Chisolm had circled around again and squinted at the streams of morning light as he lay down in the deep heather. The three remaining soldiers dragged themselves toward the military headquarters, where they were to report the successful completion of their nighttime training. Watching the soldiers in their black attire and their silhouetted shapes move in his direction, Chisolm turned away, unseen. On either side of him, the sunlight animated into a shimmer the diamondlike droplets of the morning mist touching the earth.

After fifteen minutes, the three men, grim-faced and exhausted, approached the tented headquarters. A Jeep was cruising past them in search of their missing comrades. Chisolm was standing next to two officers and three other colleagues, with four Thompsons draped over his shoulders, his own face still blackened and watching his approaching adversaries.

As the leader of the group came within several feet of Chisolm, everyone looked at him. The soldier was in his mid-twenties and the one man in the group of six for whom Chisolm had a healthy respect. Several inches shorter than Chisolm, Captain Rangle, a drop out from a Catholic seminary in his native Ireland, was as intuitive in his knowledge of guerrilla tactics and the fine art of stealth destruction as anyone he had met. Because of his former religious training and his unyielding disposition, Rangle had, in only several weeks of training, earned the sobriquet Father Aggressor. The name fit. He may not have been entirely suitable for the priesthood, but he was entirely suitable for war.

He spit on the ground at Chisolm's feet and stated menacingly, "Fuck! You're a shit! You broke the rules of engagement. You had to stay in the area. There is no way you could have gone past us without going outside the perimeter!"

The two officers stood silently while the enlisted walked away, preferring to stay out the conflict. Chisolm turned his back to the three and continued casual talk with the other officers. The frustrated and angry leader of the group then turned in the direction of the commander's tent and stood outside, awaiting an orderly to direct him inside for a debriefing.

As the early morning mist hovered on the ground and in layers all about the fields, valley, and mountains, the sun pierced it, forcing the liquescence into a soft penetration of the earth. By the time Captain Rangle was directed into the tent, the sun was up. Chisolm was still quietly talking about the night with the two officers who enjoined him to explain the night's activities during a morning tea with them after his own debriefing.

A while later, Captain Rangle walked out of the tent looking haggard and slightly forlorn. As he dragged himself past Chisolm, he paused briefly.

"You're a shit, and a fuck as well. Still, I guess you beat me and my men." He then stuck out his hand, and Chisolm took it. "I want you on our side, you shit." As he walked away, he turned again toward Chisolm. "The commander wants to see you. I said you couldn't be found."

Unable to resist a subtle taunt, Chisolm eyed the warrior monk and said, "Maybe later on you can hear my confession. Bless me, Father, for I have won."

With a sardonic grin, the captain said, "I'd rather eat shit and die. Besides, you're going to hell, just like the bloody Germans."

Chisolm smiled in response. Alluding to another of Captain Rangle's nicknames, Chisolm uttered, "You're not bad for a Roman."

"Fuckin' Ulsterman," replied Rangle as he turned away once more and headed to one of the twenty tents pitched along an imaginary line in the valley that stretched from east to west.

Tired but proud of what he had done, Chisolm walked confidently toward the tent where the commander was waiting. The orderly was holding open the screen door on a wooden frame that housed the smelly world of canvas living. Upon entering the room, Chisolm snapped to attention and saluted, not in the British method of right hand turned upside down and backward with the thumb pointed down across the right eyebrow, but in the typical American fashion, with the hand stiffly placed above the right eye, perpendicular to the forehead.

"Please, Lieutenant Chisolm," said Captain Shane, "if you're going to be in the British army, at least learn the proper way to salute; American or not."

The commander, who was seated behind a desk made out of a table top on two piles of cinder blocks, looked up serenely and said, "You're a shit they say. You broke the rules. You were to stay within the perimeter. What do you have to say for yourself?"

"I did, sir. Your men are mistaken. They think they can advance in darkness without being detected. They make too much noise and they smell."

"Are you saying you smelled them? I find that hard to believe."

"Sir, I have hunted from boyhood. I can smell prey before most men can."

"Prey? These are not animals; they are men."

"Perhaps, sir, but I understand that war makes men beasts, and I have been told that to fight in one is to surrender to the faculties that nature has given us. If you stand downwind, you can catch the smell of our men before they even know you're near them."

"As improbable as your explanation seems, there is just no other way, I suppose, to explain your success. Still, some of the men think you may have cheated. How else could you elude six men sent to capture you?"

Lieutenant Mark Chisolm was silent, still looking past the commander at the back wall of the tent, still at attention, and still utterly unconcerned about what others may have thought. The commander and captain waited for Chisolm to either deny or confirm the accusation. He did neither. His silence was insolent. Still, the commander had to respect a man who could—if in fact he had—run outside the bounds of the military training area, slip back in, and still find time to kill three adversaries.

When it became clear that Chisolm had no intention of divulging more than he had to, the commander looked up and said, "You have an uncommon athleticism, Mr. Chisolm, and I take it that you have put it to very good use. I hope that you will soon do so to the regret of our German and Italian foes. I shall interpret your silence as yet one more indication that you are either a fox or a cheat. I prefer the former. Either way, congratulations. Now get some sleep and stop fagging the men. You're destroying their morale. Your task was to elude detection and thereby help train your fellow soldiers, bolstering their confidence in their own abilities—not take *them* prisoner. Nonetheless, some day you must show me how you did it."

The commander paused for a moment, hoping Chisolm would say more, but then relented and said, "That is all. Get something to eat; you deserve it. By the way, when we get to the real thing, remember that clever as they are, foxes don't normally live very long. They're likes cats: curious and fatally inclined to overconfidence."

The commander then looked quite deliberately at Chisolm as his feral and lithe vitality radiated from beneath his black night garb.

"Some men are born great while others have greatness thrust upon them. Which is true of you?"

Not knowing if the question was rhetorical or not, Chisolm remained still. Finally, the commander smiled up at him and said, "Carry on."

Chisolm saluted, again like an American, turned tail, and walked out the tent.

The commander turned to Captain Shane and said, "He came in with four Thompsons?"

"Yes, sir, quite a show."

"What's he like?" asked the major. "Why's he here? Who sent him? Doesn't Haserling think our own boys are up to the job? Of course, our own prime minister is half of them. His mother. Still, there seems an element of impropriety about it all. Tell me what you know."

"Spartan in word but generous in deed, the men say, sir. They like him. But he's also a tad headstrong. Rugged individualist, hardy and straight-talking, as they say." The captain was then quiet, awaiting some response.

"In other words," replied the major with a grin, "he's a bona fide Scot."

"Interestingly enough, sir, his father, yes. His mother, also a yes. Some story or other about both of them immigrating to America separately but then meeting over there. Record indicates that they married in North Carolina, where both already had relatives. Married in 1920, sir. I wish we knew more, but the Americans, you know how they are. They expect much of us but give us very little information in return. Still, they are expecting to help some."

"Some," responded the major reflectively.

There was an awkward silence as the major looked out the opened canvas flap of his quarters and make-shift office toward the newly constructed plywood and tented barracks.

"Still, the boy's done very well. Commend him, captain. Thank you."

The captain saluted and turned away. He then stopped at the tent door and turned back as the major interrupted his leaving. "He was sent by command, someone of President Roosevelt's staff. When Sir Winston made it known that he would be training special forces, Roosevelt thought it appropriate for the Americans to send an observer. He seems much more than an observer. He's good—he's very good, but I still want to know how he outsmarted us. The fox should not be able to outrun or even outsmart the hounds."

CHAPTER 2

TIGHT LIPS AND BANTER

Shaman, why does my back quiver?

—"White Pawnee," Victor Landrieu

—COMMANDO BARRACKS

THAT EVENING IN THE BARRACKS, CHISOLM'S FELLOW SOLDIERS recounted the training ordeals of the day to anyone who would listen or who couldn't help but do so. Some of the men taunted one another, playfully invoking references to their own prowess while deriding that of anyone whom they may have bettered. Others staged recreations of their guerrilla mastery and reenacted the mistakes of their colleagues, who could only join in the laughter at seeing someone mimic their movements.

One soldier who had a knack for imitation carried out charades that burlesqued episodes from their training that had taken on near legendary status among men who were fit, confident, and irreverent. Like dueling bards, they each sought to embellish a kernel of fact with adornments that took the edge off the grimness of their training. Farce reigned. Hitler, Tojo, and Mussolini, and even Churchill, Stalin, and Roosevelt made nightly appearances among the men in the form of stocking puppets. German, Italian, Japanese, and Russian-accented English spilled from their woolen and cotton lips. Puppets with mustaches, cigars, and other signature paraphernalia of the premier leaders of the world sang duets, made political commentary, and gave advice on how to pick up women. Nothing seemed sacred. Each Saturday night, the men watched newsreels that provided fresh grist for their mills of derisive commentary and served as firm reminders that their training had a purpose.

Chisolm, still tired, sat on the edge of his cot in a kind of bemused detachment. While others joked, he read Tacitus in Latin. Since his high school days, he had shown a fondness for languages. Their usage was something his practical father had questioned but was happy to ignore when the academic awards were bestowed on him. In high school as well as his first two years of college, he maintained a keen interest. At the instigation of his teachers, he added French. Again his gift for languages was apparent. The war had broken his concentration but not his gifts or his interest in linguistic fare.

Once, while still in high school, he had blended his language talents with his athleticism in a most unexpected way. At half time of a basketball game in which he had shown himself to be high on aggression but light on the soft-handed finesse that marked the urban dwellers who seemed to have learned basketball in the womb, he walked over to his coach, who had attempted to communicate plays in the form of hand signals. He complained that the hand gestures were a little like playing charades. Everybody had the opportunity to eventually interpret their meaning, including the opposition. At Chisolm's urging, the coach, who was also his Latin teacher, agreed to shout out the series of plays based upon Latin declension endings. Since Chisolm and three of the other starters were all studying Latin, it worked. The coach found the whole exercise amusing while the opposition found it confusing. Still, Chisolm thought the game a bit prissy until his coach told him to think of it as steer rustling without a rope, with the ball taking the place of cattle. This image of thievery yoked to fun matched his clandestine urges and a sometime rebellious temperament that desired adventure without reproofs and admonitions.

*   *   *   *   *

On the opposite side of the plywood and tented housing, Lieutenant Wirtz sat in a dim corner near other tired soldiers. He spied Mark Chisolm from a distance. Chisolm had always felt a slight unease when this man was at his back. The expression "I've got your back" was not yet in vogue among the soldiers, but if it had been, Wirtz would have applied it in ways that Chisolm would have found uninvitingly true. As

Wirtz stared, Chisolm, sensing a certain something, turned and looked over his shoulder and then turned away again. As he did so, his observer bristled at the Yank's celebrity status.

What business has he in interfering in this war? The spoils of victory as well as the humiliations of defeat at the hands of the fascists were theirs to enjoy and bear. *Americans don't belong here,* he thought. Unfortunately, Chisolm thought otherwise.

"Why wait?" Chisolm would have responded. America would be dragged into the war sooner or later. As in the First World War, America would side with Great Britain—no slight to the Germans or even the French. It's just that Hitler and his boys weren't civilized and weren't trustworthy. And the French were civilized but somewhat cynical, it seemed, about everything.

Later, while others played cards, Lieutenant Wirtz racked his Thompson, as everyone was required to do, and then unholstered his Webley. As the evening wore on, the laughter abated as fatigue took hold. While a few others engaged in subdued conversations, he simply stared off into space, smiling occasionally as training mates passed his cot.

＊　　＊　　＊　　＊　　＊

Several times, Chisolm glanced round to see Wirtz staring over at him. A disconcerting unease enveloped Chisolm. Something didn't feel right. The hairs on the back of his neck stood up.

A short time later, another soldier, named Dennis Bernard, with whom Chisolm had exchanged several pleasantries, sat on his own cot nearby and offered, "Did you get some sleep this afternoon? Last night must have been a real challenge. We heard about your exploits. The hounds seem to be begging for mercy, Mr. Fox."

He continued, "I heard about a film the other day. It's playing in London, maybe Edinburg, maybe even Glasgow. It's about a war correspondent—an American, I think—and some German sympathizer in the plane together. It crashes. Somehow or another, they all find out that the girl in the movie has a father who's on board. She's English, I think, but her father is secretly favoring the Germans. The American in the plane thinks that eventually America will enter the war on our side. I heard about it and thought of you."

He paused, held out his hand, and said, "Thanks for coming. When we get some time away from here, maybe we can go see it."

Chisolm returned the smile and shook his hand. "Thanks for having me," he said. "It's about to be our war, too."

Dennis was two years older than Chisolm and had already served five years with the British army. He was fit, trim, and just slightly shorter than Chisolm. His gaunt, almost Gallic-looking face was creased with lines of perpetual good humor and a thin-lipped smile, as if he knew something that others didn't. Sitting in his stocking feet, he unbuttoned his trousers and shirt as he considered the most recent addition to his own six-man training team. He was the chief of the team to which Chisolm had been added only a couple of hours before, something about which Chisolm had not yet been informed.

"It's official. You are now with me and my team. Two of the men I trained departed today for unknown places. They'll be part of a new team expected to go abroad soon. A long day tomorrow," he said. "We'll get briefed at 0700. Then we'll do last-minute preparation. Then we nap. The games begin at 2000 hours. The sun will be going down about then, but it won't be completely dark. But when it is, remember, darkness is our friend. I suppose you know that better than anybody else. I think we'll make you a hound. But, of course, we're all members of a team."

"I only wish everyone in the unit were," replied Chisolm.

Dennis returned a quizzical look. Chisolm responded with a theatrical sidelong glance at the other young man, Lieutenant Wirtz, who looked away again as Dennis turned his head in his direction.

"Oh, him," responded Dennis. "He's just different. He's a bit like you: not quite one of us. He's South African. I talked to him a time or two; seems all right. Came to settle things between England and Germany. One hell of a rugby player, they say. Used to pitch, too. A cricket man. Those South African boys are tough. Wirtz—Guy Wirtz's his name."

"Will he kill?" asked Chisolm.

Dennis hesitated a moment before letting down his own defenses. "More than he has to, I think."

"Guy Wirtz," responded Chisolm. He shot Wirtz another glance. "Would that he were fatter."

Dennis, himself an aficionado of the theater and one who had spent a year at Oxford before the war, chuckled and whispered, "Et tu, my brother. His mother's Scottish; that's why he's here. How a bonnie lass came to marry a Dutchman is something I've yet to learn. But the others say something about his mother's clan being from this country, these hills. I'll find out what I can. It's good to know about the men you'll be fighting alongside."

Wirtz sat on the edge of his own cot with his back to everyone as he paged through a stack of letters from his homeland. As tired as the rest, he placed them under his pillow and lay down in his cot with his shoes still on. He pulled the blanket over his broad shoulders and then up over his ears.

The barracks grew quiet, and the lights were put out. Wirtz, in the darkness, reached to his left. He brushed his fingers against his Webley.

Chisolm turned to one side to sleep and wondered if he were still being watched as he reminisced about his hunting days in Montana. Visions from his hunting forays came back as his mind and body relaxed and drifted off.

A red fox lingered in a three-point pose, echoing the silence of the white snow as it stepped softly toward the paw prints where the half woods grew. Its coal black eyes punctuated the face as snowflakes fell on its smoldering frame, a blushing ember ready to flare. A finger of wind prodded a white rabbit from its burrow as it jolted and swirled blindly into the jaws of the quick red flame.

Chisolm's body jerked involuntarily, and he awoke. Then, in the darkness, the face of his father appeared, looking at one of his brilliantly colored maps of the Mississippi and Missouri flyway, showing the migratory patterns of geese from Canada to the Gulf of Mexico. The black lines that marked the bridges sutured America. East and west were pulled together as if by a doctor's care, with stitch work that healed old rifts between sedate Easterners and rambunctious Westerners and mountain men. As the images flowed into a mind already fatigued and open to the depths of himself, he remembered how, on both sides of the river, gunmen brought down their prey as feathers and flesh splashed goose grease onto the hard winter waters of the Big Muddy. Better to be the hunter than the hunted; better to be the fox than the …

CHAPTER 3

THE VOICE OF DIAMONDS

What is the most precious of all stones?
What is the sweetest of all sounds?

—Ancient Syrian tale

STEAMING JUNGLE FOLIAGE CREPT UP ON EITHER SIDE OF THE RIVER while only several hundred feet away, on one side of the river, lay a mixture of brush, stunted trees, and bushes mixed with nearly impenetrable thorns and thistles. Tendrils of ceaselessly growing vines snuck out of the jungle canopy onto the dry clay compound area of over a hundred thatched-roof buildings as well as tents. The compound was really a mobile village designed for efficiency of movement rather than comfort of living. It lay somewhere in that nebulous and constantly moving border country in sub-Sahara Africa—somewhere south of Somalia and Chad, somewhere east of Zaire, and somewhere west of the newly emerging political entity and ethnically purified nation that was yet to be named.

Melissa Millinson stared uneasily at the assemblage before her. She was the team leader of six journalists and film documentarians from Cassandra International News Channel, CINC, covering a story of worldwide significance. For more than twenty years, the Christ's Army of Liberation had led a brutal faction of heavily armed insurgents against the governments of Uganda, Kenya, and Tanzania. On this day, the team of journalists would finally be allowed a rare firsthand look at its administrative session, along with the accompanying ceremony.

CINC had been granted privileged status over all other news

organizations in return for a promise to be fair in its reporting. This seemed a simple enough agreement. CINC's director of production, John Robertson, surmised that continuing to do what he thought CINC had always done was hardly an unrealistic expectation. Yes, they would be fair. What else?

However, the rebel group's leader, Jomo Raphael, had also insisted that photos be taken only at moments that he designated. No audio recordings were allowed unless Raphael first approved them.

That evening, the journalists had arrived after seven days of arduous travels on foot through brush and jungle as well as desert plains. They were led by several of Jomo's soldiers and one of Raphael's most trusted lieutenants, Marx St. George.

Robertson had worked for years through various back channels and diplomatic contacts to make these arrangements. He did so despite the warnings that any efforts to engage Jomo Raphael and his followers were fraught with peril.

Three years earlier, two French journalists affiliated with the French newspaper *LeMond* had attempted to make contact with the rebel group through their own back channel overtures in eastern Africa. They waited almost eighteen months for any kind of response. None came. Therefore, in a bit of daring, perhaps augmented by a bit of hauteur, the two reporters hired some of the locals in villages in west central Uganda to help lead them down trails and through dense foliage into a vicinity in which the elusive Raphael and his followers were said to be based. They never returned; neither did their guides.

Several weeks after the journalists and their guides disappeared, a clash occurred between United Nations peace-keeping forces in western Tanzania and members of Raphael's Christ's Army. Four of the insurgents were killed and one was taken alive. Each of the insurgents wore an amulet of a tethered human ear with a diamond stud pierced into the lobe. Two of them were the ears of white people. Later DNA testing confirmed that these were the remains of the French journalists.

When the survivor, who was only a boy of fourteen, was asked to explain where the ears had come from, he said he did not know but that they had been a gift from God. Further attempts to clarify this god's name were unsuccessful. When asked why God had given him this gift, he told them that the ears were intended as a reminder that they must listen to God, who was in the diamond itself. God, he explained, also heard everything, so those guilty of blasphemy would be punished even if no one else were around to hear it. God heard everything. However, the boy's interrogation was brief because of the nature of his wounds and a desire on his part to die so that he could see, as he said, the inside of the diamond.

Eventually he was transferred to a United Nations contract hospital near Nairobi, Kenya. He expired but not before he asked for his amulet back, which by then was on its way to a French hospital in Djibouti with limited DNA testing facilities and then onto Paris for complete testing. The young man's failure to provide more detailed information on the operations of Christ's Army of Liberation and its leader merely added to the already frustrating experience of Colonel Pedro Sanchez, a Spanish army officer and then the UN's commander of peace-keeping forces in the area. In two years of operations in the area, he had lost thirty-seven men in various engagements while killing only twelve of the enemy and taking only three prisoners, including the boy. One had committed suicide by cutting his own throat upon seizing a knife from a field interrogator; another had starved himself, which only compounded the life-threatening peril of three gunshot wounds sustained in his attack upon the UN forces; and the third was the boy.

* * * * *

Melissa Millinson and her assistant team leader, Michael Constantine, sat in the tented enclosure. The interior was dimly lit by one kerosene lantern but was immaculately clean. Even the earthen floor had apparently been swept down to its clay base. Each of them sat on six-inch-high stools, in a circle, facing one another, as they had been directed.

They waited inside with the door of the hut open on a frame made from mahogany and a lintel of smoothed red rock. Finally, Marx St. George entered and stood before them.

He beamed, "Jomo Raphael will see you soon. As you can tell, our brothers and sisters in Christ are now assembling. Soon it will be dark and the meeting will begin. You will be a part of it. First, I must give each of you a token. You must wear it at all times when Jomo speaks or you will not hear him and his many voices."

He handed each of them a necklace consisting of a leather strap holding a brightly beaded pouch with a silver wire cinch to keep it closed.

A member of the team, Jeremy Democowicz, looked at each of the others as they took the necklace and placed it around their necks. As he was handed his, Jeremy began to pull at the cinch. Marx St. George slapped his hand and yelled, "No. It is not for you to open these."

"But what's in them?" asked Jeremy, now somewhat bemused and frightened at the same time.

"A gift from God. Do not open these. Jomo is coming. Do not make him angry. Your sins have already done this."

After spending several days in the wilderness with St. George, they had thought they knew him a bit but were confounded by his reaction. He stood before them with his eyes open wide and his lips firmly compressed as if to add emphasis to his remarks. His face reminded Melissa of a boiler ready to explode. Moments later, Jomo Raphael arrived outside the hut with a small entourage of armed retainers whom he beckoned to stay there. He entered.

As he did so, St. George nodded obsequiously and stepped aside to allow Raphael access to the CINC crew. All stood to greet him, and he bowed slightly in acknowledgement.

His presence was truly captivating. He stood six feet six inches tall, weighed almost three hundred pounds, and had long arms and large hands. He had a round, full face and closely cropped hair. His eyes were also large and round. His complexion was smooth, with a dark brown hue and several scars of about an inch or two each on his left side, from his ear down along his neck—a shrapnel wound from an engagement with Tanzanians troops more than ten years ago.

As Melissa stood at the top of the circle, she extended her hand first. Raphael was slightly taken aback at this, for in his world, women were not so assertive and would not presume to initiate an important social occasion.

Raphael then smiled fixedly, ignoring Melissa's hand, and extended his arms fully like some ebony Buddha. "I am wisdom come to you." He paused as if reflecting for a moment, his great arms still extended. His eyes rolled to look upward and to his right. Then, paraphrasing Jesus, he remarked, "If you have eyes, let you see; if you have ears, and I know you do," he added slyly, "prepare to hear."

"Please be seated, while I, your servant, Jomo Raphael, speak to you of our great operations. First, as you must know, I am named Jomo after the great Jomo Kenyatta, the first great liberator of my people. And of my last name, this you shall come to know soon enough. For all members of Christ's Army of Liberation take on new names when they are baptized into our great cause."

For the next hour and a half, Jomo Raphael harangued them, praised them for their courage in coming, and then invited questions, to which he responded with the words, "Not yet, my child. Only when you have been tested."

Some thought that Jomo's real name was something else entirely. At an early age, his mother had taken him to a local missionary to be baptized in the Roman Catholic Church. It was the same missionary school in which he been taught from the age of six. His gifts for memorization, languages, and athletics had distinguished him among his peers.

That this was not an infant baptism was reflected in the fact that Raphael enjoyed recounting the day, and indeed the very moment, when God first spoke to him. As the CINC crew listened, he explained how he had stood next to the baptismal font in his church when he heard a sweet voice beckoning him. He related that he then ascended to the top of the church and sat next to Jesus, who said, "You are wise like me and must cleanse the temple of infidels. You are my rock, and upon you I will build a great empire."

He further relayed how God or Jesus, depending upon the moment, showed him all the kingdoms of the world, including America and Russia, and asked which he would want. He told Jesus that he loved his people and would not leave them, even for the greatest kingdom in the world—not for America, Russia, or even all of Asia. Jesus told him that he would give him a chariot with wheels within wheels as a reward for his loyalty to the cause of his people, something, he added, which he expected to see very soon. That gift from Jesus would come from strangers, and he explained that that was why God had sent him the people from CINC.

When he was finished, he knelt down and indicated that they were to do the same. He began to pray. "Our father who art in heaven …"

Melissa and Jeremy hesitated but then knelt and joined in, "Thy kingdom come." The others followed.

He concluded the prayer and spoke solemnly, again, with seeming fear and piety. "Father, if you can take this cup from me." He bowed his head and was silent for a long minute. As the prayer ended, Raphael stood up while they remained kneeling.

Raphael motioned for them to stand up. As they did so, he moved forward and extended his arms once more and then waved his fingertips to have them come closer. As they did so, he reached out and embraced them, changing his position several times so that each could feel the warmth and strength of his full embrace. Melissa was smothered in his arm pit and caught the odor of a man who had sweated and perhaps worked arduously for at least the past day.

One of the other crew members had his face crushed against the shoulder board epaulets on his slightly wrinkled uniform.

When he finally released them, he smiled warmly and said, "Notice my very good English. I am a Christian and therefore I know to read the Bible is important. So as a boy in Botswana, I learned it well. I was the best in my class. My English is almost perfect. I listen to BBC every day, and I read American magazines and have seen many movies. I have geeks to teach us of DVDs and iPods. I also have a cellular phone."

He then motioned to St. George, who had remained standing quietly during all of this. "He is one of my geeks.

"You will join me for dinner. I love you." He smiled, turned, and walked out the door, where his retainers followed immediately behind.

After he left, they stood looking blankly at one another. "He scares me," said Jeremy.

Melissa half spoke, half whispered, "I feel like I've been raped and charmed by a snake at the same time. Just show me the apple."

They discussed quietly what they had been through and the bewildering comment about the chariot with wheels within wheels. None of them had a clue. They waited inside the hut for the evening's business and festivities to begin.

Their cameraman checked his equipment and summarized all of their feelings when he said, "I want to get out of here but I can't help but think that this could be a great story."

Melissa and the others discussed their options. As Raphael's guests, they seemed to have few.

Raphael had returned to his own domicile, a large tent with a makeshift desk and two other tents connected by zipper flaps. He went into the larger of the two adjoining tents and then stood motionless as two women, both in their teens and with large breasts—naked breasts—entered. They stood before him with their eyes downcast. Raphael snapped his fingers.

Both of them, as if on cue, approached him and said, "If we but touch you, we are healed."

Jomo looked directly to the heavens above, as if his eyes could penetrate the canvas roof. Each of the teenage girls, who were of a deep bronze, beautiful, and with black hair pulled back in Western-style ponytails, smiled at him imploringly. The younger of the two girls let out a small, nervous laugh and seemed to be on the verge of fainting, her eyes almost rolling back up into her head, even as she touched him with trembling hands. The other girl, perhaps of eighteen years, unbuttoned Jomo's uniform and unfastened his pants and boots. The younger girl disrobed him. He stood before them completely naked. The older one then knelt before him and performed fellatio. The younger girl watched as if being instructed and then did likewise until he was satisfied and pushed them away in disgust.

Then he smiled and said, "Thank you," and told them to prepare his vestments. These they laid out on his bed, which was a large wooden-framed cot. One of the items was a white smock with a Roman collar. There was also a great chainmail shirt, which must have been purchased from some medieval armory or a company that custom fit William de Wallace and Goliath-type figures whose girth far exceeded that of normal men. These were intended to thwart any attempts at assassination as he executed the word of God.

With the help of his two female attendees, he lifted these items over himself and allowed them to descend his length. Then the women strained to lift a military flak jacket that lay underneath the cot, wrapped in a blanket. On one side "U.S. Army" was stenciled in. Then, over all of this, a brightly beaded chasuble with sparkling jewels was placed above his huge form as he sat on a stool so that the women could more easily perform their sartorial tasks.

The chasuble had obviously not been made for one so large and had therefore been modified with various cuts and native stitch work to encompass his form. He then rose like a black mountain draped in snow and sun-bedecked ice, folded his hands prayerfully, bowed to each of his attendees as they held back the tent flaps to the main corridor of canvas, and then walked outside to his awaiting minions.

As he walked toward the center of the tented village, Melissa and the others awaited him as part of his official dinner party. St. George stood nearby and directed them to a long table of plywood and saw horses, on which there were thirteen handwoven placemats and various eating utensils taken from a variety of houses, hotels, motels, and other places to which Raphael had been. Next to each of the plates, which were equally varied, were plastic cups of different shapes and sizes, representing different sport teams and fast food restaurants. One large plastic beverage container read "Chicago White Sox World Champs 2005." Another said "Subway." All the others were equally decorous and showed off Raphael's eclectic taste.

As he approached the table, a dozen or so children scampered alongside him to take him by the hand or to beg for a ride on his huge shoulders.

"Papa, Papa," they yelled. At a signal from him, various women came to claim his offspring.

He stopped near the table and looked directly at Jeremy Democowicz.

"I am a father to my people. I hope you are not a homosexual." Jeremy, married and the father of two sons, was nonplussed.

As Raphael came to the table, he centered himself so that six chairs were to either side. His hardwood chair was large and simple except for a red beach towel draped over the back that contained a one and half foot in diameter circular emblem of the United States Marines. He waited until all of his guests were led to stand next to their chairs.

Five of the CINC crew had been led to chairs on either side of his: three to one side and two to the other. Melissa had been led aside by a female who explained that no woman may sit at such a table of honor but that she would be allowed to participate once the festivities had begun.

At first, she blushed with embarrassment and then drew back as two women attempted to escort her to a separate hut.

"Wait a minute," she said. "What the hell is this? I'm a journalist."

St. George was only a short distance away, and he came by and reassured her all would be well. It was only a custom. "Go with them. Besides, women do not wear pants in our country."

"Yes, but they go bare-breasted. What's so bad about slacks?" she said angrily.

The other five were already out of sight.

Melissa started to turn back toward the five CINC men when St. George stepped in front to block her way. "It is our custom," he said firmly.

As the two women grabbed her by either arm, St. George nudged her from behind with one hand solidly on her right shoulder.

*   *   *   *   *

After Raphael and the others were seated, various fruits and vegetables were brought to the table, along with several large bottles of wine, all of which sat unopened before the dinner guests. Seven other guests, each of whom wore camouflage uniforms with the usual black, green, and brown motley pattern, joined the CINC crew. Everyone had removed their caps and sat as Raphael had directed them.

Once they sat, Raphael beckoned for each of the guests to be served. Bare-breasted women hustled about, attending to the dinner guests' needs. Each guest was then poured a large glass of water from Perrier bottles.

One of the crew members, seated farthest from Raphael, held up the glass of water, smelled it, and put it back down without drinking. The others closest to him, noticing his actions, did likewise, while those on the far side of Raphael, less suspicious, sipped politely. However, all members of the team had spent enough time in Africa to know that Perrier was not a readily available commodity, especially in the more remote regions. Even those who sipped both out of thirst and for fear of offending Raphael suspected that each of the bottles may have been opened previously and merely filled with filtered water from the local rivers. All of them had been taking daily the tablets distributed by the physician hired by CINC to protect them from the usual intestinal distress that seemed to afflict foreigners uninformed as to the parasites, flora, and fauna of certain areas of Africa.

As his guests dined on fruit and vegetables, Raphael regaled them with tales of his youth and stories of how God had protected him and his followers from various disasters. The CINC crew ate uneasily, still wondering but afraid to ask of Melissa's whereabouts.

Finally, the main course of boar and chicken was brought forth. Each of them was served individually. The CINC crew observed that no one touched their food. They sat waiting as Raphael first bowed his head and then looked heavenward as he took a loaf of bread into his hands and broke off thirteen pieces. Then he took a piece of bread and raised it above his head and said, "This is my body." He paused and then waited as the wines were opened on cue by the women. They were nervous and seemed distressed at the slowness with which each of the corks were unscrewed. One youngish woman in particular seemed completely unfamiliar with the process of uncorking a bottle of wine, and dropped first the cork screw and then the whole bottle on the table and ran off in tears.

Raphael ignored her while several other women went after her. Scolding voices were heard in the distance, followed by thumping sounds and screams. Then it stopped.

Silently, the wine was poured into various plastic cups by an older woman who looked knowingly at Raphael. Raphael then tilted his head backwards and closed his eyes as he faced the heavens and lifted his Chicago White Sox World Series Championship cup. "This is my blood."

His priestly invocations seemingly finished, he looked around the table as if to say, "Drink." As they did so, he passed one of the remaining twelve pieces of bread to each. Several guests knowingly dipped it in their wine before eating it. The CINC crew, Christian and non, followed suit.

As they began to eat the meat and Raphael spoke loudly to one member of the crew, Jeremy leaned toward one of the others and whispered, "I'd have more of an appetite if I knew where Melissa was. This whole thing with the torches and the weirdness reminds me of Disney's *Fantasia*, like the part with the song 'Night on Bald Mountain.'"

At that moment, Melissa appeared at the edge of the crowd of women, children, and gawking soldiers who encircled the table at a respectful distance. She looked worried and had to be pulled and pushed forward by her keepers. She now wore a long, reddish smock that covered her down to her ankles. Her long brown hair had been up in a bun and was now hanging down, unencumbered by ribbons, bobby pins, or any other feminine adornments. She was led, in her bare feet, to the right side of Raphael. As she stood at his side, she glared at him through tears of anger and fear.

He then leaned down and grabbed a handful of loose dirt and sprinkled it on his bootless feet. Then he looked at her and said, "Are you crying?"

She was silent.

"Good," he said. "You will need your tears. Clean my feet."

"What?" she gasped

"Clean my feet," he said calmly but firmly.

"Why?"

"Can you speak the truth?" he asked.

Everyone looked on in silence. The CINC crew glanced at one another in bewilderment.

He then reached up at the leather pouch that still hung around her neck and said, "How is it you do not hear?"

With that, he grabbed her violently by the hair, so hard her chin knocked against one of his knees with a smack. He then pushed her face down to the ground as her keepers pushed her hands to her hair, indicating that she was to clean his feet with it.

The CINC crew jumped up but were immediately restrained by the clicks of rounds chambered by the soldiers now standing behind them. Melissa whimpered and slowly began to wipe his feet with her hair.

Raphael informed her, "See, I told you, you need your tears."

After two minutes, she looked up and begged, "May I go now?"

"What about your pictures? Your story? Don't you want to know how I came to lead a great nation?" He sat silently, waiting for her answer.

"Yes," she whispered.

"Good. You shall have a great prophet to write about. Imagine what it would have been like to have been a journalist following Abraham. Such an opportunity you now have."

After another pause, he told her that after everyone had finished eating, his greatness would be revealed, but only to those who had been tested.

An hour later, the table was cleared except for the remaining wine, in which the non-CINC guests were now indulging. Raphael then snapped his fingers loudly, and one of his older lieutenants came to his side. He then whispered something in the man's ear and watched as he scampered away.

A minute later, the man returned with a small pouch, much like those which the others wore around their necks. Raphael loosened the drawstring, reached in, and pulled out a small, sparkling object. "This is the soul of man," he said. "It is also God, and unless you eat of it, you shall die."

He then passed one to each of the CINC crew and to Melissa, who still stood stunned and withdrawn at his side, too frightened to move. Each crew member now held a small uncut diamond in hand. They were not certain if his warning were to be taken symbolically or literally, until he slammed his left fist down on the table, causing it to shake. "Eat the soul! Eat God or you shall die!"

He then took yet another diamond out and placed it on his tongue, reached for his Chicago White Sox cup, and swallowed it with a gulp.

Slowly and reluctantly, the CINC team, all except Melissa, were forced to swallow the diamond. She continued holding it in her right hand until one of the women attending to her took it and handed it back to Jomo. He threw it at a distance where several children scampered after it in the darkness. Melissa and the other CINC crew members neither understood the gesture nor what response Raphael expected from them.

"You are wise men," he uttered. Then he rose from his chair and said, "Now you will see the power of God."

Everyone stood. Raphael walked toward a large opening that had been cleared for him, with his lieutenants pushing many back to enlarge the circle.

St. George positioned himself about forty feet in front of Raphael, pulled out his nine-millimeter Beretta, and held it in his right hand. Raphael stared at him accusingly, pointed his right index finger, and angrily said, "You were trusted. But you have betrayed me, Judas! You have betrayed me! Better you had not been born!"

With that, St. George said loudly, "I am a sinner. Forgive me!"

He fired a shot directly into the chest of Raphael, who staggered back a step but planted his feet firmly again. "You ... have ... betrayed ... me!"

St. George fired again.

Raphael wobbled and went to one knee. Again, he rose to both feet and yelled as he pointed, "You have betrayed me, Judas!"

Again, St. George fired, and again Raphael fell, this time to both knees. With a moan of pain, he fell to all fours. He began to crawl. After going ahead several more feet, he collapsed as the crowd gasped.

A torchbearer approached with the White Sox cup and gave Raphael a sip of wine. Raphael raised his head and, in a loud voice, yelled out, "Elia, Elia, shalom, shalom, sabba alla do." He then dropped his head and did not move. The torchbearer looked up to the crowd and said, "My lord is dead." A long pause followed in which everyone was silent. Minutes passed, and the crew and Melissa looked on, transfixed.

Then another torchbearer approached and passed the firebrand over Raphael's body three times. After the third pass, Raphael lifted his head and slowly, solemnly, and triumphantly rose from the ground. Everyone clapped and sang out, "Papa! Papa!"—even his erstwhile Judas. The people laughed and hugged one another and rejoiced, and all night long, they cavorted like the rioters in a Cecil B. DeMille production. The crew looked on in amazement. Disney's "Night on Bald Mountain" animation could not compare. But the morning would bring even more to amaze.

CHAPTER 4
BROKEN VOWS

*Be not too hasty to trust or to admire the teachers of morality:
they discourse like angels, but they live like men.*

—Samuel Johnson, *Rasselas*

—THE MISSION PELLA, SOUTH AFRICA

THE EXTERIOR OF THE CHURCH HAD A YELLOWISH HUE AS IF IT HAD been bleached and, at the same time, stained by the golden glow of too many suns. It also looked strangely out of place. It had the design and features of an old Spanish mission from the American Southwest. Yet here it was, not far from the road in the middle of the dry and undulating hills of central South Africa.

Father Matteo Ricci sat in a pew with head bowed, his gray hair rather longish and swept back, still full and vital, matching bushy eyebrows that covered a long face creased and darkened by years of exposure in the vineyard of his labors.

The nightmares of his own life had unfolded in ways that only God could have foreseen and only the devil could have orchestrated. Satan's beguiling ways were truly menacing in their supreme subtlety of deceit.

Today, Father Ricci sat and waited. Someone would come. The church was an out-of-the-way place. Perhaps his whereabouts were already known. In Johannesburg, he had tried to blend in and move back into the anonymous world of a grade school teacher living out his days in charity. Changing the world would have to be left to someone else.

Two days earlier, he had received a hand-delivered message. Someone had slid it under the front door of his residence near the school. It was

33

written in the beautiful longhand he immediately recognized, requesting that he return to his people at once. His disappearance from his former place of mission in Kenya had not gone unnoticed. Moreover, if he were to fall into the hands of the South African Special Police, might they not question him about his knowledge of Jomo Raphael's activities? Did he intend his disappearance as a declaration of his no longer being willing to use his connections in the dark side of the international diamond market as a means of procuring cash and even weaponry itself?

Despite his vocation, Ricci had been Faust to his own Mephistopheles, who had played him like a fiddle. Yes, he had danced for the devil. How unaware he was. Truly, he had an intellect of extraordinary capability but one subject to all the vanity of the weakest of men.

Named for the great Italian linguist of the late sixteenth century, Ricci had never doubted his ability to live up to the legacy of this extraordinary man. *That* Matteo Ricci of the Renaissance had a genius for languages and mathematics. A man of exceptional warmth and cultural sensitivities, he had translated the classics of ancient Greece and Rome into Chinese, thereby blending Western and Eastern culture in ways that few could have foreseen. *This* Matteo Ricci hoped and fully expected to carry on the religious and linguistic legacy of his fellow Italian. That the Jesuit order could have embraced not one but two such extraordinary men of religious piety and linguistic capability, separated only by four hundred years of history, seemed the stuff that spiked the order with the comments of detractors who accused it of sometimes heeding the call of secular knowledge over the spiritual call of the Gospels.

But there was a twist in his heritage. His mother was Jewish. In consenting to rear her children Catholic upon marrying his father, she had insisted that their children nonetheless be steeped in Jewish traditions. One of these was that of learning Hebrew. So at an early age, Matteo had sat at the knee of a young Reform rabbi, a rarity in Italy before World War II, who agreed to teach the child Hebrew along with its application to the interpretation of certain biblical texts. His mother's family had both applauded as well as condemned this enterprise. They praised it for preserving the boy's roots of a mystical lineage to the ancient past but condemned it as a waste of the good rabbi's time. So much for Reform. After all, if the boy were never to have a *bar mitzvah*, what was the point?

Still, even those not inclined to praise the attempt at inculcating Jewish culture into the boy secretly hoped that, step-by-step, he might be converted to the faith of Abraham. His father, however, eyed his instruction warily and made certain that did not happen. Saturday morning Hebrew instruction was pitted against Catholic grade school in his boyhood home of Milan, and the daily recitation of both the Rosary and Mass. There were crucifixes in each of the bedrooms and a picture of the pope prominently displayed in the living room.

On this particular evening, he remained seated for a long time, trying to hear God's voice. He heard only the silence and softly wept as he wondered how he strayed so far and how he would once again, if ever, hear the voice of his beloved and administer the sacraments, especially those of confession and Communion, without feeling like the worst of hypocrites.

Father Matteo Ricci represented an element of Italian society that had come of age in the tumultuous sixties and seventies. To them, Rudy the Red, the sixties' radical of the Sorbonne students, had been a hero and Karl Marx had merely secularized and attempted to implement that which surely Augustine and Aquinas has implied, if not stated outright. And Catholic teaching had long supported the quest of establishing a kind of city of God right here, right now, however impossible and unattainable this vision seemed.

His mother and father both had died before they could see the full effect of the law of unintended consequences. Though his own linguistic achievements were celebrated by both sides of his family, his mother's side had introduced him not just to elements of Jewish culture but to secularized elements of it in the form of Communism.

Through the influence of a family that had escaped the calamity of the Nazis during World War II, he had been introduced to the quasi anti-capitalistic sentiments of his mother's older brother. His uncle held up an ideal of human conduct that matched almost everything he heard in his catechism and his Catholic upbringing.

Indeed, the sharing of not only the means of production but also of the end product itself seemed like Catholicism without the pageantry of the church and without the necessity of God. Ironically, his uncle was a gemologist in Geneva who had invited his nephew to spend several weeks during his summer vacations as his willing assistant. There, as a boy and a teenager, Matteo sat at the hand of a denouncer of capitalism, a practitioner of its skills, and a recipient of its fruits.

His interest in his summer visits was augmented by his uncle's genuine kindness, his own desire not to disappoint, and a weekly pay. He learned how to assess the value of an uncut stone and the means of making it even more valuable through the art of precision cutting. Half of everything he earned he set aside for the poor.

Later, in his early teens, as he began to understand the larger world in which others proselytized on the Lord's behalf, he specified that whatever sum he turned over to the nuns be sent to those missionaries sponsored by his parish and others of the Milan diocese working among the heathens of Africa. Because of his own generosity, he received several letters over the years from priests who baptized the poor, afflicted, and dying, as well as others new to the faith of Christ. In return for his generosity, the priests even offered to let him pick the baptismal names of the soon-to-be-christened orphans. Eagerly, he sent back replies that included names from the panoply of saints that he hoped would be models for these saved children of the orphanages of the Congo, Rhodesia, and Kenya. These little souls were being saved and their bellies filled through the kindness of thousands of youthful Matteo Riccis.

As he grew into manhood, the breadth of his language skills increased to include German, French, and, of course, Latin and Greek. The zeal for languages was matched only by his passion for the message of the Gospels.

Like others before him, he wished to change the world. But to do that, he needed an instrument of execution. So at the age of twenty, three years into this college career at the University of Milan, he approached the Jesuits. No other priesthood matched their academic reputation. They had been the school masters of Europe, and in the estimation of many, they still deserved to be.

The academicians as well as the saintly among the Jesuits encouraged him to finish his degree in classical languages with additional course work in French and German. And after dutifully following the suggestions of the Jesuits, he was sent, in recognition of his language skills, to Campion Hall at Oxford, thereby requiring that he also learn English. Sending someone who had not even completed his basic requirements as a novitiate in the Jesuit order was an extraordinary step, a deficiency that would be filled by his more experienced colleagues from America. They were young priests who tarred capitalism, even in the aftermath of World War II, in sermon and action as they espoused the Marxist-tinged philosophy that would later become known throughout Latin America as liberation theology.

He continued his studies in Hebrew by explicating ancient texts as part of his pursuit of a master's degree in theological studies from Oxford. His religious convictions of childhood remained, along with the gentlemanly pursuit of various other academic disciplines. These blended with the increasingly exciting and sometime controversial elements of Jesuit social activism.

At the age of thirty-two, he was ordained a Roman Catholic priest by the order of Melchisedec. He then went on to obtain a doctorate in theological studies at the University of Rome. He was now a fully armed and fully committed soldier of Christ.

*　　*　　*　　*　　*

Teaching the children of Botswana their rudimentary catechism along with English language studies had proven exhilarating and exhausting at the same time. The children had been extraordinarily receptive. Like those who had come before him, Matteo appealed to those back home in the capitalistic West to alleviate the injustices pervading post-colonial Africa with gifts of money and prayers. Gifts of guilt as well as some of genuine generosity flowed in.

He taught with an enthusiasm tinged with the influence of his uncle and the idealism of the church itself. Indeed, Marx increasingly looked like one for whom the halo was deserved, if not already earned, in the next life.

His early charges had included a phenomenal young man whom he had the good fortune to instruct once he took a position later in one of the missionary schools outside Nairobi. There he met the exuberant, athletic, and extraordinarily charismatic fourteen-year-old Jomo Raphael.

The boy's exceptional leadership qualities were apparent for all to see. He could command the class with his mere presence. Others were drawn to him. In one extraordinary display of his almost mystical insights into the use of his leadership ability, Raphael one day walked several of his classmates to a soccer field near his grade school. There, he took out a bag of bird seed and sprinkled it on the ground. As the birds fluttered over to feed, he turned to his classmates. "As I feed them, I will someday feed you and all my people."

Ricci watched from a distance. As the other students related the incident to him, he knew. Raphael was the means; he was the instrument.

Jomo had been a vessel waiting to be filled with the Word, or, really, any word. Father Matteo Ricci had provided that. Together they plotted the establishing of God's kingdom here on earth, at first playfully, and then, as Jomo grew and moved back to his native Tanzania with his mother, in earnest. The City on the Hill would be right here, right now, in Africa.

As he sat in the church of Mission Pella with his eyes closed, Father Robert Wirtz, a longtime associate, approached quietly. Ricci had telephoned him at his residence outside the Soweto area. Although twenty years younger, Wirtz, already in his mid-forties, had a worldliness about him that Ricci admired and trusted. Unlike some of his other associates, this one would not preach at him for his failings, moral and otherwise.

After all, it was Ricci who had used his influence to get him transferred to two other parishes when word got out of Wirtz's "sexual experimentation" with his adolescent charges. Ricci felt sorry for him and, yes, his victims too, but it seemed such a waste of talent to send him off to prison or on some solitary quest, praying for the redemption of souls long departed. Wirtz had a flair for the classroom. He had this evening come in recognition of Ricci's services to him and to the priestly community in general in its works on behalf of the wretched of the earth.

As Wirtz moved toward Ricci from the front of the dimly lit church, Ricci stood up and stepped into the aisle. He smiled as Wirtz opened his arms in greeting. They embraced and patted one another on the back.

"Father, father," said the younger of the two men.

"Ah, my son, how is it with you?"

After several minutes of cordialities and invitations to each to prevent more long years of separation from coming between them again, they both grew solemn.

"You must wonder why I called you after all these years."

"Why should you not, yes? What excuses need old friends to call one another?"

Ricci was silent. Wirtz seemed to know that he would have to fill the void with a remark, something about the reason for which Ricci had called him.

"When you left the high school in Nairobi and I replaced you, Jomo would frequently come by when he came back from his studies abroad. I'm surprised he did not tell you. We became great friends, great friends." The last sentence seemed as pregnant with meaning as had been Ricci's silence only moments before.

Ricci looked at him with a tinge of disbelief and, at the same time, the realization that it could also be true. But he would refrain from further inquiry at this moment.

"We too were great friends."

At first Wirtz was uncertain if Ricci were referring to himself and Ricci or Ricci and Jomo. But then he went on.

"We had a vision of a new Africa, one free of its colonial vestiges. A vision of Africa for Africans."

"Yes, yes, I remember," added Wirtz.

"But then, I perhaps became indiscreet. I encouraged him to do what was necessary to bring about the kingdom here on earth, now."

"Yes, yes," said Wirtz as he nodded his head up and down. "Yes, he followed your dream with a lust that few would have anticipated."

"But his cruelty. Hacking off limbs—do you know that? Hacking off ears and cutting off their lips of those whom he deemed unworthy of his revolution, then cooking their flesh in front of their wives and making them eat it or threatening to do the same to their children."

"Yes, yes, I know." But then he surprised Ricci with a look of disgust as he said, "And where did he get the weapons? Where did he get the machetes? Who bought them? Where did he get the cash? Through you and your diamond-cutting friends who would sell their mothers for access to the diamond mines that not even the DeBeers can get their hands on."

Ricci was stunned and sat in silence, staring at Wirtz.

"Look," said Wirtz, "you and I are much alike. You are a Marxist who acts like a priest—a revolutionary who lost control of his revolution. Yes, you fooled us all for a while, even me. I admired you. When I learned more, I still stayed in the priesthood because I no longer cared about my soul. You taught me that. Yes, 'The ends,' you said, 'sometimes do justify the means.' You pretended not to see the blood as you went on saying Mass for your killer. You never chastised as long as he did it for *the people.* You used the priesthood as a cover just I have all these years. Yes, I admit it. You have long known what I am. Surely, surely, you knew that. But did you ever chastise me for my conduct with the altar boys or the others? No, you indulged me by allowing me to merely move on to yet another group of unsuspecting victims. And so I did."

Wirtz smiled and then smirked cynically. Then his face softened and he spoke almost reflectively. "Remember the stories you taught in Latin about Nero and how he once sent a letter to his old teacher, Seneca? How the pupil turned on his teacher and threatened to kill him and disinherit his family unless he did it himself? Well, *your* Nero sent you a letter to."

Again, Ricci looked up, this time fearfully. "How did you know about the letter?"

"You fool. I delivered it." He laughed and taunted, "Surely some revelation is at hand."

Yeats had once been Ricci's favorite poet.

He got up past Wirtz and raced from the pew. He stumbled as he did so and then lunged toward the church door. It was locked. Wirtz calmly followed him, smiling, and then put his hand on Ricci's shoulder reassuringly and knocked on the door. It was opened from without. Then he pulled Ricci gently forward into the twilight where a 2007 black Chevrolet Trailblazer with tinted windows waited. Two stocky black men stood at its side and opened the door.

They sped away with Father Ricci sitting silently between the two black men, both of whom were dressed in black dress shirts and black suits. Father Wirtz drove.

After driving all night, stopping only for gas, they arrived at the cape town of Alexander Bay, one of the most important diamond producing areas of the country. Here, it was said, even the sea produced diamonds. Father Ricci had contacts in Alexander Bay who would be very, very happy to see him.

They drove on to the airport, a facility that looked out of place. The main terminal was painted turquoise. One almost expected Navaho craftsmen to be standing next to their stalls, ready to sell.

CHAPTER 5
THRILLING THE MESSENGER

The American will be seeking to capture something he feels he needs.

—Paul Bowles, "American in Search of a Past"

—LONDON

THE UNION JACK CLUB WAS SITUATED NEAR WATERLOO TRAIN Station in London. Its location was ideal for servicemen and servicewomen of Her Majesty's Armed Forces to spend time in the city at affordable prices. Created at the turn of the twentieth century for enlisted and noncommissioned officers, it now provides its comforts to American soldiers and those of the Commonwealth past and present.

With a modern and unadorned exterior, the club was squeezed vertically onto a concise horizontal plane in a crowded area of the city. Its comfortable sitting rooms and good table fare for breakfast, lunch, or dinner helped to make a most genial atmosphere for those far from home, as well as those soldiers of other eras, to meet with their brothers in arms as they reenact battles both real and imagined.

Walls were decorated with plaques and pictures commemorating the achievements of Her Majesty's Armed Forces in the wars of the past one hundred years. The walls chronicled a living history, and those who had done so much for their country could bring their families and point to a picture or some other commemorative and say, "This is what I did during those years I was away."

A pub with the typical British beer and Scottish whiskeys stayed open every evening until eleven, allowing the tavern crowd to stay on past the dinner hour.

Past the pub and through two usually closed doors was a reading room with comfortable chairs, magazines, and books on history, geography, and even anthropology. Travel writings also found a place on the shelves, presumably because many had been written by members of the military services who had at one time or another stayed here. They had therefore seen fit to dedicate a volume of their own work to the small but handsome library that sat open ready to be engaged.

Past this library and on the left was yet another library room, properly lit and overlooking the London street one story below. This was the T. E. Lawrence Reading Room.

Its namesake was Lawrence of Arabia, whose accomplishments were legendary. This man had, during the First World War, united Arab tribes in a war on the declining Ottoman Empire that helped deprive Germany of her allies' various resources, including men and equipment. Lawrence himself carried out a series of adventurous raids, which displayed not only his military prowess but also his scholarly bent. The scholar soldier had a long tradition in the British military.

On this particular Tuesday afternoon, Dennis Bernard was sitting in the Lawrence Reading Room doing what he often did as one long retired from the British army. He was doing research both on the military campaigns of which he had been a part during World War II as well as those of his long dead cousin, T. E. Lawrence.

But he was also biding time. He was waiting to see if the young man from the United States with whom he had corresponded would indeed appear. Over the decades, Dennis Bernard had written now and again to the widow of his friend, hoping to console as well as to merely stay in touch with someone who could remember the past. For as his own wartime colleagues departed this life, he sought more and more strongly to keep their memories alive by touching the lives of their descendants. And as something of a scholar soldier himself, Dennis had a lifelong interest in the arcane, the past and its connection to the present, and the relationship of his own existence to the puzzle of life.

Dennis thought that everyone in life had a purpose. The great quest, he imagined, was to determine exactly what that purpose was. He also thought that what one did in life resonated throughout one's own days as well as in the next life.

He thought that if a certain young man walked through the reading room door, his own purpose might be coming to fruition. It was a feeling, not a certainty. Not a mathematical truism, but a feeling that had been with him for some time.

Now in his eighties, he wondered if there was time enough left to bequeath his legacy to someone who would deem it worthy of remembrance. It was a legacy that had come to him in dribbles, in years of experience as well scholarly endeavor. Why had this passion gripped him? And why was this young man coming here now, today, if indeed he were?

As he sat there with several books open, he mused on the story of Winston Churchill's boyhood, of his once falling into a bog and sinking rapidly, unable to escape. A farmer by the last name of Flemming heard the boy's cries and ran to the rescue, eventually pulling him from certain death. Afterward, Churchill's father had gone looking for the farmer who had saved his son's life. Lord Randolph Churchill eventually found the farmer and offered him a considerable sum of money to say thank you. The farmer refused the money, but Lord Randolph, seeing that the man had a young son, offered to send the boy to college when he came of age. Farmer Flemming accepted.

Years later, Winston Churchill grew desperately ill. He was treated with a new medicine, penicillin, a recent discovery of a young medical doctor by the last name of Flemming—the same Flemming whose education had been paid for by Churchill's father. It was a wonderful story illustrating the reciprocity of a person's actions. Somehow, Dennis felt that everything he had done to date would be remembered by someone.

At that moment, a young man was standing outside the building, looking up to confirm the address. The Union Jack. He bounded up the outdoor stairs.

*   *   *   *   *

Dennis had aged well over the years. At the age of twenty-seven, he had married a lovely woman, Catharine Wilmot, an Irish girl who had given him five children: two sons and three daughters. Each prospered and married well. Theirs was a happy marriage with happy children. But none of them shared their father's devotion to the military or his interest in the past and its connections to the present, unless it had to do with one of their still living relatives.

As he considered all this, the young man walked in the front door of the Union Jack Club. To his left stood an elderly gentleman in his sixties.

"Sir, if I could see some form of identification, please."

The young man pulled out his wallet, from which he took his military identification card. A microchip with all essential information on a person's life, or at least what seemed essential to the military, lay embedded in a two-by-three-inch rigid plastic card that identified him by name as Lieutenant Commander Grant Chisolm, United States Navy. A small black and white photograph was also embedded in the card.

The gentleman examined the card and handed it back to him with a smile. Grant, dressed in blue jeans and a red pullover sport shirt, walked to the front desk, where a pretty and petite woman in an official-looking navy blue dress, with a British flag pin on her lapel, sat waiting for the day's customers.

"Excuse me. Can you tell me where the reading room is?"

"Through the pub," she said, pointing up the four stairs that led to a bar with spacious seating area for its patrons.

"Thank you."

Through the glassed wall of the reading room, Dennis watched as Grant Chisolm strode off in his direction, turned right into the darkened seating area, stopped for a moment, and then looked up at "Reading Room" printed in black ink on a brass plate over a set of double doors. He entered but found it empty. Then he noticed to his left another door that read "T. E. Lawrence Reading Room," also on a brass plate. Dennis waited patiently as Grant took several steps and entered. Dennis greeted him with a quizzical look.

"Excuse me, sir, is your name Dennis?"

"And who wants to know?" he responded with an inviting smile as he stood, extending his hand.

"Grant Chisolm. I received your letter and then your e-mail."

He took Grant's hand firmly into his own frail but energetic grip, shaking it up and down several times, then placed his left hand on top as well.

"Welcome, welcome. I always knew one day you would come. I so wished it. I have something to tell you, and you are the man—yes, the one to whom it must be said. Sit down, please. Please, let's get acquainted. Your life, I hear, has been most interesting. Your grandmother has bragged of you often and, of course, your mother, too."

Grant sat immediately opposite Dennis at a long library table. The chairs in which both sat were comfortable with rounded, cushiony seats and firm arm rests of oak and more cushiony padding. *A person,* thought Grant, *could sit here comfortably for hours.* So they did.

*   *   *   *   *

After several hours of intense conversation, Dennis suggested that they continue their talk in the pub. Dennis bought himself a pint and ordered a drink for Grant, who indicated a Perrier.

"How long will you be here in England?" Dennis asked.

"For at least one year."

"Any time off?"

"I've a couple weeks to get settled; then I'll be doing some training."

"Have you seen the sites yet?"

There was a lull in the conversation, and Dennis thought it appropriate to mention, "When you are ready, I want you to open this."

Grant was perplexed. At that moment, he noticed Dennis's eyes twinkle as he looked to a young woman who had just walked into the pub. She looked about, saw Dennis, and came straight over. She put down her purse and kissed him on the cheek.

"This, Grant, is my niece. Or really, I should say, my great niece, Blanche DeNegris."

Grant stood and politely shook hands.

Blanche was about five feet eight inches tall, had long reddish-brown hair, a full bosom, slender waist, and shapely, firm hips. She wore on this summer day a loose-fitting paisley dress and high heels. She carried a satchel with a leather strap hung over her shoulder. Her face radiated goodness and devotion to her great uncle.

"And this, my dear, is Grant, the friend of a great friend."

She sat down at the round table in between her uncle and Grant.

"Grant and I are just becoming acquainted, Blanche."

Grant smiled at Blanche and commented, "You have a beautiful name."

"It's more French than English," she responded. "Old Norman blood, I think."

While they exchanged pleasantries, Dennis gently reached over and took the leather satchel from Blanche's shoulder and shifted it to the center of the table.

"Grant was just saying that he had not seen many of the sites yet. Perhaps you could show him around," said Dennis.

Grant continued to smile at Blanche, who seemed keen at the prospect and responded, "Anything in particular interest you? London's a great city."

"Actually," he said a bit sheepishly, "I've always wanted to go to Glastonbury Tor and to Tintangle. I can't say why. They're just places that appeal to me."

"Ah," said Blanche, "the supposed place of Camelot and of King Arthur's burial. I'd like to take you there sometime, but I'm afraid my job at the British Museum precludes my making overnight trips during the week."

"I understand."

"Well, perhaps something more modest, such as the museum itself. I'd love to show you around." Grant smiled and nodded.

Dennis quietly sipped his beer as his great niece and Grant conversed. A little while later, an old friend of his saw him and walked over. Dennis asked her to sit down. She too kissed him and said hello to Blanche, whom she already knew. Grant stood as he was introduced. The older woman, Kay, had gray hair and wore a dark blue summer dress with sleeves down to her elbows and smelled of lilac. He ordered her a pint.

After a pleasant hour of conversation, Blanche announced that she must get back to work. She and Grant made a date for later in the week. He was to call her the next day to firm up the time. He told her he would be staying at the Marriott all week as he had some work to do at the U.S. Navy's European Command Center. They exchanged phone numbers.

As Grant walked back to the table at which Dennis and Kay sat, Dennis raised his eyebrows with a smile as if to say to Kay, "Look what I just did." Although himself a widower, Dennis delighted in the prospect of one day finding a match for his scholarly and all too single niece.

About a half-hour later, Dennis explained that he had enjoyed his life greatly. He also knew that it would not go on forever and that it was important therefore to give to someone, that special someone, who could make use of the fruits of his labors. Grant listened intently.

Then Dennis leaned forward and pushed the satchel toward Grant and said, "This is one old Brit's way of saying thanks to the Yanks. You've been with us in two world wars, and we've stood side by side in the two wars in the desert and now in the war on terror. Consider it a gift—a sort of hands across the waters."

Without opening the satchel, Grant said, "Thank you."

Dennis looked at his friend Kay and then again turned to Grant.

"Call me. I know you'll have questions. All the information is in there." He nodded in the direction of the satchel.

Kay smiled. "Listen to Dennis. He's a good man." She tapped his hand gently as she sipped from her pint.

Grant looked at his watch.

"I have to go, I'm afraid. My friends will be expecting me at the King's Head. Then we're going to a play later tonight."

Grant took the satchel in his hand and departed with a strange sense of urgency. He wanted to look at the contents of the satchel but remembered his mother's advice to be patient in life in order to better enjoy its fruits.

CHAPTER 6

A SHARED MYSTIQUE

It is my duty to make the position clear to you,
so that you may not resent the
impertinence of any questions I may have to ask.

—Agatha Christie, *Murder in Mesopotamia*

—GRANT'S HOTEL ROOM, LONDON

THAT EVENING, AFTER GRANT GOT BACK FROM THE PLAY, HE RECEIVED a phone call from an acquaintance in Washington DC, telling him that a Colonel Rupert Holloway of the U.S. Air Force would meet him the next day after noon at the National Art Gallery in the second floor restaurant and reception area. An exhibition of Vermeer's works was once again being shown on the ground floor. Ignore it, he was told, and go immediately to the second floor.

For a moment, Grant wanted to object. He had only just arrived in England. He hadn't yet checked into his permanent duty assignment at RAF Alconbury, about eighty miles north of London. But the acquaintance at the other end of the phone was firm and not inclined to be put off with issues of fatigue.

The next day, Grant arrived and did as instructed. Holloway was waiting at a table in one corner, overlooking the gallery below.

Grant had been instructed not to worry about identifying Holloway. He already knew what Grant looked like and would identify himself when he came into the restaurant. Holloway stood up as Grant walked in and continued looking at Grant until he turned in Holloway's direction. Holloway motioned to him to come and sit down. As Grant approached the table at which Holloway had been seated, each extended his hand to shake and then both sat down. Before Grant had a chance to ask any questions of his own, Holloway asked, "What's in the satchel?"

"What's in the satchel?" repeated Grant.

"Yes, I saw you with it yesterday. Where is it? Is it safe?" responded Holloway.

Not easily intimidated, Grant paused before answering. Then he said, with perfect diction, "To which satchel are you referring?"

It was now Holloway's turn to pause. He was accustomed to getting what he wanted immediately. They both sat in silence. Holloway knew from years of experience as an interrogator and as a member of the special forces that silence was one of the most important ways of eliciting information. Prisoners would sometimes blurt out much-sought information just to relieve the emotional discomfort caused by the silence. Grant was not a prisoner and had no such intention. They sat in silence for over a minute, Grant looking casually around and Holloway staring at him. Holloway's steely gray eyes sat beneath gray eyebrows on a thin, almost gaunt face in which the lips seemed to have been penciled in.

Finally, a waitress approached their table, forcing both of them to look up. She asked what they wanted to drink as she handed each of them a menu. They smiled as they took the menu and glanced at it superficially.

"I'll have a coffee and the ploughman's sandwich," said Grant.

"The same," said Holloway.

After she left, Holloway said, "Look, I'm not here to play games. I've been watching you since before you arrived. We've watched Dennis for years."

"He's a very interesting man," replied Grant.

"You have no idea." Holloway softened for a moment and said, "Look, we are concerned about his safety and yours."

"Why?" asked Grant.

"We're not the only ones who have been interested in Dennis."

"What does any of this have to do with the satchel?" asked Grant.

"That," we hoped, "was something you could tell us."

"No," responded Grant. "Last night I was too tired to look at it. It was a gift, and I like to enjoy them. I'll examine it at my leisure."

"Are you aware that you are being followed?" asked Holloway. He raised his eyebrows inquisitively as though to ask the question again. For a moment, his tacit query made Grant think of a mime.

"Are you the one following me?" asked Grant.

"Yes, but we're also following someone who appears to be following you." Holloway pulled out a picture apparently taken at a distance and unbeknownst to the observed. "He has been tailing you since you arrived."

"Why? How would anyone know enough to trail me in the first place? I flew here commercial, and at customs I used a passport to enter the country, not my military orders. I never display my military ID unless I need to. Who knew I was coming? Who knows I'm here?"

Ignoring Grant's questions, Holloway said, "Look, we want to watch Dennis because Dennis is interested in you. We think that Dennis's interest is what brought this man here." Holloway showed Grant a photograph. "His name is Faisal Khan. He is of Pakistani origin but was born here in England. We also know that he has made a number of trips to Germany over the past three years, two of them directly to Hamburg while the others were to Frankfurt, Stuttgart, and Berlin. However, even in those instances, he still made contact with people from Hamburg, including the ladies."

"Al Qaeda connection?" asked Grant.

"Perhaps, but," said Holloway, "we have an excellent working relationship with MI5 and MI6. Their secret services and CIA and other special ops have worked together extremely well. We both know that this war on terrorism is going to go on for some time and we need each other. Still, there are times."

The last several words were sufficiently vague for Grant to infer that Holloway's glowing endorsement of the working relationship between the United States' intelligence services and those of the British had a caveat to it. "So they aren't sharing all the information with us on this individual. Why not?"

"We would like to know that, too, unless they think we have too many leaks in our intelligence operations."

"Okay, but why are they following me and this man?"

"His movements are clearly suspicious. He has no known livelihood. He's a graduate student at Oxford, in chemical engineering. He has a nice car and likes the night life and likes to frequent the Finsbury Mosque, or at least he used to. He may be staying away since it is a well-known secret that the mosque and its worshippers are being monitored closely these days."

"The Finsbury Mosque, the one that has imams who are clearly anti-Western, anti-American, anti-everything?" asked Grant sarcastically.

"Grant," said Holloway, addressing him by his name for the first time, "we think this guy's following you has something to do with the satchel. We also think they're tapping Dennis's phone and have hacked his e-mail. If you have occasion to meet Dennis again, it's probably best to meet him in a public place, like the Union Jack. And stay out of dark places. Your nation has spent a lot of time and money training you. We can't afford to lose you."

Grant smiled and nodded in acknowledgement. Holloway then asked, "Where's the satchel?"

Grant hardly knew Holloway and wasn't sure that he needed to know. Anticipating a possibly heated response from Holloway once he answered, he said, "It's in a very safe place."

"I thought you didn't know what was in it? Why would you put it in a very safe place?" Holloway kept his temper under control.

"I do now." Grant's silence indicated that Holloway had received as much information as he was likely to get.

After another long pause, Holloway asked, "Are you still at the Marriott?" Holloway already knew that he was but wanted to save a little face by having Grant divulge something. It was better for their future relations for Holloway to leave with a gratuitous gift of information than no gift at all.

"Yes, I am," responded Grant, who also sensed that he would need to tell this man more of what he already knew if they were to work together successfully. "I'm taking some leave. I know it's a bit unusual to be granted leave at the outset of a new assignment but nothing the military does these days seems usual. I'm staying at RAF Alconbury after this."

Holloway replied, "Stay in touch. Don't make this hard. We'll need to inform one another of our whereabouts hereafter."

Grant thought that the last remark was particularly interesting since Holloway informed him of almost nothing about himself. He knew only that he would be keeping an eye on him and that he had an encrypted cell phone device that would enable Grant to reach him twenty-four hours a day.

Holloway left the National Art Institute while Grant lingered. Grant then paid five pounds extra to see the Vermeer exhibit. He thought it rather odd that on the very first trip he had ever made to the museum that his favorite painter's works would be on display. He thought somewhat comically of the lines from the TV series, *Stranger than Fiction*. "Coincidence? I think not." But elements of serendipity that he could not yet see were already at play in his life.

While standing in the line that passed through the exhibit, he stopped to look at Vermeer's *Milkmaid* painting. He admired the artist's creation. The girl was beautiful. *She looked like Blanche*, he thought. He pulled out his cell phone to tell Blanche that he was several blocks away but that he was looking at her. She was confused and reflexively looked out her second-story office window at the British museum. He explained that if she wanted to know how he could see her from several blocks away, she would have to meet him for dinner the very next day. She agreed and suggested that they begin with a tour of the British Museum.

CHAPTER 7
GODLESS AND SILENT

Woe to him that is alone when he falls, for he has no other to help him up.

—The Wisdom of Solomon, Apocrypha

OMAR HUSSEIN ABU HUSSEIN KNELT ON THE NAKED BACK OF THE prostrate figure whose head was being sat upon by one of his assistants. Hussein then reached into his innocuous-looking fanny back and pulled out a razor-sharp carving knife.

"You are an infidel. You are stupid." He spoke his words in Turkish, deliberately and without emotion, to the priest who lay face down on the floor. Both of the priest's legs were held down by two other pairs of muscular arms.

"You must tell us where it is or you will not see your wife and children again." The priest squirmed uncomfortably and continued sweating under the pressure of the force upon his body. But he did not answer.

"You speak Turkish, but if you do not answer, perhaps you can scream in Arabic or even Greek. It makes no difference to me." Without saying another word, he yanked at a section of the priest's back flesh adjacent to his spine and just below his shoulder blades. He lifted it with a heavy pinch and began to slice with the precision of a surgeon. He created a three-and-a-half-inch cut into the flesh and inserted a small glass vial of acid with the lid still tightly sealed. The priest moaned slightly in pain but did not scream. Instead he closed his eyes and uttered a quiet prayer to the Virgin Mary.

Then Omar Hussein grabbed another piece of flesh on the other side of his spine, sliced it open, and inserted another vial of acid into the bleeding pocket. This time the priest merely whispered an act of contrition in Greek. Hussein then took out a pair of rubber gloves and put them on. He reached once more into his fanny pack and pulled out yet another vial. He then turned around and faced the priest's rear and motioned for his henchmen to pull down the priest's pants. He inserted the next vial by forcing it into the man's rectum. A one-inch-thick wooden dole acted as an instrument for forcing the vial deep into the man's bowels.

"These bottles of acid will inflict wounds that no one will at first see. Unless you tell us where it is, you will die an agonizing death. In about one to two hours, the acid will have burned through the plastic caps and will begin to drip out in agonizing fire. You will wish for hell, and there will be no mercy since you are an infidel. Once we turn you over and sit you up, the acid will move to the top end and begin to burn through. So tell us what you know, and Prince Nayez has assured us that we can remove the acid and let you go."

Omar's mentioning the prince by name told the priest that his torture was sanctioned by the head of the Saudi secret police and not likely to end quickly even if he told them what he knew. Despite his silence in the face of extreme pain, with the promise of more to come, he doubted his own goodness and had begun to wonder at the purpose of martyrdom not witnessed by his followers. But then his mind drifted back to the idea that he must pray for his enemies. Perhaps at least his enemies would be moved to do good by his example. He thought of each as a possible Saul on his way to Damascus, or Mecca, or even Islamabad. His spirit, he hoped, would linger here after and his sacrifice would protect an ancient treasure and the lives of his wife and children.

Father Cosmos lay in the all-but-unknown lowest level of the Crusader stronghold of Bodrum. A walled fortification built in the Middle Ages, it now housed the Bodrum Museum of Underwater Archaeology and the material legacy of the Knights of Malta, or, as they were otherwise known, the Knights Hospitaller. With stones and artifacts removed from the Mausoleum of Halicarnassus, one of the Seven Wonders of the Ancient World, it housed secrets that taunted the daily processionals of tourists with hints of intrigue but little revelation.

A Greek Orthodox priest being appointed as curator of a museum was not a particularly peculiar event. A Greek Orthodox priest being appointed *by the Turkish government* to an official government-funded function, even if only for the sake of a show—*that* was a near impossibility.

Still, it had happened. The Turkish prime minister, in a brazen move of religious and political ecumenism, had appointed a Greek Orthodox priest, one of the few left in Istanbul, to act as the curator of both the Underwater Museum and the fortification itself. He hoped that such beneficence would be yet another display of Turkey's Western ways, its cosmopolitanism, and its deserved entry into the European Union.

On this occasion, the priest's silence provoked his antagonists, who now turned him over to await either his cooperation or his hellish demise. However, these students, as they called themselves, never met the courage of a good and holy man.

Finally, the priest, in pain, murmured, "Who are you?"

Omar Hussein replied, "We are the students. You are a teacher; tell us what you know." He smiled at the priest even though the man could not see his tormentor's face.

"Father, do you think I enjoy this? I find it tedious. It is you who forces my hand. I would like to let you go, but I cannot do so until you teach me your secrets."

Silence. The priest's lack of cooperation was confounding. Omar knew that once the acid began to work, he would get nothing from the priest. After several more minutes, he ordered Ali, Said, and one named Shakar to turn the priest over and sit him up. The priest sat on his haunches, attempting to relieve the discomfort. And then, in an act that his assailants considered all too brazen, he began to utter a prayer in Greek. As he did so, he slipped his knees underneath himself to kneel.

His abuser again smiled and said, "You are only a man, and no one, not even Christ, can withstand the pain that I will inflict."

Silence. Not even a prayer. The priest's legs were shaking uncontrollably, and his tormentor feared that the contents of a vial might have been expelled. But the priest remained silent with his eyes closed and his head bowed.

"Father, you leave me no choice." Then he began to cut away until the priest's trousers were entirely removed. He motioned for the others to bind the priest's feet with duct tape as they had already done with his hands. Then he stood up, knelt down behind the priest, and embraced him firmly around the waist with his left arm as the others leaned on him with their full weight to prevent his moving. Omar reached around with his right hand, in which he still held the carving knife, and sliced across the man's lower abdomen. Immediately, the priest's bowels began to protrude through the four-inch incision. The tormentor reached in with his thumb and his forefinger and pulled out a loop of the priest's intestines while Shakar looped a leather cord around it. Shakar then walked the cord to a metal ring anchored in the ancient granite and limestone walls and looped it through; then he walked it back to the priest and tied the leathern cord firmly around his neck.

Then, as Omar continued to hold his intestines out about three inches, Shakar again looped the cord around the priest's intestine. He looped the leather cord to yet another ring, walked it back several feet, and again tied it firmly around the priest's neck. The priest's body shook involuntarily. He could neither sit, nor stand, nor lay but in great pain. Still, he was silent. Then his demon spoke in an almost kindly whisper.

"Open your eyes, Father. I am your deliverer. If you cooperate, I can release you. If you do not, I will leave you to your own devices. If you lean or fall forward, the cord at your back will pull your bowels out. If you fall backward, the other cord will pull your bowels out. If you move to either side, your bowels will be pulled out by both cords. Please, I do not like to see a good man suffer needlessly."

Silence.

"Father, do not try my patience," he continued in an understanding voice. "I am a most lazy man, and the nice thing about your current predicament is that I really have no more work to do. I can leave you or sit and wait. The acid will be so painful that you will writhe on the floor in torment. The vials in your back I have placed beneath your shoulder blades, where your angel wings should be, for you are a good and holy man. But the acid will destroy your wings and then it will be too late. I will not be able to help you."

The priest's whole body was quivering. He opened his eyes. "Be gone, Satan," he uttered. Ali, who stood immediately behind him, angrily kicked the priest hard in the small of the back. The bowels ripped out over a foot and wrapped around his right side as he fell forward, catching himself by twisting to the left and hitting his shoulder to the floor before hitting his head. The priest's face was awash in tears, but still he made no sound.

"Idiot! Idiot! You presume too much!" shouted Omar Hussein as he glared at Ali.

The priest righted himself, breathing heavily and catching the smell of his own body. He almost gagged on his foulness as well as the pain and realization that he was being disemboweled by willful men of malediction.

His tormentor then reached out gently with one hand.

"I'm bored."

He touched the priest's face and then firmly and incrementally pulled at the front cord and watched as the priest's eyes closed in pain but not terror. Omar pulled another full foot of intestines and tied it in a knot to tighten the pull of the rope yet again.

Shaking and feeling immensely fatigued, the priest, a middle-aged man of rare faith, keeled forward. He was unconscious, and his body shook convulsively. The intestines had been ripped out another two feet, and his bodily fluids spilled from his bowels. Though still breathing, his pulse was weakening, and Omar realized that this man's death was only minutes away. Soon the acid would begin to drip from three different place as it ate through the plastic bottle caps.

Omar Hussein then looked at Ali and said, "You have yet to learn patience. But you are young. Now we must leave, and you and the others must seek another source for the information we desire." Omar pulled from his pants pocket a change purse, from which he extracted a ring made of blue stone.

"This, Father, is the same blue stone out of which Moses carved the Ten Commandments. I have met a holy man, and to such as you, I bequeath this emblem of respect." He placed the ring on the finger of the still bound hands. He then sighed and said for all to hear, "I do not hate you, infidel. I am just a man with no imagination and one so steeped in blood I can find no reason to do other than I do."

Omar rose and climbed the stone passageway that led to the iron grating, which two of them lifted open with difficulty. They ascended into the sanctuary of the old Crusader Church. As they left it and walked into the courtyard of the ancient fortification, Omar Hussein thought to himself, *I am a good man, for I make holy men better and bad men worse. I so enjoy my work.*

CHAPTER 8

THE VANITY OF HUMAN WISHES

The wheels had the sparkling appearance of chrysolite,
and all four of them looked the same.

—Ezekiel 1:16

—JOMO RAPHAEL'S ENCAMPMENT

ALL NIGHT LONG, MELISSA MILLINSON AND THE OTHERS LISTENED TO the revelry. It was a frightening combination of unabashed debauchery and violence in which the soldiers of Christ's Army of Liberation had their way with the wine as well as the women. Gunshots occasionally went off, although even Jomo had limitations in what he would endure. Besides, it gave away their position and wasted ammunition. Finally, at about four o'clock in the morning, the revelry came to an end. Those still awake vomited their fill in nature's retribution for intemperate vice. Women who gave themselves willingly and sportively to their own lust and that of the soldiers had twinges of remorse. One was seen walking around and around her tent, reciting the rosary in compensation. Most of the young men slept where they fell in their inebriation. The village looked like a battlefield in which Bacchus had wounded the lot and left them to their retching and headachy wounds.

Jomo did not drink. Even when he was seen taking drink from a wine bottle, it was in fact grape juice that he had poured into the bottle to replace the wine he had secretly poured out. To make the deception complete, he would always rub a small amount of wine around the mouth of the bottle so that the smell was completely and verifiably that of *vino*. Sometimes he would even allow one of the women devotees to sniff the cork drenched in wine as a gesture of gentlemanly conduct as he had seen done in Paris at Hiramatsu Restaurant. Then, in a gesture of benign largesse, he gave her the cork as a token of his appreciation for her services to their cause. He told her to burn the cork and smear the ash on her forehead if she wished to be fertile, and he himself would fulfill her wish. Whether she were married or not, Jomo would humbly submit to her request.

Melissa and her crew had been ushered back to their tent at about two in the morning, where they lay in fear all the night. Several hours later, after the sun came up, Jomo sent Marx St. George to fetch the group some coffee and bread. After they ate and drank, St. George returned to tell them that Jomo wished to see them.

St. George led them out to Jomo's tent, which was several hundred feet away. Despite the lateness of the morning, many of the young men were still hung over from their revelry, and even the children were still asleep in most of the village. For the most part, only the women stirred as they went about their daily chores and rituals.

Melissa was not her usual self. Her confidence had been shattered the evening before, and she only managed to doze off occasionally, racked by the pain and convulsions of her humiliation at the feet of Jomo. Moreover, she was aware that her treatment at his hands may have diminished her authority, even in the eyes of her own crew. She had cried in their presence. She also viewed her own humiliation as something directed at her womanhood itself, something to degrade as well as to control. At this moment, she simply wanted to go home.

As Melissa and her crew were brought into Jomo's tent, they eyed him suspiciously and then sat immediately opposite him in canvas-backed folding chairs. Each sat upright, tense and still confused and frightened. Jomo sensed this and attempted to put them at ease. They were learning how his mercurial temper could be alluring as well as horrifying.

He sat in a large chair for a large man. He was in his camouflage uniform, which he had designed and bedecked himself. It was arrayed with Israelis jump school wings, a U.S. Army Ranger insignia, and a U.S. Seventh Cavalry crossed sword insignia. He had even had epaulet straps sewn on the uniform so that he could display the rank of admiral, British navy. He might have seemed clownish had he been less physically imposing. But his strength and bulk, along with a radiant charm, could overcome all the contradictions and superfluities of his sartorial splendor. He remained impressive.

"How are my friends this morning?"

They responded with flickers of eye contact and silence.

He smiled brightly, warmly, and empathically. "Yes, I know," he said. "Our ways can be troubling to foreigners. But you are no longer foreigners to us. Now you are friends."

He made the last remark as he gestured to the young men who stood on either side of him. They were about eighteen and were dressed in camouflage also, but without his accoutrements and without weapons. Jomo, on the other hand, wore a holster and two pistols.

St. George, as usual, stood off to one side. Jomo looked at Jeremy Democowicz.

"You look strong. Do you hunt? Do you fish?"

Jeremy waited to make certain that Jomo was finished speaking before answering.

"I don't anymore, but I did as a kid. Washington is a great place for both."

"Good, good. Perhaps while you are with us, you can do both," Jomo responded.

"And you, my friends, you have at last your interviews, and I a new group of friends to whom I owe so much. So let me hear about *your* lives. How did you become reporters? Where do you live now? Where did you go to school?" Then he looked at Melissa and smiled.

She glowered in response with tears of intense displeasure and fear pooling in her eyes.

"And you, you," he said, pointing at Michael Constantine. "You must also hunt with me sometime." With that, he pulled out both of his revolvers and placed them in a slow, seemingly meaningful gesture, on the table in front of them. Michael grew tense and gripped hard at the wooden chair.

"No, no, my friends; do not be frightened. These guns are new, from

Brazil, and I wish for you to see them. I am very proud of them. When we go hunting, I will let you use them. You may do so now." He pushed each pistol a couple more inches toward them and said, "Take. Take. Look at them, but please be careful; they are loaded." He said the last word as they if he were warning a child, and he simultaneously wagged his right index finger.

Hesitantly, Michael picked up the pistol. He noticed that the safety was on. Jeremy did the same.

"Look, look," said Jomo. He raised his hands above his head in a mock gesture of surrender. "I have been captured by CINC crew. They will make me give them an interview and speak to the entire world."

Jomo dropped his hands and said again, "Look, look here." He reached across, making an open-handed gesture to Michael to surrender the pistol. Jeremy continued to hold the other, not quite certain what to do with it. He was no longer a hunter and not a handgun aficionado. He watched as Jomo explained the appeal of this particular pistol.

"You see, I have two of these. I have had many other pistols but never ever have I worn two at one time as I do now because these are so beautiful."

His genuine enthusiasm was infectious. Even Melissa had to look up at them.

Sensing a lessening of the tension, Jomo smiled radiantly.

"Look, look at my books." He made extravagant gestures with both arms to indicate the plastic crates on top of one another in which a small but impressive library was on display all around them. Immediately over his right shoulder were several works in English, T. E. Lawrence's *Seven Pillars of Wisdom*, Bulloch's *Stalin*, Custer's *My Life on the Plains*, Field Marshal Montgomery's war annals, *Montgomery of El Alamain* and sundry other works on contemporary warfare. Next to these was a complete collection of Copleston's *History of Philosophy* and St. Augustine's *City of God*. Next to these was a three-volume set of Tennyson's collected works.

Over his left shoulder were *Mein Kampf*, works by Camus, *My Islamic Journey* by V. S. Naipaul, *The Puzzle Palace* by James Bamford, and works of geography and tour books on virtually every country in Europe and several in Africa.

As Melissa scanned the rest of the room, she saw works by Teilhard de Chardin, Adam Smith, Dostoevsky, and Joseph Conrad. Oddly enough, she also saw *My Life* by Bill Clinton and several old issues of *Time* and *Newsweek*, as well as several recent issues of the British periodical *The Economist*.

On top of the shelves directly behind them sat a twelve-inch statue of the Virgin Mary and a picture of Jesus pointing to his heart wrapped in thorns. To either side were small stone busts of men with African features. Next to these were pictures of Mother Theresa, Elvis Presley, Tim McGraw, and Karl Marx, as well as several pictures of Jomo shaking hands with various personalities, the political movers and shakers of Africa and much of the rest of the world as well.

Throughout the room were rolled up maps and paperweights from the capitals of Europe. On others were VHS copies of battle depictions from BBC and a series entitled *The Great Commanders*. Several works by John Forsyth were also on display.

Jomo caught Melissa's glance at the VHS selections and smiled.

"I have many works on DVD, as well," he said. "I also have many American films, too. I love *Patton*. I could watch it a thousand times."

Then, parodying a line from the film, he said, "When this war is over, I will not have to say I shoveled shit in Mozambique," and laughed loudly, as did the young soldiers on either side. They laughed because he laughed. They felt it their duty. They had no idea what he had just said since neither of them had seen the film. They did, however, speak English, as Jomo had insisted on its instruction for all the youth. He promised that English would eventually be the primary language spoken in the nation that he was creating.

Before him, on his makeshift desk of plywood on two construction horses, was a map of the world laid out under a sheet of Plexiglas. On the map were red stars, such as those which a teacher might put on a child's paper for good work. He motioned to the map with his right hand.

"I have been to all those places on the map where a red star is stuck," he said proudly.

His stars blanketed Europe, North Africa, Israel, Jordan, Saudi Arabia, the Horn of Africa, and all the countries in Africa south of the Sahara.

"I have also been to America, Washington DC, Fort Bragg, North Carolina, and even the Bahamas. The Bahamas are beautiful. But nothing is like Rome. I have been there twice but I have never seen the pope."

He smiled up at them again and said, "Now you have had your interview. Now where is my van?"

All of them responded with a perplexed look. "Excuse me," said Jeremy. "Did you say *van?*"

"Of course. Perhaps you are planning a surprise. CINC will deliver it by helicopter? When will it arrive? I know you did not bring it with you," he added almost playfully.

Michael Constantine said, "We don't know anything about a van, Mr. Raphael."

"Ah, you should know by now to address me as General Raphael. Try again, only this time, do it better." Jomo waited.

Jeremy Democowicz said again, "We don't know anything about a van, General Raphael. No one told us anything."

Raphael looked genuinely disappointed.

"Perhaps," he said, "you misunderstand. You promised me an SUV if I gave you this interview. I have done my part. Now where is it? Perhaps you did not know where to deliver it."

Michael pleaded, "We don't even know for sure where we are. How could we deliver *anything* to you?"

Jomo now looked menacingly at each of them as he said, "Did I not pay you last night?" There was silence. "Well, were you not paid as well as given an interview?"

Knowing the danger they were in, Jeremy said delicately, "Sir, general, what pay are you referring to?"

Jomo glared at him and then raised his right hand and pointed his index finger at Michael and said, very slowly, in a low, controlled voice, "Did you accept the diamonds last night?"

Fearing where this was going, Michael glanced at Jeremy, and he at Melissa, looking for an escape. The remainder were dead quiet.

"Well?" asked Jomo.

"Please, we only took them because we thought they were gifts, an act of generosity. We have heard so much about your kindness and your hospitality," said Michael.

"How could you know of my hospitality? This is the first time you have been here." Jomo was breathing heavily and seemed as if he were about to explode. Then he leaned back and said in a relaxed, smiling pose, "You will give back my diamonds. You are not friends unless I get my SUV."

He looked at each of them individually.

"Go. You are not wise. You do not know the truth. You have stolen my diamonds."

Next, St. George motioned for them to get up. He led them out.

Melissa then stepped to his side and asked in a whisper, "Marx, can you help us? We're frightened." He looked at her with a furrowed brow, said nothing, and walked on, looking off into the distance.

Jomo remained seated in his chair in his tent and examined a four-month-old issue of *Time* in which appeared a full-page advertisement for a Chevrolet Trailblazer. Two of his sons looked over shoulders.

CHAPTER 9

MIND THE GAP

If you strike the heart, you steel the hide.

—Anonymous

GRANT HAD HIS DATE WITH BLANCHE. THE PLAN WAS TO MEET AT the British Museum, have an early dinner, and then go for a stroll down Drury Lane.

At one o'clock sharp, Grant met Blanche at the entrance to the museum. Grant carried the satchel that Dennis had given him. He was hoping to ask Blanche about the significance of the contents as a conversation starter.

Blanche wore a summery white sleeveless dress with a sky blue belt and matching pumps. Grant was clean-shaven as a baby, with a hint of aftershave lotion. His blond hair was clearly longer than military regulations yet not something he intended to cut any time soon. His black shoes were freshly shined. He wore a red, white, and blue pullover that gave him a patriotic look, and navy blue slacks. More taken by Blanche than he wished to admit, he smiled gallantly as she extended her hand.

"Hi, it's good to see you," she said.

"Likewise," he responded, in his inadvertently businesslike manner.

She immediately escorted him in past security and upstairs to her office. She showed him in and asked what was in the satchel. He responded, "I hoped you could tell me. Your uncle has an interesting way of communicating."

Blanche looked at him quizzically and then smiled. "He always loved puzzles—puzzles of all kinds. Did you know that about him?"

"No, I didn't," responded Grant.

"Well, you'll typically find him at the Union Jack working on the daily crossword or reading something or other on the nature of code breaking. In fact, he's working on a book of sorts on the special forces, I think. He reads a lot but doesn't like to explain so much as he likes to have others ferret out what it is he's doing. It's the way he is, but this time he's unusually quiet, almost guarded, about his work. I thought it was the legacy of T. E. Lawrence, but now I think it's more than that. At times it seems as though it's all part of the game. A family game. We all know that Dennis lives off his military pension, but he seems to have more income than anyone can fully account for. He retired and then took on some sort of government work that he seldom mentioned. Then he retired from that and did a bit of broadcasting for the BBC. Did you know that? In Bermuda, for several years."

"Well, I've only known Dennis as a result of hearing my grandmother and mother talk about him. They corresponded for years as I understand it. My grandmother said that Dennis began writing to her after the war, trying to find out if she knew what became of his friend, her husband. You see, my grandfather returned from the war in 1945. I understand that he seemed bothered—bothered by something that few seemed to understand. He wouldn't talk about it except to say that it was one of their missions. He was part of a joint U.S.-British commando unit, but he was the only American in it. On one of their missions, he felt they had been betrayed by one of their own.

"Then in 1947, he returned to England for a reunion of sorts. He came to London and indicated to some of the men there that he intended to return to the north, Scotland, and revisit their old training grounds. At this point, he had demobilized from the U.S. army and was on the verge of taking on another position with the U.S. government. As near as we can tell, he was to take a position with the OSS, which in that same year became the CIA. They never heard from him again.

"He and my grandmother had married only a year before. She was six months pregnant at the time he left. She tells me she was angry at his departure, but he had explained to her he had to; he needed to find out something. She never knew what that something was. A few months later, my father was born. Fortunately for my grandmother, relatives on both sides of the family were able to help her out. She tells me that for years she wondered about his disappearance—still does. She even wondered if he were dissatisfied with their marriage; maybe he orchestrated his own disappearance. But she also knew, she said, that he loved her and she loved him, too."

Blanche looked at him sympathetically and said, "It's a sad story. I'm sorry." But sensing that things were getting a little too glum for a date, she raised her eyebrows and said, "But you, what about you? Where do you come from? Where did you go to school? Why the navy and not the army like your grandfather?"

Grant smiled.

"Oh, no," he said. "Ladies first." She laughed and flirtatiously glanced at Grant.

"Well," she said, "you already know I'm an archaeologist, but I'm a specialist in Carthaginian lore and artifacts. I'm afraid my Latin teacher actually inspired me—four years of Latin in high school and four years at the university, along with some Homeric Greek and the usual assortment of so-called dead languages. But living or dead, I just love to study them. They're so intriguing. Let's see," she paused, "what else can I tell you? I'm the youngest of three—two brothers and me. They're both much more practical. They actually enjoy making money. My oldest brother lives in New York. He works for BP and seems to be in Alaska doing something with the pipeline most of the time. Now what about you?"

"Ah, not so fast, young lady. You still haven't told me where you went to university."

"Oh that, University of ..." She paused dramatically, raised her eyebrows, and said, "Guess."

"Oh, that's easy," Grant said. "Oxford or Cambridge?"

"Not even close," she smiled. "Keep going."

"University of Edinburgh," he guessed.

"Oh my, you're getting even colder."

"I give," he said. "Wait, I take it back. You were home schooled by Dennis. Tata!"

"Wow, you're getting colder. I can't let you go on or you'll freeze to death. Norway, the University of Norway. I majored in archaeology, and there were fellowship and summer programs available that assured hands-on experience. Then, it was graduate school. But you'll never guess where that occurred, so I had better tell you. The University of Cincinnati."

Grant looked perplexed.

"Why there?" he asked. "It seems like a long way to go."

"Oh, they have a great program, so much so that they control access to some of the most spectacular digs in the world, like Troy," she replied.

"Oh yes, like Troy," he responded appreciatively. "I'll bet you launched a few ships," continued Grant.

The obvious flirtation and the none-too-subtle complement caused Blanche to blush. Grant was confounded by his own lack of restraint. He was obviously taken with Blanche despite himself. She then looked back up and said, "Now you."

Trying to catch himself from falling too far and too quickly, Grant responded with the brevity of a one-page resume.

"Class of '99, Ohio State University and NROTC—that is, Naval Reserve Officer Training Corps. Enlisted in the United States Navy upon graduation, trained in various locations, then attended Monterey, California, School of Languages. Graduated in Farsi and then did further training and went back again for a year in Arabic." Sensing that the litany of accomplishments sounded a bit like the self-adulation of a beauty pageant, Grant tried a bit of self-deprecating humor, continuing, "I enjoy languages, cattle rustling, baton twirling, and world peace." The last sentence caught Blanche by surprise and took her more than a moment to respond to.

"Oh, oh," she said with a beaming smile of realization. "You don't *really* like baton twirling." Embarrassed at how nervous she was and how stupid she must have sounded, she rolled her eyes and burst into laughter at the same moment that Grant did. Then she looked at him seriously, trying to regain her composure and asked, "You said 'further training.' Care to explain?"

"If I could, I would. But it's classified, and it's best you don't know. Besides, you'd find it all pretty boring. Just think post office box 777," he said, referring to the address that American Special Forces used during World War II to get mail when they didn't wish to disclose their actual location. "Besides, I have my own questions about the content of that satchel. I tried to call Dennis, but there's no answer and no answering machine."

"I know; that's just like Dennis," she added. "So what's in the satchel?" she asked.

Grant paused for dramatic effect and scratched his head in mock consternation. "A strange collection of books."

"Like what?"

"Well, for starters, there's a book by Christian de Tois entitled *Parzival*. There's another by Bernard Lewis entitled *The Assassins*, and still another on the history of the United States with a picture Franklin Roosevelt as a young man, digging with a shovel. It's an actual photograph slid into the book as a kind of marker. I don't understand why all of this is there."

She smiled and said, "Two of the items, I have no idea. But the book by Christian de Tois is about the quest for the Holy Grail. Parzival was one of Arthur's knights. And since you mentioned wanting to go to Glastonbury Tor, the legendary home of Camelot and Arthur ..."

"But," interrupted Grant, "I didn't say anything about this to Dennis until after we met. He brought the satchel with him. How could he have known?"

"Anything else?" she asked.

"Perhaps, but I'll wait until later. Maybe we should begin our tour. I'm anxious to see a number of the artifacts here," said Grant.

Blanche began by taking Grant to the most intriguing archaeological find of the past two hundred years plus, the Rosetta Stone. She virtually lit up as she explained, "First discovered by troops of Napoleon Bonaparte in 1799 upon their invasion of Egypt, it proved to be a most remarkable find, enabling linguists to decode the language of the Egyptian hieroglyphics. For almost seventeen hundred years, the key to unlocking their meaning had remained hidden. As you will see, this stone is only about three feet by three feet and consists of script in three different languages: ancient Egyptian, demotic or conversational Greek, and classical Greek. Since scholars already knew how to read demotic Greek and classical Greek, their ability to do the same with hieroglyphics was before them. The other two languages provided a known construct against which the other could be successfully reconstructed. It was a discovery for the ages."

She was about to say more when Grant stopped her with a broad grin.

"You sound just like a tour guide. Do I have to pay for this?"She blushed at her own enthusiasm and took Grant's arm gently to lead him forward.

As they approached the stone, a group of Japanese tourists converged and surrounded it. They each sought to take pictures of the stone itself and then to have their pictures taken with it. It was over twenty minutes before Grant and Blanche could get close.

*   *   *   *   *

Late afternoon, Grant and Blanche left the museum after again stopping by her office to pick up the satchel. Afterwards, they headed toward what she referred to as "a fish and chips haven." They decided to take the tube by Charring Cross.

Standing in a group of people next to the tube tracks as a train approached, Grant and Blanche joked about the constancy of the loud speaker advising them to "Mind the gap, please. Mind the gap." As they were talking, a tall blond-haired man standing behind Blanche violently bumped her into the still moving train, and as Grant reached to grab her, the man ripped the satchel from the unsuspecting Grant. Blanche was tossed back from the train as the stranger ran like a wild bull through the crowd and up the escalator. Grant would have given chase, but he looked at Blanche staggering back to her feet. He lifted her gently by both arms. She appeared to be all right but was not without a look of fear and shock. As she stood up, she gazed at Grant, and it was apparent that she was shaken and stirred to anger.

"What was that about?" she blurted out.

Several bystanders asked if she were all right. One older man with a cane offered his name and phone number, as he had witnessed everything. The train now stopped, the conductor appeared to offer assistance. Blanche and Grant spent the next while answering questions before police showed up and the train was waved on.

"Now I know what they mean by 'Mind the gap, please!'" said Blanche.

As Grant and Blanche were escorted out the subway tunnel and into a police room adjoining one of the platforms, Grant noticed that Blanche had not cried or expressed any sentiment but anger.

He heard the loud speaker repeat, "Mind the gap, please."

CHAPTER 10

A GATHERING

Strike terror into the hearts of the enemies of Allah and your enemies.

—The Koran, 8:60

—SUBURBAN LONDON

HOLLOWAY SAT WITH HIS HANDS GRIPPED AROUND A PINT OF Guinness in the local pub near Sheffield, outside of London. His eyes darted from side to side. He eyed everyone who came into the pub and noticed their attire, their demeanor, and whether or not they were alone. He also looked to see what kind of shoes they wore and whether or not they carried any parcels.

Holloway had received a message slipped underneath his door, asking for a visit. The writer had indicated that he knew that Holloway was interested in the satchel formerly possessed by Lieutenant Commander Grant Chisolm. This person offered to discover the whereabouts of the satchel and bring it to him if he could first meet Holloway. The writer also revealed that if it were even suspected that Holloway were accompanied by the police or followed by MI6, the deal would be off. Against his better judgment, Holloway decided to follow the instructions of the letter. He suspected that the writer must already have him under surveillance or else how would that person know enough to contact him at his hotel room?

Late in the afternoon, he descended into one of London's few underground parking garages, got into his Toyota Nissan, and followed the M-25 on his way to Sheffield. As early evening approached, his years of military training fought against his desire to discover something that he hoped would eventually earn the promotion to general. But freelancing—that is, seeking information without official designation by U.S. government agencies, classified or otherwise—was frowned upon, and even a find could cause his lord and master back in Washington DC to look askance at what Holloway had done to make the discovery. Still, the fact that the writer could make such an offer affirmed his suspicion that the satchel contained some sort of valuable information.

He sat there in his agitation, noticing that the time of the scheduled meeting was only a minute or two away and there was still no sign of a likely contact. He had only sipped at his beer and thought to himself that the bitterness of the hops might very well match his disposition. Of late, even he could not help but notice how he had changed in recent years. The death of his wife three years earlier in a traffic accident in the DC area had left him emotionally and spiritually adrift. She had been his anchor and his solace. No matter how aggravating or how tiring his days had been, she brought levity to his life. However childless, theirs had been a happy marriage, a boon to his heart.

Lately, he had become abrupt, disconsolate, and a workaholic; he had aged more than at any other time in his life. He seemed to have lost his bearings. He needed something, some reason to go on. A good soldier with experience in combat with special forces in Desert Storm, the Balkans, and the Global War on Terrorism in the Philippines, he was respected and very much a patriot. But the years of working quietly and without any significant recognition for his time away from home while infiltrating enemy havens and training others do the same had left him feeling unwanted, like an old derelict who had seen its glory fade. He yearned for someone to recognize what he had accomplished.

Holloway sat in the pub, declining to order a meal despite several subtle attempts by the waitress to prompt him to do so. It was a Friday evening, the pub was crowded, and the table for four at which he sat was needed, especially if the companion he mentioned didn't show up and he didn't order. The man who would supposedly tell him about the satchel was now an hour late. So he drank down his Guinness and then ordered another.

Finally, at 9:01 exactly, he got up from the table and laid down a ten pound note for his two pints of Guinness and a small tip. He left the pub and walked out into the cool and misty evening, into the parking lot. But as he neared his car, two men emerged from a mini-van nearby. Two others came up behind him. Sensing his predicament before a word was said, he attempted to open his car door quickly. The four men converged. Two of them grabbed his car door so that he could not close it. The other two grabbed him from behind. As he struggled to escape, he felt a sharp pain his back. He immediately felt himself lose his balance. His muscle control disappeared and he blacked out.

*   *   *   *   *

Several hours later, Holloway came to. His head hurt, and his muscles ached and felt like mush. He reached back and attempted to feel the bruised area where he had felt the sharp pain. It was still sensitive. There was a scratch straight across his forehead, about an inch above his eyes.

He was lying on a damp concrete floor in a windowless, dark room. He smelled and felt moisture all around him. He was completely disoriented. He heard the rushing sound of a furnace turning on. He could also hear the sound and feel the vibrations of a passing car. Muffled voices speaking a language he knew and that bode ill for him came from the wall on his right.

In all his years of training, he had never before even come close to being captured. He had always been the pursuer. But in this one instance, he had failed to follow his training, and he was paying for it. He sat up. The room was pitch black. Even after several minutes, he could see absolutely nothing. He wanted to die.

Despite his despair, he compulsively rewound the evening's events and imagined himself in a film, a documentary in which his true-life adventure would be seen by millions of his countrymen. He began feeling his way around the room on his hands and knees, crawling the entire perimeter of the room. He estimated that it was no more than eight by eight. He tried to stand up. Before he could reach his full height, his head hit a metal pipe, making a soft bumping sound. Touching the pipe with one hand, he realized it was covered with some sort of protective cloth and slightly warm to the touch.

He continued exploring the room like a mime in a trance. Marcel

PIERCING THE VEIL ✠ 75

Marceau in the abyss. He then sat down and barely breathed. He did not know how long he had been here or whether or not this room would be his crypt. Then he heard footsteps on the floor above him. The voices stopped. The steps continued above. Then a door seemed to be opening, and the steps continued at a different pitch. In the darkness, he neither knew night nor day, only desolation. Beyond fear, he awaited his destiny.

A door to his cubicle opened. It was thick and insulated on the inside with quilted pads. On the outside, the door was covered with an ornately decorated rug that hid the hinges and the lintel. The silhouette of four heads appeared. As a flashlight flicked on, Holloway raised his right hand to shield his eyes from the blinding light.

The four men came to him, and one said, "Get up." As he attempted to raise himself, he glanced at their faces. Even with his distorted vision, he thought he recognized one of them. He stood shakily, and two of them grabbed him by his arms and dragged him out of the room into the adjoining area, which appeared to be a recreational room.

Slowly, his eyes regained their focus. The men sat him down in a sturdy wooden chair with arm rests, at a round table. The two who had dragged him out stood behind him. A small chandelier with eight bulbs hung directly over the table. He sat upright but groggily in the chair. The other two men sat directly opposite him.

One of the men smiled and asked, "Perhaps you would like some tea. It is very, very good, from India, if I may say so myself."

Holloway looked at the chandelier, his focus getting sharper but still not quite right. The man sat alongside Holloway, silently smiling.

"Yes, yes," Holloway finally murmured.

The tea was brought to him and set at his right hand. He took a sip and put it down. He then focused his attention on the man sitting opposite and to his left. The man neither smiled nor grimaced but waited passively for Holloway's acknowledgement. A look of recognition passed over Holloway's face.

Holloway looked at the man knowingly and said, "You have me. Now what do you want? And what do you intend to do with me?"

"It is for us to ask the questions," responded the Ali Kahn. He, like all the others, had a dark complexion.

Middle Eastern. Pakistani, thought Holloway.

But their accents varied. The larger of the two sitting opposite him had a trim mustache and was dressed in a gray suit with a white collared shirt and tie, and spoke English with an Urdu accent. The other was an all-too-familiar face, the man he had been following for weeks, Ali Kahn. He had never heard the man speak before. Ali looked calm in his blue Nike running outfit. He was clean-shaven and had a crew cut and spoke with a British accent.

"Good evening, Colonel Holloway."

Holloway recorded everything mentally; his calm demeanor would play well in his imaginary black and white documentary. Holloway did not want to be interrogated. So instead of waiting to be asked any questions, he began with a complement on their ruse to get him here. He also knew by their not concealing their identities that they did not intend to let him go.

Already, he thought, *I am a dead man.*

Then he looked around the room, noticing the several different calendars on the walls, some secular and Western. Four Muslim lunar calendars, whose religious significance Holloway knew well, hung neatly next to each other. For three years, he had been attached to the United States embassy in Islamabad, Pakistan.

"Mr. Holloway," said Ali in a gentle, almost womanly voice, "I am pleased at last to meet you. Tell me, what is your interest in me?"

"Nothing," responded Holloway.

"Nothing?" asked Ali.

"Nothing," said Holloway.

He responded with King Learean provocation, "Speak again, lest you mar your fortunes."

Holloway replied in kind with a glint of humor and knowledge, "Nothing."

Ali responded in their Shakespearean repartee with, "Nothing? Well then, nothing will come of nothing."

Holloway broke the act by simply stating, "I know."

Unaware of the literary gamesmanship that was going on before him, the man with the trim mustache asked, "Mr. Holloway, we hope you will cooperate."

Holloway again glanced around the room and asked the man sitting opposite him in Urdu, "*Kya aap ka wasta Finsbury Masjid say hay?*" (Are you with the Finsbury Mosque?)

The other man raised his eyebrows in surprise and pleasure. "Very good, Mr. Holloway. I am impressed."

Holloway said, "I recognize the accent. Lahore?" The reference to a specific city in northern Pakistan was even more discerning and indicative of a man with a facility with the languages of that country.

"Indeed," responded the man in his accented English. "You are well chosen for your profession. Unfortunately, this is where it has led you. You have been to Lahore?"

Holloway hesitated and then asked, "What do you want? These pleasantries are a ruse, just like the trip to the pub for our meeting."

"On the contrary. We did meet you, just not in the manner that you had expected. I'm sorry, nonetheless, that you find our hospitality so … so unacceptable. Perhaps I am at fault. I am Colonel Mohammed Khan. No, we are not related," he added as he gestured toward Ali.

"That's unfortunate," said Holloway.

"Unfortunate? How do you mean, Mr. Holloway?"

"Colonel, you can address me in the same way. As you know, I am also a colonel."

"Yes, I am sorry for the impropriety."

"My suspicion is that you are with the Pakistani secret police," Holloway said. Then he waited.

"Colonel Holloway, you still have not told me why you said, 'Unfortunate,' a moment ago. I would like to know."

"Colonel, you have revealed your identity. You intend to kill me. Stop me if I am wrong." Even Holloway was surprised at his own candor and calm. But he thought to himself, *This will play well in the video.*

Ali responded, "Colonel Holloway, you misjudge us. We are not your enemy. We are not what you think: Islamic fanatics. It does have some appeal, but we are not allied with any Wahabi sect or Al Qaeda. This room is for entertainment. We must present the right appearance. Perhaps you will judge us less harshly. But, tell me, why are we of such interest to you?"

"'We'? I don't know you."

"Stop pretending. We suspect that you seek the same piece of information that we do. Tell us, what is in the satchel? And where is it?"

"I think you might know that. After all, you took it. Besides, I wouldn't tell you if I knew." *Defiance plays well in the documentary.*

"Spoken bravely, but if you have no information for us, then, of course, you realize that you are, what is the word? Ah, yes, *expendable.*"

Holloway didn't flinch. Instead, he asked for more tea. Then he added, "I pity you and your mistaken jihadists. There will be no virgins for any of you. Just pigs. You can have sex with the porkers in hell." He looked again at his half-empty tea cup.

"Colonel Khan, I don't quite believe that you or your cohorts are trustworthy. But, if I may, let me tell you a brief story." As he looked directly at the man whose accent he had so precisely identified, he asked Colonel Mohammed Khan if he knew the name General "Black Jack" Pershing.

"Of course I know the name, Colonel Holloway," responded Khan. "After all, I have studied American military history."

"Well," said Holloway, "in about 1900, he was sent to the Philippines to contend with insurgents on the island of Mindanao. The insurgents were then, as now, Muslim. The rebels refused to submit to the authority of the United States government. Instead, they killed Americans and Filipinos in the name of Islam. Pershing took over the campaign against the Muslims. Every man the Americans killed was buried in a shallow grave with pig's blood poured over 'em and with their heads pointed away from Mecca. The same will happen to you."

"You are an arrogant man," responded Colonel Khan.

Then Colonel Khan looked at him quizzically, almost sympathetically, unaware that the uncooperative Colonel was still filming his imaginary documentary and seeking a climactic and heroic moment. One of the men behind him brought him some more tea. Holloway brought it to his lips to test it. His lips burned, and he immediately threw it in the face of Colonel Khan.

The colonel almost fell out of his chair and yelled, "Bastard American! Fuck you!"

The others held Holloway down in his chair while one applied a choke hold. He applied pressure until the colonel stopped resisting. Colonel Khan stood in his now tea-stained gray suit and glared at Holloway. "Did you think we truly needed your cooperation, Mr. Holloway? We have your notebook that was in your jacket, along with your Blackberry. Fool, we have the addresses and phone numbers of all the others we most wish to contact."

Colonel Khan signaled the others to release Holloway, but the prisoner's strength had returned and he responded with a punch to the face of the man on his right. The others grabbed hold of his arms and his jacket. He felt the prick again.

Colonel Holloway, when next he regained consciousness, was sitting in the back seat of a Mercedes, traveling parallel to the coast. His two guards from the house were on either side. Colonel Kahn drove, and Ali sat in the passenger seat. Holloway looked up and focused long enough to see a sign that said "Cardiff." The lights of each passing motorist temporarily blinded him.

Then somewhere beyond Cardiff, the car pulled off to a single-lane highway, which ended in a dark parking lot by the beach. The car came to a stop, and the men got out, the backseat guards pulling Holloway out on the driver's side. They dragged him behind a sand dune. One of them was carrying something wrapped in a four-foot-long sheath of cloth. Colonel Khan pulled out his lighter, held its flame before Colonel Holloway's face, and said, "Kneel down. You were right. We are going to kill you."

The two guards let go of Holloway, who involuntarily fell to his knees. The sound of the ocean breeze kicking up sand mingled with the sound of hard steel being slid from its scabbard. The concealing cloth slipped from his assailant's hand and fluttered against Holloway's chest and to the ground in front of him. He dropped his head cooperatively. He had made his statement of defiance. Now he was too weak to add to his performance. He awaited the fatal blow. He felt nothing as his documentary ended with the fading lights of the harbor and stars disappearing into a world of complete darkness. He had fought the good fight—firmly, resolutely. He would be a martyr, an example of all the toughness that is an American soldier. He would die a patriot. *Allah Akbar* was the last thing he heard.

CHAPTER 11
MILITARY BEARINGS

What little soul they had.

—Ivor Gurney, "The Bohemians"

THE NEXT DAY, GRANT ARRIVED AT THE UNITED STATES Headquarters European Command at 0700 hours for a meeting with personnel with whom he was only vaguely familiar. Names were shared but, it seemed to him, reluctantly. They had heard about the theft of the satchel from their own sources but kept quiet about it to see if Grant would bring it up. Given his clearance level, Grant was expected to inform his superiors about unusual or suspicious occurrences. He had tried to contact Holloway late the previous evening, but there was no answer. He had left a message for Holloway to call him, indicating he could be reached any time, night or day.

This morning's meeting was planned by the navy in an attempt to ferret out from Grant Chisolm information denied to them. There were directives that indicated they didn't need to know more than they already did about the operations in which Grant was involved—or in which he would be involved. The coincidence of the previous night's occurrence had actually come to them through the British Ministry of Defense. They had been informed by the police investigating the assault on Blanche. Grant had been forced to divulge his military ID to the police and to give his address at the Marriott, as well as show his military orders to explain why he was in England in the first place.

80

Twenty minutes into the interview, it became apparent that he was being subtly pressured by the uniform discipline of the navy. Three captains questioned him. He sensed they were using their rank and their understood nearness to the admiral of the European Command as a means of finding out what he had been advised not to disclose by his contacts in DC. Suspecting that they already knew at least some of the answers to the questions they were asking him, he thought it best to remain silent whenever possible for fear of inviting even more probing queries.

Still, when he was through explaining the incident, one of the captains stared hard at him and said, "You're in our theater now, not in the States, and you need to be more careful about fraternizing with foreigners, Mr. Chisolm."

He surmised that the warning was more than merely a chastisement for dating a foreign national. His clearance, however, required that he report all such contacts. Technically, even his meetings with Dennis were something he was to report to the security manager at his unit at the Royal Air Force base in Alconbury. But since he hadn't begun work there yet, and since he was part of a special operations unit, he didn't know to whom he should report these contacts, other than Holloway.

Finally, the captain with steely gray hair and eyes looked up from a file in front of him and asked, "For whom do you work, Mr. Chisolm?"

Grant hesitated, but then his training took over and he replied crisply, "The United States Navy, sir."

"Do you?" the captain replied with an unfriendly gaze.

It was not a question; it was an accusation. Grant was annoyed but calm. He said nothing. The captain looked at the other two officers.

Grant noticed something odd. Though they were in kakis, none of them were wearing their name tags.

Then, the captain again looked hard at Grant and said, "You will be available for the next several days. Someone else may want to speak with you." The captain got up to leave. Grant stood respectfully, silently. The others rose without looking at him and left the room. Grant walked past security and out into the early London morning.

CHAPTER 12
OZIFICATION

And heart meets heart and mind and hand
Although it cannot understand.

—Burns Singer, "Nothing"

—LONDON

GRANT WALKED LEISURELY BACK TO THE MARRIOTT. HE WAS perplexed at the relative harshness and coldness of those who were ostensibly on the same side as he was. Like Holloway, they irritated him. The morning air was already warm and slightly muggy, and he needed some time to clear his head. His meeting had not gone particularly well, and he was aware that ticking off an admiral of the sixth fleet, which handled the Atlantic and Mediterranean, was a fast track to Tierra Del Fuego or Diego Garcia, the latter an island archipelago lost in the vastness of the Indian Ocean. Grant had no desire to visit either.

He approached the Marriott and stood outside for a moment as if the interior of the hotel would shut out thought as well as sunlight. Lingering outside for several minutes, he considered spending the morning reading the books that Dennis had placed in the satchel. He would simply get copies at one of the local book stores. As he walked inside, he turned to the in-house newsstand and purchased *USA Today* to check the sports and get the U.S. perspective on the world events, along with a copy of *LeMonde* to get an antagonistic and typically French perspective.

He immediately headed toward the hallway and to his room. As he did so, the concierge approached him and said, "Mr. Chisolm."

Grant turned around, surprised to hear his name uttered across the lobby. He waited as the concierge approached.

"I apologize, Mr. Chisolm. It is not my practice to call the names of our guests so loudly across an open space. But there is a man in the lobby tavern waiting to see you. It's upstairs and to your left."

"Who is it?"

"I don't know, sir," he replied.

Grant looked at the young man's name tag and said, "Thank you, Ali," and immediately walked up the stairs to the restaurant and bar. As he had turned away, he could have sworn that Ali had batted his eyes at him. He looked back and noticed that Ali was still watching him.

As he climbed the steps, thoughts about old friends in the military flooded his brain. After all, who else would know him here? Entering the room, he looked first to his left, where several couples were eating breakfast. As he turned to his right, a man in a dark brown suit got up from a table in the corner near a window. A couple of inches shorter than Chisolm and in his fifties, he attempted to make his way over to Grant through an obstacle course of tables and chairs clumped together and filled with the fluff of American tourists.

Halfway to Grant, he smiled and waved him over, indicating that he should join him at his table. The man then turned away, retreating to his table. Grant followed. As Grant approached, the man thrust out his hand and shook Grant's vigorously.

"I'm glad to see you, Grant. It's been a while."

"It's a pleasure," said Grant.

The gentleman eased himself into the chair and motioned for Grant to sit. Grant's blank expression must have registered with him because before Grant could even pose a question, the man said, "I'll explain. But first, would you like some breakfast? I just got here myself and could use a good meal."

Grant said some toast and coffee would be fine. "I have a workout yet to get in this morning," he added.

"Admirable," replied the other man. "Apparently, we picked the right man. I can see that." The man had a distinctive air about him and was dressed impeccably. His hair was full and gray, and his suit could not disguise his large shoulders and well-toned structure. He also seemed to know more than Grant felt comfortable acknowledging.

"How have things gone thus far?" he asked Grant.

Grant hesitated. Again, the fact that someone whom he could not recognize would speak so familiarly to him was slightly disconcerting but also aroused Grant's curiosity.

"Do you remember your training days at Fort Huachuca, Arizona, a few years ago? At that time, you were chosen to be in a highly select group of personnel who would be part of a force of officers trained in intelligence gathering, cryptography, language skills, and combat." The man paused and waited for Grant to catch up with him. "Do you know me now?"

Grant sat quietly and thought.

"Were you the man who sat in back during the briefings we were required to give at the end of the program there?"

"Well done," the man replied.

He stuck out his hand again and said, "Frank Oz. I'm the man behind the curtain. You may call me Oz. I recommended you."

Grant was still uneasy. His training had never mentioned this man. But Grant was struck by the fact that the man clearly knew about him and the special group to which he belonged.

Then Oz reached into his inner coat pocket. He hesitated as the waitress appeared. They both ordered. She walked away, and Frank Oz reached into his pocket again and pulled out a diagram. He placed it in front of Grant and, like a salesman with the ability to read things upside down while making sure his customer saw everything, Oz pointed to a sequence of squares identifying various agencies and a series of nodes with terse explanations of their activities. "Do you know for whom you work?" Oz asked.

Grant had the feeling that he was going to find out it wasn't the United States Navy. Still, he remained silent.

Oz pointed to a rectangle on the diagram that read "Department of Defense" and said, "Of course, your monthly salary comes from here. But you're actually now functioning, along with a select number of cohorts from Great Britain and other branches of the United States military, as a part of *this* agency." His finger pointed to a blank space on the sheet, about an inch or two above the Department of Defense rectangle and just below the square that read, "President, Executive Branch." He waited.

Grant recognized the silence as his cue to chime in. "There's nothing there."

"Exactly," responded Oz. "And my name is all you'll need to know until we know how you do and how well this program operates. The previous administration was hostile to the idea of a joint command with the Brits that would enable us—in fact, require us— to share with them. The previous administration was hostile to the military in general. We have been established as a result of the personal trust between our president and the prime minister of Great Britain. And, for the time being, you work for me. Your contacts in DC and elsewhere know that."

Then Oz paused, waiting for Grant to ask the question that he sensed must be on his mind.

"Isn't there someone else who is being left out of the loop?"

Oz replied in a low whisper, "Holloway is dead. Beachgoers near Cardiff found his body yesterday morning. His head had been cut off. There was no message, no request for ransom. Police are keeping it quiet. MI5 has been brought in. He *was* your liaison. You'll soon be at RAF Alconbury, but technically, you're still on leave. However, you need to be available. Your cell phone is fine for local calls, but when you call me, use this."

He reached into yet another coat pocket, pulled out a cell phone, and handed it to Grant. Chisolm was struck by the abruptness of Oz's remark. There was no expression of regret or feeling of loss over this man's death. Was Oz indifferent, a hard ass, or just an unfeeling slob? Grant wanted to say something but let Oz continue.

"This cell phone has an encryption device. Anyone picking up your transmission will get a garbled message. It must be with you at all times. There are only a handful of these. They are being distributed to your brothers in arms. By the way, the people who got Holloway may have gotten his little black book. He was watching you and watching those others watching you. They'll have your phone number and address along with those with whom you've been in contact. Be careful. And one more thing. I'll be local for a while. You and I will be talking again soon. When you want to reach me, dial 'PO BOX 1776.' The letters, of course, convert to numbers. You're part of a new world order, and you will keep the number in your head. Do not write it down."

Oz then folded the diagram and placed it back in his coat pocket.

Grant felt both complemented and miffed by the whole experience of this morning. He had been a part of special operations in North Africa as well as the Middle East. Some of his military companions had been killed, but the knowledge that he and others might not be safe even in London brought back the statement of his commander even before he left for England: "You will go to where you are needed, even before the need has been known." *For what need have I been brought here?* he thought to himself.

The waitress then brought their meals, and each ate deliberately—Grant with a certain amount of circumspection. He was now in virgin territory. They exchanged pleasantries about the sites of England, Wales, and Scotland. It was apparent that Oz had been here a number of times before.

As they finished their meal, Grant asked, "Is there a light side to any of this?"

"I'm afraid," replied Oz, "that the only light in all of this is in your saber. Keep it handy. Darth Vader appears to be on the loose. The arrangements have been made with the British government. You're now licensed to carry. Your weapon of choice is still the Glock, I assume."

"Yes, it is," replied Chisolm.

"When you get to Alconbury, you're to see a Chief Warrant Officer Perez. He will make certain you have access to the shooting range daily. You'll need it."

Oz then smiled and said, "By the way, Grant, Dennis is a good man, and you'll want to heed his advice. He's very well informed and connected. Learn from him."

They both finished their meals amidst pleasantries about the weather and the many attractions in London. Oz urged Grant to see Greenwich and the British Naval Museum, as well as several others that would be of particular interest to someone with a nautical or military background. Then Oz added, "Oh, I wanted you to know that your motorcycle has already been delivered to Alconbury. She's beautiful!"

"Yes," smiled Grant. "She's my 2006 V-Rod. Harley doesn't make a better bike." His details concerning the motor and its capabilities made it obvious to Oz that bikes were among Grant's passions. He spoke about the bike's features with the animation and excitement of a child.

When Grant finished, Oz rose from the table, and said, "The bill's on me. It's taken care of." Grant thanked him.

"I'll be in touch," Oz added. "But if you need anything at all, call me."

Grant left the room, and as he walked down the steps to the lobby, he was not at all surprised to see Ali standing at its foot, reading a newspaper, apparently on break and in the right place to see when Oz and Grant departed the restaurant.

*   *   *   *   *

As Blanche was returning home that evening, she had an uneasy feeling. She hadn't heard from Grant in two days.

Men, she thought, *can't they give a girl a break? Why doesn't he call?*

After she stepped off the tube, she bumped and cajoled her way through the crowd. She rose from the depths on the escalator and walked out past the train platforms and into daylight.

Each time she heard the expression over the PA system, "Mind the gap, please. Mind the gap," she instinctively tensed in an attempt to thwart another imaginary assault. As she turned to her right and began to walk past the various shops toward her flat, Grant stepped out from the entranceway of a jewelry shop and said, "Hello, beautiful lady." Blanche was startled and delighted.

"Grant," she said with more pleasure than she intended. "What a surprise! What are you doing here?"

"Waiting for you."

"What?" she said with a smile, "Are you stalking me?"

"I would if I were to stalk anyone," he replied. "Actually," he explained, "I needed to speak with you."

Wow, she thought, *this may be going faster than I thought.*

"The assault on you the other night still hasn't turned up any leads, has it? The police haven't said anything more to you, have they?" asked Grant.

"No, they haven't, and to you?" she replied.

"Nothing. There appear to be no leads."

They continued walking as Grant explained the nature of his concern.

"I was worried, you know, about your safety. Have you noticed anything suspicious?"

"Nothing at all. Everything seems normal, except for one thing. One evening, two nights ago, there was a car sitting outside my flat. It stayed there for several hours. There were two men in it. They were dark, or maybe it was just the fact that it was dark outside. I don't know. I've never seen them before. It just seemed a little strange."

Grant thought back to Holloway's warning about the men watching him since his arrival. *If he could find me*, he thought, *he could find Blanche just as well. But why? Does all of this relate to the satchel?*

As they turned up the street to Blanche's flat, they saw several police cars had blocked off most of the street. The flashing lights of the cars and the luminescent green of the police vests made the street look like a ghoulish Christmas pageant in July. Blanche approached one of the policemen and asked, "I live here. What's going on?"

"There's been a murder, miss. Who are you?"

"I'm a resident. I live right there."

She pointed to her flat, the second story of a three-story building. The officer insisted on seeing her identification. He took out a small green notebook and copied down her name and address. "You'll have to walk around to the other side and enter your flat from the back, miss. The street has been secured. This is a crime scene and not something we wish to have contaminated. We may wish to speak with you later, miss." He then looked at Grant and asked, "And you, sir?"

"I'm with her, a friend." He began to walk away. Trained in the art of detection, the policeman eyed Grant up and down and then said, "What's a Yank doing here, if I may ask?" He smiled and waited for Grant to respond.

Grant stopped midway in his turn and smiled back. "Just touring the country."

"May I see you passport, sir?"

Grant produced it from the breast pocket of his sport coat. The policeman said, "Show me the stamp indicating the day and time of arrival."

Grant opened up his passport to the appropriate page. The

policeman wrote down the information in his green notebook and then took Grant's passport long enough to copy down his passport number, date of issuance, and his name. Then he asked for his address while staying in England.

The address of the Marriott seemed a wiser decision than giving his address of the RAF base at Alconbury. Since the policeman didn't question his address, Grant didn't mention that he might be there for only a few more days or a couple of weeks at the most.

Grant and Blanche walked down a side street that enabled them to enter the stairwell of her flat from the rear. There were already two policemen combing the street for clues. As Grant and Blanche paused while she got out her key, Grant noticed one of the policemen take out a plastic bag and a pair of tweezers with which he lifted up about six or seven cigarette butts. Someone had been waiting near the rear entrance of Blanche's flat for some time.

Blanche unlocked the door, and Grant followed her up the creaky stairs to her flat. They entered and immediately walked to the front window and looked out. A tow truck was maneuvering through the various parked cars, toward a blue Mercedes. There were several bullet holes in the windshield, and even the driver's side window was cracked. They could not see if there were any shattered windows on the far side. There was an ambulance nearby. Two gurneys behind it were covered with sheets that draped over bodies that blood-stained their whiteness and left telltale signs on the street.

These were lifted into the rear by several men. The ambulance drove off, and the police filled in the wake as they continued looking for the unexpected. Grant knew that the police, in their zeal to search for clues, were inadvertently guilty of contaminating the scene. But the area had now been cordoned off. Several people stood at the end of the street, perhaps because they lived on it and were trying to get home or because they were curious and just happened to be passing by when they saw the commotion.

Grant had spent two more hours at Blanche's when he suggested she find another place to stay temporarily. The combination of a murder in front of her building and the assault of three nights earlier had unnerved her. She felt vulnerable and was easily swayed. Grant brought up her uncle Dennis, but she didn't have the key to his flat and, on second thought, she mightn't be safe there either. Moreover, she, like Grant, hadn't heard from Dennis in a while. "He's like a magician," said Blanche. "He seems to disappear at will."

Finally, Blanche asked, "Does all of this have to do with the satchel?"

Grant responded, "I don't know, but it might. Strange things have been happening of late."

Blanche packed a bag. Grant invited her to stay at his room at the Marriott, but, she called a girlfriend and told him that given the circumstances of late, she was tempted to go north to Scotland for a few days if she could make arrangements to see a friend there. Grant escorted her to the tube and then to her friend's apartment in another area of the city. On the way back, Grant stopped at a park bench and dialed "P O Box 1776." He told Oz all that had happened. Oz suggested he head up to Alconbury sooner rather than later. He explained that he would short circuit the unwelcome intrusion into Grant's life by Naval Investigative Services. It was their reporting of the incident about the satchel that had brought about his unorthodox treatment at the hands of his superiors at European Command Headquarters.

The agency for which he now worked apparently hadn't covered all the bases or all their tracks. Compounding the difficulties of the agency's using Grant's service in the navy as an ongoing cover was the fact that he was attached to an intelligence unit. His access led him to the nose bleed regions of what was called the "high side" of intel. There was a real aversion to allowing anyone with this kind of access into a tactical or special forces unit where there was the possibility of death or captivity leading to the compromise of highly classified material.

The next day, the local tabloids reported the murder of the two men outside Blanche's flat as they had been sitting on Pinkton Street. Both men were identified as Pakistani nationals who worked for an import/export house with ties in London, Glasgow, Inverness, and Cardiff. Their home base was said to be Islamabad, Pakistan. Neither of the dead was a British citizen. The headline in one paper simply read, "Murder Again. Guns Galore." The more sedate *London Times* reported the murder with the same decorum as a high tea: dignified and to be experienced only by the few.

CHAPTER 13

GUNS

To any sailor, a letter is a symbol of hope.

—Chief Petty Officer Marcus Renard,
United States Navy

—ROYAL AIR FORCE BASE, ALCONBURY

GRANT CHISOLM WAS IN-PROCESSING AT RAF ALCONBURY. HE had very little luggage with him since most of his gear had been flown directly there by the U.S. military. He had been stationed at Fort Bragg for eight months prior to his arrival in Britain. But the base had served as merely a staging area.

Since his special training had begun, he was also finding that more and more of the routine paper work associated with military moves was either being waved or directly handled by another contact named Shannon Simone. She worked somewhere at a facility outside of Kansas City and apparently had the contacts and resources to grease the skids for all the clerical and bureaucratic tasks he had to endure. To his knowledge, he had never met her. She was just a lovely voice over the phone who once told him that she could get anything done on his behalf as long as she worked with the chief petty officers in the navy and their counterparts in the other branches of the military.

After getting Oz's message, he had checked out of his hotel with the understanding that the details of certain unexplained activities on his part would be forgotten. The navy would have no further questions, at least not at its London office. As he left the hotel that morning, he noticed that the ever so friendly, almost coquettish Ali was not there. What a relief. Grant found his friendliness oppressive and humiliatingly obsequious. He had then walked several blocks and taken the train at Charring Cross Station in London to Huntington, about eighty miles north. From there, he took a cab to the Royal Air Force base in Alconbury.

Despite the fact that it was a British air base, Americans of all branches of the United States military had been operating out of this facility since the heady and equally worrisome days of World War II. It was primarily a United States Air Force base on British soil. Like all such United States facilities, a Ministry of Defense administrative and security office stood just outside and adjacent to the base's main gate. And like all air force bases touched by the hand of the air force's landscape and design committee, it set the military standard for aesthetic composition and culinary craftsmanship. The presentation of its facilities, with their floral and shrub outlines, made its military component seem anomalous. The military might was disguised by an ambiance that any gardener would love.

Shortly after arriving at the base, Grant checked into the Hotel Britannia, the primary on-base housing facility for officers. Despite the fact that others checking in immediately before and after him were forced to live on the economy, off-base housing because of a lack of room on base, Grant had a reservation at the hotel itself, even though he hadn't requested any.

Shannon Simmone again, he thought.

Grant used the afternoon time upon arrival to check in at the motor pool. His bike, or as he called her, the Silver Beast, sat securely in one area of the on-base compound, covered with a tarp and away from all the other vehicles to prevent its being dented by the on-base tows brought in. She was speed incarnate and steely cold under duress.

Later on that evening, Grant walked over to the Stukely Inn, just a half mile outside the main gate of the base. He had a meal of curried lamb. It was a first for him. He had underestimated the infernal flames that curried anything could generate. The advertisement for the evening special had read "Subcontinent special." It failed to either say "hot" or show flames indicating the heat this dish provided. He had often wondered and marveled at the ability of the Indian government to maintain relative peace and equilibrium in a country of one billion people, most of who lived in varying degrees of poverty. He thought he now had the answer.

If they ate this stuff, he thought, *they were simply too burned out to rebel, protest, or even approve anything.* Whew! He was smoking! He was forced to wash the meal down with two cold waters.

Later that evening, Grant put on his motorcycle helmet and decided to cruise the English countryside despite the fact that everyone drove on the wrong side. His was the American perspective that wondered why most of the world and, ironically, most of the British Commonwealth, drove on the right side of the road.

Compounding matters, Grant thought, *they drive with the steering wheel on the wrong side.* However, the British perspective was one in which two wrongs certainly do make a right.

The next morning, Grant rode his bike down various back roads on his way to JAC Molesworth—Joint Analysis Center—another British air base with a storied history of bombing heroics from World War II to the days of the U-2 amidst the Cold War. His mind idled and wandered as he rode down the quiet country lanes, seeing occasional pheasants scurrying to cover in a hedgerow and catching the unintended humor in a hand-painted sign outside a farm house that read "Free! Range Eggs." However much the local signs and countryside amused him, Chisolm could not help but think—and, to a degree, worry—about Blanche.

Grant spent the morning checking into various buildings to get his orders stamped, and then finally he went to security to have his badge issued and to obtain his login ID and password so that he could use the classified computers in the building in which he would be working. But even before he could be shown the facilities or introduced to the others with whom he would be working, Grant was greeted by a Marine gunny who explained that he had orders to take Grant directly to the firing range for two hours of practice. This was to be part of his daily routine. Grant explained that his side arm had not yet been provided. However, the gunny, who was also an assistant to the range officer, knew that his preferred side arms were a nine-millimeter Beretta and a Glock. Both would be provided.

Grant was at home on the range in more ways than one. After all, his father had begun his shooting instruction when Grant was only six years old. But when he arrived at the range, he found that the weapons provided were his own.

"Damn, these guys are good," he whispered to himself.

Additionally, he received instruction from the range master on the use of the M-4. Grant had shot it many times before in various stages of training, as well as in combat, but never with such intensity of purpose. He sensed that all of his training would soon come in handy. It was just a feeling, but his feelings were something he was learning to trust. And at the moment, he was feeling as though he wanted to see Blanche again. He wanted her to be safe.

After two hours of shooting, the range master explained that as long as he was in uniform, he could carry a concealed weapon, or any weapon, while in England. Or at least that was usually the case. He warned Grant that this right had not been affirmed for any American service men since the end of World War II.

"Be judicious," he said.

At the end of practice, Grant carefully cleaned his pistols. He assured the range master that he would be back again in another day to hone his skills even more, even though he was a crack shot with both pistols. He then took them back to his room in a briefcase that Oz had had delivered to the range master.

Grant reported to his immediate supervisor, a civilian by the name of Dr. Tommie Grizwold. Grizwold was retired army and had a background as an analyst and Russian linguist. Like so many others who trained for the confrontation with the Soviet Union, he had found a need to retrain after the Berlin Wall came down and the Soviet Union disintegrated. He went back to school for computer programming after retiring from the military and parleyed that new degree, along with his overall geopolitical awareness and leadership skills in the military, into a G-13 government position. He now led a group of analysts who kept their eyes focused on the world of intrigue enveloping vast tracts of Africa.

Grizwold explained that access would be provided to all the message traffic concerning any country or political entity about which Grant might need to learn. Again, Grant had the feeling that the skids had been greased and that he would have access to certain material without their being too many expectations regarding actual production.

That evening, Grant biked back to his room at Alconbury. When he arrived at the Hotel Britannia, there was a message waiting for him at the front desk, indicating that a package had been dropped off at the front gate by a Federal Express driver. It wouldn't be allowed onto the base unless Grant came over and signed for it. He walked the three hundred or so feet to the gate. The guard directed him to the MOD, who ushered him into an office and asked him if recognized the return address on the package. He saw the name Dennis Bernard and recognized the address as well. MOD explained that they had already put it through their own scanner to prevent any contraband or explosive packages from being brought onto the base. Grant signed for the package and brought it back to his room.

Grant opened the package and found a satchel. It was identical to the one that Dennis had given him at the Union Jack club.

At first, Chisolm wondered if somehow the London police had managed to find the one stolen several days earlier. But when he reached inside, he found not the books that Dennis had apparently intended for him to read but instead a large brown envelope folded in two. He opened the envelope and pulled out four inch-thick stacks of letters still in their envelopes. Many of them looked worn and were yellowed by age. Each batch was neatly tied with plain white string. He looked at the envelopes of the first stack and found that each was addressed to Dennis, although to a different address than the one at which he now lived.

He examined the others and found the same. *All* the letters were addressed to Dennis. He looked at one pile in which the postage mark read September 11, 1945. He looked through the remainder of the letters in this same stack and found they were dated between 1945 and 1947. He opened the letter with the earliest date and began to read. The letter was a thank you to Dennis for his friendship and his invaluable advice when getting around London after the war. The letters were signed in a neatly written hand by Mark Chisolm, Grant's grandfather. Grant could hardly believe the wealth of ancestral memories he now held in his hands.

That evening, Grant stayed in his room, even forgetting about dinner as he read all the letters in the first stack. Some were seven or eight pages long. The gist of the letters was that Chisolm would eventually return to England to track down the traitor in their midst.

The details of his grandfather's life had always been nebulous at best. Like many veterans of World War II, he wasn't particularly fond of relating his exploits as though they were somehow deserving of recognition or celebration for heroism, although they were. Instead, his grandfather conveyed details of an episode that had been painful for him as well as Dennis. What the letters revealed was information about which little official recognition had been accorded military members in the United States. Official United States government attempts to provide comparable details concerning those men who fought as part of certain special operations or commando units of World War II would be less valuable than the letters now held in his hands. A devastating fire in the St. Louis National Archives in 1975 had destroyed the wartime records of thousand of United States soldiers. The accomplishments of Grant's grandfather had been among those.

In 1943, a unit of commandos had been sent to North Africa to capture the genius of the Germany army, Field Marshal Erwin Rommel. The mission had failed and, according to all official British records, several men had been killed and twenty-two captured. What was not mentioned in those same records was the fact that three men who were part of the raid had eluded detection completely: one South African commando who trained with the British and also spoke fluent German; one British commando from the London area, Dennis Bernard; and Grant's grandfather, an American.

Moreover, one of the letters alluded to a new position that Mark had taken with the United States government after the war. It was with an unnamed agency, but from the details, one could infer that Grant's grandfather had gone to work for the OSS, the precursor to the CIA.

In one letter, Mark explained that in one of those ironies of fate, he had been assigned the task of interrogating German prisoners of war concerning certain missions. He had been selected to interview several officers, as well as a couple of enlisted men, who had been part of Rommel's entourage in 1943.

When events of 1943 were brought up, Rommel's men were asked what they knew about the unsuccessful attempt by the British commandos to capture Rommel. Two of the German officers explained that the attempt might have succeeded except that they had been tipped off from someone in their Berlin office several days before the raid had actually taken place. They had therefore removed Rommel to a safe distance and awaited the arrival of the commandoes in full force. However, they indicated that they knew nothing about any men escaping.

The letter was important because it confirmed his grandfather's feelings that the commandos had been betrayed. And since the full details, including the intention of the operation, were known only to a few men—those in the unit and their officers—someone in their own group must have betrayed them. In ominous words at the conclusion of one of the letters, Mark Chisolm stated that he intended to find out who that someone was.

In one of his later letters, he wrote Dennis indicating that he had written to all the other surviving members of their group to say that he would be coming to London for a reunion soon. Dennis and Colonel Marshal Lyndhurst had arranged it themselves. It was on this trip that Grant's grandfather had disappeared.

Grant spent the rest of the evening going through the other three stacks. Those had all been written between 1947 and 2006. They included letters from his grandmother asking repeatedly over the years for any kind of help in finding her dear husband. She finally recognized his disappearance in 1950. The rest of the letters were sad but also engaging in the intimacy of an otherwise private grief that his grandmother harbored and for the details of his own father's upbringing; he was born three months after Mark's disappearance.

Grant's mother then became part of the correspondence, especially once her husband found himself stationed at the Scottish submarine base located at Holy Loch. While there, Grant's father wrote several letters to Dennis, thanking him for his hospitality, something which his father had alluded to occasionally but which Dennis modestly never mentioned. The letters were a treasure trove of the sentiment of his family and of the affinity of soldiers who had shared experiences during World War II.

Then, as the evening wore on, Grant put down the letters and once more reached into the satchel. There was another letter, this one in a conventional business envelope. Inside was a handwritten note from Dennis

It simply said, "Your purpose is much more than you know. Go to

Scotland and speak with Regis MacArthur. He knows that you are coming."

His address and phone number were written at the bottom. Then there was a P.S. "Sorry to keep you in the dark about all of this, but you'll understand in due time." It was too late in the evening to call, so Grant rolled over on his bed and tried to sleep. Though he was tired, his head was in turmoil.

Dennis's letter also assured Grant that his need to travel to Scotland would be appreciated by his higher ups and should require very little hassle. Although Grant would normally have thought such a statement to be presumptuous, he was learning that Dennis was a resource that he would need to tap for answers to questions he had not yet fully formed. He looked at a map of Scotland and found the location.

It is close enough to Glasgow, he thought, *to visit an old friend.*

CHAPTER 14
ANCIENT LORE

Time acts like a filter, refining the past into the most precious of gems.

—Mark Charles, "Buried"

The past itself, as historical change continues to accelerate, has become the most surreal of subjects—making it possible ... to see a new beauty in what is vanishing.

—Susan Sontag, "Melancholy Objects"

—NORTHWESTERN SCOTLAND

DR. REX CARRUTHERS FROM THE GLASGOW INSTITUTE OF Archaeological Studies of Western Scotland sped north on his Harley Davidson. His leather outfit of black pants and jacket with a red racing stripe that went from his shoulder to his black, steel-toed boots blended with his black and red demon cycle. If he were indeed hell on wheels, as his friends had said of him, then it must have something to do with his mode of transportation. The reflective sedentary life of a scholar seemed out of keeping with his lust for all things mechanical and fast, whether the latter were of the combustible two-wheeled kind or his women.

At thirty-two years of age, his enthusiasm for even the most arcane of ancient debris was blended with a passion for the people who had produced the stuff that is the very essence of archaeology. Moreover, when discussing his archaeological studies, he had an aura about him that seduced others with its mystery. Formerly of the British Royal

Marines, Carruthers' background was sufficiently murky as to read like something out of a British crime novel. Academically, he was the cause of envy among his peers, and socially, he was ingratiatingly kind and flirtatious with women and fixedly antagonistic to his wooing rivals. In short, he liked women exceedingly, loved archaeology as few men did, and thought of himself as a man destined to reconcile the otherwise improbable elements of his military training and his lust for speed with the other assets of his being only on his death bed. The strain and tension of these conflicting elements made him a man of intrigue who mystified everyone, including himself.

Only yesterday, he had received a phone call of incredibly preposterous information. Nonetheless, he had cancelled his next morning's classes: a survey course on archaeology through the ages and another on archaeological finds and their anthropological implications. Like a clairvoyant whose expertise had at last been called for, he flew north, he assumed, to set things right and find the truth behind assertions that he knew were false—or at least not the stuff of true archaeological findings.

But the beauty of the Highlands and their antiquarian atmosphere, as he attempted to go faster on the sparsely traveled northern highways, teased him with obstinate sheep that crowded the single-lane highways in exercises of professional slow walking. He would learn to hate mutton and forebear all woolen products if they didn't get out of his way.

While visiting Los Angeles with his family as an eighteen-year-old, he had tried stunt jumping in hopes of getting a film contract. A broken arm and a fractured skull had put an end to his Evil Knievelish daredevil ways before he ever had the opportunity to prove that man can indeed fly if given enough velocity and risky behavior. Aware of the risk that his desire for an adrenalin rush required, he simply shrugged and said, "If you speed, you bleed. It's the cycle of life." His Harley pressed on, past glens; up hills and down; past rivers and streams, Munros, and sheep.

When he arrived at Heather Inn, he found Dr. Mermac Collins of the Highland Archaeology Society, who had called him. His two sons were also there, standing awkwardly and excitedly next to their backpacks from another excursion to their newfound site of interest.

Mermac was man of indistinct features. Everything about him was common or average. He was neither handsome nor ugly. He was of medium height and build, and clean-shaven, with thinning hair and brown eyes that on this occasion seemed to be glinting with delight. He was forty years of age, married, very happy, and proud of his two sons.

Carruthers immediately got off his cycle and extended his hand to a fellow scholar. Collins was in many ways the exact opposite of Carruthers. His personality was certainly better suited to family life than was that of Carruthers, whose IndianaJones-type forays into the world of motorcycles would have unnerved his older friend.

Having worked on several archaeological endeavors together in the west of England and another in Norway only a year ago, they had discovered in one another the delight of digging up old stuff, touching it, and, by such tactile means, communicating with the past.

Collins' two sons were similarly inclined to follow in their father's footsteps. But by the way they eyed Carruthers' bike, it was likely they would spice their own work as adults with a bit of hair-raising adventure. Both shook hands with Carruthers after their father and then turned toward him to see how he wanted to proceed. He looked at Rex and said, "Let's go inside"

The inn's dark interior was touched with the musty foulness induced by years of never completely drying out from the Atlantic winds that swept the country. The dimly lit corridors gave the place a coziness and an ancient feel that archaeologists might well have felt to be a tribute to their own desire to recreate the past in their daily lives.

As they sat, Collins looked at his two sons proudly and began.

"You know, Rex, that both of my boys are archaeologists—not formally yet, but they've accompanied me on several digs and they enjoy it as much as I do. Well, last week, they were hiking the environs, doing some camping. They happened to be in the Ben Nevis area and decided to go down to the bottom to get some water."

He paused and looked over again at his boys.

"Why am I doing the talking? You boys tell it yourselves." The youngest boy, who was fourteen, immediately jumped in.

"We were just pumping water out near the place the mountain cascade feeds into the lake. I had my water filtration pump out, and I dipped it into the water. As I was pumping, something caught my eye—something bright and shiny. I reached in, and I found these." He then pulled out a small change purse and handed it to Rex.

"Look, Rex, we called you because we don't want the press. You're someone we know, we trust. You have a background in geology as well as archaeology. Besides, all the others would want to take credit—if credit is truly due—for this."

The oldest boy, sixteen, looked on respectfully and then added, "We wanted to know if they're real."

Rex listened attentively and then took the change purse and opened it. Inside were several blue and white diamonds, cut as well as uncut. He wanted to hold them up to the light to affirm their brilliance but chose not to for fear that the innkeeper might notice and become a bit more curious than any of them wished.

Keeping his voice low, Rex said, "I'm not William Smith, but I'd say these are real. You found them where?"

The boys talked excitedly over one another as their father urged them to keep their voices down.

"In the water by Loch Milston."

"But I found them first."

"But we both found some."

"We'll show you where."

"Who's William Smith?" asked the youngest boy.

"The actor. I thought it was Will Smith," said the eldest.

"Yeah, I think he's funny. Is it the same one?"

It was now Carruthers turn. "Who's Will Smith?" he asked playfully.

"You know, *Men in Black*."

"Nope, not the same one, unless William Smith has lived much longer than anyone anticipated and changed the color of his skin along the way—although growing very old over a period of several hundred years can do that to a man."

Then Rex leaned back comfortably, no longer feeling compelled to speak conspiratorially or secretively.

"He's the father of modern geology. He mapped all of Great Britain and taught us that God may have created the world but he left it a puzzle of layers of fossilized shells and moving rocks and compressed soil. It's all predictably laid out. He taught us how to read the signs of the earth's strata. Thanks to him, we can now find oil, coal, or other elements—diamonds, for example—or at least we have an idea where to look."

He paused and added, "This can't be indigenous to this soil. These were planted—the cut ones for certain, but even the others. There have never been diamond mines in Scotland. Does anyone else know about your discovery?"

Collins shook his head, but the younger boy turned guiltily and admitted, "I told someone. I told Mom."

"We all did," added his father. "We'd have to."

"Unless you want these hills swarming with treasure hunters, keep this to yourself until we can investigate," Rex added,

"*Moms* the word," added the youngest one cheekily.

Rex smiled, Collins winced playfully, and his brother rolled his eyes.

As they sat chatting about the boys' schooling and their interest in archaeology, their father mentioned his decision to spend the night at the inn. That would give them several more hours of daylight in which to explore rather than having to drive back to Glasgow. They'd go home tomorrow, instead. Would Rex join them? Rex smiled and pointed out that he had already cancelled his classes for tomorrow and asked if they were ready to show him the whereabouts of the diamond find.

They were, and so it was agreed that right after an early dinner, they'd be going out to find the place where the iridescence of Loch Milston had seemingly crystallized into the diamonds of Ben Nevis. But as they sat there, the father's cell phone rang. With an apologetic look, he answered, saying that it was difficult to explain everything to her now, but, yes, if she did want to come up after she finished her work at the school, they would all love to have her.

"Come up, dear, if you can."

He said good-bye and turned off his phone.

He apologized to Rex but explained, "You know my wife—she's as caught up in all this now as we are. We have to make her a part of this."

Rex agreed. Besides, her vitality and feminine insights about the source of diamonds could add luster to the company of four men bristling with scholarly exuberance but having none of the pragmatism of a woman who would know by nature the value of the stones that men had to study in order to evaluate.

As they sat eating their dinner, Rex noticed a solitary hiker off in the distance, ascending a nearby Munro. He walked at a brisk pace and with the energy of a young man. He paused periodically to take in the scenery and then continued on. Rex wondered who he might be and looked on bemusedly in a moment of self-indulgence as he reminisced about those days when his love of nature had first bidden him to be a poet. Even now, as he looked at the beauty of the scene, he could recall the lines he had long ago memorized before he realized that he did not have a poet's temperament.

The curfew tolls the knell of parting day
The lowing herd winds slowly o'er the lea

He was not a greedy man, but he did not wish to live a solitary life of rueful reflections on death, lost love, and the ephemeral nature of all things sweet and good. He was much too practical for that. Or at least he thought he was. These days, only Ogden Nash among poets still appealed to him. No, he would not be an unacknowledged legislator of the world; he would instead prefer to be a renowned archaeologist for whom looking into an ancient grave is much more wondrous and fulfilling than writing about the sorrow induced by a particular soul's departure from this world. To an archaeologist, ancient dust is more interesting than fresh dirt and pietistic sentiment.

CHAPTER 15

SPEEDING TO SPEAN BRIDGE

And the holy veil of the dawn has gone.
Swiftly the brazen car comes on.

—Vachel Lindsay,
In Which a Racing Auto Comes from the East

—NORTHERN ENGLAND

Two days after arriving at RAF Alconbury, all arrangements made, Grant donned his motorcycle outfit and helmet, packed a few belongings, and headed north on the A-1 toward Scotland. His bike purred and seemed to stretch smoothly round the bends. The ride was both comforting and exhilarating. It also gave him time to think. The strangeness of his situation—in which military regimentation fell away with a simple phone call to Oz and then others to Shannon—had him feeling as though he had already left the military and entered another world of the paramilitary and individual operators. He wondered at the cloak that covered so much of the network with which he was now connected by strong but invisible threads.

On the several-hour drive, he also thought of Blanche, with whom he had not spoken in three days. He was interested but didn't want to come on too strongly. Besides, he wasn't quite sure if Blanche was as interested in him as he was in her. But, yes, she was charming, personable, and vivacious, with a quick wit that kept him on his toes.

His bike streamed past the flowers, the various hamlets, and the ubiquitous Little Chef restaurants. Several times, jet planes, Harriers, flew by over head as he approached the RAF bases of northern England.

105

He might have envied their freedom if he didn't enjoy the sensation of flirting with his own form of aviation as he sped boldly up the A-1 toward Three Corners, a well-known cross-section as one entered Scotland. Turning left took a person west into Glasgow, and turning east took a person into Edinburgh.

As he approached Glasgow, he turned north toward Lake Lemont and then to the Grampian Mountains, where the Highlands begin. He headed onto the A-25. As he sped onto the single-lane highway, he left the urbanity of Glasgow behind and eventually motored into a quiet residential neighborhood with Tudor-style townhouses. He went down an alleyway and into a parking curtain right behind a garage that dipped under the three-story townhouses. He rang the doorbell three times. A housekeeper approached the door and opened it. She seemed taken aback to see someone wearing a motorcycle outfit almost identical to Carruthers'. After Grant explained who he was, she indicated that Rex Carruthers was up north at some archaeological site. With some reluctance, she gave him the name of the inn at which he was staying for the next few days.

Grant quickly glanced at his Michelin map of Scotland and headed north again toward Loch Loman. Grant's lack of familiarity with the area did nothing to deter him from a kind of journalistic reverie as he spotted geographic details that enabled him to habitually and accurately orient himself no matter where he traveled. With a navigator's skill, he watched the clouds and the sun and noted the direction of the winds that gently buffeted him as he outlined the western shore of Loch Loman, one of the longest of the storied lakes of Scotland.

For the first several miles, the traffic was light—here and there a passing motorist. For the blind turns, Grant stopped and idled his bike before proceeding. The single lanes meant truly only one vehicle could ride the road at a time. The spots were tight, and anyone foolish enough to try his luck would find his skill deficient at trying to share the space on the highway with an oncoming car or the occasional tour bus.

In the distance, he could see the mist-covered Grampian Mountains and the winding road with small berms and the occasional inn or petrol station. The highways were well maintained, and his bike glided along as if he were a skater cruising on ice. Finally, near Fort William, he eased into a petrol station to take a short break and fill up.

After filling his tank, he walked into the station to grab a coffee and maybe a snack. As he was paying, he glanced up and noticed someone walk by his bike, pause, check the plates, and glance around. The man was dark-complected, about five foot ten, and dressed casually in a blue windbreaker. Grant might not have noticed since many bike aficionados seemed to enjoy talking with him about the cycle's characteristics and performance. But in this instance, the man looking over his bike seemed to be taking more than a casual interest in it. As Grant walked out, it occurred to him that someone who looked very much like this man had stopped in the Stukely Inn two nights earlier. The stranger turned away and climbed behind the wheel of a gray pickup truck while another man, much bigger, with a full beard and glowering dark eyes to go with his swarthy complexion, finished pumping gas and went around to the driver's side.

As Grant pulled out and casually navigated through the town of Fort William, the gray pickup followed. Two miles out of town, Grant accelerated on the lonely roads as another car fell in behind the gray pickup. Grant glanced back uneasily. Something did not feel right, and the small entourage seemed strangely out of place in the increasingly solitary roads of the Scottish Highlands.

About ten miles out of town, Grant glanced back and noticed the pickup was increasing speed and closing what had been the several-hundred-foot distance between them. The blue BMW that followed the pickup kept pace as well. Its tinted windows made detection of that driver impossible. Grant smacked down hard on the gas. The pickup responded. The BMW followed suit. Then, as Grant leveled his speed out to eighty miles per hour, he looked in his rearview mirror. The pickup continued to close the gap. The BMW did the same.

Grant's cycle changed pitch from a low vibration to high-pitch whine. The pickup and BMW kept pace. As Grant increased his speed, he crouched down over the steerage to cut down wind resistance and put distance between himself and the pickup. At over one hundred miles per hour, the pickup was still staying with him after an initial faltering.

Grant sped toward a concrete bridge over a river. As he closed the distance to the bridge, the pickup driver floored the gas pedal in a futile attempt to pull alongside and overcome Grant. Grant powered up and flew onto and over the bridge. As he did so, the BMW pulled alongside the pickup and rode in the right hand lane until the vehicles were a short distance from the bridge crossing. Then the driver of the BMW swerved left with the expertise of a stunt driver and forced the panicky driver of the pickup off the road, down the embankment, and into the water, just missing the concrete retaining wall that stretched the length of the bridge.

For a few seconds, the car floated on the water; then the front end started to sink, and the truck rolled over to the right. Since both windows were open, the truck was awash in seconds. The driver's-side door was jammed shut from the impact. The big man, however, pushed his door open and started to crawl out onto the truck, which suddenly went down. His head bobbed to the surface. He floundered and splashed about for several seconds, gulping for air and swallowing water and then sank and rose again and repeated his agony, although with less energy and more pain. He sank again and then feebly rose once more to the surface, his arms in agony and unable to even splash an appeal to the heavens to save him.

"Allah! Allah!" he shouted, and in one final gesture of desperation, he attempted to splash himself to the shore. But his blue jeans and the windbreaker filled with water and continued to weigh him down. He sank under again, his arms flailing weakly, almost helplessly. Bubbles rose to the surface from the submerged vehicle. The driver never reappeared. Within two minutes, the pickup and all evidence of two fatalities disappeared.

On the far side of the bridge, the BMW pulled over to the berm. A tall, blond man got out of the car on the still solitary highway and watched until he was certain that nothing incriminating would emerge from the depths of the river. After several minutes, he lit up a cigarette and puffed on it in satisfaction.

Grant had rounded a bend in the highway and had not seen the fate of his pursuers. He drove on in solitude, and after a couple more miles, he slowed to a modest seventy miles per hour. An hour later, he pulled into a Little Chef petrol oasis, brought his cycle around to the rear, and sat there casually, waiting to see if anyone passed him in a gray pickup or a BMW. He stopped for thirty minutes. No one followed. He wondered if he had a guardian angel, but he wasn't going to wait around to find out.

*   *   *   *   *

Grant sped out of the petrol station and headed north again. Along the way, he stopped near the town of Spean Bridge. There, he saw the monument dedicated to the commandoes of World War II. The monument stood on a hill overlooking what had been their training grounds.

The statue had a profound effect on Grant. He realized the grounds upon which he stood were the training grounds of his grandfather and that somewhere in these mountains might be the answer to the questions of his disappearance sixty years earlier. In the distance stood Ben Nevis. At its foot rested the Heather Inn, his destination, where he anticipated the reunion of men in arms who shared the thrills and trauma of combat along with the shared ineffability of fear. Grant stood looking at the statue. Walking across the flagstone on which the plinth was situated, he looked up from its base to the three bronze figures. Each gazed into some distant challenge, their posture erect and their uniforms the conventional commando togs of non-descript pants tucked into their boots, rugged-looking jackets, and caps that were a cross between a beret and a garrison cap. He wondered whose features were engraved on their faces, faces that stood yet in silent vigil to again protect a kingdom and people who knew not their protectors nor of their need for them. He looked at three bouquets of flowers at the base, and then he, a solitary figure on the plane amongst the Munros of the Highlands, realized he was not truly alone. Walking back across the flagstones, he bent down near some wildflowers and reached out, not to pick them, but to scratch out a handful of dirt around them that he held in his right hand. He turned again to the statue, walked to the plinth, and leaned his body against it, his forehead touching a foot of the figure to his right and his left hand touching the bronze laces of yet another of the three soldiers' boots. For a full minute, he remained perfectly still, barely breathing and not entirely aware that, for a brief while, he was possessed by the occasion, by the place, and by spirits that came here to rest. Then, in a gesture of communion, he rubbed some of the dirt on the right foot of each of the figures and touched some of the dirt to his own lips and then to his tongue before wiping the rest onto his right cheek. Taking three steps back, he brought his heels together, looked straight at the three figures, and saluted, his right hand leaving a slight smudge above his right eye, like a talisman of one who chose to remind the dead that he too was mortal and would one day be of dust. He would embrace them as brothers, which they knew one another to be.

Then reaching into his right pants pocket, he withdrew a long stilettolike knife, one that was an exact replica of those actually produced during World War II for the commandoes and which virtually every special force in the world had since copied. The knife had a two-sided blade with a hilt of iron and steel, which he now held firmly as he slid the blade against his left index finger, just enough to make it bleed. As several droplets of blood emerged, he dropped them each onto the dirt yet remaining on his right hand and mixed the two together, which he then wiped on the knife's blade and hilt. Turning his back on the statue, he walked to the edge of the flagstone and, with the knife, he scraped a hollow the size and depth of a shoe box next to one stone. Pausing, he kissed both the blade and the hilt of the weapon and slid it into the hollow and covered it. After stomping down firmly to conceal his digging, he walked away, got on his cycle, and sped off.

*   *   *   *   *

Chisolm pulled into Heather Inn in the early evening, tired and relieved. He found the Scottish Highlands breathtaking in their beauty and consoling in their solitude. When he arrived, he noted only a couple of cars at the inn. Yes, there was plenty of room for the night. After changing into some jeans, a brown tweed sport jacket and some loafers, Grant left his room and seated himself in the dining room next to a window looking out onto Ben Nevis. He sat there trying to make sense out of the day's events. Then he pulled out his cell phone and called Blanche.

There was no answer, so he left a simple message.

"This is Rocket Man calling. I just wanted to make sure you were all right." He hoped that referring to himself as Rocket Man, an allusion to an Elton John song, and his echoing a line in the song about "everything being all right" were light enough and detectable enough an allusion to let Blanche know that he was thinking of her in a fanciful but not too serious way. However, he did not wish to reveal his own adventure today, an adventure that had resurrected his own deeply felt concern about her safety.

He was looking out the window when the host brought him the menu. One of only six people seated in the inn's restaurant area, he ordered the day's special of bangers and mash—sausage and mashed potatoes. Later, he added a dessert of currants and strawberries in whipped cream and a cup of decaffeinated mint tea. It was late and almost everyone else was already asleep.

Grant remained in the restaurant, reading from Bernard Lewis's *The Assassins*. The book told the history of an Islamic sect of assassins in the Middle Ages whose uncanny knack for stealth and viciousness enabled them to kill a number of prominent figures throughout the Middle East, North Africa, and southeast Europe for money, power, or political expediency.

Exactly why Dennis had wanted him to read this book was something he had not yet determined. Later that evening, Grant retired to his room, where he undressed, lay down on the floor, and did fifty pushups and twenty-five crunches—just enough to tone a body that still hummed with the vibrations of his V-Rod. He lay in bed for a few minutes, glancing at a map of the Highlands, anticipating his early rising to do a little hiking before his reunion with one of the members of his own band of brothers. Fatigue set in, and he slept with the map held lightly in one hand.

CHAPTER 16

DIGGERS AND STUFF

Luck favors the prepared.

—Popular saying

EARLY THE NEXT MORNING, JUST AS THE SUN WAS COMING UP, Margaret Collins pulled her new Ford Fiesta into the gravelly parking lot of the Heather Inn. All the doors were locked, and she didn't want to wake the innkeeper or her own family. She looked at her husband's car and smiled to herself, reassured that he was resting comfortably inside along with her sons. She was surprised, however, to see not one but two motorcycles. They were unusual—both were Harleys, a rarity for this part of the country where the big bikes were considered wasteful of gasoline. After all, this was Scotland, and, of course, it was no accident that Adam Smith, as well as several of the American robber barons, had come from this country. Frugality was a way of life.

But this was a woman who had an immense curiosity about all things, especially all things familial. She had a remarkably good marriage due in no small part to her uncompromising willingness to take part in all the rigors of prescribed gentility and academic flirtations in a multiplicity of fields of inquiry in being married to a university professor. Hers was a vibrant intellect.

Her sons' precociousness and enthusiasm for sport and outdoor everything could be traced back to a motherly discipline that seldom allowed television and which required from infancy exposure to soccer, rugby, tennis, basketball, and track. Her own hands worked tirelessly in playing games of this sort before the boys ever signed onto organized youth leagues. The youngest sister of a family with three older brothers, she could and did learn the necessity of rugged play and constant pranks and teasing. She enjoyed them all as a girl and taught them to her cubs, even the one to whom she was married. And like her counterparts in the animal kingdom, she would have fought to the death for their survival. In return, her husband and sons were uncommonly devoted to the one who had taught them to live life and not merely observe it.

She and her husband bore the fruits of their familial devotion with good humor and the firm religiosity of muscular Christianity. They were devotees of faith who cherished even their burdens for the strength they elicited from themselves. That which did not kill them only served to make them stronger.

Mom was here this morning to help.

Since the world was asleep, Margaret Collins decided to begin her own investigative work. Margaret was a morning person. All five foot six inches of her taut, lithe, athletic frame were typically up before the birds, and she would indeed have gotten the worm if she had desired it. She was attractive to most men but especially to those who knew a woman of true quality. She was generous, hale, and hardy.

Margaret was dressed this morning in the khaki zipper pants that could easily be converted into shorts. This morning's mist still hovered, and a coolness lingered as if waiting for the full sun to melt away its sheen on the grass and heather.

Margaret opened the back driver's-side door of her car and pulled out a metal detector. For years, while hanging out at soccer games or languishing on the periphery of a cricket match in which her husband and later her sons played, she flitted about the bushes, the fields, the edges of roads, seeking metallic objects. A human with a ravenlike eye for detecting shiny objects, she found coins, hair clips, broken toy parts, gadgets, and junk. All of it registered on her detector, causing her to stoop over thousands of times to examine something. Her long red hair was held back with bobby pins and a yellow-green bandana as she placed the metal detector next to the car and reached in yet again.

This time, she pulled out her backpack, ever filled with a compass; a GPS; a notebook to record finds; ropes; strings; a small fishing tackle outfit and the greatest of her garage sales finds, a Pocket Popil fishing pole; and a breakfast of a ploughman's sandwich of cheese, chopped garlic, mayonnaise, and tomatoes. She also had two bottles of Highland spring water. A few prawns and two slices of bread filled her pack.

She looked at the sun, a perfect disk, with its blinding rays subdued through the mist. Ever considerate of her husband and her children's delight in telling her of their own adventures, she decided to stay away from the area near Loch Milston. She would let them show her themselves as they shared all the details of discovery.

She then checked her digital camera, tucked securely in a protected interior pocket of her backpack, threw the pack onto her back, grabbed her metal detector, and headed toward Ben Nevis. She sang softly to herself, "You take the high road, and I'll take the low road, and I'll get to Scotland afore you."

In the distance above, she eyed an outcropping on which sat the ruins of an old church. Its roof was long gone, and the stone foundation here and there was overgrown with upland grasses and flowers. She seemed like an old gray lady about whom children had garlanded the pleasantries of spring and summer in an affectionate display of reverence for an aged youth, a prophecy of what they themselves would one day become. Here it seemed even Persephone might have been content to grow old.

Gallantly laboring, Margaret trekked up the side of Ben Nevis to get a better look still, all the while singing to herself the same tune over and over, "You take the high road ..."

Occasionally using her metal detector as a sort of walking stick, she inched up the hill, and as she did so, she wondered, *Why would anyone build a church so high up that it would be difficult to access?* She labored on, huffing and puffing as her thighs and calves tightened with her ascent.

At over a thousand feet up, the church's location again struck her as rather odd. Building a castle or a fortress here she understood—but a church? Somehow it didn't seem to make sense.

As she finally stepped onto the level ground of the outcropping, she sighed satisfactorily and then sat on a section of the masonry that still partially surrounded the church.

Gazing at the beauty of the Highlands, she reasoned that God must be a Scot, for here the mountains grew to be near Him and the green was easy on His eyes. The mist was lifting like a veil that would again descend when day was done. But for now, the mist seemed to shimmer. Tiny droplets floating in the air and glistening gold shafts of the sun's power pierced the vale.

The grass had begun to dance with the morning light as droplets of dew shook themselves off in the light like liquid diamonds and crawled back into the earth or condensed into other clouds of mist. The stones too sat quiet. Margaret looked in wonder and then took her camera from the backpack and snapped a variety of pictures. She was alone and *almost*, she thought, in heaven.

After breakfasting on half a prawn sandwich and a few sips of water, she turned on her metal detector and began to walk slowly around the outside of the church.

The old walls that enclosed the church grounds surrounded it on three sides. The fourth side was the side of the mountain itself.

How many prayers, she wondered, *have ascended from here over the centuries? Or did they even need to ascend? Heaven seems close at hand already.*

After deliberately following the outline of the walls on the outside, she turned to the inside and then did the same again on the interior of the area between the church and the walls.

Finally, after finding nothing more than a couple of coins and several pieces of what may have been ancient metallic refuse, she began to walk the interior of the church in a perfect grid pattern, going back and forth slowly, east and west and back again, as she swept the church in quiet anticipation. Who knew what lay beneath the soil?

She approached the northeast corner of the church. She began to get a sporadic and then much stronger reading on the detector. But most of what lay beneath her seemed little more than dirt, with occasional stone tiles showing through the dust of the ages. The readings grew stronger as she approached the wall.

At this point, the wall was only two and a half to three feet high but, unlike the rest of the church, was only casually erected. Here there was no mortar; the stones had been merely laid on top of one another as if someone were building a cairn.

She lifted the metal detector over the wall and sat it down against the abutment that was the mountain itself. The readings were even stronger.

She took out her knife and began to prod and then jab into the soil. Despite the heavy metallic reading, the knife blade went the full four inches into the ground. On either side of this one patch was a mountain wall of four or five solid feet of granite. But her knife continued to sink in, only deflected slightly by something that seemed solid but which was somewhat moveable.

Then, in the theater of her own imagination, she heard the music of the shower scene in Hitchcock's *Psycho*. She jabbed repeatedly and fitfully. She checked again; the readings were significant. There had to be something metallic near the surface, but her slicing had produced nothing.

Then she leaned against the grassy, heathery, seemingly metal-rich side of this small part of the mountain, and with her knife, she began to dig. A full five inches down, her blade, and then her hands, touched something solid. Intuitively, she gasped and her heart leapt. Something. Something was here.

What she found was a rusted but still intact layer of metal mesh fencing, several layers thick. It was the kind of metal mesh used for cages of small animals. She scrubbed the dirt away and noticed that on either side were two-inch wide—and who knew how long—metal bars, each about a third of an inch in width. She continued to clear the soil away until she came across another piece of metal reaching across from the opposite direction. A grid.

She passed the blade horizontally along the strip of metal in an east-west direction, back and forth, and back and forth again, until she felt as if she were merely slicing air. Then she dug down slightly beneath the metal bar, which was about four feet long. Reaching under and with her right hand, she attempted to lift it. There was a slight movement as all the grass-covered earth in about a three-foot-square area rose and then lowered with each tug upward and each release. She lifted again and again, prying the earth and tangled roots of grass and flowers from three sides of the frame. The fourth side seemed to be hinged to something unseen.

She began to carve all around in a roughly three-by-four-foot rectangle. After twenty minutes of digging, she lifted again. She lifted from the bottom with all her might, with her back straining and the blood vessels of her temple and neck bulging. The earth and metal cover slapped shut with a *rumph* as she let go.

She tried again. But she first took several stones and lifted them to either side of the cover and took out a flashlight from her backpack and placed it on the ground between her legs. Lifting again, she kicked several of the stones on her left into the opening. She did the same with her right. When the bottom of the grassy and earth-covered hatch was resting on these, she then had a one-foot-high opening to look inside. While lifting again and bracing the opening on her right shoulder, she placed several more stones under the heavy metal hatch. She reversed herself and then did the same on her other side.

With a full two-foot-high opening, the bottom of the cover braced on the rocks and the hinges still intact at the top and concealed under the earth, she ducked under, reached for her flashlight and then turned it on. She had felt and now saw smooth stones like a pathway in front of her. They were oily.

She held the flashlight in her right hand and began to advance carefully, concerned that she might jar some of the stones to either side, causing the doorway to close on her. Her heart beat more and more rapidly even as she inched into the darkness.

After crawling on her hands and knees for twenty feet, she shined the light upward, toward the ceiling. Realizing that the narrow passage way had expanded and she no longer needed to crawl, she stood upright.

As she shined the flashlight all around, she realized she was in a manmade chamber. Strangely, off in the distance, she thought she heard a rumbling noise. Breathless as Alice in Wonderland and stunned like Carter first gazing into Tut's tomb, she gasped. Then she giggled with delight. Now she too would have something to tell.

But not yet. She would explore first.

*   *   *   *   *

The boys were up. As they and their father dined on an English breakfast of sausage, scones, fried eggs, and tomatoes, Rex Carruthers discussed their day's itinerary. As they did so, Mermac's cell phone rang.

"Honey," Margaret said.

"Ah, good morning, my love. How are you?"

"I'm here."

"Here?"

"Look out the window, into the parking lot."

He saw the light blue Fiesta. In recognition, he said, "You never cease to amaze me. But are you here, in the inn? I don't see you."

"No, no, I'm up the mountain. I left early. Actually, I'm *in* the mountain." The boys looked on with a smile, the youngest nodding expectantly toward his father in hopes of his surrendering the phone.

Rex looked on bemusedly.

But then, as suddenly as a smile had come to his face on first hearing his beloved's voice, Collins' brow furrowed with concern.

"What?" he said. He listened again. "Tell me exactly where you are. What do you mean you're not alone?"

The boys stopped smiling, as did Carruthers.

"She's found something," he responded to their looks of inquiry. He clicked his cell phone shut.

"What?" the boys wanted to know. Carruthers kept quiet, knowing that Collins would tell them all shortly.

"We must go," he said. He looked at the boys, smiled, and further aroused their curiosity. "Say nothing of which I'm about to tell you. Mum's the word."

"Well?" said the oldest with his eyes wide and his eyebrows lifted expectantly.

"Your mother's found a … a cavern—a very old one I suspect," he whispered.

"Is that what she meant by not being alone?" asked Carruthers.

Collins looked at him, not knowing whether to laugh or frown. He merely maintained his look of perplexity.

At precisely that moment, Blanche DeNegris walked into the dining room wearing a red summer jacket and a pair of black slacks and red flats. Mermac saw her immediately and stood up in surprise.

"Blanche, what are you doing here?"

"I just arrived. I spoke with Margaret yesterday. She said she would be coming here. I see her car, so I guess she made it."

"Yes, yes, she has," replied Mermac.

As Rex stood up, Blanche looked over and said, "Carruthers, Rex, it's good to see you."

Blanche hugged Mermac and then Carruthers as each approached her.

"The Norway digs seem so far away and long ago," she offered. "I had no idea you'd be here, Rex."

"Nor did I," replied Carruthers cryptically.

The boys remained seated and quiet until Blanche looked over at them.

"These must be your boys. I recognize them from the pictures Margaret sent."

"I'm afraid Margaret is a much better writer than I am. But these are indeed my sons. My oldest, George, and, last blessing, Jonathan. This is the woman your mother talks about. They became good friends when Mum visited me at the Norway dig. She's very smart and someone who knows a great deal about archaeology. You'll have a good deal to talk about. She works for the British Museum in London. Speaking of that, Blanche, London's a long way off."

"I know, but when I spoke with Margaret, I told her I needed to get out of the city for a few days. She invited me up. So here I am."

"And, I'd say, just in time for some professional adventure—if you can keep a secret," added Mermac.

CHAPTER 17

MOTHERS AND MAYHEM

The female bear roots, digs, and kills.
She has no equal as a warrior.

—Lakota mythology

See the pictures on the walls,
Heroes fights and festivals;
And in a corner find the toys.

—Robert Louis Stevenson, "Travel"

—MOUNTAINSIDE NEAR HEATHER INN

From a considerable distance, Margaret Collins could see her cubs approaching. She waved with both arms above her head. They all waved back, including Carruthers, who delighted in the supportive, familial atmosphere, and Blanche, who lagged behind in her now slightly uncomfortable street shoes and with the burden of an all night drive. They trooped through the heather as the boys sang, "We are marching to Praetoria, Praetoria. We are marching to Praetoria, my love," another of their mother's contributions to their learning all things strange and wonderful about the world. After a minute or so, Carruthers and Mermac joined in. The singing lasted until they began their actual climb up Ben Nevis. Mother looked on like some Celtic goddess who knows that the progeny nearing from the valley bring gifts of love and a quest for her knowledge.

As she had done, they too huffed and puffed their way up, sweating in their windbreakers and light backpacks. But they were hers, and she knew that sooner rather than later, the competitive nature she had instilled in them would come out. As she watched from a distance, first the boys, then her husband, and finally Carruthers began to pick up the pace. Each was secretly hoping to get to Mom first. Even Carruthers. Though sometimes a cad with women, he secretly wished that he too could meet a woman like Margaret. Then he might actually think about marriage. But, as several of his friends had observed, he had a knack for missing the obvious opportunities.

When they got within a hundred yards of the matron, the boys dropped all pretense of merely exerting a casual display of energy and began to laugh as they raced to see who would be first to their mother. At that, Carruthers, who had hung back all the while, suddenly burst past Mermac and then one boy and then the other. Blanche trudged along at her own pace, wondering if she had inadvertently intruded upon an all-too-familial affair.

"I'm going to get to Mommy first. I love her best."

Everyone laughed, including Margaret.

As Carruthers approached her, she opened her arms to receive him with a hug. She then gave him a loud smacking kiss on the cheek and said, "You big baby, you. I'm not your mother. When are you going to find a girl of your own and settle down?"

"Ha!" he replied. "Are you available?"

She laughed. Both her boys approached, still chortling in their excitement and exertion as they bumped into each other playfully, competing for their mother's kisses.

Mermac arrived with a smile and a deep sigh and asked, "Any consolation prizes for an old man?"

"Why do you ask, young man?" responded Margaret. "Is your grandfather with you?"

"Yes," he replied, "I knew you would inspire me. Me, a young man! Wow! I'm excited, too. Kiss me, Mama!"

He kissed her, dramatically bending her backwards while everyone looked on. Mermac stared into her eyes.

"What did you find?" he asked playfully. "More diamonds?"

"Something even better," she said. "A surprise."

"Well, dear, we've brought out own surprise," he offered as he turned to look back at Blanche as she walked up to the little circle of friends and family.

"Oh, Blanche, it's so good to see you. I hoped you would come. But it must have been quite a drive."

"It was, it was," she replied as they hugged each other.

They walked back toward the church ruins. As they examined the wall, Carruthers, still at heart a royal marine, reacted to the moment reflexively as if on another reconnaissance mission. He looked around to make certain that no other hikers were in the vicinity. Other than some stranger on the other side of the Munro, there was no one.

Margaret took them to the stone wall of the church, which she had closed up again for fear that other hikers might come upon the opening. But ominous clouds forming overhead and occasional droplets of rain might also discourage company. She looked around dramatically to entertain, causing everyone to smile. She also scanned the adjoining terrain quite purposefully. She didn't know exactly what was in the tunnel, but if it were anything of note, she didn't want anyone else stealing her discovery.

Besides, she thought, *this may have something to do with the diamonds nearby.* About a half mile away, another hiker stood off to the side of a beetling brow of the Munro down below. With his binoculars, he was likely to see more of them than they were of him.

Margaret squatted down like a weight-lifter about to do a dead lift, put her fingers underneath the bottom of the metal grate, and began to lift. Seeing her exertion, Carruthers and Mermac attempted to help on either side. As they lifted the grate to reveal the opening, Mom told the boys to pile stones up on either side to prop it open. Blanche, however tired, seemed to gain a new burst of energy as she entertained the prospect of being part of some discovery, lifting several stones herself to help brace open the hatch to Margaret's discovery.

Margaret got down on her hands and knees with her flashlight and began crawling forward. The boys and then Mermac followed. Blanche and Carruthers waited until it was clear that there was enough room for all of them before entering. As they inched forward, Margaret was the first to speak.

"Once you get here," she said, "I think you can stand." About twenty feet in, she stood upright. "This is as far as I went before I called you."

They had entered a granite-hewn, hemispherically shaped room with about a sixty foot diameter. The floor was solid rock, fairly smooth, and cool and slippery. But the walls seemed perfectly dry. Along the entire perimeter of the wall was about a three-foot-high white semi-glazed stuccolike material.

The plaster or cementlike material at the base of the hemisphere was covered with horizontally and vertically upright diagonal lines connected to each other to form an ornament of upright and upside-down Vs. The floor had amidst its smoothness a kind of lattice work of six-inch-deep cylindrical holes. Each was about the circumference of a silver dollar. Mermac stuck his fingers in one and found the hole filled with black liquid. He rubbed the liquid between his right thumb and index finger. He asked Margaret to shine the light in his direction. He continued rubbing his fingers and then put them to his tongue. "Oil?"

At first, no one said anything; instead, each looked around at his feet and then put a finger in a similar hole. Carruthers replied, "You're right."

Each of the boys made a "yuck" sound, and then the younger expressed his belief that perhaps it had once been the site of an ancient oil well. Blanche looked on in disbelief.

The oldest said, "Come on, there's no oil in Scotland. It's all in the North Sea."

Right in the center of the room was a bowl-shaped depression five and a half feet in diameter and about six inches deep. It too had several holes in it that were about one inch wide and of an indeterminate depth. The boys could not touch the bottom when they put their fingers in. Unlike the other holes, these were oily but not filled with oil.

Margaret stood in the center with her back facing the tunnel through which they had crawled. She shined the flashlight toward the far wall and noticed three different passageways that were equidistant from one another, with the center one directly opposite the tunnel entrance. The passageways were likewise covered in the plasterlike white finish as high as a man's waist.

Mermac detected a possible danger in their separating and said, "Let's stay together and explore each in its turn."

"Where are we?" uttered the oldest boy.

"In the womb," responded Carruthers.

They were too much in awe to comment further or respond.

Then Margaret said, "I wonder … one must wonder."

Her husband finished her thought with, "How old is this place?"

Blanche had similar thoughts but could hardly speak. She had arrived at the moment of discovery and seemed content merely to take it all in without commentary. Carruthers was also respectfully silent and observant. He waited to hear the direction in which the others wanted to travel. This was *their* discovery, not his. He felt privileged to be here, wherever that was.

We have treasures yet, do we, Ben Nevis? he thought to himself. *You are indeed a guardian.*

Mermac suggested that they try the passage to the left. Mermac led with his wife shining the flashlight in front of him. The floor remained smooth, level, and oily, with the holes strewn throughout. They inched their way forward. Carruthers thought he heard something other than the sound of their own shuffling about and his own heartbeat: a distant roar, faint and muted.

After about thirty feet, the passage again opened up to yet another hemispherically shaped room. This one was even larger than the first. As they looked about, Margaret flashed the light to dispel the darkness in exciting spurts. She was agitated with delight as she looked about at the various cuts and designs that covered the smoothed stone. "My God," she said. "Who did all this?"

They stared in wonder as she pointed the light toward the ceiling, where elaborate creatures were carved deep into the rock. Unlike the first room, this one had no plasterlike finish. But the walls were smooth and polished, except where a design had been carved. Mom continued to follow the ceiling with her flashlight from the zenith to the base. For a moment, it occurred to her that she was in a kind of planetarium.

The base, she thought, *might have been the equator.*

While she looked up, Carruthers took out his key light and brought it down to the floor, where there were circuitous mazes all about, carved with precision and the intricacies of a medieval Celtic manuscript. He used his tiny light to follow the contours into patterns that confounded. The soft light from the keychain looked like the bulbous bow of some deep-water submersible exploring the dark world of an ocean bottom.

A gasp from Margaret was followed by Mermac's "What the devil?"

All stopped to look in the direction of the light revealing an image of incongruity. Here, in what was assuredly a world of antiquity and ancient arts and mystery, near what appeared to be yet another passage way into another room, stood a desk, several crates, and a typewriterlike instrument, along with several small wooden boxes and pencils and pens. Margaret walked forward, illuminating something they recognized should not have been there. Hanging from the wall from caribiners used for climbing was a World War II Nazi flag and one of the old German Weimar Republic.

All about the desk were small crates and two instruments that looked like generators. One was very new, and one was very old.

"I'll be damned. So this is where Hitler's been hiding all these years," said Carruthers facetiously

Suddenly, from behind they heard, "Not quite." They were startled and jumped. Margaret almost dropped the flashlight. At the mouth of the passageway stood a figure holding a powerful flashlight whose illumination almost blinded them.

Margaret, undaunted by her own trepidation, flashed her light on a tall blond man in hiking boots, long green zipper pants like hers, and a blue windbreaker.

"Put that down!" cried the voice.

She dropped the light to her feet. He then uttered in a frighteningly deep and menacing voice, "You arrogant, obtrusive, meddling idiots!"

He spoke English with ease and with just a trace of an accent. It wasn't English. It wasn't American, but not exactly German either.

As he spoke these words, he reached around to his back and produced a pistol. The room's silence made the moments almost unbearable. No one dared to move. Then the stranger said, "I should shoot you all. But here in this cave, that would hurt my ears. Still, you aren't going anywhere." And with that, he stepped backwards into the passageway. When he was in the other room, he walked quietly back to the tunnel and lit a match. Then he dropped it and fled.

The first room, the passage leading to the outside, and then the three passageways lit up, and within seconds, the second room burned as well. The dense fire was stifling. All the holes in the floor were burning along with various culverts that had been carved throughout.

"Here! Here!" shouted Carruthers. As the room burst into flames,

Carruthers pushed each of them ahead of him into the next passageway with a smooth ascent. Here, everything was dry. But the oily smell and heat was smothering. They were temporarily safe from the flames but the smell, heat, and smoke were unbearable. All of them attempted to use their windbreakers to keep the fumes at bay, huddling together on the floor.

"Face down! Face down!" cried Carruthers. "Stay low! Stay low!"

At that moment, Carruthers' cell phone rang.

Unbelievable, he thought, *it works even here.* He reached into his jacket and flipped it open.

"Where in the hell are you?" It was Chisolm.

"Grant?" replied Carruthers.

"Who else?"

"Exactly, I'm in hell and we need help. This is no joke, my friend. If you can, come for us."

"Where are you? I had hoped to meet for breakfast. Talk to me." Chisolm was calm but attentive.

"Grant, we're in trouble. We're in a cave on Ben Nevis. We're trapped. The mountain. We're *in* it. We're in it and we're going to need someone's help to get out. We're trapped."

"What?" cried Grant, "You're breaking up."

Remembering his training in the British marines, Carruthers decided that his only hope was KISS: keep it simple stupid.

"Grant, Grant. We're trapped in the mountain! Under the church! Under the church! Bring blankets! Help! Help! Bring blankets! Fire! Fire!"

Grant tried to ask where, but the call was dropped. He looked out the window of the pub and thought he saw a whiff of smoke emanating from the side of the mountain near the church ruins. He ran to his room, grabbed the blankets off his bed and several from the closet, rushed into the bathroom, and threw them into the shower to get them wet.

He ran past the innkeeper, who was puzzled by the American carrying wet blankets outside. He didn't ask why. He had met Americans before.

Grant threw the blankets onto his bike and then rushed into the inn again, bounded up the stairs to his room, and threw on his motorcycle suit and helmet like a fireman putting on his outfit. He rushed back outside, jumped on his bike, and sped across the heather and up the path leading toward the smoke. His bike churned up rocks that created a wake of dust and din. He kept his pace right up to the old church ruins and saw again a whiff of smoke seeping out a still partially opened passageway into the mountain.

Grant reached for his phone again. This time it worked.

"Grant, Grant, where are you?"

"Just outside."

"Where are you?"

"Inside, two rooms. Go left, go left." He repeated this two more times. "Inside, inside, go left, go left. Fire! Fire!"

Grant said, "I have wet blankets. I'm coming in. Keep in contact. Don't hang up."

Grant knew that his helmet and leather outfit would help protect him from the smoke and flames. After lifting the grated cover with one hand and pushing the stones into place with the other, he grabbed the blankets. Throwing them over his back like a cape, he entered. The smoke on the inside was thick and blinding. He put his helmet back on and crawled several feet, feeling the heat all around him. His gloves offered protection but not indefinitely. He inched forward, trying to get a sense of where he was going. Periodically, he reached up to see if the ceiling would permit him to stand.

After two minutes of agonizing progress, his hands getting hot and his breathing more labored, he stood. He was amidst a number of columns of fire and smoke and a circle of fire that burned on the periphery. He headed left, but there in the passageway, everything seemed to be burning. He couldn't see to the end of the passage because the oil smoke roiled about. He looked down and saw that his pant legs were burning. The two layers of leather wouldn't hold out much longer. He wanted to call out but decided to charge right in. He didn't have time to talk; oxygen was being eaten by the fire as it was.

Holding the blankets above his head and over his back, he raced in, holding his breath to avoid scorching his lungs. Blinded by the smoke and flames, he bumped the walls on both sides before emerging into the next chamber. He lifted his helmet and yelled, while trying to avoid choking, "Where are you?"

Immediately he heard a voice.

"Grant, Grant, over here! Over here!" It was Carruthers. Then he heard others yelling, "Help! Help! We're here! We're here!"

Grant lowered his helmet over his face again and then shot past the fire, into the next chamber. Upon seeing Grant's silhouette against the flames, they all grabbed at him, choking, as he handed out blankets. He and the others then whipped at his legs and smacked them with wet blankets in an attempt to smother the burning leather.

Grant took off his helmet again and yelled, "Follow me through the tunnel, one at a time. Stay behind me. My clothes will give you protection. Keep the blankets over you."

Grant raced through the passage, first with the youngest boy, whom he actually lifted onto his back, leading him to the tunnel entrance.

He told him, "Stay here."

He then went back and grabbed the older boy and did the same. Margaret grabbed Blanche by the hand and followed, and then Mermac.

Finally, Carruthers said, "You've done enough. Run. I'm right behind you." Grant and then Carruthers sprinted through. Both were choking from the heat and smoke. Grant's outfit was again on fire. He stopped and smothered the flames by smacking his gloved hands rapidly against the smoldering leather. He caught up with the others, who were still using the blankets over their heads to ward off the flames, smoke, and heat.

He took off his helmet.

"We have to do it again. Put your blankets over your head and climb onto my back." He took each out in the same order. But as he did so, he took back the blankets once outside and placed each in front of him on the floor to help smother the flames. By the time Carruthers was again ready to go, five blankets were already laid end to end on the hot stone floor. They smoldered but didn't ignite. Carruthers looked at Grant and motioned for him to go ahead. He would follow.

When they finally emerged outside, all of them were spitting and coughing. No one could speak. Carruthers was the last to emerge, and his hands were pink from the heat of the stones and he had difficulty catching his breath. Grant was overheated from the flames, the exertion and the heat generated by his leather outfit itself. He felt as though he were simmering in his own juices.

For the first time, Grant recognized Blanche, who lay on the ground, trying to catch her breath. As he took off his helmet, she realized for the first time who her rescuer was. She mouthed his name. He smiled in response and said in a soft voice, which was little more than a whisper, "You lead an exciting life."

After several minutes, their lungs cleared and they began to talk about what had just happened and the tall, blond stranger. Grant, though tired from his exertions, listened intently and then asked for details concerning the man. Finally, Mermac spoke up and said, "Now it's time for the police."

"No," said Margaret. Everyone looked at her. "No," she repeated.

"You call the police, and these hills will be swarming—not just with police, but tourists, tomb robbers, hikers, and thrill seekers, all of them trying to get in on our discovery. No, not yet. Maybe later."

"Dear," said Mermac, "someone tried to kill us." He said it softly, almost deferentially. He looked at her pleadingly. The boys eyes were focused first upon their father as he spoke and then upon their mother, awaiting her reply.

"And he'll wish he had," fumed Margaret. "No one does this. And yet someone tried to. Why? Because of what we discovered. I feel this … this place is holy. The energy within those walls spoke to me. I feel a connection with something holy, something sacred. Let's not desecrate it any more than it's been already."

"Why the Nazi flag?" asked Carruthers. "And the machine—it's an Enigma, the World War II decoding machines of the Germans—to say nothing about the generators."

Grant listened in disbelief. But Carruthers was nothing if not honest, and indeed someone had tried to kill them. Grant asked several questions. As they spoke, they noticed that the smoke from the entrance had lessened. After about a half an hour, in which everyone speculated about the hows and whys of their experience, Grant entered the tunnel. Though the stones were hot, the flames had burned themselves out. The smoke was evaporating however slowly while the oily fumes still hung like a suffocating ether. He re-merged several minutes later with the smoldering blankets.

"Well, how will we explain these?" asked Carruthers.

"We won't," replied Grant.

"And your outfit, you have burn marks everywhere."

"Smoking in bed," he replied with a half smile.

"It actually looks rugged," replied the oldest boy, "in a Terminator sort of way."

"Yes, but it is our friend with the blond hair who may be back," replied Grant with a slight parody of Schwarzenegger's accent.

"Does what we're saying," asked the youngest boy, "mean we can't share any of this with the fellows at school?" He looked at his mother.

"Not a word," she said.

Grant had blended right in without so much as an introduction. So he reached out his hand to Margaret Collins and said, "Grant Chisolm. *Interesting* way to meet you."

She laughed at his inflection.

Mermac stood to offer his hand and said, "We owe you our lives."

The two boys introduced themselves as well while the youngest hugged Grant around the waist. Blanche stood off to Grant's side, wanting to imitate the boy's action, but was constrained by her shyness and inhibited by her own sense of decorum. As improbable as it seemed, this man had come to her rescue twice in as many weeks. Nothing she could say or do seemed entirely appropriate.

Carruthers said, "Grant, do you remember the old song called, 'Smoke Gets in Your Eyes'?"

"Yes, I do," replied Grant. "I guess you'll tell me that the moment inspired that recollection."

They shook hands and patted each other on the back. "Just like old times," said Carruthers.

They agreed to dispose of the blankets, at least temporarily, by leaving them in the cave and to seek the passageway again at a later time. But for the moment, all of them were at least a little shaken. They also agreed that they would feign ignorance regarding anything peculiar on the mountain. As far as the blankets, Grant said, only he would need to answer for those, and he would eventually come up with some plausible explanation.

In fact, when they did get back, the innkeeper got up the nerve to ask, "Excuse me, Mr. Chisolm, but I noticed you running out with wet blankets this morning. Is there anything the matter?"

With Blanche now standing at his side, Granted responded, "You see that beautiful woman? The one with the handsome young man and two boys?"

"Yes," replied the innkeeper somewhat suspiciously.

"Have you ever heard the story of Sir Walter Raleigh putting his cape down in a puddle so that Queen Elizabeth wouldn't have to walk in it?"

"Yes," replied the innkeeper slowly, now looking askance at Grant. He knew that he was being set up but was too curious as to *how* he was being set up to desist from Grant's explanation.

"Well, we crossed several streams this morning, and I didn't want her to get wet."

"But you had already made the blankets wet. Why would you do that?"

Ignoring the question like a politician, Grant responded, "Are you saying that this woman isn't as worthy as Queen Elizabeth? Or as ladylike? Or perhaps you think she isn't worthy of queenly treatment?"

The innkeeper merely nodded in surrender, to which Grant responded, "Please, I'll pay for the blankets since they're now beyond our reach. But I'll need more for the evening. It might get cold."

"Indeed, you shall," said the innkeeper as he raised his eyebrows in bemused excitement at the prospect of watching the American and his friends for the next few days. *Thankfully, they are paid in advance,* he thought. As they walked away, Blanche wondered why Grant had not used her as an example of a beautiful woman for whom he would lay down blankets in a puddle.

The smudges and oil on the faces of his guests reminded him of old daguerreotypes he had seen of Welsh coal miners. He wanted to ask how the filth on their faces had come to be, but sensed that no answer would be satisfactory. Besides, their credit cards were good and he rather liked the refreshing thought of having guests who didn't require his kindly and much-put-upon listening skills.

That evening, when he got back to his room, Grant called Oz and told him what had happened. He agreed: no police, not yet. Grant could explore for another day but then he'd have to head to Blaire to see Regis MacArthur.

The next morning, everyone arose early, especially the innkeeper, who could hardly wait to see what adventure his strange clientele would afford him today.

CHAPTER 18

A NIGHT AT THE CASTLE

A most distinguished man
Who from the day on which he first began
To ride abroad he followed chivalry
Truth, honour, generousness and courtesy.

—Geoffrey Chaucer, *The Canterbury Tales*

—REGIS MACARTHUR'S ESTATE

GRANT SAT DIRECTLY OPPOSITE REGIS MACARTHUR. A LARGE AND impressive mahogany desk lay between them. It was marred with a thousand scuffs and scratches, rich with storied marks of dignitaries, soldiers, and friends who drank tea at it and plotted intrigues, festivities, and even tributes and funerals.

"My boy," said the elderly gentleman, "have you any idea why you are here? Do you know who I am?"

"Sir," responded Grant Chisolm respectfully and honestly, "I'm a sailor and a soldier, and I attempt to follow orders when they are explicit and suggestions that are often implicit."

"Well then, I shall suggest much and imply much, and you will infer much."

The old man smiled and, in doing so, he no longer seemed so much intimidating as he did passionate about his declarations.

The elderly gentleman was one of the few whom Grant met of late who was taller than he was. His heft was that of a man half his age. His deportment was that of a onetime athlete who had secured his athleticism with countless rigorous activities from his playing days at

Cambridge. He had been on a rowing team with a deep water stroke that both inspired and shamed his teammates.

MacArthur had climbed every notable mountain in the northern hemisphere and once tried his hand at boxing but retreated from the sport after delivering a near fatal blow to a teammate on the British boxing team at the Melbourne games in 1956. He still moved with the lithe and vigor of a much younger man. And much to the dismay of his concerned friends and family, he still hiked the Munros of Scotland, competed in age-grouped bicycle races, and sailed by himself in the North Sea to keep himself and his boat in trim. All those who knew him both feared and admired him. At six feet six inches, he towered over most people and let them feel both his physical force and welcoming good nature with a handshake that possessed none of the frailty of his age but all of the passion and vigor of a man who lived with purpose and manly joy.

Grant Chisolm had the feeling that at least at the moment, discretion was indeed the better part of valor. He could challenge this old man's confident and seemingly presumptuous airs or he could listen. Long ago, his mother had taught him that we have two ears and one mouth and we should listen and speak accordingly. Moreover, she also taught him that a man of temperance is also one of discretion. He should therefore not ask many questions of anyone in a first encounter. Listen and learn.

Several times during their meeting, Regis MacArthur was silent. He waited respectfully for the younger man to fill the void with comments or queries of his own. But Grant sat quietly, confidently, and solemnly. He came to hear what this man had to say.

When it became obvious that Grant Chisolm did not intend to speak, MacArthur said, "You have not asked the right questions of me, so I must ask them for you and then answer them myself.

"You are here, but why?" he asked rhetorically.

"Because I sent for you. But why have I sent for you? Because your fate and that of countless others are inextricably linked in ways with which you must become aware. You are here because you have been selected by me. You epitomize all the military acumen and strategy and tactics that good sailors and soldiers possess. You also have an uncommonly rugged constitution, which has been put to the test on several continents. You have a gift for languages and you know how to lead because you can think on your own."

"Thank you. But why do we need this meeting?"

"Ah, a question. Finally." MacArthur's response surprised him. "Boy," he said with paternalist good will, "do you know your purpose?"

"I only know, sir," replied Chisolm, "that my military career is taking shape in ways that I had never before experienced. I think someone is planning something that involves me and perhaps some others. But exactly what that something is, I don't yet know."

"Then shall we say that I have asked for you to come here so that you may learn your purpose." The remark was not a question but a statement.

"Young man, my own life, I hope, will help you realize what your purpose is. During the Second World War, I enlisted as a seventeen-year-old in the British army. I rose through the ranks, and then in 1947, I was discharged after spending my last year as liaison between the United Kingdom and the royal family on the island of Bahrain. Like you, I had a knack for languages. I found Arabic fascinating, and I loved the Arab people. Then, after several years in the family business—and my family was involved in many—I reenlisted, keeping my commission. I found myself on board ships that traversed the globe. My strategic capabilities earned me a place at the admiral's table at the ripe old age of thirty-two, only a bit older than you, my boy.

"After stints in Malaysia and various British and American bases throughout the world, I returned to the United Kingdom and found my way into NATO offices, where I had occasion to work very closely with the other countrymen, but especially the Americans.

"Over the years and through several different military campaigns, we found a need, a need for a special force. And this is where Dennis comes in. Do you know Dennis's background?"

"Only a little," responded Grant. "I learned a few things from Blanche, but I'm not certain yet where I tie into all this."

"Patience, young man, patience." For just a moment, MacArthur's manner seemed a caricature of the cartoon chicken, Foghorn Leghorn, who was in turn a caricature of a glad-handing politician from the American South.

"For you see, Dennis is the man who devised this program, the program that you have become part of. Over the years, Dennis has fostered a number of personal relations with several prominent American political figures, all of whom have a decidedly cosmopolitan attitude toward the creation of a special forces element. A special force that is truly representative of the highest ideals of the world's great democracies. It is one which requires of those called to its banner the virtue and toughness of its people.

"These men have been trained to the highest demands of the Rangers, the SEALS, the SAS, and other special forces. They could interact in a variety of environments because of their intellectual skills—specifically, their language skills—and because of their extensive training on land, sea, and air. You need to know that though Dennis has selected you, along with several of your American colleagues, it is I and I alone who can give the final approval. And before that final approval is given, you must prove yourself in ways for which your accomplishments in Iraq and Afghanistan were only the beginning. Know that you are one of only twelve men considered for this program. Think of your subsequent ordeals as a kind of quest. And finally, young man, realize that as of this moment, your purpose is much greater than you may fully realize. Even I do not yet know its full extent."

Regis MacArthur got up from his desk, walked over to his bookshelf, and pulled out an atlas of the world. Then he opened up the front cover and pulled out a piece of paper that was folded in two. He returned to his desk opposite Grant and turned the paper over so that Grant could read it.

On the paper was a large circle with another much smaller circle in its dead center. In this smaller circle was a diagonal line that halved it. On one hemisphere it had the name Admiral Regis MacArthur and in the other, Andrew Dupree, Special Deputy to the President of the United States. Around the inner circle were twelve to thirteen lines making twelve pie like pieces into which twelve names had been inserted. Grant recognized none of them. However, MacArthur then pointed to the center and said, "You will be the lead. No others will be selected and fully included until you approve. But only Dennis and I will bring them in to ask that you work with them. Assuming that you prove your worth, you will help confirm the others."

"But why am I the first?" asked Grant.

"Only Dennis can answer that. It has something to do with the fact that it's in your blood. Or so he says. He will explain."

"But there are certain things I need to know before I can commit. I need to know a lot more about this program and who is directing my orders."

"There is no more need for me to speak with you on these matters at the moment. Rather, someone else wishes to see you. I've a matter of some importance that I must now address while you are speaking with another. Please wait here. And, by the way, you may find this all befuddling at the moment, but it has to do with your blood. It's in you. Of course, blood lines are like flood lines; no one pays attention to them until they rise to prominence." MacArthur left the room.

Grant found himself alone. For the first time, he gazed about him with a curiosity that had not been impeded by his being escorted directly to the office of MacArthur rather than being left to wander the estate. MacArthur's presence also required his undivided attention. But now he felt free to look around.

The office was really a library. Bookshelves covered three walls, except for the two areas blotted out by two immense floor-to-ceiling windows. These could fill the room with light. The shelves themselves were, he estimated, at least twice the height of a man. Beyond the first several shelves, a person would have to use one of three mobile brass ladders that moved the length of each wall on a brass track.

The collection of books in one section included numerous works on navigation, mountaineering, and even gardening. Upon seeing the books on gardening, Grant speculated that the admiral must have started out as an air force man. It was widely joked in the United States armed services that air force personnel were generally better fed and better housed than their counterparts in other services and substituted gardening and other such activities in lieu of the usual rigors of combat training. Of course, air force personnel would have objected to such assertions except that it would have interfered with the time devoted to their lawn manicures.

On several other shelves were books on travel and a number of different atlases as well as more books on gardening. These seemed expertly placed next to an array of books on oceanography.

As he walked around the room, he spied one whole section on military history. He reached up and pulled out a volume entitled *Montgomery of*

Al Alamain. This was Field Marshal Montgomery's memoir of his part in World War II as commander of the British Eighth Army. He opened it and saw a handwritten message.

> *Stay with us as long as you can. The world needs more good men like you. Let's go climbing when we can.*
> *Respectfully, Field Marshal Montgomery.*

Next to it was a map of Normandy dated June 6, 1944. It was a military map showing German military positions and was enclosed in a glass case and wooden frame. It was signed by President Dwight D. Eisenhower and dated June 6, 1954, the tenth anniversary of the Normandy invasion.

Each book and map that he inspected was signed by one famous personage or another. Then his eyes drifted to another book, T. E. Lawrence's *Seven Pillars of Wisdom.* He opened it and noted the original date of publication. On the inside was a message.

> *To my friend and mentor. Here is a volume that once belonged to my cousin. I bequeath it now to yet another scholar warrior.*
> *Dennis Bernard, June 24, 1986.*

As he looked toward the wall behind MacArthur's desk where there were no bookshelves, he noticed numerous pictures showing a tall young naval officer shaking hands with various American and British officers, as well as one with President Charles de Gaulle of France. Still several others in which he was dressed in a natty blue suit with a red tie revealed his shaking hands with Prince Phillip, Lord Mountbatten, Prince Charles, and Lady Diana. Other pictures showed members of the royal family with MacArthur conspicuously standing in the back.

In one photograph MacArthur was shaking hands with George Bush the Elder, and in another, he and Prince Charles, both dressed in kilts, stood outside Balmoral Castle. Yet another was a picture of Margaret Thatcher having tea with MacArthur in an intimate and unrecognizable location. Still several pictures were dinner scenarios with MacArthur and various personalities, such as Laurence Olivier, Sean Connery, and even Rod Stewart and Billy Connolly.

Grant could only ask himself, *How could I not know who this man is?*

As he was standing before the array of pictures, Oz walked in. Grant walked toward him and they shook hands. Oz pulled the chair out from behind MacArthur's desk and sat it alongside the desk next to where Chisolm then seated himself.

"Good to see you, Grant. Let's get down to business. You've had an exciting couple of days, and this has made you a higher profile than any of us imagined. But I suspect your excitement has just begun. Events have transpired within the past several days that may push up the dates for some of your training and subsequent execution in field operations. You'll need to be ready. Stay below the radar and don't carry your side arm, at least not yet. The Brits are very strict about carrying guns, even for their police. We can't afford to jeopardize our program before it even gets started. No incidents."

Chisolm explained the incident in the cave. Oz listened and said, "Go back and finish your investigation of the mountain. But keep things quiet. More is perhaps unfolding here than you might expect."

Grant then looked directly at Oz and asked, "How deep undercover is this program?"

Oz stared right back and said, "Son, you're in so deep that your mere presence can bend light and time."

Oz then stood abruptly and told Grant that he would stay for dinner. MacArthur had already made the arrangements.

CHAPTER 19
THE LISTENERS

Seeing is believing.

—Popular saying

THE CINC BUREAU CHIEF HAD NOT HEARD FROM HIS REPORTERS in two weeks. Melissa Millinson and her crew were missing but there was not yet any presumption of death. Perilous conditions were endemic to the trade. Reporters went to dangerous places and came back with great stories. He imagined the return of his reporters as triumphant with big game prizes, only their trophies would be stories and film that helped to tell those stories.

As a young man, had he not risked his life in the jungles of Vietnam at Khe Sahn, Hue and Saigon in its last days before the collapse of the South Vietnamese government to the Communist north? Had he not at one point filmed the triumphant march of the Khmer Rouge into Phnom Phen only to flee a week later after unsuccessfully attempting to film the butchery of its civilians? And had he not traveled the trouble spots, such as Soweto in South Africa, during the tumultuous seventies? And how many reporters like him had risked life and limb to gather stories in Lebanon as the PLO fought to establish their control there and elsewhere in the vicinity before finding itself in pitched battles with their Hashemite cousins in Jordan? Had he not, in direct violation of the rules for the inclusion of reporters with United States forces in the First Gulf War, had himself spirited into Iraq to catch a glimpse of the fighting from the perspective of the Iraqis?

140

Schwarzkopf be damned, he thought.

No one, even with the best of intentions, could deter him from going where he wanted to go to get a story he desired. His own capture by the Iraqi forces and his subsequent detention and brutal captivity before his rescue by United States forces was the basis for his greatest journalist triumph in which he became his own lead story.

How he envied the young Turks now in the field. Were he a younger man, he too would once again enter the fray, serving his readers with the nit and grit of life's crises as he and his protégés swarmed from one country to the next. The triumphs of these young reporters would be his triumphs as well. He had helped father an entire generation of journalists who lived by the adage that the facts were not nearly as important as the truth.

Never let the facts get in the way of a good story, he thought.

This was the truism by which his career had been guided. A fellow Texan was right: the truth, not the facts, are what set men free. He had sent out a team of journalists and documentarians to deal with the misunderstood and all-too-often caricatured guerrilla warriors who lived in the midst of the jungles and in the heart of the savannah, as well as the cool of the mountains. His team of reporters would get the story, and CINC would have its own "Guerrillas in the Mist: a Triumph of Humanity."

As he sat at his desk writing a letter to the CINC honchos who were as anxious as he was to get this story, he reminisced about the stories that had brought him to his place. No, these were crack reporters, and he would edit their work even before sending it back home for final editing. There would be no more awkward incidents in which anxious reporters seeking the headlines had been brought low by horribly inaccurate stories about various events in the Balkans, Rwanda, Vietnam, incidents that embarrassed the news bureau.

The term *CINC Phenomenon* was a reprehensible reference to the habit of dropping reporters into hot spots to report on a conflict in a country they had never been to before, where the people spoke a language and maintained customs with which the reporters had little or no familiarity. The incident in which a reporter had shown on the evening news over a hundred dead civilians burned and eventually killed by Serbian militia had been the worst. Those lying dead on the ground were in fact dead Serbs killed by Kosovar Albanians. Fortunately, the rest of the media and the American public never got the facts. They would have been troubled if they had, and the greater truth that he and others wanted to convey about that war-scarred peninsula in southern Europe would have been lost.

He looked out his office window and saw a delivery man drive up on a red scooter that was scraped and dented from years of hard use. The driver was neither the usual UPS man who delivered most of their mail nor was he one of the city's postmen. He was a short, stocky black man with symmetrical scars on either cheek that went from just below his eyes to his mouth. His attire was a pair of brown shorts that came to just about the knee, and he wore the usual UPS brown shirt as well. In a wire basket with a holder on either side of the rear wheel was a small package wrapped in brown paper and tied with a string.

The driver dismounted and disappeared into the entranceway. Mortimer continued looking out over the throbbing heart of Nairobi, the bustling largesse that could be frenetic and decidedly indecisive, a thriving culture of motion that suggested feverish accomplishment but that always seemed to burn itself out from the heat of its own fire. Truly, he thought, these people existed in a country living on coffee and dreams plagued by corruption in government and schemes. Internecine conflict could be just around the corner if the international community didn't do something soon to allay the concerns of Jomo Raphael and his gallant warriors to remedy the injustices perpetrated by Western stooges who still bowed to Western interests. *Uhuru*, he thought, *Uhuru*. Jomo Kenyatta, the father of the Kenyan nation, would be appalled.

He was still staring out the window when his secretary in the outer office knocked gently on his door and opened it.

"Mr. Mortimer, there's a delivery here for you, and the man with the package says he has explicit instructions to hand it to you personally."

"Where's it from?"

"I don't' know, sir. I'll ask."

"Never mind; I'll check it myself."

Mortimer walked into the outer office where the delivery man stood patiently in front of the secretary's desk. The man's symmetrical scars reminded Mortimer of cat whiskers. The scars, the round face, and the blackness of the man's complexion, as well as his physique, all suggested a non-Kenyan, someone of Bantu extraction, central or western Africa. The Kenyans tended to be lighter-complected and lithe and had less pronounced African features.

"What do you have for me?" asked Mortimer.

The young man smiled in reply and then said, "It's a special package, sir. It is for you, I think."

He spoke English well enough, with an accent that was marked by glottal stops that any native English speaker would have recognized as non-native, non-Kenyan.

Mortimer looked at the package, which the young man still held dutifully with both hands. There was a clipboard on top with a sheet for customers to sign for receipt of their packages. Mortimer asked him to put the package down on his secretary's desk. He did so. The clipboard, still on top, covered the address. Mortimer asked the young man to please remove the clipboard. The young man did so most obligingly and with an apologetic smile. He made a gentle gesture with the clipboard for Mortimer to sign.

However, Mortimer noticed that the brown-paper-wrapped package had no return address. His own was written out in a graceful, florid hand. There were no other markings of any other kind. The package was missing the usual markings indicating it had been appropriately handled, inspected, and registered at a UPS facility. Mortimer ignored the young man's gesture to sign and instead asked, "Who gave you this package?"

"Where I work," he replied. "My chief give to me. My work is to deliver on time."

He sounds like a commercial, thought Mortimer. His secretary now stood behind him, growing suspicious, not because of the package itself but because of her boss's reaction to it.

"This package did not come through the usual delivery system," Mortimer said as he looked at his secretary. The young man looked perplexed.

"Sir," he said, "I must go. Please, you sign."

"Young man," said Mortimer, "you need to stay a bit longer." He reached into his pocket and pulled out two twenty dollar bills and handed them to the delivery man. Since this was as much as he knew the young man made in a week, he was certain that this would be quite an inducement to stay longer. As he did so, he turned to his secretary and said, "U.S. Embassy. I'm suspicious. Call the U.S. Embassy and alert them to the fact that we have a suspicious package. The locals are not likely to handle it safely or knowledgeably. Tell them we'd like their advice."

The young man continued standing with his clipboard in hand along with the money, which he hesitated to put into his pocket for fear Mortimer would change his mind. Mortimer suspected a bomb and he wanted the young man to stay as long as possible. If it were a bomb, then the man's presence might insure against its detonation. Western newsmen and agencies had been the subject of repeated bombing attempts throughout Africa in recent years. Al Qaeda's success in delivering these package bombs was well-known to U.S. personnel in volatile areas. Recipients had been advised by the U.S. State Department to be cautious about receiving packages unless they knew who they were from and had confirmed their being mailed from a recognizable postal or private delivery system.

The secretary got the United States Embassy on the line. As she began to speak, Mortimer asked her to hand him in the phone. After several comments and clicks on the phone, Mortimer was speaking to the deputy ambassador of the United States Embassy in Kenya.

"Mr. Abassani, this is Lewis Mortimer at CINC news. Fine, thank you. Yes, but not today. I'm afraid lunch may be a little more leisurely an activity than I can engage in at the moment. Look, I have a suspicious package over here. Do you have personnel who can inspect it *before* or *if* I open it? The UPS man delivered it, but the package doesn't have the usual markings. I'm suspicious. We'll heed your advice."

Mortimer listened for several seconds and then responded.

"I'm attempting to. Yes, he's still here. We'll wait for your men," he replied and then hung up.

The delivery man sat quietly but uneasily.

"I have done nothing wrong. Please, sir, you will sign, and I will go."

Mortimer reached into his pocket again and pulled out two more twenty dollar bills and handed them to the young man.

"Please stay. Everything will be all right."

Half an hour later, a black Ford pulled up in front of the building. The young man remained seated, now munching on a tuna fish sandwich Mortimer's secretary had given him and sipping from a bottle of Coca-Cola. Two men walked the stairs to the third floor. Both wore gray suits with dark ties and shiny black wing-tip shoes. The crew cuts suggested that they were U.S. marines working at the embassy. They knocked, waited, and the door opened. Without ceremony, the men asked for the package. They inspected it, handling it quite carefully. For several minutes, they interrogated the young man. They then wrapped the package in a green canvas bag and left. They were crisp, efficient, and, Mortimer thought, *not entirely thorough.* They should have stayed longer and asked more questions of him and the young man, if not his secretary.

The young man finished his sandwich and Coke and then lingered. Mortimer reached into his pocket and handed him yet another twenty dollar bill. The young man smiled and picked up his still unsigned clipboard and said, "Please, sir." Mortimer signed and handed the clipboard back. The young man turned back as he approached the door and said, "Thank you, very, very much. I hope to deliver many, many more packages to you." As he left, Mortimer told his secretary to lock the door and call New York CINC headquarters. As she did so, he wondered why he had heard nothing, nothing at all from the CINC team sent to interview Jomo Raphael.

An hour later, Mortimer received a phone call from Ambassador Abassani.

"Lewis, I need you over here right away. Bring your secretary. We'll need to question both of you. I'll be waiting."

Mortimer wanted to ask questions, but Abassani hung up before he could do so. Within ten minutes, he had his secretary cancel his remaining appointments for the day and they were on their way to the U.S. Embassy.

*　　*　　*　　*　　*

When they arrived at the embassy, their car was immediately waved through by the marines who had been alerted to their coming. They parked their car in the front of the building, which was surrounded by concrete as well as steel chain link fences that were iced off with barbed wire and electronically equipped sensors that would automatically electrify the entire fence if touched by an unwary passerby.

One of the guards on the interior of the building immediately escorted them to the ambassador's office. His secretary was in the outer office, and she immediately showed them in. The office was completely enclosed—no windows. As they entered, Abassani stood to greet them. The two crew cuts who had picked up the box at his office were seated to either side of his desk. The box sat squarely on the middle of the ambassador's desk with its wrapper spread out beneath, serving as a kind of place mat.

The ambassador then told his secretary to call Dr. Chumani, their resident physician and laboratory technician. He motioned for Mortimer and his secretary, Janice LeFay, to take the chairs in front of his desk.

After they were seated, Abassani introduced Mortimer and LeFay to his aides, Charles Ringold and Bernard Sinclair.

"Mr. Mortimer, several months ago you and I had a conversation at one of our embassy functions. You will recall the occasion since it was part of our annual get-acquainted affair for some of our new embassy personnel. Here, you and other movers and shakers met them and got to know who is stirring the kettle in this part of the world. On this occasion, you spoke with me about the advisability of sending reporters into the interior of the areas in which Zaire, Uganda, Rwanda, and Kenya meet in hopes of making contact with members of Jomo Raphael's Liberation Army."

Mortimer sat silently, dreading to think what this might have to do with the contents of the box.

"I most strongly advised against any such enterprise. I warned you against attempting to make contact with one of the most vicious leaders in any insurgency in the world today. I also advised you to tell your colleagues at CINC that Raphael is unpredictable and can change almost imperceptibly from an ingratiating charmer to a cruel barbarian. Tell me, did you take my advice?"

Mortimer sat silently and looked down as he cupped his chin in his right hand. Then he looked up and asked, "What would you have me do? I'm a reporter, an editor, a seller. I can't live on rumor and myth. I must investigate or send others to report. Of course, we seek the safest means of doing so. What does any of that have to do with this box?"

Abassani then asked, "Where are your reporters now?"

"I don't know exactly. We've not heard from them in two weeks. But we're sure of their capabilities. They're resourceful, and I have faith in them."

"Lewis, read this," responded Abassani. "It was addressed to you, but I took the liberty of opening it because of the circumstances."

Lewis took the folded white letter, opened it, and began to read. As he did so, his brow furrowed and his chest felt a pang of regret. His hands tensed on the corners of the paper. He glanced at his secretary. She looked concerned. Then he put the letter down on the desk.

"How have you kept in touch with them?" asked the ambassador.

"Lately, we haven't been able to. As I said, two weeks now."

Amidst the silence that followed, Mortimer reached over and, using his right index finger, gently pulled the box to himself. With trepidation, he took the top off. Inside was another layer of crushed newspaper. He pulled the papers out and placed them on the desk. Then he looked inside. He gasped despite having already guessed what the box might contain. His secretary leaned over and threw her hand to her mouth and cried out, "Oh my God. It can't be!" Tears began to well in her eyes.

Abassani said, "Please, I know how you must feel. But using their ears as beads on this grotesque rosary …it gives us little hope that they are still alive. Still, it is only one ear from each. How many did you send?"

"Six," responded Mortimer.

"Six?" asked Abassani. "Then one may still be alive. There are only five ears here."

Everyone in the room was somber, but Abassani remained on task. "We've contacted DC already. They want more details. We'll find out soon enough what they intend to do. If your people are still alive, we'll get them out. If not, then we will punish those who did this."

∗   ∗   ∗   ∗   ∗

Within two days, satellites had been repositioned over parts of south central Africa by the U.S. government, and intelligence resources had been reconfigured to prepare for a rescue operation. Immediate recommendations to deploy United Nations envoys had been rejected by the president. Details concerning the whereabouts of the captive journalists were relayed from various channels in Africa, some of them from undisclosed locations from unknown but reliable agents. The seemingly amorphous, nondescript border between Uganda and Kenya seemed a possible and likely sanctuary for Jomo Raphael and his men.

At Fort Bragg, North Carolina, higher ups in the chain of command were alerted. Select elements of the 82nd Airborne, as well as auxiliary personnel, were told to make ready. Parachutists within the unit were singled out for a quick course on the terrain of western Kenya and eastern Uganda. Cooperation from both governments would be required. However, the moment such cooperation began, the secrecy enveloping the operation would end. CINC's own source hoped to break the story of the presumed rescue before anyone else even knew the reporters had been detained and tortured.

CHAPTER 20
CRYING WOLF

They're like a lot of bairns, they are, like children of me own,
They fondle round about owd Shep afore they're strong and
grown

—Jesse Baggaley, "Lincolnshire Shepherd"

—*LOCH MAREE REGION, SCOTLAND*

TELLY CROMARTY HAD FOLLOWED HIS DOG, SHEP SHEP, INTO THE hills. Instead of rounding up his domestic quarry of sheep, the dog had come running and barking, trying to get his master's attention.

Cromarty was a small but energetic man of fifty whose physique had weathered storms of winter rain and the heat of summer sizzle with the delight of one who had run these hills as a boy and saw each ascent as an excuse to reminisce. His calves still swelled as his heart pumped with his morning exertion. He sensed that Shep Shep was not his usual cautious self. He was not stalking to drive the sheep into a rounded mass as he did all other days. Instead, the dog was fury of barks, forward and backward motion, and swirling circles. Something was amiss.

He climbed the crest of the hill, and the dog led him down to a small hollow encircled with several bushes and dwarfed pine trees twisted by the constant winds off the ocean only several miles away. Still, mysteriously, others nearby grew straight and unbowed. The dog stood and vibrated with excitement at the opening to the wooded hollow.

Cromarty entered the depression and looked first in disbelief and

149

then in disgust and concern. Here at his feet lay three of his sheep, or at least their remains. Their throats had been torn open and their bowels ripped apart. Guts lay strewn about and their once dirty white fleece was matted in blood. The killings were fresh. Only several hours, thought Cromarty, separated the moment of death from his discovery. He knelt down by their sides and spit.

He knew that his own dogs were unlikely culprits in this instance. Even if they had done it, the telltale sight and smell of blood on their muzzles would have been obvious. Either other dogs or something akin to a dog did this.

Best, he thought, *if the sheep remains are buried or burned immediately.*

But before he destroyed the evidence, he decided to pay a visit to the village constable. He would also take pictures of the crime scene before the evidence was eliminated.

As he walked around the site attempting to detect tracks or some evidence of the predator's nature, he spotted a cigarette butt. He bent down to pick it up. It was a Shimmer, a Dutch brand. How strange that it lay among carcasses of sheep. Had someone else already been here? He had seen enough Agatha Christie movies and Christielike films that he knew the cigarette could be a clue. He placed it in the pocket of his heavy tweed coat. Before he descended the hill, he sent Shep Shep ahead to pull the other sheep down off the mountain. He watched Shep Shep do his work and wondered at the relatively small number of sheep on this part of the mountain. Suspecting that the predator had scared the sheep away from its own lair, he looked to see where his flock was primarily gathered. It would be away from the predator's haunt. Behind him lay thousands of acres of mountainous terrain, empty of human habitation and, on this particular morning, empty of sheep as well. He looked north to the emptiness, north to the path he knew led to the predator. In that vicinity, there was only one house—one very large house—and an array of stables, barns, and other buildings belonging to a wealthy, reclusive Dutchman. Approaching him might take some gumption on Cromarty's part, along with a little bit of tact.

In the distance he could see a winding road that led up from the single-lane motorway to the top of the mountain. A BMW was just entering the highway from the base of the mountain. Cromarty watched as the car kicked up dust as it sped along at the base and gradually ascended in a sinuous motion. The car gradually disappeared on the far side of the mountain. Cromarty felt again the cigarette in his pocket and canted down the mountain.

Later in the day, he called the local constable, who was then afield, investigating supposed violations of the legal limit for whiskey distillation. As in the days gone by, some Scots were known to create a whiskey in their private stills that was commercially viable in terms of taste but commercially dead without the appropriate licenses. The constable would enforce the law and proffer the suggestion that the violator stop selling his whiskey unless he wanted to start paying taxes on it and get the appropriate permits. The cry of the Crown had long been "no distillation without taxation."

Cromarty simmered all afternoon at this violation of his property. Unwilling if not unable to wait for the return of the constable, he decided to cool off by visiting the local pub. A pint and a shot could calm him and slow his heart rate. He was angry at someone or something, and he disliked the sensation. He was, after all, a kind man who thought of the sheep as a substitute for the children he never had.

He walked into the pub late in the afternoon with six photos that he had processed only a couple of hours after he took them. Even the photo lab technician had made a comment on the gruesome quality of the pictures. Cromarty had nodded in assent and avoided conversation with the unknown technician. But at the pub, he would be among trusted neighbors and friends.

Later at the pub, Cromarty pulled out his photos and laid them on the bar. The pub was a most plebian establishment. That was its appeal. It had been established in 1703 but shut down for lack of business after the Battle of Culloden and the subsequent clearing of the Highlands. It had been re-opened after the Jacobite fever diminished and had remained open ever since. It was said that the stone and brick had been dragged from older homes deserted during one of the clan wars of the seventeenth century, but no one was entirely certain. But it was a very good place to tell a story and to be heard.

The bartender looked at the photos and said, "Hmm. Perhaps we still have dogs that do the dirty work for men who want mutton but don't want to pay for it."

"Ha," chimed in another. "Ha again. I say, If sheep are found dead, it's because of the negligence of the owner himself. And you, Mr. Cromarty, should be ashamed. What kind of steward of God's blessing are you?"

"Oh, you can go to, Mr. Puckett. I know my blessings and my sheep. I keep both close to me. Go back to your drink."

For a moment, an old, distinguished-looking gentleman who sat sucking on an unlit pipe looked up. The scene itself reminded him of one from Thomas Hardy's *Far From the Madding Crowd*. Cromarty, the bartender, and the other patrons continued talking. He discerned that the photographs that Cromarty's fellow drinkers now held up accusingly were the catalyst for the exchange and that Cromarty had lost some sheep.

Nonchalantly the professorial-looking individual—tall, thin, almost gaunt, and wearing a blue shirt and red tie with a bluish tweed jacket and black pants—got up from behind his small, round table and eased himself to the bar to Cromarty's side. He stood still, his presence acknowledged by others with a knowing look.

After about a minute, he asked Cromarty his own theories concerning the culprit. Cromarty said he had to assume it was dogs, perhaps strays that occasionally coursed through the wilds of the mountains and well-known now and again to take down a deer from among several herds of the red deer for which Scotland was justifiably famous.

"Excuse me," he said, "I'm Iris Reid. I'm sorry for your loss. However, none of you have mentioned the strange goings on of late."

"Goings on?" asked Cromarty.

"Yes. You know, I'm a retired college teacher and so I have more time on my hands than I know what to do with. So I read police reports. But within the past several months, many people have reported seeing a large dog, usually on the night of the full moon and always aglow."

Cromarty smiled at the story, thinking that he was being set up for some kind of joke. "What do you mean 'glowing dog'?"

"I really can't say. It's strange but it appears to be true. Several people, adults as well as some teens, have called to report it. At first, the police dismissed the sightings as some of kind of prank. But your photographs suggest another possibility, namely, a kind of rabid dog that rather likes lamb chops."

"But," said the bartender, "do you remember a few years ago when

the Dutchman moved in? He was the one went to Colinburgh to see
if he could get the law changed so that he could bring wolves back to
Scotland. He wanted to release them into the wild."

"I remember," offered Cromarty. "I'm glad our representatives didn't
listen to such foolishness. I could be devastating to our livestock."

"Perhaps they did listen," offered the elder gentleman. "I recall that
he offered a compromise of some sort that was later passed, I thought,
by our parliament, whereby he could keep wolves on his own property
provided they were properly contained."

The others knew of no such provisions in the law and were silent.
Realizing he had inadvertently quelled the conversation, he bought a
round of drinks for the pub's five patrons, including himself, and went
and sat back down where he sucked on his pipe and his beer.

*　　*　　*　　*　　*

In northern Scotland lay a twenty-mile-long body of water known
as Loch Maree. The water was fresh and eventually flowed out into the
North Sea by way of a town and fishing village known as Gairloch. The
surrounding country was hilly, mountainous, precipitous, conifered,
rugged, barren, and misty. The body of water was clear and filled with
trout and dotted with islands of historic significance. It sat like a solitary
giant waiting for victims. But aside from Loch Maree Inn, the terrain
was uninhabited. This was one of the most beautiful and lonely places
in Scotland.

On the eastern side of the lake lay a stretch of largely uninhabited
land on whose towering cliffs near the south end sat an historic estate.
It could, however, be seen by no one as it lay far from the edge of the
cliffs that fell into the lake and too far from the highways that circled
its mountain base. The original estate dated from the twelfth century.
But the families of the past, as well as its present owners, demolished
much of the original enclosure to build an even more impressive
façade. Its current owner was rumored to be a mysterious Dutchman
of considerable wealth who had invested wisely and sought to buy a
building whose antiquity would give him regal stature to accompany his
wealth. He had over the years amassed a fortune, which he exhibited in
a gaudy display of baronial statuary and walls that protected a fantastic
house of stone. It was an encapsulated form of a medieval castle with

every clichéd adornment. This was Elvis's Graceland without the good taste. Even medieval Celticlike crosses were planted and painted queer florescent colors so that they would glow in the dark. As one delivery man had said upon dropping off a package at the estate, its owner had "taken the God out of gaudy."

Inside, a large living room looked like a cross between a Hilton hotel party room and an Oxford don's library, lively and untidy. But art objects were strewn about with the same care with which people display those velvet art works at Sunday afternoon specials at gas stations in America.

Into the room, Byron Vanderkin rolled his wheelchair. The flush of anger on his ruddy complexion bespoke a clear irritation. He murmured to himself as he eased his still strong but pained body to the window, looking over the vastness of his estate. Next to him was a coffee table with the morning paper. He held the paper in his hands and then threw it down in disgust.

As he did so, a tall blond-haired man in his early thirties entered the room. He started to walk across the room to greet his great uncle when the man in the wheelchair swore at him.

"Damn it! Damn it! You pig! You leave your crap wherever you go. Did you do this? Is this your idea of a joke?"

He eyed the young man with contempt. With that, he picked up the paper again and threw it at him. The paper fluttered to the floor, coming unsheathed so that the loose pages scattered. He watched as his great nephew, Martin Vanderkin—tall, tough, rugged, and not accustomed to being sworn at, except by his great uncle—looked down at the floor. Despite his chagrin at the unorthodox greeting, Martin bent down and gathered the newspaper. His uncle watched for any glimmer of recognition on his great nephew's face as he reassembled it and looked at the front page. In the lower left-hand side of the front page was the headline "Basking Hound Haunts the Mountains." The article read:

> *In a story reminiscent of a work by Sir Arthur Conan Doyle, a large mastifflike creature with a glowing coat has been reported traversing the hills east of the village of Morley. Last night, yet another sighting occurred under the full moon. It was the fourth such sighting in the last three*

weeks. The mastiff's appearance was at first dismissed as a possible prank or a kind of hallucination. However, recent sightings suggest that some unusually large dog or a small deer has taken on extraterrestrial qualities. Police continue their investigation.

✱   ✱   ✱   ✱   ✱

Martin Vanderkin was an embodiment of the Nordic ideal. His good looks and godly physique were unfortunately marred by a scowl that often crossed his face. But like a god without a heart, he treated most mere mortals with contempt. There were, however, creatures of the night for whom he had an affinity. He identified with them and their quest for survival.

"Your carelessness works against us. If your parents were still alive, they would be shamed by the futility of attempting to educate you. If you paid as much attention to cleaning up after yourself as you do to your damned wolves, then we could live without the prospect of discovery. Our obscurity keeps us from the prying eyes of the police and our inquisitive neighbors," said Byron.

"If obscurity was what you wanted, you shouldn't have purchased several thousand acres of Scottish countryside," replied the young man.

"This acreage and these buildings are my rightful possession. And if you don't mess things up too badly, all this will be yours. Guard it, take care of it, and stop bringing unwanted attention to us. Remember who you are. This is my legacy. It is yours, as well."

The young man waited.

"Get me a whiskey," said the older man.

His great nephew turned toward a large wooden bar of an antique nature that looked as if it were something stolen from a fight scene at a saloon in a cowboy film. It was large, ornate, and encrusted with wooden cherubs and fleshy nude women who lay in various seductive postures. The flat surface was polished but stained with the ovals of drinking glasses and the nicks of broken bottles and sharp hunting knives. In fact, the bar was an American import from an estate sale of an old tavern in Kansas City, Missouri. Several years earlier, while drinking in a restaurant/tavern being readied for demolition, Vanderkin heard that everything in the building would be auctioned off. Days later, he outbid everyone and paid a sum of seventy thousand dollars after a robust bidding war with a restaurant outfitter from Outback and another from Old Corral restaurants.

The young man poured his uncle a large whiskey, part of his daily medicine. The whiskey came from a nearby distillery that epitomized the traditions and tastes of Scotland—whiskey that was smooth and powerful, just like the man to whom it was now being given. The older man's mood instantly mellowed.

As he sat looking out the large window overlooking his estate, a drizzle began. Clouds were followed by a heavy mist from the North Sea. It soon spread over the mountainside, blotting out what little sun had filtered through the clouds and crawling about the estate like a giant cat smothering and obscuring those within and without. The white mist enveloped the fields, the barns, and the hills like a poison gas that would soon seep beneath the door sills and insinuate itself into a man's soul.

But this mist was more likely to be infected than to infect. Its whiteness was, however, a portend of the stagnant, lifeless, and selfish world of those who are self-contained, too self-assured, unduly righteous, and always revolving about their own psychic solar system, with their own ego acting like the sun, the center of everything.

"Sit, sit," said the older man.

The young man, his scowled lifted, sat by his great uncle.

"I had intended that our wealth would provide us with security and the chance to recover what is rightfully ours. But to do this we must live quietly, with occasional forays into the world of the well connected and the celebrated to cultivate the masters of wealth and deception. They're usually related."

He paused, took a deep breath, and began again.

"No one must suspect. Lately, our flow of diamonds has been disrupted. The Kimberly Process has made things most difficult. Our liaisons have been touched and perhaps apprehended. Those who are interfering with us must be dealt with. Unfortunately, Al Qaeda and even the handlers for the drug cartels have attempted to move in on our near monopoly of illegal trafficking. Our blood diamonds aren't getting much good press at this point. Like a submarine, we have to temporarily surface to fix the damage and then submerge again. Tell me, what have you learned? Our own investigations tell us their links are only incidentally connected to the Pakistani government. Their real financiers and promoters are local Al Qaeda connections operating out of our very own Londonistan."

"Londonistan?" queried the younger man.

"Yes, if we are not careful, the Muslims will soon rule this country, and that would be worse than having even the English do it. Diamonds, and a few other ventures, built this estate, this fortune. Jomo Raphael has of late, it seems, failed to deliver. We can deliver the guns and munitions he needs only after he deals us the diamonds. But I understand that even those which we have secured for our own personal finances have not been delivered to our financiers. Where are they?"

"Uncle, they have disappeared."

"Disappeared? Disappeared? What kind of fool do you think I am? Diamonds don't just disappear. They may be lost, but they don't just disappear."

"After the last shipment of munitions to Jomo I did as you instructed. I went to the our hideaway to divest ourselves of some diamonds to finance our endeavors. But the last rain in the mountains flooded the tunnel where you kept the *sparkle*. The wall collapsed. The rivulet had formed and broke through. The cache was partially washed away."

"You're a fool. Why can't you take care of things?"

"Uncle," the younger man uttered in exasperation. "No one could have known the wall would break."

"Perhaps I should have sent you back to South Africa long ago. There you can live with the Kafirs. You're as stupid as they are."

The old man paused and then said, "We will surface. We are going to reestablish contact with old friends and enemies. From now on, we will hide in public. I think it is time for a little celebration. Everyone needs a party now and then. We will have one. We shall invite the good, the bad, and the ugly, to say nothing of the smug. I myself shall be in charge of this affair. But there is yet another matter: the satchel. Where is it and what's in it?"

"The risk was not worth the reward," replied the young man. "Only books."

"Books?" asked Vanderkin incredulously.

"Yes, books. I brought them. I can't understand why they were of such concern."

"What kind of books?"

"Nothing special. One on Arab assassins by Bernard Lewis, and the others, well, not worth mentioning," said the young man.

"Well there are certainly some other things worth mentioning. Your wolves. Your damned pet wolves. Against my better judgment, I allowed you to import them here. Now they have become a source of concern. Melika tells me they roamed into the pastures, and last night he tracked them into a den. He said he found three dead sheep. Despite your permit, this incident will probably bring us into contention with our neighbors and I will once again have to pay for your foolery."

The young man hung his head and then said, "But the wolves are the one thing I love that I know will love me back."

"You are indeed a fool. They can't love any more than you can."

The young man sighed and smiled. No matter his efforts, he would never attain the approval he sought. He stood up and walked out the back door of the study into yet another huge room and then through the kitchen and bar and out yet another door into the vastness of the late afternoon and early evening mist. He disappeared into the whiteness as he headed toward the barn where his wolves were kept.

CHAPTER 21
A LIVE GRENADE

Behold the preparations, fire and iron.

—Wilfred Owen,
"The Parable of the Old Man and the Young"

—*FORT BRAGG, NORTH CAROLINA*

MAJOR SHELBY CRANE WAS FIVE FOOT TEN INCHES OF PISS AND vinegar. At the age of thirty-one, he lived for the opportunity to prove himself. His idea of fun was a day in the Carolina swamps in wartime training maneuvers in which he and his team would perform stealth envelopments. The night, the swamps, the danger of insects and venomous snakes, and the fog—these he regarded as friendlies who helped him secure his own positions and destroy others. With two tours of duty in Afghanistan and one hunting Al Qaeda with the Filipino forces in the southern Philippines, his mettle had been tested. But his last mission in Iraq had been shortened as a result of shrapnel embedded in his left shoulder and across his back from an engagement with insurgents in Baghdad. His recovery time with his family and friends had left him not with joy but with anxiety. He wanted to get back to the action. Even having to take required recovery time had not suited him. Against doctor's orders, he had begun working out again and shooting at the range only a couple of weeks after his surgery. As a result of this required down time, he was, by his own admission, as well conditioned and well rested as any time in his first nine years in the army. He was a live grenade looking for a target.

On a Sunday morning, he had gotten some of his buddies to open the range for him early so he could test the new weapon of choice for the select U.S. Special Forces, the SOCOM II, the newly updated modular M1A.

"Compact but deadly, heavy but accurate, and modified for those wishing to be glorified," was the way one army officer, who had been instrumental in its adoption by experimental units and some elements of the special forces, described it. Still, in any mission, his men would be divided among those who carried the SOCOM II and those with the traditional and reliable firepower of the M-4.

After an hour of practice with his SOCOM II, he switched to his Glock. Almost all U.S. forces in the field carried the nine-millimeter Beretta, but Crane still preferred the Glock. Lighter, more powerful, and easier to maintain, it was the weapon most American forces would have preferred. But NATO didn't deem it advantages sufficiently strong to outweigh those of keeping Italian gun manufacturers and their political supporters entirely happy. So in the name of NATO familial harmony, the Beretta was used by many but preferred by few.

As he chambered several more rounds, his cell phone rang. He was back in action. He was to lead a platoon of eighteen highly trained men into the territory held by Jomo Raphael and his rebel forces.

Seven days later, Major Crane and his unit were assembled at Patrick Air Force base in Florida. The next morning, they left for Ascension Island in the South Atlantic in a C-130. Hours later, a backup platoon of eighteen other men followed.

*   *   *   *   *

The planes carrying Major Crane and the platoon of backup personnel had rendezvoused at Wakewake Airfield on Ascension Island. There they were briefed by British and American military as well as civilian personnel and CIA operatives regarding the situation with those who were still presumed to be alive. The reporters, however, could already be dead, in which case, this operation could be futile. The lives of Major Crane and his men were just as valuable and not to be thrown away. They were to gain entry into what was thought to be Jomo Raphael's primary facilities, where it was likely that the hostages were being held.

The British officers were particularly helpful in terms of explaining the difficulties of the terrain that they would face. Two of them had trained members of the Kenyan armed forces and had accidentally engaged a contingent of Raphael's forces in western Kenya while conducting nighttime reconnaissance training on two separate occasions.

They observed that his own tactics were anything but amateurish, as he had attained the benefits of the finest training available as a young man. British, American, and Israel forces had put the young Raphael through his paces after he had distinguished himself as a most clever and charismatic Kenyan officer. He eventually found the electoral process of Kenyan democracy antiquated and stacked against his own self-declared brilliance. Moreover, the concept of a nation-state was too confining for his own vision of Africa as the embodiment of a new Christendom. This would replace the soft self-indulgence of the effete Europeans who were showing an ever increasing penchant to bow before the new Islamic onslaught, covert jihadism in the form of illegal immigration into virtually all of the European states. Raphael would rally a new nation to fight the Islamic invasion that was already subduing Europe and looking to do the same to all of Africa.

After several briefs, Major Crane and both platoons were shown satellite imagery of Jomo's compound. Points of ingress and egress were considered. Finally, they broke for a late lunch. Afterwards, plans were finalized. If the hostages were dead, Crane and his men were told to minimize engagements and to break them off if they had already begun. Whether the hostages were alive or dead, Crane and his men were to retreat to one of several staging areas where helicopters could land and take them back to safe haven. All of this, of course, was to be accomplished without the Kenyans knowing anything about it.

The next morning, the C-130s were revved. Crane and his men were launched for a nighttime high-altitude insertion about twenty miles from Jomo's main encampment. They would rest in the morning and day, and toward dusk begin to converge upon the objective.

As the C-130s began their long flight across the Atlantic and over the air space of various African nations, Crane wondered how any maneuvers could be kept secret with the African government being so susceptible to bribery. Everything seemed to be for sale and, if Raphael were as swamp-foxlike as he had been led to believe, then certainly he had contacts and sympathizers higher up in the Kenyan, Ugandan, and who knew what other African governments.

As the planes hummed across the Atlantic and then the west coastline and interior of Africa, they did so in a close enough formation that radar would detect one plane, not two. As they actually converged upon the drop site, the plane carrying Crane and his men would peel off to the north while the other plane would continue west in a large circle, essentially hovering and awaiting the return of Crane's empty transport. Both would then assume their cloaked flying formation until approaching an abandoned airfield almost on the Ugandan border. As they approached, Crane's plane would again peal north at low altitude and then out to sea and out of weapons' range for refueling at the British/American air base of Diego Garcia. The other plane would land publicly at an airfield near Nairobi as part of a protocol gesture—American forces just dropping in and keeping everybody's attention on them while their comrades did the real work. This was a charade that could also suggest that the Americans had indeed come in through western Kenya and that, of course, this matter had been cleared with the appropriate diplomatic and military authorities. Only, it hadn't.

On the long day's flight, Crane's men rested, soothed to sleep by the drone of the C-130's humming engines. One of his men leaned on his rucksack, reciting the rosary quietly, the beads gently filtering through his fingers with the *amen* that marked the conclusion of each Our Father, Hail Mary, or Glory Be to God. Another read from a leather-covered pocket version the New Testament while still another read the last *Harry Potter*. Most simply slept.

Chapter 22

RIFTING TOWARD BETHLEHEM

Kýrie eléison

—Words from the Catholic Mass

—BORDER REGION BETWEEN KENYA AND UGANDA

CRANE WAS AT HOME. THE MUCK OF THEIR LOCATION WAS uncomfortable, but it was also the gook that was least likely to invite company. Neither Kenyans nor Ugandans were likely to be wandering this area of the Rift Valley at this time of night. An unusually heavy summer rain had deluged the rendezvous of his men. But within minutes of the drop, everyone was in radio contact with one another. Using their night vision equipment, they converged upon Crane, who remained stationary. The others kept in contact as he reaffirmed their position with GPS. Within an hour and half, they had found their way through the mixture of savannahs and jungle to Crane's position. With several hours of night left and with no moon, they moved in the direction of the last known whereabouts of Jomo's camp.

At one point, they dropped to rest. As they did so, one of the men at the front of the formation, Captain Jeremy Hickman, put his left hand back to cushion himself as he was about to sit on the ground. The moment his hand touched the ground, he felt two sensations, a slithering movement beneath his hand and a sharp pain in his wrist of his gun hand. He yelled out, "Oh, shit!" In the darkness, he could see little, but the excruciating pain now traveling up his left arm was enough to tell him that something had just unleashed its venom. He flipped down his night vision goggles to see a puff adder slithering away, almost nonchalantly, into the tall vegetation. Angry and pained, he reached out with the butt of his rifle and clamped down hard on the tail of the adder and then jumped up and down onto the coiling snake's body. Its body took the full force of his weight with its head sticking out from beneath his boot. He reached down with his K-bar and sliced off its head.

As the others gathered round, he stomped on its head until it was crushed as its body convulsed and twisted helplessly. Within two minutes, he was lying on the ground, sweating and grimacing from the pain in his arm. Fear, frustration and anger now converged. The poison was already at work as the unit's medic grabbed his arm and began to administer anti-snake venom. The commando was now a burden to the unit. He would have to stay behind and wait for their return. One of the medics would stay with him, effectively diminishing the team's overall firepower and medical readiness in the event of further injuries or combat casualties.

Before dawn, Crane and fifteen others were already moving. Their GPS told them exactly where they were and how far they had to go to their destination. As far as they knew, their drop and subsequent movement had been the stuff of textbook maneuvers. Now, as the sun came up, they sought the refuge of increasingly dense foliage as they hugged a river bank that would lead them to Jomo's compound.

Their movements were swift, silent, and, even at a distance from their destination, perilous. Raphael had eluded whole contingents of Kenyan, Ugandan, and Tanzanian armies in the past, moving with the speed and stealth of classically trained guerrillas. The only handicap was that of Raphael's instinctive military brilliance leading to his own self-acclaimed infallibility in all things violent, tactical, and strategic. In short, he was now unpredictable even to himself as his ego assumed command of his rationality. His idealism and self-indulgent cruelty no longer seemed politically charged but the stuff of gratuitous violence and evil incarnate.

Crane's men were a mixture of veterans like himself who had served in the remotest and most dangerous campaigns against the Taliban and Al Qaeda in southeast Afghanistan. Others had served with distinction in Mosul, Fallujah, Basra, Baghdad, and other areas of Iraq.

Despite their stealth, mobility, and fire power, if they were discovered prematurely, sixteen men against several hundred well-armed members of the Liberation Army of Christ, who fought on their home turf, could suffer disaster. Still, special operations forces are nothing if not confident in their own ability and optimistic about the prospect of happy endings.

About noon, Crane brought his men to a standstill on the edge of a flat treeless field of dry ground and sand that drew back several hundred feet from the water's edge and lay several hundred feet across. Crane might have moved across, hunkering close to the ground once he emerged from the jungle, except for the fact that directly opposite from them could be seen two boys of about twelve who were only a couple of hundred feet away. If they spotted Crane's forces, they could alert Raphael or anyone who was nearby. And much of this area was either sympathetic to Raphael; dependent upon him for money, food, or safety; or simply too afraid not to side with him in all matters.

Crane and his men waited and watched as the boys played at the warrior's art, hurling sticks like spears into imaginary prey. After about fifteen minutes, the boys turned away and moved east, away from Crane and into the forest. Still, Crane felt exposed and vulnerable, so he motioned for his men to pull back into the jungle about one hundred feet. Sheltered from the heat and the prospect of discovery, he and his men broke out provisions. They would eat and sleep now and move again at dusk.

*　　*　　*　　*　　*

The summer heat made the jungle cover into a kind of broiler. The combination of heat and insects seemed a mild form of torture intended to test the patience of men. Most men snoozed intermittently, their nets keeping some insects at bay while others slithered beneath and still others stung and bit through the tiny openings in the mesh pressed against flesh.

At dusk, the men—rested, if not wholly refreshed—slipped out into the twilight, miming their words and signaling concerns and instructions. As the darkness fell, they moved within sight of a depression in the mix of jungle and savannah. Here would be Jomo's encampment.

From a distance, the encampment could barely be discerned. Their night vision goggles were indispensable. The village stretched for over one half mile in an east-west direction and was nearly a quarter mile wide. This was by no means a temporary settlement but rather a long-standing village that Jomo had co-opted more than eight years earlier in his quest to establish a base of operations for his Soldiers of Christ. Still, its essential components could be packed and moved on very short notice. Strewn about the depression there stood corrals for cattle and pigs and huts for those who tended to them. Crane observed that there were no palisades protecting any parts of the village. The whole terrain seemed open, exposed, and susceptible to attack. Strangely, Raphael's village was entirely quiet. No movement.

Based on aerial intelligence as well as undisclosed informers, the deduction was that the CINC crew would be kept in a hut or compound near Jomo's. But which was his? All of them were round, traditional huts with thatched roofs or large military-style tents. No guards appeared to be posted anywhere. Crane found it maddening. For a secret operation to stumble upon what appeared to be a deserted village was ominous. Something didn't feel right. There was no sound. No crying infants, no barking dogs, and no traipsing about by late night revelers. Nothing. The silence could not have been more foreboding.

Crane called two of his squad leaders to his side. He and eleven other men would move forward and attempt to reconnoiter the vicinity of the tents, looking for either Jomo, who they were authorized to kill, or the CINC crew, their primary objective.

Four others would stay back in the event that the bad guys attempted to cut off their retreat. They were equipped with the heaviest and most deadly pieces of equipment. The advance unit with Crane was lethal but had to be capable of moving quickly even though encumbered by their heavy rucksacks, which they would leave and dump into the river if need be.

Crane's contingent advanced to the periphery of the village. Neither sound nor sight revealed any of the enemy. The silence itself seemed increasingly threatening. Then Crane sent three men forward to the first large tent. Quickly, one of them slipped behind a tent that was canvas draped over a sturdy frame of wood, with several adjoining smaller tents that connected to yet another very large one. One of the men took out a knife and sliced through the canvas. With his night vision goggles, he peered inside. The room was furnished with a table, some chairs, maps, books, and clothing in a makeshift closet. But there were no people. He whispered to the two men next to him, "Empty." One of them radioed back to the others, whose radios were also embedded into their clothing with the microphone knit into their collars.

In the meantime, one of the four men in the rear contingent closest to the river thought he heard sounds like splashing water down river. The sound was faint; he could be mistaken. There were also water fowl and other animals in the area. He turned several times, listening. He whispered to the others that he thought that maybe they weren't alone. Each of the men also wore experimental text message wrist guards into which was embedded an LED. However, trying to type in a message, even with night vision goggles, was cumbersome. It may have negated the necessity of talking but it also took time. Even Crane was skeptical as to its utility.

As the four men sat in the darkness, anxiously but confidently awaiting their fellow soldiers' return with the hostages, Captain Reno, situated on the opposite flank of the four, thought that he too heard a faint sound on the water; but it was coming from the opposite direction reported by the other flanker.

Crane kept three men in their current position but then ordered the remainder to advance with him toward the other large tents. The ground over which they moved was hard and well trampled, and despite their graceful movements, their boots made a slight shuffling sound. The men continued, inspecting two other tents as they moved deeper into the village. Two more inspected, two more empty. But there was one rounded hut in the middle of the large tents.

One of Crane's men peered through the doorway while two others guarded his back. Through the darkness of the enclosure, he saw the hostages. Each was bound hand and foot, not with rope but with duct tape, which had also been wound about their mouths five or six times each. Captain O'Rourke, the man peering in, radioed to Crane that all but one of the captives appeared to be in the room.

"There's no woman," he said. The others were attached to one another by a long rope, which was wound about in back of each of the captives. The rope was tied securely around the wrist already bound with duct tape, then wrapped repeatedly around a pole in the center of the hut, and finally wrapped again around the neck of each of the captives. In short, if any one of them moved or squirmed much, it would cause the rope to tighten about the neck of everyone. Their eyes were also taped shut. Crane radioed back to be cautious as they might be booby trapped.

O'Rourke peeled and cut the tape from each, so they could speak. Their faces were dirty. When he peeled their tape away, he was momentarily stunned as each began to spit blood. Each had had his tongue cut out. Their eyes, even at their moment of rescue, were beseeching with fear and horror. Their attempts at communication horrified both O'Rourke and the others as the two other men peered in at the ghastly sight. But even before O'Rourke could complete freeing the captives, gunshots broke out by the river—first single shots and then machine guns.

The fire was heavy. The guttural sound of the AK47 was distinctly different from the American-made weapons. The AK47 fire was on both flanks of the American position. The hostages were quickly freed and brought out of the hut when heavy gunfire emerged from the north. Immediately, two men outside the hut fell. O'Rourke kept moving with the hostages toward the river as other men came forward and tried to reach the wounded but still moving men. As they did so, there was more gun fire. But this time, Crane's men had seen the barrel bursts, which, with their night vision goggles, enabled them to spray the vicinity with accuracy. The fire from behind them was growing in intensity while that near the hut was also increasing. Crane realized that the firing was now coming from all sides. He was nearly surrounded and would have to fight his way out with the hostages.

He ordered his men to hold their ground near the river to prevent a complete envelopment. But even as he did so, he heard another yelp as Captain Mack Brady fell and lay bleeding profusely from a wound to the neck. The darkness was still a blessing to Crane. His men could see while Raphael's men were presumably shooting blindly in the darkness. Despite the harm that Crane's men inflicted, it was apparent that at least five of his own men were dead or wounded.

As he and his men moved back to the river, O'Rourke ordered the hostages to stay low. Even as he did so, a bullet grazed his forehead while another entered his left shoulder, hitting his clavicle and exiting his back near the base of his neck. He fell while the hostages froze and hovered over him, afraid to go any farther on their own. O'Rourke got on his hands and knees and radioed to Crane.

"Hit! Hit! O'Rourke! Need help!"

"Stay where you are," said Crane. "We'll come to you." But the firefight's intensity prevented Crane's movement. His men had moved back toward the river when another enfilade exploded from the far side. At first, several men yelled out. They were Raphael's men being hit by gunfire from his own men. But then their spray splashed into the water near the position at which Crane had originally set his rear guardsmen. Bit by bit and shot by shot, the splashing in the water came closer. The darkness prevented Jomo's men from complete accuracy, but they could see occasional splashes and foam in the water, indicating that they were not yet hitting the embankment to which Crane and his men were retreating.

The firing continued apace for fifteen minutes, with both sides frozen in their positions. Crane and two other men eventually broke for the hostages. Crane escorted them while the other two carried O'Rourke. But as they neared their own base near the river, one of the men carrying O'Rourke fell backwards, dead—a head shot. Jomo's men on the far side of the river had found their range even in the darkness.

Finally, Crane gave the order to evacuate by moving north along the river bank, which he hoped would prevent a near envelopment on his left flank. But as he and the hostages and his wounded moved north out of the clearing toward the jungle, the intensity of gunfire in front of him doubled. Three more of Crane's men fell with wounds of varying severity. Before he could fully assess the damage, the gunfire slacked on the far side of the river. It was the same on his right flank, then his rear, and finally on his front. The only shots were those still being fired by his own men. Crane ordered his men to stop firing. There was complete silence.

Then in the silence emerged a voice.

"I am the horseman of the Apocalypse. I can give life, and I can take it. I wish to give you life, brave American soldiers. I am one like you. I too have suffered and toiled for my people. But I have risen again, and I come to bring you good news. Today, even Death is your friend, for I wish for you to live. For you are rangers, and I once trained with you. I know about ranger danger. How can you possibly win when you must fight a fellow ranger and Death at the same time? We are brothers. Do not be afraid. I am your friend. Over you, Death shall have no dominion, but only life. I alone can give you this."

There was a long pause. The voice was Jomo's. Crane recognized it from the videos he had seen of the younger version when he spoke after leading student revolts against the Kenyan government years earlier.

Jomo waited for a response. Crane was silent, not wishing to speak and thereby give away his exact position.

Jomo waited and then raised the megaphone again. "Major Crane, you and I are brothers in Christ. For you too are a Christian. We fight for the one true God, not Allah, not Krishna, not Buddha. Speak. I wish to help you. I admire American fighting men. I am your brother. I too wear the ranger patch. Soon it will be daylight. You are surrounded. By friends. Many friends. My men are many, for you are rangers and only the many can defeat the few like you. Let me help you. You have many wounded and some already dead. I have a priest who can bless them, for we are all Christians. We will have communion together. I have forgiven you seventy times seventy already, for you and I are brothers."

He paused again. Then one of the hostages abruptly stood up and started to run toward the voice in a vain attempt to yell, "Fuck you." But it was an exercise in self-mockery. He attempted as well to yell out, "Kill me! Kill me!" but the sound was like that of a pig being slaughtered. "Ill meeah, Ill meeah!" The hostage then ran in a circle, crying. He fell to his knees and sobbed uncontrollably.

Jomo stopped and, betraying his own charm and what little humanity he had left, began to laugh. Then he added, "I have the gift of tongues and you do not. You stole my diamonds. Hahaha!"

Crane looked in the direction of the voice, trying to see Jomo. He prayed for a sighting and one good shot. But Jomo was concealed in the jungle.

Again silence. The pause gave Crane yet another opportunity to assess his predicament. He was under strict orders to get the hostages back to a safe place. Failure was not an option, not even a possibility. As he spoke with his men, he heard two of the hostages now whimpering while yet another continued to sob. He then heard the most ungodly sound.

"Kýrie, Kýrie, eléison, Kýrie eléison." Jomo was singing the Greek hymn of the Catholic Mass, "Lord, have mercy." As if on cue, his men joined in on all sides. If there had been any doubt about their being surrounded before, all doubts were now lifted. Crane, a graduate of the Reserve Officer Training Program at Cincinnati Xavier University listened with consternation. What could he and his men expect of a man who mutilated the living, offered forgiveness, asserted his respect for brother rangers, and sang part of the Roman Catholic Mass during a lull in a fire fight?

As though he knew what Crane was thinking, O'Rourke whispered to him, "No surrender, sir. He's a butcher. Make him bleed if he wants us." As Crane contemplated his options, he considered the translation of the Kýrie: Lord, have mercy. Crane then spoke to his men and told them that on his signal, they should move forward toward the jungle and cut a path through the enemy back toward the path on which they had come. As Jomo sang the last of the Kýrie, he went right into yet another song, the Agnus Dei. The song was in Latin and literally translated as *Lamb of God*. As Jomo sang, Crane stood up and fired in the direction of the voice in the darkness.

He heard laughter. As Crane and his men charged forward, the forest erupted with gunfire. Raphael had anticipated their move and brought his heaviest concentration of men and weapons to the area toward which they were now headed.

Crane responded with grenades in an all-out drive to get to the jungle. Even firing wildly in the darkness, Raphael's men hit several more of Crane's men. As Raphael retreated deeper into the forest, the others behind Crane fired—at first sporadically for fear of hitting their own men. But then, as though gradualism itself could justify their actions, they steadily increased the intensity of their fire even though Crane and several others were still in front of the rangers. One of the rangers went down dead, hit in back with rifle fire by one of his own men. The screams, the blood, the curses, the smell. Crane now lay on the ground with two bullets in his back, one in his shoulder, and two more in his left hamstring. He lay in agony, bleeding, almost helpless, unable to advance.

Again there was silence. Crane's men were still exposed on the edge of the jungle. Raphael's men closed in. The sun was beginning to show a pinkish luster on the horizon. The hostages merely huddled helplessly, afraid to move.

As the sun slowly rose, Raphael's men crept forward. The flies were already gathering. Crane was floating in and out of consciousness. He no longer knew where he was until one of Jomo's men came alongside him and put the muzzle of an AK47 against his forehead. Crane passed out.

Two hours later, Crane awoke in excruciating pain. As he came to, his blurred vision detected the movement of a bearded elderly man. He was white and slightly stoop-shouldered. Crane tried to sit up on the bedding made of a cushiony straw mat and a pillow made of a burlap bag stuffed with pieces of cloth.

Crane barely had enough strength to lift his head. Even as he did, he reached helplessly with his right arm toward the figure that hovered above him. As the elderly man moved about the hut, Crane's effort to sit up caught his eye.

"No, no, please rest. You are hurt, and we must stop the bleeding. Moving only makes it worse." The man spoke English fluently but with a slight accent.

Crane continued to try to raise himself up, but the pain in his back and legs reverberated throughout his entire body. Involuntarily, he began to shake all over despite the fact that the air was hot.

The old man came to his side and sat on a plastic crate. He looked sad, tired, timid, and kind.

"You should drink this."

He offered a small clay cup of water, bringing it to Crane's lips. Crane collapsed backwards, his whole body now shaking almost violently. He lay there breathing quickly and convulsively.

Crane looked up, bewildered not at what the old man had said but at his own body's involuntary reaction. It continued to shake and chill despite the heat. As he tried to sit up again, the old man gently pressed down on his chest to encourage him to rest.

"Listen," he said, "Jomo tells me you must live for you are a great warrior. You are worthy of joining him. You in particular. The others are being cared for by some of the women, but you—you are mine. He wishes for you to live, and if you die, that is not good for me. So rest and listen.

"Jomo was once my student. Whatever demon he now is, I helped create. In him I have sinned and sinned greatly. I have long known that he was capable of achieving more than any student I have ever taught. But his methods have also been a horrible reminder that the ends do not always justify the means. He is a guerrilla genius. He even got you and your men."

As Crane was finally able to focus his eyes, he noticed for the first time that his caretaker was wearing a Roman collar. Nothing could have seemed stranger to him. For a moment, he wondered if he had somehow been transported to a mission hospital.

"My men, Father. How are they?"

"How many did you have?"

"I came with sixteen."

"You have been brave, but now you must be even braver."

"Why?" asked Crane.

"Jomo says that nine of your men are already dead. Two more may die soon. They are badly hurt. The others were also wounded but they should live if Jomo wills it. He is unpredictable."

Crane then asked, "The nine who are dead and the two who are likely to die—that is only eleven. I make twelve. What of the other four? Are they also wounded?"

"Perhaps, but only three are being cared for by the women. It is possible one of your men escaped."

Crane was silent. Could he trust this man? Then Crane asked as his body began to convulse again, "Why are you here?"

"Because I am a fool, not for Christ but for the devil. I have created him. As a child, his education was entrusted to me. I taught him to channel his great talents into helping the poor attain justice. But I never taught him mercy. Justice is a most severe taskmaster. I believe at one time Jomo wished to be its instrument. But power does indeed corrupt. And Jomo is its child.

"Soon he will test you, you and your men. You must show yourself to be worthy to live or he will kill you. Do not underestimate him; his intelligence and his cruelty are both without peer."

Crane listened and then, softly, he asked the priest, "And the hostages?"

"Better where they are now than where they were. They could not live long given the condition they were in. Jomo left them only half human, only half men."

Then, as if he were physically ill, he ran outside and vomited. Crane again collapsed back onto the mat.

Crane lay there, breathing shallowly and spasmodically, wondering about the woman he was to rescue. Where was she? Was she dead? He had no chance to speak with the other hostages.

Father Ricci came back in and sat again next to Crane. "Your life has been spared, but Jomo is coming. Do not make him angry."

Moments later, Jomo and St. George walked into the room. Jomo pulled a chair over next to Crane as Father Ricci got up and walked to the other side and stood. Jomo glared at the priest, who then left. St. George remained standing near the doorway.

CHAPTER 23
LOCH MAREE'S GUEST

Scotland was a beautiful woman who's treasure the Vikings left in runes.

—Popular saying

—GAIRLOCH REGION, SCOTLAND

WITHIN A WEEK, AN INVITATION HAD BEEN PREPARED AND SENT out to a group of the most celebrated, infamous, famous, and interesting people of the British Isles. A summertime party was to be held at Teutonic Nights Estate, an estate that represented an unsuccessful blend of kitsch and modernity wrapped around medieval barns and the remnants of old-time stone castles that still haunted the Highlands like an ugly ghost that refused to leave. As one visitor who had once visited Elvis' Graceland observed, Elvis may have had bad taste, but the Vanderkins seemed to have none. On this particular occasion, a party would be held not for fun, but for profit. It was a means of schmoozing with the *hoi polloi*, a means of informing the financially insecure, and even some of the not so insecure, who their financial betters were.

*　　*　　*　　*　　*

For several days, Grant Chisolm had made plans for an extended trip to northern Scotland. Regis MacArthur had called him, and Oz had set up another meeting. Grant was told that he would be taking time to visit Loch Maree. Loch Maree was a twenty-mile-long lake that emptied into the North Sea. The landscape was forbidding, frequently under a mist and surrounded by forest that still abounded in red deer. The area was sparsely populated, and on the entire lake there was only one inn, the Loch Maree Inn, which had been around since the 1870s. Grant was told of the invitation that Regis MacArthur had received. MacArthur had informed Grant that he would be attending the function with him. Grant was to make the moment as casual and convincing as possible. MacArthur would make the arrangements with Vanderkin, a longtime acquaintance. He also advised Grant that a woman's presence would help him hide his true intentions. When Grant asked why he was being sent on such a nebulous mission, Regis reminded him that he would frequently be called upon to go to different places before he was apparently needed. He would therefore go to Loch Maree, secure a room as a tourist at the Loch Maree Inn, and do touristy things.

Two days later, Grant was at the inn. He pulled up in a 2005 Cooper S and walked into the main entrance. The entry was warm and cozy, with old oak floors and several prints on the wall depicting English fox-hunting scenes. Grant walked immediately to a guest registry, which was a rather small, dark, waist-high desk on which sat a bell and a large, green-covered guest book. No one was behind the desk and no one appeared even after Grant rang the bell twice. Thinking that someone would eventually appear, he entertained himself opening the thick guest book to the first page.

The date set in the left-hand side was June, 1937. The list of names going down the page was all handwritten, often in lovely cursive and only occasionally in printed letters.

As he looked at the beautifully scripted letters of the pre-computer age, he reflected upon the hundreds and perhaps thousands of names of the guests represented, a by-gone generation, many of whom stopped here before World War II. The later signatures might have been part of that same generation that went onto fight in the same war. He perused the names, almost all of which were English, Scottish, or Irish. Some wrote their names with the flourish of Irish monastics about to decorate some ancient manuscript with calligraphic marks of patiently lined and exquisitely conceived beauty. Some were bold and masculine. But all were florid and stilted with the mannered restraint of disciplined hands. Grant admired the artistry of letters slanted with the consistency of an accordion fold, each cursive letter standing parallel to the next. Most listed as part of their address cities and towns with which he had a passing familiarity because of his having seen the names on maps of the surrounding area. Still others identified London, Dublin, York, Edinburgh, Glasgow, the great cities of the British Isles. Here and there, but only rarely, other cities were mentioned, like Oslo or Paris and even Berlin. As he turned the pages, Grant noticed the apparent infestation of German tourists to the area in late 1937 and throughout 1938. Thereafter, the guest registry grew thin with names, with the number of tourists dropping off rapidly in 1939. *World War II*, he thought.

He noticed, however, that even in 1940–41, tourists still trickled in, even one from South Africa. He wondered if there was a story there. He was turning the pages when a friendly gentleman appeared behind the desk, wearing a white shirt and tie with a bib apron wrapped around him.

"Good afternoon, sir, and welcome," he said with the affability and self-assured delight of one who seemed to be genuinely concerned about the well-being of his guests.

"My name is Chisolm, Grant Chisolm. I called several days ago. I believe you have a room for me."

"Yes, I believe we do. Please, if you wouldn't mind, sign into our hotel guest book. Cash or credit card, sir?"

"Credit card," replied Grant.

"Very good, and how long will you be staying, sir?"

"One week, maybe two."

"Fine. Here to see the sites, are you?"

"Yes, I enjoy travel."

Grant turned to the last pages of the hotel guest book and signed in as thousands before him had done.

"This is quite interesting—your guest book."

"Oh yes, Mr. Chisolm," he responded. "It's a very interesting book. It's a sort of history of the place. May I ask, Mr. Chisolm, if you've an itinerary for your holiday?"

"Not quite," responded Grant. "I have a guide book of the area. But I'm open to suggestions."

"Tell me then, what are your interests?"

"Oh, I could enjoy some of the historic sites; I understand you have your fair share."

"Yes, we do and, if such interests you, I suggest that you drive to Gairloch. It's only a few miles farther north and has a museum along with a most interesting curator. You may also wish to take in the arts festival there. It's going on now."

"Sounds good. I also understand that Scotland is renowned for its trout fishing. Any chance of my doing any of that here?"

"Oh, yes, we have gillies who would be happy to take you out on the lake. And since you're interested in history, they could even show you some of the islands. A lot of history there—the Vikings, the Irish, and all. But unfortunately, you can only look at the islands. You can't go on unless you are an archaeologist."

"Well the fishing sounds just fine," replied Grant.

"I'll call one of the gillies."

"Gillies?" asked Grant.

"Yes, you will need a guide with a boat. And, if you catch a big one, we can even have our chef prepare it for you."

"Sounds like a plan."

Grant handed him his credit card. As the innkeeper processed it, he told Grant of the dining services available and then handed him his key.

"Room 22, second floor overlooking the lake. You'll enjoy the view. Bathroom at the end of the hallway. Hope you enjoy it. Oh, and one more thing. Will you be dining with us this evening?"

"Yes, I think so. What time?"

"Six thirty. Very good fare. I think you'll like it."

"I hope to. Thank you."

Grant climbed the narrow steps to the second floor. They creaked with age. Upstairs, the darkly carpeted hallway, even with the light through the windows, was dusky. He arrived at his room, went in, and immediately fell asleep on the old and well-tried bed.

When he awoke only an hour later, he was refreshed. His room was small but comfortable, with a television, two lamps, and a wash basin. He looked out the window. It did indeed overlook the lake, and across on the far side was a steep, rocky declivity of several hundred feet on which the mist still lingered on what was otherwise a fairly bright Scottish day.

Grant then walked out to his car, opened the trunk, and pulled out his suitcase and a duffle bag filled with his running equipment. In his room, he changed and then trotted down the steps and out into the late afternoon air. The day was warm but hardly oppressive, and a gentle breeze blew off the north end of the lake, cooling him as he jogged north along the highway. Although quiet, three cars passed him, but only one of them on his side of the road. Oddly, the car looked familiar. Grant took mental notes of the color and license plate and moved on.

After a half an hour, he turned around. He jogged back with the wind at his back, covering the same distance in only twenty-eight minutes. As he approached the hotel, he sprinted the last one hundred or so yards, determined to steal the gold medal from the imaginary Kenyan runner who was favored to win by the entire world. Of course, it was a world that did not know Grant Chisolm, the most muscular and competitive and tallest runner in the ten-thousand-meter field. Fresh from his victory, Grant jogged triumphantly to his room, grabbed a towel and robe, and headed toward the communal bathroom to take a shower. The bathroom was small but adequate. Grant showered, sauntered back to his room in a bathrobe, and then changed into casual attire to prepare for a well-deserved dinner.

* * * * *

The waitress's accent seemed odd to Grant—neither English nor Scottish, but nonetheless British with a twist of something else. She came to his table, and he placed an order of chicken and garlic mashed potatoes. After several pleasantries concerning his comfort at the hotel, Grant asked about her accent. She smiled and said, "Guess."

The waitress was twentyish and attractive, with long legs, a winning smile, and an air of vulnerability. Her "Guess" seemed to suggest more than merely an invitation to ascertain her country or origin.

Grant smiled and said, "British colonial, I'd say; maybe South African."

She raised her eyebrows appreciatively and said, "Very good. You're a good guesser. But then, I'll bet you don't know where I live."

Grant smiled again and said, "Gairloch."

"Very good again, sir. But absolutely wrong. I live right here on the first floor, room 2. Isn't that nice? That makes us neighbors."

Grant half laughed at the none-too-subtle flirtation as she sashayed out of the dining room with his order.

When she came back with his food, she placed it before him silently but appealingly glancing at him as she did so. She lingered a little too long thereafter to see if he were looking at her. He was.

She then hurried to attend other diners. Several of the couples at the other tables seemed by their accents to be American.

After dinner, Grant wandered into the reading room, where he glanced at several books on hunting and fishing. As he did so, the innkeeper approached him and said, "Mr. Chisolm, very good news. I have a gillie for you: Mr. Michael Marty. He'll be here promptly at seven tomorrow morning to pick you up and go out to fish. He's very good. You'll certainly catch a fish or two."

"Thank you, I look forward to it."

That evening, Grant lingered in the reading room and then later in the bar area, where he maintained his abstemious ways, sipping several sparkling waters while he conversed casually with the wait staff. To his surprise, the bartender, the barmaid—who also waited on the tables— and the cook were all from South Africa. When Grant asked why, one of them responded, "Because we get a fair number of Germans here. South Africans speak English as well as German. We're bilingual by birth, you might say."

The cook, who was behind the kitchen wall, overheard the remark and stuck his head through the food window. "And don't forget. A South African owns this place—the bloke across the way. Or maybe he's Dutch," he said as he made a thumb throw over his right shoulder.

Grant sat and listened at the evening's banter between the staff members and the relaxed conversation of the inn's patrons.

The next morning, Grant arose early and settled himself, with a newspaper, in the dining area. The waitress from yesterday looked at him with pleasant satisfaction, offering him a smile with his coffee, scrambled eggs, and fried tomatoes. However aware he was of the waitress's flirtations, he kept thinking of Blanche.

After breakfast, he went back to his room and called her. Blanche sounded absolutely delighted to hear from him. At the same time, she grew quiet when he asked her if she would consider coming up to Loch Maree in a couple of weeks to attend a party.

"Grant, I'd love to, but a co-worker, someone I used to date, has asked me out to a concert that same weekend. We're going along with some mutual friends. I'm sorry. I wish you had called sooner. Maybe we can get together the following weekend."

"Sure," Grant said. "That would be good." Despite his disappointment, Grant detected that Blanche was sincere and really did wish he had called sooner. Next time he would do so. But Grant immediately bounced back and said, "Yes, we'll plan for the following weekend."

"Besides," she added, "we have a thousand things to talk about. I have exciting news. I want to share it with friends."

"What is it?" Grant asked.

"It's a secret. I'll tell you when we get together. But, Grant, I'm still at work and I have people waiting to see me. Call me later. I'd love to talk."

They said their good-byes, and Grant began to think, *Where am I going to find a date?*

The next morning, Grant was up at five o' clock. He put on his running shorts, shoes, and T-shirt. The morning air had a bite to it, but he knew that his run would quickly find him hot and sweaty. He maintained a consistent pace as he once again jogged for thirty minutes in one direction, north toward Gairloch. On the way back, he frequently looked at his watch, determined to run faster than he had the day before. There was a slight mist coming off the loch, and he found himself running in and out of low layers of fog. It was a phenomenon that pilots referred to as "running popeye," going in and out of clouds or fog banks. Each patch of fog he ran into seemed to amplify the sound of his steps and his breathing. He ran the same distance on the way back in twenty-seven minutes and six seconds.

*　　*　　*　　*　　*

Upon his walking into the inn, he could smell the early morning eggs and bacon being prepared for the guests. His own appetite increased with the aroma. He quickly went back to his room, then the bathroom, where he showered and shaved and changed. Within fifteen minutes, he was seated in the bar area, having his own English breakfast.

Moments later, the gillie, Michael Marty, walked in. He was a hearty-looking man of thirty or so with red hair and red stubble. He was a big man with large hands and a stocky physique that looked as though it should be moving cargo on the wharfs.

Since Grant was the only one still eating, Michael went immediately to his table and said, "Are you the Yank, Grant Chisolm?"

"Yes, I am."

"Well, it's a good day for fishin'. A few clouds, a bit of a breeze, maybe even a storm front moving in, the kind that make the fish bite."

One of the kitchen staff came in with a cup of coffee and set it down at Grant's table for the gillie.

"Tell me, what are my best prospects on Loch Maree?"

"Prospects? I assume you mean fish. The pike might bite, but I'm thinkin' more salmon. You ever fish before?"

"Many times," replied Grant. "Many times. But I'm not particular. I'll fish whatever and however you suggest."

"That you will, because I'm the best gillie in these parts."

"Did you say 'filly'? You been keepin' secrets from us," joked the bartender.

"You should know, you pervert."

He looked back at Grant and asked, "Now you tell me, have you ever fly fished?"

"Yes, I have. I enjoy it."

"Well, I'll betcha you've never fly fished the way we do here."

"What? Do you use real flies or something?" smiled Grant in response.

"No, better than that. I'll show you when we get out on the lake."

Within the hour, Grant and the gillie had shoved off from the shore in a wooden boat with a covered bow, teak side boards, and gunnels that suggested the boat was made more for rough ocean waters than those of an inlet body of water like Loch Maree. The boat was fourteen feet long and sturdy, with oar locks on either side and a small, low horse-powered motor that the gillie started with a ripcord and some fiddling with the choke.

With the motor puttering along heartily like a little motor who knew he could, the boat covered the distance from its mooring behind the inn to the middle of the lake, where the gillie brought it to a standstill. He cut the motor, allowing the boat to drift slowly south.

He picked up one of the long fishing poles, brought the tip toward his face, and pulled on the line to extend it several feet. Then he opened a tackle box at his feet with his free hand and pulled out a seven- or eight-foot length of red yarn and tied it to the end of his line. Then, as Grant watched, he pulled the yarn slowly through his tightly compressed forefinger and thumb, flattening the yarn into a long plane.

"This," he said, "will catch the wind. It acts like a sail." To the end of the yarn, he tied a small black fly. Then he handed the pole to Grant.

"Now cast out. The line and the yarn are all the weight you need."

Grant brought the pole back to the two o'clock position over his right shoulder and whipped the line over the side of the boat, onto the water. The gillie was right; the yarn acted like a sail, causing the black fly to dance upon the water with the delicate dappling dance of a real fly. As the wind momentarily gushed, the fly lifted from the water and seemingly flew to yet another space on the water's surface. Grant had never before seen such a realistic presentation of bait upon the water. As he drew the fly back slightly to cast farther from the boat, a trout lifted his head out of the water, snapping at the fly and hooking his glittering snout. What ensued was a belly-flopping fight on the small waves as Grant jerked on the pole to set the hook and begin to take his prey.

The gillie encouraged Grant. "There she is, there she is! Keep the line taut. Reel her in. I've the net, I've the net!"

As Grant reeled his trophy to the side of the boat, the gillie lifted her out with his net, unhooked her with a deft fingering of the unbarbed hook, and then held the fish out for Grant to see.

"Fourteen, fifteen inches! This is your dinner!"

Grant beamed with delight, surprised by his own success on only one cast. The gillie dropped the fish into a large yellow bucket filled with fresh water from the lake. The trout immediately began to swim in a panicky circle.

Grant then cast out again, watching the fly dapple upon the water. He spent the next hour and a half reeling them in, the fish seemingly biting at anything as a light drizzle clouded the morning.

After the morning's success in which the gillie and Grant kept only two of the eleven fish Grant landed, he asked the gillie, "What about this lake? Any sites of interests? I hear there might be a few."

"Well, over there," said the gillie, pointing to his right, "that's Witch's

Point. Called so because in the past, that's where the witches were taken to be burned."

"And that island over there, what of it?" asked Grant

"That's the most important place in Scottish history." And with that remark, the gillie angled the boat with their backs to the wind and moved toward the far side of it. As they came within thirty or so feet of it, the gillie pointed behind Grant and said, "Look."

Grant turned to look and saw nothing but the vastness of the lake itself. "From here you can see everything, including ..." He paused dramatically and raised his eyebrows, "Viking ships. This part of the island is called Lookout Point. From here, the alarm would go up. They could see the Vikings coming up the lake quite nicely."

Grant then asked, "What about the island? Any significance?"

"Yes, but I'm afraid we can't go there. It's a part of the National Trust of Scotland. Only archaeologists with permission from the government can go there."

"Why, what's on it?"

"An ancient Viking burial ground. And it also happens to be the place where St. Columba began preaching and converting the Scots to Christianity. It's sacred ground even if it's forgotten."

"Why aren't people allowed to go there? Maybe that's why it's forgotten."

"They're afraid people will deface the tombs or steal things from the island. You're not allowed to take even a rock or pebbles from it."

"Have you been on it?"

"Yes, but I live here, don't I?"

"Perhaps others could also visit if they promised not to disturb anything," hinted Grant.

"Remember, not even a pebble," replied the gillie, even as the boat's hull scraped the rocky shore. Grant stepped out and then the gillie as he killed the motor.

The island seemed to be an invention of musical gods. The waves rhythmically washed against the shore. The trees that hugged the shoreline and the short embankment responded to the gusts of wind in an ages old symbiosis. Wind without sound seemed more than merely voiceless but like a mime without purpose. Here the trees moved and voiced their delight at dancing to the musicality of the sea wind's invisible hands. Everything was in harmony in the continuing light drizzle. The entire island seemed at first to be covered in trees and shrubs. The gillie led Grant through the narrow pathways, condensed even further by low-hung branches that forced both of them to bend down and duck. Moments later, the interior of the island opened up like a vaulted cavern in which the ancient trees hung over the peace and troubles of those long departed.

Here, in a wide circle, stood ancient stones hewn out of nearby cliffs to mark the burial sites of Vikings lords. From the first, Grant thought of it as a kind of Stonehenge, only smaller and less public.

After a while, Grant followed the gillie to a tree that stood by itself. At first, Grant could not believe his eyes. There, in the midst of the morning drizzle, stood a tree shimmering with rain and coins of the realm. Before Grant could ask, the gillie offered that the tree was ages old and that the coins embedded in its bark were the result of tourists and archaeologists coming to the island over the years.

"It is said that once Queen Victoria herself came ashore with her Scotsman, Mr. Brown. She put a crown into the bark of the tree to pay for passages of the dead into the next world. But after she had gone back to the boat, Mr. Brown made some excuse to go back and relieve himself, whereupon, like a true Scotsman, he took the coin back. No use wasting it on the dead."

The gillie then pointed to a part of the circle of stone opposite from where they stood and said, "The money tree is interesting all right, but here is something else you won't see back in America. In your country, like mine, they often bury husband and wife side by side. But not here, not the Vikings. Here you see the site of two Viking nobles. One woman, one man. Husband and wife. You see how they're buried, foot to foot. Well, that's so that on Judgment Day, they can rise up and face each other and embrace as they go to heaven. A nice thought. I hope it's true. Then maybe my wife and I can get together – at least in death, because we're not doin' so well now."

"Divorced?" asked Grant

"Yes, and hatin' every minute of it."

Grant was dutifully silent and offered no more. Then, after several more minutes, the guide said that they should go.

"Before we are seen. Don't mention this to anyone; I'm not supposed to take people here."

As they approached the boat, Grant asked, "Why is the money tree here? Why not on the mainland?"

"Legend says that the tree actually grows from the wealth planted here a long time ago. The coins now are almost all recent, maybe twenty or thirty years old. But before that, there were still other coins. I suppose kids in the area or descendants of Mr. Brown kept sneaking in to take the coins for themselves. What wealth would be planted here, no one knows—just legend."

"But," said Grant, "don't many legends have a kernel of fact about them?"

"I suppose, but who's to know?"

Grant stepped into the boat as the gillie, with his boots on, stepped into the water, pushed the boat off, jumped in, and started the motor with two cranks.

As they scooted through the small whitecaps, the morning drizzle ceased and a rainbow appeared immediately above them and to the west, one end of the arc touching down on the island they had just left.

Chapter 24
SURVIVOR'S GUILT

Whoever you are holding me now in hand,
Without one thing all will be useless,
I give you fair warning before you attempt me further,
I am not what you supposed, but far different

> —Walt Whitman,
> "Whoever You Are Holding Me Now in Hand"

—JOMO'S ENCAMPMENT

THE TUMULT IN CRANE'S HEAD WAS MATCHED BY THE SEVERITY OF the spasms of his legs and back. The pain was attenuated only by the knowledge that he was still alive.

Jomo had seemed pleased to have a man of Crane's military bearing and training in his presence. In fact, after their first visit, he had even sent two lovelies to bath Crane and to remove his blood-stained clothes. Crane was too weak to resist. They treated him tenderly, smiling at him all the while. He attempted to smile back, only dimly aware of their touch. Though naked, he was too disoriented to care. He passed out and only came to several hours later when Father Ricci once again returned to his side.

Father Ricci placed a wet cloth over his forehead and spoke softly.

"You must have done well. He says he likes you and that you are to be well treated since you are a brave man. He says you have already been tested and you are worthy to be one of his warriors."

Crane listened as Ricci explained that several of his most trusted advisors were military men from the armies of Kenya, Uganda,

Tanzania – all men whom Jomo had captured in battle. Though they were wounded, Jomo had them nursed back to health. He had even had missionary doctors kidnapped for the explicit purpose of caring for them. Unfortunately, once the doctors were through with their task, Jomo had them executed.

"It's his way. He admires their skill but insists that they cannot be trusted to not lead others to his headquarters. Therefore ..." Father Ricci paused and said, "Your comrades are to recover also. But Jomo's hospitality always demands a repayment."

Crane whispered amidst his pain, "Why the SUV? Hasn't the man enough money to buy one hundred of them? Why an SUV? It's sick."

"Sick? Perhaps," replied Father Ricci. "But rather he is evil, a child with an intellect that few can match. But the SUV is tribute. He wishes that the world pay him tribute. He is a king. Kings have their subjects, and they must pay him tribute in recognition of his greatness. Besides, here no one could drive a car through the jungle. There are no roads. Therefore, he must have them flown in, and even Jomo cannot have SUVs flown in without bringing in Kenyan or Ugandan forces."

"And you?" whispered Crane. "How? Why are you here?"

Ricci smiled in resignation and said, "I am Seneca, and he is my Nero. I am Arthur, and he is my Mordred." And then, almost angrily, he spit out the words, "I am Judas, and he is my lord. Only I have followed the false prophet that I myself created. I was a fool. *Lasciate ogni speranza, o voi che entrate* (Abandon all hope, ye who enter here).'"

Crane wondered at the Italian. But before he could ask, several small heads peered around the doorway, wide-eyed and curious. The children had returned to the village with the women. They had heard of the American soldiers. One of them, about seven or eight years of age, taller than the rest, stepped into the room while the others lingered. He walked over to Ricci and asked in English, "Is he the devil?"

"No," said Ricci. "He is a messenger. He brings a message to your father. So you must treat him well, for he is a friend of your father."

The boy looked blankly at Crane, who still lay naked. As the boy moved nearer, he reached out to touch Crane's arm. Crane's forearm had an eagle tattooed on it. He touched it delicately and then suddenly pinched it hard. Crane pulled his arm away. The boy was about to do it again when Ricci grasped the boy's arm and firmly led him back outside. The boy did not resist. Crane could hear him admonish the boy.

"If you are not kind, then you cannot have a good communion. Go."

The boy, Moshe MacArthur, ran off with the other younger children.

Then, as Crane drifted off again to sleep, Ricci lifted his eyes to heaven but saw only the thatched roof of the hut and sighed. *I am heaven's folly* he thought. *I pretend a goodness and cannot undo the bastard I have created.* He looked at Crane and said quietly, "I am a black robe who carries water for Satan and mimics the good actions of good men. I am a parody of goodness. *Pater Noster, qui es angelis ...* My sins must keep me hidden from God's sight. I cannot even hear a whisper of his voice." He left the room in despair.

CHAPTER 25

NOTHING IS SACRED

There is no moral vice, no moral virtue, which has not its precise prototype in the art of painting; so that you may at your will illustrate the moral habit by the art, or the art by the moral habit.

—John Ruskin,
"The Analogy of Art and Morals"

—VANDERKIN ESTATE, SCOTLAND

VANDERKIN'S PARTY WAS AN EVENT INTENDED TO RAISE MONEY for his special charity, which invariably gave him an opportunity to hob knob with Scottish and English celebrities. Academics, business people, and certain entertainers of renown attended. The event was also a cause célèbre for artists and musicians to show off their wares or to perform. Vanderkin was not beneath showing off his own skewed talent for recognizing artists of mediocrity and mistaking their eccentricities for *avant-garde* conceptions. But Vanderkin himself could never truly appreciate art, only consume it. The word *philistine* might have been created with him in mind. He sought solace in art's presence as though his feints at aesthetic contemplation could provide him with spirituality where only greed and kitsch were harbored. In short, he was a Getty in search of a soul.

The evening's entertainment was a mirror of Vanderkin's own eclectic taste. In the first room off the foyer was one of his own favorite groups, a local talent composed of part-time musicians who studied paleontology at the local university, *The Trilobites of Concordia and the Musicians of*

Gloom. Their one original song had been a parody of Scottish excess of sentimentality for all things pre-battle of Culloden, a song about the good old days when Rome sent its soldiers on forays into the Highlands to subdue Scots and Picts entitled "A Roman in the Glommin.'" Their musical virtuosity was questionable but their sense of the ridiculous and humor was not. That Vanderkin saw through their sometime maudlin sentimentality to their true intent suggested that he was not without the possibility of redemption, at least when it came to having some sense of artistic imagination.

In the next room was Vanderkin's tribute to kitsch unlimited, a soft rock band that admired the greatness of such American soft rockers as John Tesh and Barry Manilow. However, they mistook cleverness for art as they pantomimed their own favorite artists with introductions of the various band members in the sashay sway of gentle background drumming. As if their audience really cared.

"Hi, my name is Al Zach, and this is our lead singer, Lorain. And over here on my right is Penelope Ceylon, our backup vocalist, along with Trudy Badour. Be nice to them and they'll be nice to you."

Then in the dance room, a Versailleslike rendition of extravagance, performed the choicest of Vanderkin's finds, a group of musicians that mimed their vocals and instrumentation. Their brazenness was such that their own silence had been drowned out by the applause of the intelligentsia in London and elsewhere. Those who mocked them were denounced as low brows who failed to appreciate the sheer genius of their silent vocalization and musicality. The failure of anyone to criticize their choreographed sways and hand motions attested to their greatness; and the London elite condemned the petty bourgeoisie for a failure to provide acclaim and MTV type sales in a loud chorus that drowned out their silence. Theirs was a Chaplinesque interpretation of the quiet life. Performing without shoes, they thought of themselves as musical monks on a mission, Trappists without soles.

And finally, in the great hall itself, local artists displayed their paintings and sculpting. Here again Vanderkin outdid himself, providing a venue for Titi Leola, a local talent who engaged in performance art as she squeezed cut-in-half grapefruits onto a tight T-shirt, which she was able to drench entirely in the course of an hour-long show. Since she was without peer, she invariably won her own version of the wet T-shirt

192 ✠ Eric Wentz

contest. To each passerby, she would plead, "I am insouciance," and then would close her eyes in reflection or meditation.

Rendition Monet was another of Vanderkin's delights. An attractive woman sat on a stool with a dog collar wrapped around her neck connected to a leash. She was completely nude and sat behind a white sheet of rice paper with a bright yellow light behind her that cast her full-bosomed shadow onto the screen. Her brochure indicated that her performance art was to bring attention to the plight of artists worldwide suffering from lack of government funding for their artistic endeavors. It was this failure of the people and their government that forced her and others into exiting the British Isles into a kind of rendition where they were tortured by the ignorance of the British masses and others. Even the Americans did not suffer them gladly.

Vanderkin, like the patron of art that he was, wheeled his chair through the halls, savoring the ephemeral nature of true beauty. His guests had arrived and were already being regaled with the incipient knowledge that seeped into the house of art like a poison gas, silently and overwhelmingly. It was a knowledge that was hidden to them but which he was certain would profoundly affect them. It was the knowledge known to Vanderkin that few mortals could expend such *dolors* on the unappreciative *hoi polloi* that he attempted to educate at his parties.

As he roamed the halls and rooms in his wheelchair, he met his guests and engaged them in friendly banter and self-deprecating remarks as they all praised him for his kindness on behalf of mankind. Then, as he engaged an elderly couple who had come up from Edinburgh for the evening's affair, a black Rolls Royce pulled up in front of the estate.

Immediately, two lithe and almost feminine-looking men walked to either side of the car. Both were dressed in the livery of Vanderkin's estate, a patch over dark blue jackets with the emblem of a Chinese dragon. The mix of cultural symbolism carried by young African men working on a Scottish estate owned by a Dutchman was not lost on MacArthur as he exited the rear seat with his own guests, Grant and his lovely date, Miss Pamela Credo.

MacArthur and Grant were dressed in black suits with black bow ties, suitable attire for such an august event, for which each person paid one thousand pounds. MacArthur had called and asked Vanderkin's permission to bring his nephew from America along and his date.

Vanderkin had offered that they could attend for free but MacArthur had insisted upon paying the full one thousand pounds for each in the name of Vanderkin's charity. Since MacArthur did have a sister living in America, it was quite possible if not probable that he would in fact have a nephew of about Grant's age.

Grant's date was dressed in a deep lavender gown that hugged her curves with a subtle elegance that belied her own touch of anxiety at attending such a function of high-powered brokers of commerce and the arts. The dignitaries were unknown to her but not to those who read the business section of the *Edinburgh Press*.

As the two African men opened the doors, MacArthur's driver stepped out of the Rolls. He was about six feet tall, wore a suit identical to MacArthur and Grant's, and moved with quiet stealth. The fluidity of his motion contradicted his present occupation and suggested an athletic background. Still, to all other appearances, Thomas Patel was a driver. Like the young Africans, his dark Indian complexion was an oddity among the evening's attendees.

As Grant and Pamela began to walk away, MacArthur stepped to Thomas's side and asked if he had worked out that day.

"No, sir."

"Good. Then I recommend a brisk evening walk once you've parked. Take in the entire grounds. Come back tired and sweaty. Did you bring your running shoes?"

"Yes, sir."

"I'll see you in three hours or so."

"Yes, sir." MacArthur turned and walked away to join Grant and his date.

"Oh, and Thomas, by the looks of the physiques of several of the groundskeepers and other attendees of the duke of the Dutch, I'd say they're Kenyans. Quite good runners. Be careful."

"Yes, sir." Thomas smiled as they walked away.

Before they entered the house, Grant noticed Pamela's momentary hesitation. She stopped abruptly for a split second. Then she reached down to grab at one of her heels as if it were loose.

"I seldom wear heels these days," she offered to Grant as she grasped his arm for balance just a little too tightly. Grant sensed a certain unease in her but sloughed it off to the nature of the company, which was sufficiently intimidating to browbeat just about any it dared.

Once inside, the young Africans escorted them into the great hall where a man with a build that looked all too familiar stood in the entranceway, greeting guests and engaging in conversation with all within his sphere. Tall, blond, and exact in his movements, he reminded Grant of a boxer. His physique was telling, with strong back and shoulder muscles that filled his dark evening jacket. As he turned, he smiled at MacArthur, whom he knew by reputation if not personally. Martin Vanderkin raised his eyebrows appreciatively as he eyed Pamela and then returned to his naturally suspicious nature as he was introduced to Grant Chisolm, who placed his hand on Pamela's shoulder as if to say, "Look but don't touch." Each locked his eyes on the other as they shook hands in a quiet test of strength. Grant suppressed his surprise at the appearance of the other and concealed the full extent of his suspicion. However, Grant's near exclamation of contempt for Vanderkin was enough to make MacArthur take notice. Vanderkin responded with his own suppressed anger, squeezing Grant's hand with all his strength. Grant nonetheless smiled, and Pamela, however excited and anxious, stood by silently within the aura of masculine competition.

A middle-aged couple, all smiles, came up alongside Grant and introduced themselves. "Hello, Martin. We wanted to pay our respects. Thanks for the invitation. Always a special time."

The couple's interruption enabled Grant and Vanderkin's nephew to break off their quiet confrontation naturally and without either conceding power to the other. As they walked away, MacArthur asked Grant, "Do you know each other?"

"Fortunately, now I do."

As they wandered from room to room taking in the various ostentatious displays of wealth, MacArthur counted the rooms, looked for doors and windows, and counted the number of staff members. Grant counted the number of locked doorways to which no access was granted and imagined how many alarms would go off with the opening of one of them. Without his being told, Grant was discovering why he was being asked to visit northern Scotland before he was apparently needed.

With the density of the evening's crowd, Grant found it easy to nonchalantly approach any door or room he wished without arousing suspicion. But doing so required that he temporarily dispose of his lovely but now burdensome date.

So Grant escorted her into one of the comfortable rooms where chamber musicians played the baroque music that antiquarians love. He and his date sat on a loveseat and listened. Then Grant offered to get her a drink. She answered, "A white wine, please."

Grant left to find one of the bars and to see if he could ease his way into one of the non-traditional venues for a Vanderkin party, perhaps one that lay behind locked doors that led into the nether regions of the house.

Pamela was sitting listening to the music when Vanderkin's nephew approached and offered her a drink. He already had a glass of white wine in one hand.

How coy, she thought. "How did you know what I like?"

"I don't, but that has never stopped me from approaching a beautiful woman who sits alone in splendid isolation."

He stopped before her, and she reached up for the wine, saying, "One now, and one later."

"Where is your friend?" asked Vanderkin's nephew.

"He's gone to get a drink, one just like this."

Martin Vanderkin smiled even as he sat down beside her. He then offered her a toast, reaching over to clink glasses, "To your health."

"And to yours," she replied.

Both sipped almost as if on guard.

"Tell me, what brings a sweet kitten like you to the remote Teutonic Nights?"

"Did you say *'sweet kitten'*? Come on, you can do better than that." She took another sip and noticed a certain lightheadedness. "Say, what's in this drink?"

"Nothing, my kitten."

"I may be a kitten, but I'm not going to become catatonic." With that, she stood up and poured the remainder of the wine into the pot of a nearby plant. She walked out of the room, looking for Grant, but had to grasp the door frame and a couple pieces of furniture to prevent herself from falling. Then she sat down in an easy chair, looking warily about her even as her eyes closed and she drifted off to sleep.

Like a spider, Vanderkin's nephew watched her weave her way

through his web with lustful deviousness. With Grant still out of sight, he went over to her side and spoke softly to her. Anonymous in the presence of the crowd, he then lifted her as a gentleman bearing the burdens of a host who felt duty bound to care for his guests' many needs. Tenderly, softly, he escorted her into a back hallway and then unlocked one of the doors and put her down.

CHAPTER 26
KNOSSOS REVISITED

Beware of false prophets who come to you in sheep's clothing but inwardly are ravenous as wolves.

—Matthew 7:15

—VANDERKIN ESTATE

THE VANDERKIN ESTATE WAS NOTHING IF NOT CONVOLUTED. LIKE the syntax of a professional intellectual whose puffery was long-winded and seemingly without purpose, the hallways meandered in a pretense of mystery and a perversion of grandeur. The house was a Cretan maze in which the Minotaur would have died in a frenzy of dizzying missteps while searching for his victims. Like Theseus, Grant wandered in search of the menace he thought might dwell beneath the apparent lack of design, within the bowels of the house. But to find its entrance was a task even King Minos of Knossos himself would have found amazing.

Grant eventually winded his way down a darkened hall, where he tested two doors on his right. Both were locked. He moved onto his left and tried yet another, which opened easily. The room was dimly lit with a series of elaborate rotogravure posters depicting highly stylized wolves in pursuit of equally stylized deer and, in one instance, what appeared to be a man. The pack of wolves was in full assault, striding after a man who was already glancing back at the horror in pursuit.

On the other wall were several paintings depicting Indians and animals of the American West: bison, antelope, horses, and bears. In each instance, the animals were themselves being pursued and attacked by a pack of wolves or, in the paintings with Indians in them, the Indians were looking about either in panic or fear as the wolves closed in. But against still another wall was a large painting of what should have been a pastoral scene with gray wolves in an orgy of blood, ripping out the throats and bowels of a flock of sheep while others were attempting to escape by diving over a cliff to their deaths. In one corner, the shepherd was pressed with his back against a tree with a look of wide-eyed dread as he held his crook out in a vain attempt to thwart an avalanche of white teeth and snapping jaws. In the background, another shepherd, with his feet facing the viewers, lay naked on the ground while wolves were pulling out his intestines and chewing off his head.

"Like a primitive cave man," murmured Grant to himself. "He's enacting the hunt. Humph."

The painting was draped on either side by large billowy drapes to frame it. Grant went to move the drapes aside to see if the painting extended only to find the frame of a narrow door with an old knob well sunken into its oak solidity.

As Grant reached out for the knob, he noticed that the door was already slightly ajar. He pushed it open. The door swung easily and silently on its hinges and revealed a long, narrow hallway almost entirely dark. Only small lights running along the concrete floor on either side, like those along the floor of a passenger airliner, illuminated the darkness.

Grant stepped cautiously into the near darkness, feeling along the walls for guidance and eyeing the lights for indications of the length and curves of the hallway. The walls were cool to the touch, the concrete floor hard, and the lights gradually fading to the left at a distance of thirty or so feet. As Grant approached the bend, he saw that the lights extended down a flight of twenty or so steps into a room softly lit with blue light. Quietly, he descended. The ceiling narrowed until he had to duck as he took the last step. As he did, he saw the room unfold into a soft but garish blue den complete with rugs, large cushiony chairs, a davenport, and several more paintings, each of which represented a provocatively posed Rubenesque nude in some none too subtle form of sexual ecstasy. *Kitsch on canvas*, thought Grant.

Grant smiled at the erotica as he continued through the labyrinth, wishing he had some bread crumbs to make a path for his return. Sensing the need to establish a pattern of his own, Grant made it a point at each divide in the ongoing pathway to always turn left, knowing that on the way back he must always turn right.

As he approached yet another divide, Grant thought in the near gloom that he smelled a slight hint of kerosene. He took several steps to the left into a large cavern complete with a ceiling of unpolished rock and nine or ten foot tall walls that had been plastered over in white stucco and fashioned to conceal the rough rock beneath. The room was spacious and again furnished with comfortable chairs. Grant wondered at anyone's ability to get such items through the narrow hallways. All the items were plush and red.

On the far side of the room, another pathway beckoned. As Grant walked the passage, it gradually grew taller and wider. The ceiling was vaulted and much more finely hewn than the other parts of the labyrinth, and here and there were niches with burning lamps about the walls on either side. This, then, was the source of the kerosene. At the far end of a fifty-foot stretch, the passage rose slightly to another room, on the far side of which stood a large, white-painted door.

Grant approached it cautiously and then reached for the brass door knob. As his hand touched the handle, he heard a faint sound behind him and then a cold voice,

"Good evening, Mr. Bond."

Despite his military training, Grant had been taken unaware. He turned suddenly. Standing no more than ten feet from Grant was Vanderkin's nephew, Martin. He smiled menacingly at Grant and said, "You are a most curious cat."

Grant recovered quickly enough and responded, "You just called me Bond."

"Yes. James, to be precise, Mr. 007. I trust you were not shaken when I stirred. For I think your presence here may mean you are looking for me. Perhaps I have not been a good host. I'm sure anyone associated with Mr. MacArthur is by nature a most curious adventurer."

Then, as though he had been transformed by his momentary pleasantries, he relaxed and smiled pleasingly. "Allow me to show you those parts of the house that you might find interesting."

"Yes, I'd like that," said Grant. But having been taken unaware, he hoped not to let it happen again. He viewed the invitation most suspiciously.

Vanderkin's nephew pushed the door open. The room was a great sunken den.

"This," he said, "is my personal study." The room was brightly lit, and on one wall was a series of paintings. Grant glanced at them.

"Those are interesting," he said. "There appears to be a theme."

"I suppose it's hard to miss. These are works that I painted, depicting scenes in various pieces of famous literature in which my favorite creature, the wolf, finally gets the upper hand over mankind—mankind, the most vicious and voracious creature of all. You see, it is only man who consistently takes what he neither needs nor owns."

"You don't exactly appear to be a poor boy yourself," replied Grant. "There must have been some taking along the way by members of your own family."

"True, but only to exact revenge or to acquire the means by which I may assist in the restoration of a kind of balance in nature. I rather think of myself as God's playful tinkerer. I fix what man has broken and God has ignored."

"See here," he then said, pointing to a painting of a pack of wolves tearing apart a young woman and man apparently thrown from a sled being pulled by two horses. The driver and his companion looked back on them in terror.

"This is a scene from an American novel entitled *My Antonia*, in which two Russian characters named Peter and Pavel drive off in their sled after throwing the bride and her bridegroom over to lighten their load as the wolves come down upon them. They are haunted by the memory. I, on the other hand, am pleased by the scene. It is only right now and then that nature exact revenge for the injustices perpetrated against it by humanity. Only right."

"You seem to take a very dim view of humanity."

"I see it as it is. As in this scene," he continued. "Few know of Daniel Defoe's depiction of wolves in his works."

Grant moved to look at the next painting. Again, a pack of wolves appeared to have converged, this time upon a woman and child who were fleeing through the streets of some nondescript city at night."

"Apparently you don't even see the innocent as deserving of being spared—mother and child."

"There are no innocents. The women give birth to the children, who grow to become the avaricious adults who plague the world today. The wolf only kills to eat, to live. It can act alone but seems to prefer to act in concert with others. It knows true companionship."

"I'd like to see more."

"I'm certain you would. However, your intrusion is most unwelcome. For you, sir, have been an immense nuisance to me and my operations. But no longer." Vanderkin's nephew pulled out a pistol."

Grant looked at the gun and said, "A Glock, Austrian engineering at its finest."

"Don't be smart, Mr. Chisolm. I'm sure you recognize me just as I recognize you. You wanted to see the house, and so you shall. You'll find its subterranean features are twice the size of the estate that sits atop it. Unfortunately, you shall not soon see the upper regions again. For you, this ancient Celtic labyrinth is but the nether world. Dante would have recognized it for what it will surely be to you: the bottom rung of hell. Move."

He pointed toward the door through which they had come and found that waiting on the outside were two young men dressed in Vanderkin livery.

"My young Kenyans shall help escort you out, and I shall be behind you as well. The Glock is fully loaded." As he walked by one of the forks in the underground labyrinth, where Grant would have turned right to find his way back, the Kenyans on either side of him pushed him to the opening on the left—another dimly lit passageway that descended steeply into complete darkness. As the passageway narrowed, one Kenyan slipped in front of him while the other stayed behind him with one hand on Grant's shoulder.

*　*　*　*　*

Upstairs in the largest of all the rooms, Byron Vanderkin wheeled himself to a raised dais. Behind him sat several young, black Africans as well as others who were white and a bit older. Above him, suspended from a rope attached to the ceiling, was a large white banner with bold black and red block letters, "Tudor Scholarship Program."

Stepping to the dais was a black-garbed, fortyish, slender priest. He had a ruddy complexion and partially sun-bleached hair. He looked out with a broad, friendly smile into a sea of equally friendly faces at several dozen tables at which were seated an array of guests from London to Peterborough, Edinburgh to Inverness, from the Isle of Man to the Orkneys. The wealth before him was old, cool, and quite liberal in its generosity. All cared deeply for the disadvantaged.

The conversations filled the air with a steady drone. At first, many did not notice the priest standing patiently at the dais. Gradually, the loud drone of blended conversation died down to an expectant murmur.

As if on cue, the priest raised his hands above his head to ask for a cessation of sound. The murmur was replaced not with silence but with a round of applause. It was the applause of the generous for those who till in the Lord's vineyard among the wretched of the earth. Poor souls, but for themselves, they knew that the lot of those now before them would be lives of destitution and ignorance. Again the priest raised his hands above his head to call for silence but was instead greeted with a swelling of continued applause and calls of "Hear! Hear!" The priest surrendered to the accolades and smiled benignly upon the assemblage, a horde of tuxedoed privilege and largess fanned by the plumage of well-feathered fashion from the finest boutiques in Europe.

The plumaged fanned their feathers in grand gestures while conversing about their children to old acquaintances and about world events to any who needed their insights concerning the world stage. Finally, the applause petered out and the priest began.

"Ladies and gentlemen, today I stand before you as a humble servant of those here who have so long given their lives to benefit those less fortunate. You have made me an instrument of your beneficence. In so doing, you have given me the privilege of acting on your behalf. For that, I am most thankful. For that, I am most lucky. I, a poor boy from Johannesburg, today am showered in the wealth of your prayers and in the nearness to your most generous hearts.

"For more than twenty years I have had the rare privilege to work with a celebrated and now, sadly, very ill but still inspirational figure, Father Matteo Ricci. I sought to do as he did, make the world a better place. He then, along with another noble individual, set upon a plan to rid Africa of the ignorance and injustices that have so long plagued that most sick and poorly used continent. They sought to do this by providing scholarships for worthy young men and women for whom education might otherwise have been an unfulfilled dream.

"So in 1991, an uncommon visionary, a rebel with a true cause, and that great man of faith, Father Matteo Ricci, started the programs that you have so graciously funded. Today it is my pleasure to introduce my inspiration and, I hope, yours, the man who gave us social concern with dynamic action, Mr. Byron Vanderkin."

Vanderkin, who had been hidden off stage behind a curtain, emerged in his wheelchair, smiling and wheeling himself to the microphone. The applause was just the beginning. As he stopped next to Father Wirtz, the audience stood and clapped in adulation. With dramatic effort and a grimace, Vanderkin lifted himself from the chair and leaned slightly against Father Wirtz. Then he reached for the microphone stand with both hands and said, "You can't keep a good man down."

The applause increased again to a new height. He held up both hands with fingers in the shape of Vs for victory, ala Winston Churchill. Then he put both hands together and bowed his head, bringing the prayerful hands to his forehead like a Hindu. Only after another thirty seconds or so did the hands of his audience tire. Finally, they sat back down. He spoke.

"Today you see behind me those who have come so far, both geographically as well as educationally, through your help. Years ago, Father Ricci and I started a program to help my disadvantaged countrymen, young boys and girls who deserved better than life had doled out for them. You may ask why I call them countrymen. After all, I am a Dutchman of sorts, but I am also South African. And yet these young men and women are from Tanzania, Kenya, Rwanda, Botswana, and Burundi. Still, humanity knows no boundaries. I am therefore proud to call them countrymen." He paused as applause broke out once again.

"To help those who had the least hope, we started in that country which had suffered the most, Rwanda. And from the suffering of those who were caught in the ugliest of wars came the program of Father Ricci and myself, TUDOR. TUDOR helped raise money for scholarships for those who are ..." here he paused for dramatic effect, "the real TUDORS, not of England but of Africa. Ladies and gentlemen, this year's TUDORS, The Uncut Diamonds of Rwanda. The crescendo in his voice fomented an explosion of clapping hands, and once again everyone stood as Vanderkin looked out with a grin and his arms extended on either side. The six students behind him smiled and waved timidly. Two of the six were white and hardly Rwandans.

"These are the future, Africa's hope." Another chorus of applause. "And, yes, I know what you are thinking. So let me explain. When we started this program, Rwanda was in the throes of a terrible war. But even amidst the worst of times, there is always hope. And from the ashes of a burned out country rose a phoenix, the phoenix of hope. And these are the feathers of that great bird. But it is a bird that has flown beyond the borders of that small country. It has flown to Kenya, to Burundi, to Tanzania, to South Africa, and to the rest of Africa. And this bird is one of many colors. Race does not matter to this great bird. So, students of all races are and have been part of this program. White, black, brown— all beautiful feathers.

"Today is a great day for these young people. They now have a future, one that marks the end of poverty and the beginning of a great adventure. These young scholars will study here in Scotland or England or in any institution that can hope to slacken their thirst for knowledge. They are," he looked down at his notes for the first time, "Nelson Raphael." A tall, well-built young man of sixteen stood. "Chinua Lamumba, Marsh Vandaniken, and Chad Jones." He then paused momentarily and said, "But our TUDOR scholars are not only bright but beautiful as well." He then turned to his right, where the two females, one black and one white, had been led to his side. He reached out with both hands to grasp one of each of the girls' as he looked smilingly at them and then at a photographer who sought to memorialize the moments. Looking again at the girls, he then said, "These are the flowers of Africa."

Applause broke forth again as he once more held his arms out like a vulture hovering above a would-be meal. Then one of his servants escorted the TUDOR scholars to tables where they were expected to meet with their benefactors.

Shortly afterwards, while Vanderkin was again being congratulated on his beneficence and kindness, a slight commotion stirred in the hallway immediately outside the room in which the dinner and celebration were being held. Only a few people toward the back seemed to notice. But as Vanderkin continued to make the rounds among his guests, one of his servants, a burly man of forty or so with a thick Scottish accent to match an equally thick, black mustache, came to Vanderkin's side and whispered in his ear. A wave of concern and then a flush of anger crossed his face before he regained his composure. He smiled again as he continued to now haphazardly shake hands, and then he wheeled himself deliberately toward the site of the commotion.

*   *   *   *   *

As a former high school champion wrestler as well an NCAA finalist in his weight class, Chisolm had learned the art of wrestling blindfolded. His coach at both levels had him and his teammates wrestle with blindfolds so that they could learn to wrestle by feel. His high school coach, with a touch of humor, would tell them, "Feel the force." In this case, the force was their own energy and, as he explained, the force of their opponent, both physical and spiritual. They must, he explained, manifest their *kokorazasu*, their ambition and determination, through knowledge of self. Since Grant's high school coach was Japanese, a former national wrestling champion of Japan who went to college at Iowa State University, the wrestling Mecca of America, Grant and his teammates listened. Grant had learned to feel his opponent's force and position even before he could see them. The blackness worked to his advantage.

As Grant and his escorts moved on in the darkness, he could feel the dankness being enlivened by a breath of sweet and slightly salty air. Any opening to the sea could only be one that exited to the sheer declivity that fell about two hundred feet into the rocks that abounded on Loch Maree. It was a step he did not intend to take.

They turned right at another corner, where a touch of moonlight had filtered through the evening's mist, enough to give any figure standing in the opening a slight silhouette. The Kenyans were both behind him, pushing him forward by either shoulder. Then as one pushed on his right shoulder, Grant grabbed the hand with both of his own, wrenched it violently down and under his own arm. He pulled the Kenyan's arm across the taut muscles of his abdomen as he bumped hard backwards against his captor and thrust both legs against the other side of the wall, walking up its side. The Kenyan called out in pain as Chisolm flipped himself over in an exaggerated form of what wrestlers called the Granby role. He came down the other side of the wall with the Kenyan's shoulder completely twisted out of its socket. The crunching sound as the sinew snapped was as loud as a man's voice.

His partner had reached out in the darkness and, at first, had actually helped Grant by accidentally punching his cohort sharply in the back of the head. With Grant's flip and subsequent destruction of the other's right shoulder, he spun on the other escort. As the second man attempted to fall upon Grant, he felt a blow that crushed his Adam's apple, and he now lay on his fellow Kenyan, gasping for air.

Martin Vanderkin had refrained from shooting in the darkness, not out of concern for his own men but for fear that a gunshot so close to the opening would be heard by others. He stepped back, where he caught Grant's silhouette and announced forcefully, "It's over, Mr. Chisolm. Now back up slowly. As an old navy man, you'll appreciate the fact that you are about to walk the plank."

The two Kenyans were writhing in pain as Grant stood.

"Aren't you afraid I'll scream?"

"Perhaps, but most men who fall from cliffs while strolling about do. You should have known better than to take a walk where you weren't supposed to be."

"What about your paintings? Don't want to show me some more?"

"Mr. Chisolm, the plank is waiting. Turn and walk or I'll shoot now. Guests or no guests."

He brought his pistol up again, grinning as he pointed it at Grant's forehead. Grant could vaguely make out the motion of Martin Vanderkin's gesture in the darkness. Suddenly, Vanderkin's nephew jerked backwards and the gun went off. A bullet ricocheted off the stone ceiling and slapped into the forehead of the Kenyan who had begun to stand back up. He quietly sat back down, stunned with the bullet embedded one half inch into his skull and his crushed Adam's apple. He breathed heavily in pain.

Grant had ducked at the gunshot and moved forward at his adversary, who was struggling, choking, and breathing haltingly and heavily. As he jumped to Vanderkin's nephew, he grabbed onto his shirt and suit, only to feel the arms of someone else already around Martin's chest and arms.

"Grab his gun!" yelled a familiar voice.

"Thomas!" exclaimed Grant.

"Not bad for a chauffeur," responded Thomas.

"What are you doing here?"

"Right now I'm trying to restrain your would-be assailant." He then reached across Vanderkin's face and placed his hand firmly over his mouth.

Grant tried to feel for the gun until he felt its muzzle braced against his neck. The Kenyan with the broken shoulder had heard the gun fall and grabbed it as Vanderkin's nephew, Thomas, and Grant struggled. Grant lurched upward violently, his head smacking hard against the Kenyan's chin and rocking him backwards. Grant turned and grabbed him with both arms, grasped at the gun hand, and headbutted the Kenyan, sending him staggering. He stepped twice and fell into the void, the gun still in his hand. He was only semi-conscious as he fell over the cliffs of Loch Maree into the rocks below. The other Kenyan lay still, his breathing having stopped. Martin Vanderkin was still struggling, but Thomas continued to muffle his cries.

Standing over him, Grant said, "Mr. Vanderkin, we appear to have a problem. We can hardly let you go."

Then Thomas removed his hands from Martin's mouth.

"You also cannot say anything to the police," replied Vanderkin's nephew. "No one will believe you. You're the intruder. You'll create another international incident, another American cowboy. This is Scotland. Not Iraq. Not Afghanistan. Besides, my great uncle and I are benefactors of the oppressed. You are the demons of Western imperialism."

Grant remembered MacArthur's warning about moving about inconspicuously. This seemed to be a violation of all he had been told to do. He reached down and grabbed Vanderkin's nephew by his lapel and pulled him up as Thomas let go. Thomas got up and stood behind him.

Recapturing his composure, Martin Vanderkin dusted himself off and walked away. Thomas and Grant followed. As they did so, Grant wondered what fate awaited him. Martin Vanderkin had just killed a man and did not even need to secret the body, and another had fallen into the abyss and yet there was no concern.

Emerging once again from the labyrinth, Vanderkin turned to Chisolm and Thomas and said, "I have not yet decided whether or not to prosecute you for intruding and for murder."

"I don't think you'll get away with that," replied Grant. "You're the one who shot your own man."

Martin Vanderkin looked at his assailant, Thomas. For the first time, he realized that his newfound enemy was a dark-skinned Indian.

"But your finger prints are on the gun, Mr. Bond," he said tauntingly. "Oh, and tell your sidekick that we may provide a special scholarship to him. We are merciful to the great unwashed masses."

"I'm hardly unwashed," responded Thomas.

"Then merely smelly," replied Vanderkin's nephew. "Perhaps a little too much curry. Be careful, it's bad for your intestines."

"The only thing here nauseating is you."

"Surprisingly insolent for a colonial. No doubt you've picked up another bad habit from the American. But beware or you may find your intestines strung out in one of my yet to be painted scenes of your demise. Perhaps your cowboy *compadre* can tell you about them. By the way, I must complement you. You're surprisingly talkative for an Indian, Tonto."

Vanderkin's nephew spun and walked away toward the room to which he had previously taken the South African girl. Grant and Thomas turned and walked toward the main room in which others were still chatting. As they entered, they almost bumped into Regis MacArthur.

"Where have you been?" he asked. "Your dinner is getting cold, and I can't fend off the none-too-interesting conversation of my fellow diners without your help."

Grant looked at Thomas, whose slightly dirty chauffeur's jacket had caught Regis's attention.

"Is there a story here?" asked Regis.

"More than I can now speak, Sahib," responded Thomas.

MacArthur smiled at the playful response. Thomas then walked away, intending to appear like the chauffer he surely was not.

Grant and Thomas walked back into the room as MacArthur asked, "Where's Miss South Africa?"

CHAPTER 27

GRATITUDE

We that are bound by vows, and by promotion,
With pomp of holy sacrifice and rites.

—Fulke Greville, Lord Brooke, *Mustapha*

—VANDERKIN ESTATE

A LARGE MUSTACHIOED MAN WHO HAD WHISPERED INTO VANDERKIN'S ear at the dinner for the TUDORS now stood over Pamela Credo. She looked up from the couch on which she lay. Her head felt heavy as a rock. Her shoes had been removed, and Vanderkin sat in his wheelchair off to her left. She rolled over to get a better look at him. In her drug-induced state of wooziness, she took several seconds to focus her eyes. She attempted to blink away the eyes' failure to focus steadily on any one object in the room. Only when Vanderkin spoke her name did she recognize him.

As she attempted to sit up and then stand, she tottered. Suddenly she noticed the man standing next to her. She was slightly taken aback by his menacing look and the firmness of his hand as he attempted to stop her from falling over again.

"What did you do to me? Where am I?"

"My dear," responded Vanderkin, "I suggest that you sit back down before you fall down."

She sat and immediately put her face in her hands, holding up her head and trying to wipe away the heaviness and drowsiness that weighed down her entire body.

The room was dimly lit by a couple of small end table lamps. It was cozy and looked like a parlor designed by someone who actually had a sense of perspective and style.

A designer must have actually gotten his way, she thought.

Vanderkin wheeled his chair closer to her and remained silent as he waited for her to regain her composure. She looked up at him with a pained look on her face.

"My dear, it is one thing to be here at my event. It is another thing entirely for you to be here with someone who, shall we say, may be antagonistic to me and my designs."

She remained silent.

"You're here with a young man. Are you attracted to him?"

"That's not your business," she replied testily.

"Oh, but it is. Apparently you have forgotten who you are and why you are here."

"You're a pimp," she spit out.

"Oh, now you're angry! But it is only I who should be angry. But you are an attractive young woman. It is only, I suppose, natural. Unfortunately, you have, I fear, fallen for someone with whom you can have no future."

"I haven't fallen for anyone!" she seethed. "Why did you drug me?"

"You cannot continue …"

She interrupted him. "I am a free woman. But since you're so interested, I came with Regis MacArthur."

"Mr. MacArthur only asked my permission to bring a couple more guests. He never mentioned the names. But that is not his fault. It's yours. You should have informed me. Apparently, you have lost your memory. Alzheimer's should not so affect one so young."

"I haven't forgotten anything."

"He is an attractive young man. But perhaps your future can intertwine with his after all. He has information. We would like to get it. You have a woman's ways. You could use them."

"No, I won't help."

"Yes, you will. You forget that it is I who brought you here. Were it not for me and the TUDOR program, you would still be living in the slums of Johannesburg. The death of your parents in Rwanda was, of course, unfortunate. But good Christian missionaries must know that life is filled with risks." He paused. "What kind of parents would take their child to the hell that is miserable Africa? You are lucky to be alive. You find my means of livelihood contemptible—pimp is a most ugly word. But it was my being in the midst of my unsavory world that enabled me to find you. I was once a *kind* old man. Now I feel that you think of me as merely *old*. I could have left you to perish in the slums or in the jungles or some South African orphanage. It is I who saved you. It is I who paid for your education. Even now you work for me. Where is your gratitude?"

"Where is my gratitude? Where are your morals?"

"Dear, my morals are represented in your very existence. You have life. You have a job. You have safety and security. Without me, you would have none of these."

She sat silently. Then she lifted her face again to look at him. Her eyes were wet. She spoke softly. "I am not ungrateful. I just like him. He's sweet. He's good. Please don't ask me to do more. I can't."

"You may continue to see him but you must learn what we need to know. He may already know too much. You will find out for us. Now, if you're feeling better, you can go back to the great hall. He'll no doubt be looking for you."

Silently, she rose, wiped her eyes with tissue, and began to walk toward the door. She then paused, turned to look at the mustachioed henchman, and said, "Robert, thank you for picking me up. And, yes, I am truly grateful for everything." She turned again and walked out the door.

Mincing her steps somewhat slowly to the great hall, she saw the table at which Regis was now seated with three others. As she walked with the pallor of one who felt the humiliation of having just been chastened, she heard a voice behind her.

"There you are. We've been looking for you."

Grant came to her side to escort her to the table. Regis stood and smiled as they approached, as did two other gentlemen who were then introduced. A short while later, Byron Vanderkin reentered the room with his mustachioed friend. As he did so, Grant looked up, expecting to see his nephew at his side. His absence the rest of the evening was conspicuous.

Pamela's soberness was tangible and hovered over the table. She glanced furtively at Grant several times as though to be reassured by his presence and wondered at the futility of apparently falling for one whose future she had the audacity to hope might be tied to hers in a most pleasant way. He looked back at her quizzically at one point. Their eyes meeting in a private exchange, even amidst the attempts at conviviality of the other guests, prompted her to say, "I just wasn't feeling well. I'm better now." Her smile throughout the remainder of the evening was forced, and she sought solace by gently touching Grant's hand as it sat next to hers. She slightly and almost imperceptibly moved closer to him, calming her tumultuous feelings by noting his kindly smile and the slight scent of his aftershave lotion.

CHAPTER 28

UNLEASHED

Oh, let us howl some heavy note,
Some deadly dogged howl,
Sounding as from the threatening throat
Of beasts

—John Webster, "The Madman's Song"

—VANDERKIN ESTATE

LATE IN THE EVENING, THOMAS STOOD OUTSIDE REGIS'S ROLLS ROYCE, trying to act like a genuine chauffer. With his cell phone on, he decided to step into the back seat of the car and lay down while he waited for Sahib. After a couple of minutes, he came to at the sound of something jangling beneath the car. He lay still and listened. He slowly sat up without making any sound. The jangling continued.

Thomas then looked out and saw nothing except the other cars parked around the estate, most of them unwatched. Chauffeurs were a rarity these days, even among the well-to-do. Thomas placed his left hand on the door latch and slowly pulled it out. The door opened with a slight click. The jangling sound stopped. Thomas stepped deliberately out of the car with one foot and then the other.

As he stooped down to look under the car, he saw a figure emerge on the far side, rolling out from under and sprinting quickly away. Thomas was inclined to give chase but decided not to risk creating a scene. He instead opened up the front passenger's side of the car and grabbed a flashlight from under the seat. He examined the underside of the car and saw a chain. He reached for it, realizing it had been partially wrapped around the axel. He attempted to pull it out but it had also been wrapped around the springs. It took him a couple of minutes to fully undo it. It was a dog's leash.

As he stood looking at it, wondering at the intruder's purpose, MacArthur, Pamela, and Grant walked out of the house. When they arrived at the car, he stood silently holding the leash in both hands.

Thomas said, "Someone tied this underneath the car, around the axel and supports. It's a dog's leash."

Grant reached for it and said, "Looks like someone is warning us."

"But what is the message?" asked Regis.

"Perhaps," said Grant, "someone is telling us that he has unleashed the dogs on us."

"Perhaps," replied Regis. "I've always admired masters of symbolic gestures and those who can interpret them."

Thomas had a doubtful expression on his face. Regis smiled and said, "Please, Thomas, try not to live up to your name."

Grant gazed at Pamela. She looked worried but said nothing. Thomas opened the doors of the car in keeping with his charade. They drove away.

Later they stopped at the Loch Maree Inn. Grant and Pamela got out. "I'll speak with you soon, Grant," said MacArthur.

"Not soon enough," replied Grant.

They walked into the inn. Grant had intended to escort her to her quarters for the inn's personnel in an attached building. But as they stepped into the entrance way, she turned to him and, with an air of coldness, said, "It was interesting tonight." She then turned and walked away. Grant stood there frozen by her abruptness. She slipped into the darkness of the hallway and through the doorway into the adjoining facilities. As he walked back to his room, he asked himself again, *Why a dog leash?*

CHAPTER 29

CHATTER

My very heart feints and my whole soul grieves.

—Alfred Lord Tennyson,
"A spirit haunts the year's last hours"

WITH THE DISAPPEARANCE OF AN EIGHTEEN-MAN PLATOON IN THE jungles of south-central Africa, the United States government found itself in a quandary. The lack of intelligence on their whereabouts and their condition made Defense Intelligence Agency personnel anxious and deeply concerned. Members of the Joint Chiefs of Staff were nonplussed. Their men were too well trained to simply disappear. Still, Raphael's ability to escape traps and to instead spawn his own was legendary. Keeping their disappearance from the press and family members would prove extremely difficult even in the furtive world known as black ops, those guerrilla type operations involving soldiers whose missions and activities were secrets to which even family members were not privy.

In the period since he and his men had been lured into a trap by Raphael, Crane and the other survivors had been visited daily by Father Ricci. Crane recuperated slowly. He was allowed no contact with any of his men, if there were indeed any among the survivors, and knew even less about those whom he was to have rescued. He had seen some of the CINC team during the battle but none since. No one, not even Ricci, offered him any details concerning who was still alive.

After three weeks, Crane was hearty enough to walk about, but not without three armed guards and extreme pain in his legs and shoulder.

He attempted to get to know his guards and found them contrastingly reserved and stoical or friendly and generous with their cigarettes and candy. One of them, Abraham Jones, spoke English flawlessly and observed to Crane that he too was a great admirer of the United States military and that one day he would like to train with it.

Crane remained silent on what he thought were the young man's prospects. But Jones's persistence was intriguing. Crane thought the he might be able to play it. However, to do so, he'd have to have an opportunity to speak to the young man alone. So after one of his afternoon walks around the village, Crane went back to his hut and invited everyone in for some tea. Jones thanked him but said that he and the others had additional tasks. Seemingly disappointed, Crane suggested that Jones send the others on their way while he explained more about special forces to him. Jones's hesitancy evaporated at the prospect of receiving special knowledge.

Crane, who had majored in psychology as an undergraduate and while attending graduate school at the University of North Carolina, recognized that Jones was childlike in some ways. Despite the fact that he had been one of the men against whom Crane had fought just several weeks ago, he had about him a certain innocence. He had an infectious smile and a readiness to listen to Crane's stories because of a deep thirst for knowledge, especially about all things American.

"Jones, tell me, what makes a man like you tick?"

"Tick? You mean like a clock?"

"Yes, what makes you go? Why do you work so hard?" Crane asked as he escorted Jones into what he was now calling his hut.

"Oh, I see. I am wanting to be a very good soldier. I want to be the leader of my country."

"The leader? I thought Jomo was the leader."

Jones paused as if he had made a mistake. Crane caught the hesitancy, the unwanted self-revelation. Then he added, "Oh, yes, I love it almost as much as Raphael. But he loves it more than any man. No one loves it like he does, and he loves God, and God also loves him very much. That is why he is our leader. God has chosen him like David. He will slay the bad leaders in this part of the world. Someday maybe he will take me to America with him to meet the president when he too becomes the president."

"President of what?"

"President of our new country. We are all Christian brothers, even though your country sometime has Jewish leaders like Truman and Roosevelt."

"What do you mean?"

"We know that the Americans like Israel so very much, even though it is not a Christian country, because so many of your leaders are Jews."

Crane decided not to confront the obvious inculcation of faulty notions of history. Instead, he played to the young man's enthusiasm for America.

"If you met the president of the United States, what would you say to him?"

"I will salute him and I will say, 'Mr. President, you are the leader of the greatest Christian country in the world. I want to shake your hand. Someday you will come to my country and I will show you why we too are a great people and why we win all the golden medals in the Olympics.'"

"Oh, so you think of your country as Kenya. The great runners like Kip Keino and all the others great distance runners."

"Yes, but I am more than Kenyan. I am African. Sometime Kenyan, Tanzanian, or Botswanan. We will all be one people, and I will be one of the leaders. This Jomo tells me."

"So, I must tell you, you would be a good American. Maybe if you go to America, you will not leave. Many people stay."

"Yes, I would work for the American president," he replied with a broad smile.

"You know, many of the great runners of Kenya and Ethiopia and South Africa now live in America. They are United States citizens."

"Maybe if you teach me about the United States Army, I can be one of them."

"Perhaps, but I must get back to America first. But if I do, I would want to take you with me."

Suddenly, Jones looked at him suspiciously.

Crane sensed that he had gone too far too fast. So he changed the subject and said, "Tell me, what do you think is the most beautiful part of Africa?"

Jones was silent and then replied, "I will tell you. It is Lake Victoria. Someday I will go there again."

"I've heard it is quite beautiful."

Jones had not returned to his previous state of affability. Instead, he turned to walk out of the hut. He hesitated and then turned again and smiled, "America is my dream. Maybe sometime you will get there again."

"If I do, I'll buy you a beer."

For the next several days, these visits continued, getting longer and longer. Finally, one of them ran late into the evening, long enough for Father Ricci to come in as they were speaking. At Ricci's arrival, Jones excused himself, promising Crane that he would speak with him again tomorrow.

Ricci busied himself in preparing an evening meal for Crane.

Crane had never been entirely certain if he could trust Ricci. But amidst the casual discussions over the evening's meal, Ricci was frequently solicitous about Crane's health. Crane still walked with a notable limp. Then Ricci turned the conversation to his relationship with Jones.

"Be careful. Anything you discuss, Jomo will know. Jones admires him greatly. He will do anything that he asks."

"Father, why are you here? You seem like a good man."

"I am here because I am an idealist without a brain. You know the story of the Wizard of Oz?"

"Of course. Every American is familiar with this story."

"I am the scarecrow. Only, I can't dance," he added with a smile.

"Tell me, Father, where are the others?"

"I told you once before, it is better not to know. But now I will tell you. Your men are dead. All of them. Most died fighting. Others died within days, even hours of the fight. Their wounds were much more severe than yours."

"Where are the hostages?"

"You mean hostage. They too are dead, with the exception of their leader. She is to become Jomo's bride."

"Where is she?"

"You'll find her mourning over her wedding day."

"Wedding day?"

"Did you not hear what I said? Jomo intends for her to be his wife.

He has several already. But he has no American wives. Besides, he contends that he has the ability to save and that she is going to go to heaven with him someday. He will save her."

"Where is she?"

"Jomo keeps her in the women's compound. They are purifying her for the occasion." Ricci detected the inquisitive expression on Crane's face and added, "Yes, Jomo and some of his followers have the idea that women are inherently inferior. To be married, they must first be made worthy."

"But what do they have to do to make themselves worthy?"

"For the most part, I do not know. That is special knowledge of the women. As a priest, I have had too many occasions to look into the depths of the human heart. I have not enjoyed the vision. I try to know less about humanity than I once desired to know.

"However, since you ask and I can tell a little … they make her sit alone in a hut, where she is allowed to see no one except the women who bring her food and drink. The food is specially prepared and includes plants that are thought to have special powers to make the woman fertile."

"This sounds primitive."

"It's worse than that. Jomo will rape her in front of the village after the ceremony. Poor thing, she does not know the humiliation she will suffer. And once she is publicly raped, Jomo will announce if she satisfies him or not. If she does not, he will publicly reject her and turn her over to the other men, to be raped by all who wish. At that point, she may wish she were dead."

"Can you do nothing for her?"

"You see me as I am, a broken priest. All the good that I once sought to do is gone. I am a broken priest. Yet Jomo is my son. I helped convince him that he could be the leader of a great nation. I told him once that he would lead his people from social injustice to a new kind of utopia. He believed me and then, for a while, I believed him. But you see that his cruelty is his paramount characteristic along with a lustful profligacy. He seems to think that he is Abraham and Christ reborn. He is, I think, merely demented, and I am his fool."

"Do you have access to outside communication?"

Ricci was silent.

"I need to get out of here. I'd like to take her with me."

Again Ricci was silent.

"Can't you help?"

Ricci looked at him with an expression of woe and sadness. Then he looked again at Crane and asked, "Do you believe that man is inherently good?"

"Yes, I think so."

"I used to as well, but I think he is inherently cowardly. A man can be both. I am both. God made me good. But I am a coward. I am tired of living and wish to end my cowardice. But even that frightens me. I think, like Faust, I have made the pursuit of knowledge a substitute for actions. And I do not act because I am tired. Fatigue has made me a coward. I tried running, but Jomo and his friends found me. I am back among them."

"Why did Jomo bring you back?"

"Because I have contacts. You see, I am a priest, a Jesuit priest. I can travel anywhere in the world, and I am thought to be above reproach. And a number of my colleagues believe that social injustices are the result of the capitalistic system. You would say some of us are Marxist and we believe that anything that brings about this revolution is fair. I was once one who thought like this. Jomo was a student who seemed capable of bringing about such a revolution. But he is not a Marxist—anything but. He sees nothing wrong with killing, but it's not to bring about the revolution I envisioned. No, he is much more interested in the Christianity that he sees as necessary to purge the world of evil. It is I who taught him that the ends do indeed justify the means. I have done Satan's handiwork."

Now it was Crane's turn to be silent.

Crane looked sympathetically toward the priest, who went on for several more minutes. Finally, when he had stopped, Crane looked at him and said, "It ain't over yet. You can still do good."

Ricci smiled meekly and said, "Faith may move mountains, but I think I have become a reed shaken in the wind."

Crane, recognizing the biblical allusion, replied in kind, "The Lord is my shepherd, I shall not want."

He paused and, as if the pause were a further invitation to self-revelation, Ricci said, "Do you have any idea why I am still here?"

"I think you might like to tell me."

"For a military man, you are surprisingly … sensitive."

"It's popular misconception that military people can't be sensitive. We love our children, too, and we even miss them when we are away from them."

"I no longer know what or where my country is." He smiled again and added, "Even soccer cannot elicit feelings of patriotism. I no longer care if Italy wins or Kenya, or South Africa. I am no longer attached. Even if the Vatican or the Jesuits had a team, I wouldn't care. Some days I am sorry to be alive."

"Will you help me?"

"Why?"

"Because I still want to live. I still have a family to go back to." Even as he said the words, a pang of consternation ripped through his chest at the thought of not seeing his wife and children again. He involuntarily closed his eyes, looked down at the ground, and moved his right hand to his forehead as if to touch a thought of his family and grasp it before it faded. His face was slightly flushed and his eyes glistened with moisture. He wondered what his family was doing at this moment and if they missed him. He wondered what his government had told them, if anything.

Instinctively, the priest reached out to touch Crane's shoulder in a gentle gesture of support. Crane grabbed the priest's hand, held it firmly, and closed his eyes again. He held Ricci's hand tightly closed for a minute, then slowly and with a slight expression of embarrassment, he released it.

Ricci said softly, "You should see them again. Perhaps I will see mine someday, too. My mother is still alive. She lives in Bari, a beautiful town on the east coast of Italy. If you and I survive this, someday you can visit us both there."

Crane recovered and then looked into Ricci's sad eyes and asked, "So, why are you here?"

Ricci saw no point in subterfuge since he regarded escape as improbable at best and impossible at the worst.

"I am, as some would say, a carrier, a mule, a diamond aficionado. I transport diamonds routinely from Africa to Europe, where I meet old contacts."

"Where in Europe?"

"Obviously Italy, but also Amsterdam, Brussels. Even England. My contacts call me the DP, diamond priest. I am a whore for Jomo and his henchmen. I enable him to sell the diamonds to the rich people of the world, who in turn provide Raphael with his weapons and the dollars he needs to feed and clothe his army, to bribe various officials, and to aid him in his bloody revolution. But I am just a whore."

"You know, wasn't Mary Magdalene a prostitute?"

"You are too kind. Yes, she was and, yes, Jesus did forgive her."

"So then there is always hope."

"Perhaps there is," replied Ricci with a wan expression that belied the momentary flicker in eyes that had long seemed lifeless.

"Once, I believed that with all my heart. I, like all the Jesuits, went through the Spiritual Exercises of Ignatius Loyola, the founder of our order. And in the beginning, I found them exhilarating. They seemed to cleanse the soul. But as the years passed on, living in the world that has been my home these last several decades took my strength and my soul. Even when I went back to Rome for spiritual rejuvenation, a retreat from the world, I carried the chatter of the world with me. I could no longer hear God in the silence of the quiet countryside. I heard only the chatter of the world. The chatter of my own voice. I could only think and think. I could no longer be. I talked to myself, and even I did not listen. I talked so much that I could not have heard God's voice even if he had spoken." Crane sat silently listening.

CHAPTER 30

OF BLOOD LINES AND
NORDIC KNIGHTS

The glories of our blood and state
Are shadows, not substantial things.

—James Shirley,
"The Glories of Our Blood and State"

—MACARTHUR ESTATE

"PEOPLE LIKE JOMO RAPHAEL AND THEIR ILK ARE ALLOWED TO WREAK havoc on the world because the so-called civilized refuse to do anything about it. The intelligentsia and the ruling elites have as their middle name Complicity. They often will not rid the world of the plague that afflicts others because in some way or another they see themselves as benefiting from it. Until the scourge, in its blood thirst, becomes a threat to them, they will not act. Unless, of course, the citizenry of a country or countries has sufficient self-righteous indignation to rise up and force the hand of its own ruling elite." Regis MacArthur then paused. "However, I would like to think that some of us who might seem to be members of the ruling class still have some backbone. Perhaps we even see our own self-interest in trying to establish a ruling elite that is first and foremost a people who rule by virtue of our own spiritual force.

"As you know, Grant, the United Nations cannot or will not act in most cases unless its hand is forced. At the moment, it is paralyzed by the burden of its own corruption. Jomo's activities continue without much likelihood of serious opposition. South-central Africa is increasingly looking like a country within a series of countries. Borders seem ill-conceived or merely lines on maps, nothing representative of reality. The corruption there has provided much low-hanging fruit that Jomo may find irresistible to pluck, but I fear that he and his henchmen will only make things worse. He has created a cult of personality. Your government and mine would like to end it. Your own country has a reason for doing so that the world at large is not yet aware of."

"Sir, I am not at all certain what any of this has to do with Vanderkin or anything else."

"You will. But first you must become familiar with your purpose. You've been selected by your government and mine to carry on a tradition of stealth warfare against the power of truly evil men that goes back well beyond World War II. We suspect it is in your blood to do so. You've a destiny that will be divulged to you in good time."

"By whom?"

"By me, by Oz, and by Dennis. But before that can happen, you must prove yourself. Thus far, you've shown yourself to be quite resourceful. We intend to put that resourceful to the test. You see, we think one of the scourges that plagues humanity is Byron Vanderkin. We cannot, however, prove it. His wealth, its ultimate source, remains baffling, but we suspect it to be more unseemly than the world would ever imagine. Murder, mayhem, and prostitution are all part of his background. We think that his time in Africa has been the source of his fortune. To bring him low, we must get him to act, to make a mistake. One way of doing that is to eliminate one of his sources of income. We think that source is Jomo Raphael and his blood diamonds—diamonds sold to buy arms that he uses to spread his terror. But to eliminate him would require the cooperation of half a dozen African nations.

"The leaders of these nations would, however, feign cooperation while still eliminating the reformers and others of good will who would really like to bring Jomo and his henchmen to justice. These corrupt government officials stand to continue to benefit from Jomo's largess; he pays them to ignore his illegal diamond trafficking. If that trafficking were eliminated, so too would be a source of their own income. So neither the UN nor any other agency requiring government cooperation can be used to get Raphael. Besides, Raphael is most charismatic and able to hold his Liberation Army together as few others might. We want him dead. Are you up to the challenge?"

For the first time, Grant felt his blood race. "This is what I've trained for."

"You'll not be acting alone. Thomas will be with you."

"Thomas?"

"Yes. You see, Thomas like you has a knack for languages and quite an unusual background. He has recruited from the Royal Marines. His father and grandfather were in the British army before him. He was born in India, in a small Christian community that goes back to the days of Christ. It's one, interesting enough, to which even Alfred the Great sent aid a thousand-plus years ago to help sustain the faith there. Thomas immigrated to England with his mother and father when he was seven. He still speaks his native tongue along with some Urdu and other languages as well. Good man to have with you. Very strong, rugged, and extremely well trained. Well I was hoping you'd say yes, and I've taken the liberty of making preparations for you. Oz will contact you shortly. You'll then rendezvous with some extraordinary gentlemen and Thomas for a special bit of training to enhance the prospect of your success."

Grant had listened with patience but now dared to ask, "What about the package, the satchel? How am I to interpret its contents?"

"With the help of a magician. And he will appear. By the way, I understand from speaking with Oz and Dennis that you are quite the outdoorsman. You camp, climb, hunt, fish, and canoe."

"Yes, I love the outdoors."

"Then you won't mind my reminding you of the true outdoorsman's creed. It applies to your mission as well."

"And what is that, sir?"

"Leave no trace."

*   *   *   *   *

Two days later, Grant was on a military transport at RAF Mildenhall in southern England. He climbed aboard the C-130, and within moments the plane was embarking. It rolled down the runway and, like a great albatross, it lifted off and immediately turned northeast to head toward Oleg Island in Norway, a facility so remote that virtually any type of military exercises could be carried on there without even the Norwegians knowing about it.

Several hours later, as Grant's flight came to an end, the C-130 rolled to a gentle stop near the gray-green terminal. The rear cargo door opened, and Grant watched as several unmarked crates were inspected for possible damage. Grant then squeezed by the cargo and walked down the ramp to a cool and bright blue day. He began walking toward the terminal with his black duffle bag and backpack containing maps and other materials for those who wish to be attuned to the cultures of sub-Saharan Africa. Before he could reach the terminal, he saw a figure inside the tinted windows of the flight control tower who seemed to be waving to him. He strained his eyes to see through the tinted Plexiglas and realized it was Thomas Patel.

Once he entered the lobby, he looked around and saw Thomas descending steps from an area marked "Restricted." For the first time, he saw Thomas for whom he was. He was wearing a British military desert camouflage uniform with the black captain's device sewn onto the collars. Thomas was actually Captain Patel, British Royal Marines.

"Glad to see you, Grant."

"I should say the same. But really, why wasn't I told? You're certainly not a run of the mill chauffeur. If you were, I'd insist upon calling you James."

Thomas laughed. "We Indians, or should I say British of Indian ancestry, have a long tradition of being part of the British military. Surely, you know your Rudyard Kipling. If my new appearance makes you uncomfortable, you may call me Mowgli," he said, referring to the principal character in Rudyard Kipling's *The Jungle Book*.

Grant stopped and looked quizzically at Thomas. "Given your ability to turn up unexpectedly and with ..." he motioned at his captain's insignia, "I'd say you are sufficiently menacing to have earned the sobriquet Shere Khan."

This allusion to the tiger in *The Jungle Book* who attempted to kill Mowgli made Thomas smile. He replied, "No, I am much too nice for a tiger. I would never eat anybody."

"Well, then," said Grant, "let's hope in light of where we're going, no one eats us."

"I don't think that will happen. I have eaten too much curry. I'm too hot for most palates. I am a great lover, not a killer. You know, the *Kama Sutra* and all that."

"Casanova, I only hope your charms will help us where we are going."

"It must. Have you seen the Taj Mahal?"

"You mean in person? No, I haven't, just in pictures."

"You know it was built by a great raj for his wife. Yesterday, I bought it. It's now mine, and so now I have a lover's monument but no lover. But, like Mowgli, I hope someday to have one."

As they exited the terminal, a black Hummer pulled up with a civilian at the wheel wearing a brown leather, fur-collared jacket. It looked like a pilot's jacket but it had no markings on it. Thomas opened the back door. Grant crawled in, squeezing his long legs behind the front seat while Thomas seated himself in front next to the driver.

"I hope you don't mind sitting in back. It's just that I must now give directions to our driver, James." The driver smiled at his new name. Grant looked into the front rear-view mirror where he caught the brilliant eyes of the fiftyish red-faired driver who smiled familiarly. Grant continued looking into the mirror as he offered, "Grant, Grant Chisolm."

"I don't need to know your name, sir."

Slightly surprised at the abrupt response, Grant leaned back for the next hour while Thomas and the driver conversed about the terrain and their destination.

*   *   *   *   *

The facility was not immediately observable. The road simply ended before a granite outcropping. Thomas then got out and waved to an unseen camera. He then motioned to Grant to do the same. Without another word, the driver removed Grant's gear and put it outside the car, got back in, and turned the vehicle around. Grant and Thomas watched as the Hummer disappeared down the rugged dirt road in a cloud of dust. A couple of minutes later, two men wearing non-descript uniforms, absent name tags, appeared from behind the outcropping.

Thomas and Grant walked toward them. These were slender, hard-looking men, each holding a Heckler and Koch machine gun. One of them turned his back to lead while Grant and Thomas fell in line behind him and the other behind them. They walked through sparse tundra where, off in the distance, two caribou grazed on the slowly rising landscape. After twenty minutes of walking, they approached an enclosed compound with a heavy chain link fence and guard post at a roadless entrance.

As they approached, two guards waved them through. The enclosure was almost perfectly flat for what appeared to be a half-mile square. Here and there, vents appeared about a foot above ground. Except for the guards, the entire area was deserted—at least on the surface.

As they trudged with their gear another one hundred or so yards on the uneven tundra, toward the center of the compound, where there was a low-lying outcropping of about twenty square feet, it began to slowly rise up out of the turf. Grant, Thomas, and their escort stood by watching until the entire rock had risen to an elevation of about ten feet above the ground. The area immediately beneath a rock look-alike consisted of a solid square of steel powered up and down by an unseen hydraulic system. A door opened to a flat-floored bin. One of the still silent escorts walked inside, followed by Grant, Thomas, and the other guard.

The last man in closed the metal, windowless door and then pressed a button that read "Thor." Beneath this button were two others: Valkerie and Woton, the names of Viking supernatural beings. As the elevator landed at Thor, the doors opened. A sign immediately opposite the elevator doors as they opened read, "Please remember where you parked."

At least someone has a sense of humor, thought Grant.

Grant and Thomas then walked down a brightly lit white hallway. There were doors on either side with names on each that read like something out of *Bulfinch's Mythology:* Zeus, Mercury, and Juno. Finally, they were escorted to a door that read "Kansas." The lead escort knocked, and an attractive blond woman opened it. She was dressed in something akin to a U.S. Air Force flight suit, but again with no markings, names, or insignia.

"We've been expecting you," she said. "Please be seated." She spoke with only the slightest trace of a British accent. Grant speculated that she might actually be Norwegian with ample exposure to the BBC.

Grant and Thomas sat in adjacent comfortable chairs opposite a large steel desk that might have been plucked from army surplus. Behind the desk were four four-drawer safes. Above the safes was a picture of Richard the Lionhearted with sword upraised as he was about to lead his men into battle. Grant had seen the original once before at a museum in Cambridge. Next to it was a framed sign that read "Thomas Wolf was right: you can't go home again unless I say so." Then on top of one of the safes was a pair of black patent leather military dress shoes. Beneath them was a hand-painted poster board sign that read "If you click your heels together three times and make a wish, you'll go straight to hell. Wishes are for dreamers; here all are schemers." Beneath that was yet another sign, again hand-lettered, that read "I hate Jung." A reference, Grant assumed, to the psychoanalyst Karl Jung who spent his life studying dreams and their importance.

The secretary asked if either of them would like some tea, to which Thomas replied, "Yes, of course. Am I not English?"

Grant hesitated and said, "Why not? After all, we Americans are your bloody cousins." Thomas chuckled and raised his eyebrows at the first indication he had really seen of Grant's sense of humor. The secretary left.

Grant and Thomas waited. After about a minute, the speaker on the desk crackled and they heard, "I am the great and powerful Oz." Thomas and Grant wondered what was going on when Grant turned to Thomas and said, "Did you notice the sign on the door?"

"You mean the one that says 'Kansas'?"

"Yes, I don't think it's true. I've never been there. Maybe we took the wrong cyclone."

Thomas, who was better read in American literature than most Americans, replied, "No, that would make you Pecos Bill and maybe I would be Tonto."

Surprisingly, it was Grant who had to profess ignorance, "Tonto?"

"Yes, remember Vanderkin used the term in reference to me? Tonto was an Indian like me, only not as bright or as good-looking. At least that is what I've heard. Moreover, he was an *American* Indian."

"Funny, somehow I thought you were English."

Before the banter could continue, a door on their right opened. A familiar figure in an olive green jump suit and a pair of all-terrain boots walked in. It was Oz himself.

"Welcome to Kansas, boys."

"That's strange. I didn't see any yellow brick road," replied Grant.

Twice in one day, thought Thomas. *Sahib is right.*

"Nor will you ever see such a road, if all goes to plan. Remember, this is Kansas, not Oz. Our location is remote, as are any suspicions that something unusual might actually be going on here."

"Is there?" asked Grant.

"Now that you and Thomas are here, yes. Let's get you up to speed. First of all, you both have the necessary clearance to be a part of the programs here. And nothing, absolutely nothing, that is going on here can ever be revealed. Only a handful of people even know that this program and this facility exist."

Grant immediately picked up on the ultra sensitivity of the program and asked, "How deep is this program?"

"So deep that if Dorothy had made it in, Toto would have been shot for yapping too much and even the wizard could not get out and back home again."

Well, that clears things up, thought Thomas.

"Gentlemen, as a rule I would prefer that we spin a wide web and ensnare the unsuspecting villains of the world. However, there are some villains who would prefer to ensnare us. The most demanding task for us is to ensnare the ensnarers."

"Sir, may I inject a note of concern?" asked Grant. "If all that we do here is deep, deep cover, where are the security badges?"

"There are none. Within two days, you will personally know everyone, and everyone involved in this program will know you. Badges require paperwork to create and they can be stolen and compromised. They even tell certain people who is here by virtue of an electric scanning process. No, you won't use them here since we don't really exist and neither do you. Your disappearance is to be of no concern to the outside world. Anonymity gives you freedom."

Grant nodded while Thomas stared back blankly. As Oz glanced at Thomas, it occurred to him that Thomas's indecipherable expression would have made him a good poker player.

Oz looked directly at Grant and then again at Thomas. "You are our best. You will have a chance to prove it. You are to be trained in the use of equipment that has been tested but has hardly seen the light of day. It is advanced beyond what most people can even fathom. So, tell me, boys, do either of you recall the 1984 Olympics?"

"I've only read about them. I never saw them. I was a little young at the time," replied Grant.

"Same here, sir," said Thomas.

"During the 1984 Olympics, during the opening ceremony, a huge Americans flag was floated across the stadium, above the crowd. It was kept aloft by eight men wearing rocket packs, like Buck Rogers or some other comic book characters. Each of them had a handle on the flag so that if they kept to their rectangular formation, the flag would remain extended and visible to everyone below in the stadium. For most Americans, this was their first exposure to science fiction come to actual life. Rocket man was real. However, if you were standing next to one of these rocket men, you would also know that the sound was deafening. It was like standing next a Harrier jet. Even throughout the stadium a couple hundred feet below, talking to anyone was completely out of the question because of the noise. So rocket packs, along with their fuel inefficiency, were abandoned by the U.S. Army as a legitimate vehicle for either combat soldiers or for rescue operations. Even recon was ruled out with these. But someone else took it up."

"I smell a skunk," said Grant, alluding to the legendary research and development facility in the remotest area of Nevada.

"And well you should. However, these days even Skunk Works draws too much public attention. Every conspiracy buff and no-need-to-know fool on the planet is watching the facility, especially Area 51, to find out what we really did with the aliens who crashed near Roswell. So the program twenty years ago was reexamined and then it reemerged here. For twenty years, we've had people working to do three things: one, lighten the rocket pack itself; two, extend its range with greater fuel efficiency; and three, shut it the hell up. This thing was so loud that it would be impossible to sneak into a rock concert. The noise ... just too much.

"Here," Oz paused for dramatic effect, "here," he repeated, "at this location. Well, we've done it! We've done it! Now it's quieter than anyone could imagine!"

"How does this affect us?" asked Grant.

What kind of bird am I? thought Thomas. *I'd like to be an eagle. Will this make me an eagle?* He kept silent even as he anticipated where Oz's remarks might be headed.

"You two will use this technological marvel on your mission. If you're alive and you read the newspapers, you know that central Africa is menaced by a warlord of sorts named Jomo Raphael. What you did not know is that several weeks ago, CINC sent in a documentary team to interview him. Not long afterwards, the ears of several of the members were sent to CINC's headquarters in Nairobi. Apparently, Jomo is holding them hostage in return for an unbelievable reward. He says he wants an SUV."

"An SUV?" asked Thomas. "Can't he buy one?"

"The SUV is just an excuse," said Oz. "The man is a sadist and he enjoys manipulating his victims for personal reasons. The man seems to enjoy humiliating his victims for no other reason than that he can."

"Why not just give him the SUV in return for the hostages?"

"Because we have already reason enough for punishing him. We don't want to reward him or no journalist in Africa or Asia will be safe. Besides, he knows what we think of his request." Then he paused before explaining the matter that had consumed him and others for the past several days.

"Two weeks ago, we sent in an eighteen-man platoon to find the hostages and to get them out. Someone, somewhere, somehow seems to have tipped them off. The entire platoon has disappeared. We have an inside source who tells us that most of the men were killed; a few may be alive, but we're not sure. We also don't know what happened to the CINC team. All we have are their ears. But one source seems to know about them. At most, four of the soldiers and CINC members may still be alive. The rest, we believe, are already dead."

Grant and Thomas listened as Oz went over the details of their training for the next week. They would be accompanied on their mission by two teachers, expert soldiers who also had a background in what they liked to call "advanced gadgetry." One was British and the other was Norwegian.

Just then, the woman who had greeted them walked in with tea and a small dish of pastry, placed it on Oz's desk, and left. As they sipped their teas, Oz explained the mechanics of the rocket pack that gave them the possibility of limited, controlled flight.

"We've come up with a rocket pack that represents a quantum leap. It enables us to improve flight time from the mere forty-five seconds of the eighties to an astonishing twelve minutes! Twelve minutes! Enough to surprise the bad guys, defeat them, and then fly back to safety!" Oz positively glowed with excitement as he continued speaking.

"The rocket pack has been around since World War II. The Germans had a thing called the *Himmelstrumer*. Skystormer. It consisted of two tubes that enabled a man to jump several hundred feet. But the device was never implemented, and it disappeared after being handed over to the Americans.

"Interestingly, Wendell Moore, an American who may have seen the German belt, invented his own rocket belt. In the sixties, we made another that operated on kerosene. It was functional but extremely difficult to make. It was also very expensive."

"Why not just use helicopters instead?" asked Thomas.

"Because helos are big and conspicuous. It's hard to sneak in upon the enemy with such a big bird."

Thomas could not stop thinking about the fact that he would rather be an eagle than someone dropping out of a helicopter or a man with a fuel tank strapped to his back.

"The belt is a big jump forward. Before this, we experimented with rocket belts fueled by nitrogen and then later by hydrogen peroxide. Once again, the project was temporarily surrendered when Wendell Moore died. Since then, there have been numerous attempts to improve the pack—even the Finns, just next door, have tried building flight packs. Only theirs have wings as well as a rocket pack. However, our pack is better than anything anywhere! You two will be the first men in history to take them into a combat setting."

Both Thomas and Grant were excited but also tried to sip their tea calmly so as to not betray an entirely too enthusiastic response. However, neither of them knew how dangerous their mission would be in and of itself but had been trained to expect the worse. Adding untried-in-combat rocket packs lent an element of anxiety to any endeavor that might now unfold before them. Oz was oblivious to their concern.

CHAPTER 31

WITH FRIENDS LIKE THESE

These oak-hearted warriors
Lured me to this land

—"Icelandic Sagas"

—NORTHERN NORWAY

THE ROCKET PACKS, DESPITE THEIR POWER AND EFFICIENCY, WEIGHED only twenty-eight pounds, considerably lighter than some of the earlier versions. After ten straight days of training in their use, along with preparations for their insertion into northern Tanzania near the Kenyan border, Grant and Thomas and their two accomplices were ready.

Their British technician was more than a mere engineer. He had graduated from Sandhurst, the British military academy, two years earlier and gone immediately into British Black Ops. He stood five feet nine inches tall and was barrel-chested and extremely fit. Every day during training, he arose at four in the morning to run five miles or to lift weights. His uniform was like the new ones issued to Grant and Thomas: black, brown, gray, and white camouflage with no insignia to indicate rank, name, or nation. He had a quick smile, a ready laugh, and a rugged constitution that thrived on extreme tasks. He actually enjoyed seeing how much pain he could tolerate. At one point, his ability to run the four hundred meters in less than forty-seven seconds had given him reason to pause about his determination to have a military career. The Commonwealth Games or even the Olympics seemed a worthy aspiration. But a family of militarily accomplished individuals had caused him to reassert the primacy of the warrior ethos in his own life.

He still ran routinely as part of his training, and he trained extremely because he wanted to overcome pain. At twenty-four years of age, Giles Peterson was the youngest member of the team.

The Norwegian team member was a stereotype: blond-haired, blue-eyed, and muscular. A thin pink scar went across his forehead from the middle of his brow down over his nose and extended to his left cheek. His name was Tellef and he was thirty-three, the oldest member of the team.

"What happened to your face?" asked Thomas

"I bit a dog; he bit back." He spoke English with an American accent, revealing the fact that he had attended college at the University of Virginia, where he had majored in mathematics and computer technology as well as advanced kayaking and rock climbing. He had once killed a man as part of a covert operation into northern Pakistan.

Certain Taliban leaders were said to be gathered in a border village south of Kandahar. He, along with two others from the Norwegian Special Operation Forces, had snuck into the village and found the location of their adversary, and while others kept watch, Tellef had slipped into his mud and stone house without a sound. He had identified his enemy, who awoke just as Tellef's knife blade slid across his throat. Then without awakening anyone else in the house, he and his team stole out of the village and into darkness.

No one in the village was even aware of the assassination until Tellef and his men were back in safe territory. Tellef thought that trouble, challenge, and enjoyment were one and the same. His operations were generally of such a black nature that he told people even he didn't know what he did. He secretly reveled in his Viking ancestry, still considering America part of the Viking empire, which he liked to think he had already extended to Afghanistan and now to parts of Africa. He and some of his close friends were as apt to refer to America as Vinland or Nova Norway as Brits were occasionally and with good humor apt to refer to America as the colonies. Like his British counterpart, he had been selected to assist Grant and Thomas in part for his toughness as well as his experience, overall fitness, and ingenuity. He was mechanically adept and could handle or fix all sorts of equipment.

All four left Norway after their training in various civilians flights. They would rendezvous in two days in Nairobi. Their equipment would be shipped as special diplomatically secured material to the United States Embassy, free from the prying eyes of customs' officials. Duplicate containers of the same equipment would also be shipped to the island of Ascension in the event that Kenyan officials seemed to sense something and a backup plan was needed.

Someone had also secured the assistance of two Brits living in the bush country. These were two renowned big game hunters who knew the terrain and had curried favor with the locals since they often hired them to assist them and their customers on their trips into the African interior. These two hunters also had the advantage of having trained mercenaries operating in various Congolese and Nigerian conflicts. They were both cynics about the goodness of human nature, including their own, but deeply loyal to their motherland of England. They also loved the peoples of Kenya and Tanzania as well as those of Burundi and Botswana, but they mistrusted all the governments of the region since all of them had at one time or another sought them out privately in hopes of enlisting their support to kill one political adversary or another.

As Huntley, the older of the two, pointed out to a would-be employer, "We're bloody mercenaries, not bloody assassins. We don't get involved in politics." The distinction was lost on most who inquired of their services but was sufficient to give them a pretense of morality and a strict code of conduct. They wished to at least appear to be above the fray of the toiling masses and their chaos even if they contributed to it.

CHAPTER 32

THE STUFF OF DREAMS

Dreams are the X-rays of the soul.

—Terry Margolies

"It's incredible, the possibilities. I knew it had to have been recorded somewhere, Uncle. I spent an entire week of my vacation at the library trying to find it. It was something I had read years ago. But I found it, and I think it connects." Blanche DeNigris's whole being practically dilated with excitement.

Dennis listened with the patient kindliness that had marked his relationship with his niece since her childhood. Her enthusiasm for history and archaeology was arresting. She had contacted him, or at least attempted to, several times since her own short disappearance. Dennis, who understood from his own sources the travail to which his niece had been subject both in London as well as in the archaeological site in Scotland, had surmised where and why she might be hiding out, especially after she explained her episodes to the management of the British Museum.

"And what exactly have you found?" asked Dennis.

"Uncle, do you know the name William Smith?"

"Do you mean *the* William Smith? The father of modern day geology? Well, my dear, I have even seen the map that he drew. His map of England, Scotland, and Wales is a masterpiece. He mapped, if you will, Middle Earth long before Tolkien was born. I once spent an afternoon at Burlington House in London's Piccadilly gazing at it. Why do you ask?"

"Are you aware that in the nineties, a portfolio of his unpublished papers was found at the Sheldonian Theatre at Oxford?"

"No, no, I wasn't aware of that. Are they of any value? Are they interesting?"

"Uncle, they mention something. Something that I think may prove quite interesting. You see, he drew a map of the area around Ben Nevis and a line representing a canal that he suggested be built between the Irish Sea at Fort William, all the way through Spean Bridge, Invergarry, Fort Augustus and finally through to Inverness on the east coast of Scotland. But his notations also reference caverns on the south side of the would-be canal. He outlines them. He shows them as going at least a couple of miles into the interior of the terrain near what is now Kyle of Iten. He even wrote about them, the caverns. He states that he found them, or at least an opening to them, while digging to examine some substrata near the canal's present-day location. And this was years before the canal was actually constructed."

"Well, if he knew about it, then why didn't others find it, especially when they dug the canal?"

"I was wondering the same thing. But then it occurred to me. Unless he mentioned his find to somebody, how would they know? Even people—" She stopped suddenly.

"Uncle, do you remember a few years ago when the tomb of Ramses II's children was found in the Valley of the Kings?"

"Oh, yes," he replied, "Quite. It was an extraordinary find."

"Do you remember any of the details of the find?"

"Well, yes, if I recollect correctly, was the tomb's entrance only a couple hundred feet from another tomb of another pharaoh, one that tourists had been visiting for years?"

"Yes, and do you remember why no one had seen the entrance before?"

"Hmm, something about the debris. Yes, that's it; the debris removed from the area around the entrance to another tomb had been piled in the entrance of this other tomb. After a while, I suppose people forgot it was there."

"Until some contemporary archaeologist remembered that some

sketches made by Sir Richard Burkhart, who had visited the area in the early nineteenth century, revealed a tomb entrance that no one in recent years had seen. But the drawings prompted one man to attempt to find the opening to what appeared to be a tomb. He surmised it was only a stone's throw from the opening of pharaoh's tomb."

She paused and wiped a tear of excitement from her eye.

"Uncle, look at this." She unfolded a sheet of paper on which there was an image of what looked like the cutaway of a hillside, with several different labels identifying various subterranean features of the land.

"Look here." She pointed to a hole blackened in and appearing at about sight level.

"I see," he said. "But again, how is it that no one has mentioned this cavern or at least its entrance in all these years?"

"Well, I think it's like the Egyptian tomb. While the workmen were digging the Inverness Canal, they simply covered it over. They needed a place to throw their debris, and they found it."

"My dear, your excitement is contagious."

"Oh, he says in one of his remarks that the cavern may go on for miles. What if it's connected to the site that we found?"

"That, my dear, would be extraordinary. I suppose we'll have to get the site reopened. But, of course, we can do that only when you're safety is assured."

"Uncle, I know you are a man of considerable resourcefulness."

"Oh, my dear, I could deny you nothing."

He reached across from his chair and patted his niece's cheek.

*   *   *   *   *

Two men, looking very much like backpackers, settled down on the mountainside near the ruins of the old church, seemingly oblivious to the secret entranceway only feet from where they rested. But their eyes were constantly moving, inspecting any other hikers in the area. Their binoculars would now and then focus on a bird and then move subtly to inspect someone or something else. Despite their appearance, these were not ordinary backpackers or mere day-trippers.

Regis MacArthur, by virtue of his position as Earl of Atholl, had access to the only private army in the British Isles. Going back to the fourteenth century, the legacy of his earldom had been the envy of other self-styled monarchs. However, his army actually had the blessing of the House of Windsor. The occasions upon which this force had been activated were few. Still, without exception, the judgment to employ that force was exclusively in the earl's hands. In this instance, the earl had activated two of his most trusted men to scrutinize the hillside near Ben Nevis to assure its remaining secure. He now listened as Blanche made her case.

"Sir, my uncle has advised me that you're the man I should see to gain access to our find without too many others becoming aware of our discovery and without imperiling our own safety."

"And can I possibly do so much?"

"My uncle tells me that you are a man of many resources and considerable talent."

"I'm afraid that I am most prone to flattery. Dennis has long known my weakness. However, I must ask, why is it so imperative that this site be opened now? You've had quite enough excitement in your life of late, I should think."

"Because this is an archaeologist's dream—to see and to touch something that may have gone unnoticed for who knows how many years—hundreds, maybe even thousands. I could feel it when I was there. There's something mystical about that place. It's holy, I know it. I think this may be one of the sacred places of the ancient Celts."

"But didn't you tell me that you found modern equipment there and nearby? Didn't you find diamonds? Diamonds. That alone gives me reason to think that this place may be something other than holy, unless it is a holiness that has been corrupted. Tell me, is it true about William Smith? Do you really think that your find could possibly stretch for miles? If so, I must say it sounds positively delicious. Something out of the imagination of my old friend, Tolkien. Middle Earth, you know."

"Yes, but this is real," she said.

"My attention, you have it. What exactly do you want? My men are already guarding it. I assure you that no one will find, or if they do, none will go inside it. They shall see to that. When the time is right, we shall open it again. But ..." He paused and looked into her eyes, which were watery with frustrated desire.

He smiled. "You do not wish merely to protect the site. Your purpose is certainly larger."

She blushed in embarrassment. "I'm an archaeologist. This discovery is the stuff of dreams. I felt as though I were, if for only a few minutes, Howard Carter peering into Tut's tomb. What relics lay within? I yearn to be the first to touch them."

"What of your friends? I understand that several others, as well as a certain American friend, a handsome fellow at that, all played a part in this matter."

"Yes, and they shall again. We can all do it together. But even before that can happen, we need your blessing and your protection."

Regis then looked at her and replied, "There are more pressing matters at this moment that require my individual attention. I expect such matters to be resolved within a month. Until that time," he said most gently, "you must wait. Then I shall call you and we shall see."

Feeling slightly encouraged at his remarks and also frustrated at the delay, she smiled and asked, "May I call you in thirty days?"

"Yes, and I shall take your call and respond honestly. No false hope, but neither unnecessary delays."

With the matter at least temporarily settled, Regis ushered her into his garden to examine the blossoms of summer on which his servant had spent the last thirty years working.

"When I first took over the estate, it seemed barren to me. But with my own love of gardening and the good fortune of hiring Roland Gardner—it really is his name—I rather think we have made the barren once again fertile, and the land again brims with life, with color."

As they strolled through the garden, Regis said, "The American, you ignored my reference to him. You like him very much, don't you?"

Blanche blushed like one of the red flowers in his garden and looked at him almost girlishly. "Is it that obvious?"

"Yes, and I suspect he'd enjoy seeing you in your role as Howard Carter. Perhaps he could switch his sex as well and he'll be Nefertiti."

She laughed and then continued walking. He assured her that she would see Grant again. He had imagined correctly that her not hearing from Grant while at Loch Maree and again during training in Norway left her with a sense of doubt regarding her own appeal. His comment, however brief, momentarily whet her appetite to hear Grant speak her name again.

CHAPTER 33
PREPARATIONS

Soldiers are sworn to action; they must win
Some flaming, fatal climax with their lives.

—Siegfried Sassoon, "Dreamers"

—SKIES OVER EUROPE

ONLY HOURS AFTER TAKEOFF, THE TWO CIVILIAN AIRLINERS, CARRYING Grant, Thomas, Tellef, and Giles, landed in Rome, a routine stop on the way to Nairobi. There, each of them was met by Oz, who informed them that their plans had been changed. Kenyan officials had grown suspicious and attempted to confiscate the undisclosed materials brought into their country. The rocket packs and everything else had been stymied by customs despite diplomatic protocol and were being sent back. Grant and company disembarked and headed by car to the U.S. Air Force base in Aviano, Italy, where a C-130 awaited them.

*　　*　　*　　*　　*

"Did you ever see the movie or read the book about Graystoke?" asked Grant.

"You mean about the ape man? Tarzan?" replied Thomas.

"Yep, that's the one. I'm thinking about it. I wonder how he would handle this situation."

"He would yell, 'Ah aaaaah aaaaah,'" replied Thomas in a weak

242

imitation of a Tarzan yell. "And then would tell the elephants to crush the village and the apes to take all the women for themselves."

"That Tarzan sounds like a bright fellow," said Grant.

Their two accompanying geek soldiers smiled but said nothing. The hum of the C-130 acted like a drug, inducing a feeling of comfort, a sort of meditative state in which a person could, just for a while, enjoy the mere state of being. After a flight of too many hours and too many miles from Ascension, in the remotest regions of the south Atlantic, the plane, in the dead of night, maintained its unearthly levitation of thirty thousand feet.

From the cockpit, this truly looked like the Dark Continent. Only a couple of hours before, each of the men had been given a pre-cooked meal of steak and potatoes, and among the four they emptied a half pot of coffee. Thomas, however, insisted upon tea, Indian tea.

Oz, who was in charge of the operation, sat in a dark corner of the plane looking through a head lamp perched on his forehead at a map of the terrain. He had been over it repeatedly in the last two weeks. He looked again at the army grid system and matched it with satellite photography to establish and once again affirm the latitude and longitude marks as well as the GTM coordinates, the universal transverse Mercator system of identification and positioning.

Just for a couple of minutes, Grant drifted off and saw Jomo's face before him, painted sky blue and with his hair raised up in a macabre mohawk with his mouth open and bees coming from it. They swarmed toward Grant, who woke with a start, sweat beading on his brow.

Thomas remained calm. Oz moved out of the shadows. Together they went over the operation one last time. Ten minutes later, the co-pilot came back and said, "We're approaching our objective. Get your gear ready."

Minutes later, the four soldiers lined up behind one another: Tellef, then Thomas, Giles, and finally Grant. As the rear cargo door opened, they gazed skyward into the moonless night, stars shining brightly and in contrast to the dark abyss below. Each placed his oxygen device for high-altitude descent over his face. The HALO (high altitude, low opening) commenced. One by one, they fell silent and jumped. On his descent, Grant momentarily gazed skyward.

Star light, star bright, the first star I see tonight.

Then he looked earthward, where he imagined ignorant armies clashing by a moonless night.

As Thomas fell from the sky, he amused himself with a silent parody of the time-honored tradition of American chutzpa to yell "Geronimo" as his mind echoed with the sound of "Ghandiiiiiiiiii." The fall was fleeting and less than fun despite the tranquility of their descent. And as the four chutists fell, another pack dropped a few seconds behind them. A large box tethered to a closed chute contained the rocket packs. A barometric device would pop the chute open at just over one thousand feet above the ground.

As each man fell, he looked at his altimeter attached to his left forearm and two lights: a red one that glowed until the altimeter activated the green light that signaled the chute to open. One by one, their chutes bloomed only one thousand feet above the brush and scattered trees.

They each directed their chutes to the openings in the brush discerned through their night vision goggles. Each landed with a running motion as the wind continued pulling at their billowy chutes, yanking them backwards as they attempted to twist themselves out from the cords. As they descended and landed, two sets of eyes desperate with fear and wide with hope watched from the brush.

Everyone had landed within sight of one another while the packs dropped amidst some heavy brush. But the wind kept the chute buffeting about so that in the darkness, the flopping created enough sound that they could have found it even without their night vision goggles.

Twelve miles from Jomo's camp, and opposite the side on which the American Special Forces crew had been dropped several weeks earlier, they fell upon the rocket packs. There were sixteen rocket packs in all. The objective was to space them out over several miles at pre-determined points of egress from the camp so they could escape Jomo's men to the next site where they could drop their empty rocket packs in a river or any other large bodies of water over which they flew as they strapped on their new ones. Buoyancy deflators were programmed into each canister to force the packs to sink after they were empty. Corrosives were to be simultaneously released on the inside of the canisters destroying all computer boards quickly in the event that an enemy attempted to retrieve them. Only the team leader had a detonating device that could be triggered if the packs fell into enemy hands while still fully operational.

From the crate they pulled out two canvas collapsible boats and two battery-operated trolling motors. Within fifteen minutes, they had buried the crate and its chute and were headed toward the river.

Floating up stream with their supplies in two boats, they stayed low. Once they had traveled four miles, they GPS'd their location and planted four rocket packs, complete with honing transmitters. Four more miles later, they did the same on a small tree-infested island near the middle of the river.

Finally, they quietly approached a promontory less than four miles from the village. Despite its elevation, satellite imagery had revealed that the density of its foliage made it a good hiding place but not a good place from which to observe the surrounding area. After several minutes of struggling up the hillside, parts of which were nearly impenetrable, they cleared out a small area at the top and lay down the remaining eight rocket packs. They went back down the hill and then climbed back up, towing their rucksacks and the boats, once again in case they would be needed on the way back. When everything was in place, they broke out some charcoal-heated meals of chicken and rice and some filtered water. They ate and then they slept.

*   *   *   *   *

Jomo rose early. It was his wedding day.

"Bring me my sword." Making a grand gesture of bowing as if before a monarch, Marx St. George considered the order and exited, walking toward a special supply tent. His keys hanging at his side, he searched through a pile of wooden crates until he found the one marked with stenciled letters, "U.S.A." He unlocked the crate and lifted the lid. Inside on top were two United-States-Army-issued M-4 rifles. He moved the rifles and pushed the packing materials aside as he rummaged about until he found the long, thin cardboard box. He pulled it out and opened it. Inside was a three-and-half-foot-long sword engraved with "To an Army of One, Jomo Raphael, 82nd Airborne, Fort Bragg, NC, 1994."

In the woman's compound, the women arose early. The bride was reluctant but too fearful to actively resist. She stood before her attendees, most of whom went about their tasks with a carefree air and perhaps a touch of envy. They stripped her to bathe her and to affirm that she was not menstruating, an event which would require a ritualistic cleansing before her bedding.

Melissa Millinson stood erect and tense for the inspection in her long brown hair now being twisted into neat rows and festooned with red, blue, and yellow beads. Her eyes were red and swollen from incessant crying the night before. As one of the elderly women inspected her for signs of menstruation, she gasped and bit her lower lip. One of the women laughed and said, "Don't worry. Jomo will please you. He is a man."

During the humiliating inspection, her mind wandered. She thought of her first husband. *How did I come to be here? Who would have imagined? Is this the adventure I had wished for? Will I ever awaken from this nightmare?*

One elderly woman who sat silently and unconcernedly caught Melissa's eye and smiled in a kindly fashion. The old woman's attention was focused on her. She smiled again and then nodded toward her as if to say that everything would be all right. This woman's smile was her sole consolation.

One by one, the women circled her, touched her on the cheek, and softly said, "Sister.'" Melissa did not understand the gesture and remained fixated on the kindly elder who sat cross-legged on the periphery.

Then, with the women chattering about her, she looked toward the doorway of the hut as a tall young woman entered holding a long garment draped over two arms. As she entered, she looked to her right to the old woman on whom Melissa had focused. The elderly woman extended both arms, and the woman carefully placed the garment gently in her arms.

One of the women then came forward with yet another all white garment. She then placed it on a clean green and yellow palm strand weave at the American's feet.

Finally, the elder woman rose from the floor and clapped her hands together several times. Everyone in the room left hurriedly. She then cocked her head and again smiled as she stood before the American. Melissa continued to look straight at her. Gently, the elder reached out with her right hand and stroked her cheek and said, "He will not harm you. I will see to that."

Feeling entirely vulnerable and wishing at last to confide in someone,

Melissa burst into tears. For two solid minutes the woman stood stoically before her, waiting for the tears to stop.

When she could see no sign of abatement, the old woman reached up with her right hand and pressed it against Melissa's cheek.

"Listen," she said, "dress now and rejoice at the celebration and count yourself blessed. The Lord will prevail. And Jomo will not harm you. I know. Now put this on."

"But what is to stop him? He fears nothing."

"He fears one thing."

"What? What does he fear?"

"Put this on," she repeated. "Now listen to me. Our ways may be strange to you. But they are our ways. Do as I say, and no one will harm you."

"But what does he fear?"

"Me. Now put this on. Several men are about to enter this room on my signal. Before they enter, you must drink."

She then stepped back, turned, and stooped to pick up a plastic white canister filled with water. As she did so, Melissa put on the long white garment by sliding it over her head and down her torso. It draped below her knees. She looked like a catechist about to be baptized.

The elderly woman took the lid and held the liter of water before her and said, "You must drink it all. All. It will purify you."

Melissa reached for it and began to drink, droplets of water splashing on her white dress. She gulped down the entire liter, forcing her stomach to protrude beneath the garment. After she finished the canister, she handed it back to the old woman. She placed it on the ground, turned, and took the American girl by the hand.

"When I tell them to, these men will enter. They are Jomo's brothers, some real, some imaginary; they were adopted. The eldest among them will have a stool with him. He will enter first and will place the stool before you. You will pull up your dress and place your bottom on it. Your skin must be upon the stool. Only your flesh must touch the stool, not the dress. Then you must pee."

"What?" exclaimed Melissa. "Pee?"

"Yes, and do not object. It will do no good."

"Why?"

"It is a custom. But listen to me, there is more. The men, they will place their hands under you. You must pee on their hands."

"What?"

"You must pee on their hands. As I said, our ways must be strange to you. I will stay with you to help. I know you must be uncomfortable."

"Strange? Uncomfortable? More like crazy!"

"Yes, I know. Sometimes I think so myself. But you must try to understand."

"But why?"

"The peeing, it is a tribal tradition. The men whose hands you pee on may have sex with you when Jomo is away."

"What? Pee and sex!"

The old woman looked down and then backed up and said simply, "It is our way. But no one will harm you. But you must not resist."

"Why? This is rape!"

"No, they will not hurt you. You must learn to be soft with them. They will not harm you for they fear me."

Melissa stood silent in disbelief. She believed and yet she could not believe. Then the old woman turned and walked toward the doorway. She clapped her hands twice. Four men ran toward the hut. One of them carried a stool.

*   *   *   *   *

Late in the afternoon, Grant and the others arose from their daytime slumber. They prepared for the raid.

"Okay, boys, remember," said Grant. "We will leave no trace."

They waited. The sun went down. Darkness fell. They slipped down the hillside with their rocket packs strapped to their backs. Each man carried his weapons and eight grenades.

As they merged with the darkness, Thomas prayed to himself, "Hail Mary, full of grace ..." The others spoke of nothing but merely envisioned the path before them. It took them six hours to traverse the last four miles, stepping through the jungle, avoiding foot paths and even the semblance of a road to prevent detection. At one point, the tangle of brush and rugged terrain slowed their progress to a crawl. Grant stopped and told them to rest a while as he pulled out a Tyvek map and checked pre-determined locations against his own GPS readings with a small red-bulbed flashlight.

"We're exactly where we want to be," he whispered.

"That's what I thought," joked Thomas. "I'm in complete darkness with three white guys who're trying to look like me." Thomas's own dark skin produced little or no shine in the darkness. But the others knew that even the slightest shine from their white skin could give them away. They had blackened their faces so that each could only see the others' eyes. When they gathered around the map and Grant's flashlight, he looked at their intense blackened faces.

"If I didn't know better, I'd say you guys escaped from a New Orleans restaurant where they serve everything blackened, or you were a bunch of rejects from a minstrel show." Thomas and the Brit laughed while the Norwegian smiled good-naturedly, wondering what people in a minstrel show were supposed to look like. He assumed they were black people who did not look like Vikings.

After a fifteen-minute rest, they advanced in the darkness like four red-eyed demons.

"We're within two miles of the village. We stay together and move in silence."

By dawn, they stood on a declivity overlooking an area of the river within site of the village. The vegetation shrouded their movements. They again rested.

"This evening, we move in. But first we find out where the hostages are. Satellite imaging points to this hut as Jomo's. Here in a separate compound is the women's section. And, according to our friends at the U.S. Embassy, there is someone in Nairobi who not only works for Jomo but who also enjoys being paid by the word. He seems to be in near constant contact with our personnel. He says that the woman is still alive. Let's go over our plan one more time."

CHAPTER 34

SHAKING HANDS

Alien they seemed to be.

—Thomas Hardy,
"The Convergence of the Twain"

—*U.S. EMBASSY, NAIROBI*

WAITING IN THE OUTER OFFICE OF THE UNITED STATES AMBASSADOR to Kenya stood a tall, thin, and distinguished-looking gentleman wearing an off-white suit with a silver tie. His Gatsbyesque appearance notwithstanding, Dr. Richard Dripple was a noted anthropologist, a writer, and, of late, a diplomat for hire. His considerable academic credentials along with his native Kenyan birth and his recent scientific best-seller, *The Eighth Sin*—an analysis of man's abuse of his environment and the likely results—provided him with easy access to both international academic as well as diplomatic circles. His being white in a black sub-Saharan Africa made him an anomaly. Behind his back, people called him White Chocolate, something he smiled at. When a somewhat intoxicated diplomat referred to him as such to his face at a state function, Dr. Richard Dripple had responded graciously. When the man persisted in a loud, obnoxious manner, Dripple responded, "Sir, you need more milk to go with your vodka."

"Why? Why do I need milk?" he asked.

"It's the only thing to go with an Oreo, sir."

This pejorative reference to a black man who dressed and acted like a white man caught the attention and excited the laughter of the two Americans nearby. The Africans in earshot ignored the comment, and the obnoxious Ugandan who had been pestering Dripple left him alone thereafter as he attempted to find out why he should like milk. He didn't get it.

Dripple wasn't so much witty as he was a man with an exceptional memory who drew parallels between his own life and those of noteworthy people who had come before him. On still another occasion, a young woman who resented Dr. Dripple's notoriety and his multiplicity of talents commented on the fact that Dripple was drunk, something she found most disgusting for a man of his international stature. In a Churchillian parody, he replied, "Yes, madam, I am indeed drunk, but you, madam, are ugly. Tomorrow when I awake, I will be sober."

Deft at laying verbal traps, Dripple had to be listened to and spoken to most carefully.

As the door opened to the U.S. ambassador's office, Dripple stood with a smile and extended his hand to James Mavor II, U.S. ambassador to Kenya.

"Dr. Dripple, it's always a delight. Come in, come in." They shook hands firmly. Mavor closed the door and sat in a chair behind his desk while Dripple sat immediately in front of it in a large, cushiony, and very comfortable chair. The desk between them was Mavor's way of saying, "I assume this is not a friendly social call but rather an official visit."

"Ambassador Mavor," began Dripple.

Mavor was right; Dripple referring to him as Ambassador instead of Jamie said that this call was strictly business.

Two minutes past the formalities of inquiring after each other's health and the welfare of their wives and children, James said, "Dick, this is not a social call."

"No, no, it's not. My government has asked me to broach a most delicate matter. As you know, Kenya considers its relationship with the United States most valuable. In many ways, we consider ourselves America's greatest ally in this part of the world. Many of our own citizens aspire to be nothing so much in life as American: in dress, in conduct, and even in terms of their democratic government. Truly, we treasure your good will and trust that you treasure ours."

"This is true; we do indeed treasure that relationship," responded Mavor.

Mavor paused as if to offer Dripple the opportunity to transition from statements of diplomatic civility and currency to those that represented the less sanguine aspects of life.

"We know that your war on terrorism has many fronts: some of them in Asia, some in your own country, and some in Africa. And as your ally in this part of the world, we trust that any attempt to fight against terrorists would nonetheless be respectful of international boundaries. If there were, for example, unsavory figures that my own government were pursuing in your country, we would certainly come to you and ask for your assistance and that of the FBI and perhaps even the CIA. We would not, however, presume to enter your country to pursue such figures ourselves."

Mavor knew where this meeting was headed but he remained silent.

Dripple paused for a full twenty seconds. He knew that Mavor's failure to fill in the gap was a statement in and of itself.

Dripple then rose from his chair, saying, "I will take no more of your time. Please be assured that we would work with you concerning any matter of international terrorism and trust that unilateralism on your part in this area of the world would be unnecessary."

Mavor also stood and reached across his desk to shake Dripple's hand. The coolness in Dripple's demeanor was not at all typical, and he sensed from that more than anything else that the Kenyan government was very upset with the United States. Dripple himself had dual citizenship, British and Kenyan. But on this occasion, his demeanor was that of a Kenyan who was personally as well as diplomatically offended at being left out in the cold by United States' activities in his own country. And if those actions were indeed taken and successful, how much more tarnished would the Kenyan nation's image be? It would come across to the rest of the world as yet another sub-Saharan government of incompetence and corruption which could not offer reasonable guarantees of safety to visiting foreigners. What did that say about the competency of its police and its military?

And if the United States' efforts, whatever they might be, were not successful, how much more emboldened would its own terrorists become? How much longer would the United States tolerate the Kenyan bureaucrats that blocked nearly every effort by the United States to follow the money trail of illegal diamond trafficking that led to the very heart of sub-Saharan Africa?

Upon Dripple's departure, Mavor called his secretary into his office and said, "Get me the secretary of defense."

Moments later, Mavor was on the phone to Phillip Kazarian.

"Mr. Secretary, I just had a short, crisp, and cool visit from Dr. Richard Dripple. We knew it was only a matter of time. They know about our operations."

CHAPTER 35
WEDDING GIFTS

A vast military wedding
Somewhere advanced one step.

—James Dickey, "Drinking from Helmets"

The lady is mine and I am hers and I will do with her as I
please.

—Chretien de Troyes, *Erec and Enide*

—*JOMO'S ENCAMPMENT*

AFTER WATCHING THE ENERGETIC BUT DELIBERATE ACTIVITIES IN THE
encampment all day long, Grant and the others were struck by the near
frenzy that began in the evening.

Jomo Raphael's village began to stir with alarm. Watching from the
heavy vegetation of the hill, Grant likewise felt the alarm and wondered
if someone had spotted him and his men. With his binoculars, he
surveyed the swirl of activity. Armed men moved rapidly throughout the
village, but none of them in the direction of Grant and his men. Instead,
hundreds of black and brown specs seemed to be pulled inexorably
toward an unseen force on the far side of the compound. Grant thought
they looked like iron filings being drawn toward a magnet.

After a half an hour of frenetic activity, the village seemed to regain
its composure. Then, without explanation, the black and brown specs

reversed their movement and many reentered the compound area waving their arms and shooting their guns off. Grant saw two men in the uniforms of the Kenyan military being pushed and dragged to a large, open area. A circle formed with the men in the middle, with several of Jomo's men standing at their backs.

A large man, resplendent in what appeared to be a white military uniform with a golden-handled sword at his side, walked toward the two men. As he approached them, one of the gunmen hit them in the backs with the butt of his rifle.

Even at a distance, Grant and his men could see that the man in the white uniform stood out in height as well as girth. His appearance was in sharp contrast to the T-shirts and camouflage uniforms mixed with celebratory pink and yellow shirts. They looked strangely festive despite their black and green military-style pants.

For several more minutes, Grant watched. Like a silent film, the plot unfolded with extravagant gestures and a pantomime of anger and disgust as the white uniformed man swept his arms up in grand gestures. His hands lifted to the sky as if in parody of some Old Testament prophet beseeching God to throw down a plague upon his enemies. The man wagged his index finger on his left hand and then his right at the now kneeling men. Then the soldiers raised their eyes to the towering figure and threw up their hands in a gesture of prayer mixed with a desperate cry for mercy.

The men were led away. The white-clad figure pulled out his sword and raised it so that it glinted in the sun. Simultaneously, a cheer erupted from the assembled multitude, which could be detected even at a distance. The white figure then turned and walked away. The crowd parted.

Grant put down his binoculars and turned to the others, who put down their eye pieces as well.

"I'm not sure what we just witnessed, but I do know that those men kneeling were wearing Kenyan military uniforms."

"Maybe they're here to help us," joked Thomas.

Grant looked back toward the compound and offered, "I think we may have to help them."

"That's not our mission," replied the Norwegian.

Grant and the others were silent. The sun was setting, but the village was being lit with torches that formed a pathway from the largest tent in the compound to the enclosed circle, in which a kind of makeshift platform was being assembled.

Then all was silent. The darkness descended. The villagers formed a large circle and began to sing a kind of hymn. Grant and the others could not make out the exact words, but the melody sounded vaguely familiar.

Finally, someone entered the circle with a megaphone. Now they could hear even at a distance.

"Amazing Grace, how great thou art ..."

Thomas smiled and hummed along and said, "I thought Jomo was Catholic. It's a Protestant hymn."

After about a minute, Giles said, "What are we waiting for?"

"Opportunity," said Grant. "And this doesn't appear to be it. Everyone's up and about. We need their cooperation. Too bad they don't seem to know that."

Then one torch at the far end of the lit path was raised up and down three times, and the assemblage began clapping, singing, and swaying. The man with the megaphone stood upon the platform and said, "Jomo, man of God, Jomo, man of God." He said it over and over again.

Finally, a dark-robed figure stepped onto the makeshift platform. He stood with stooped shoulders and seemed frail. At his side stood a pale figure in camouflage. Both were white. The black-robed figure stepped down and stood in front of the platform and looked out toward the row of lit torches.

At this point, the whole village seemed to be swaying, undulating, and vibrating. At the far end of the pathway, one man with yet another torch in hand began to move slowly toward the great circle. Behind him, a large white-clad figure emerged from the shadows.

As he walked, the villagers continued to sing and applaud. He was followed by what appeared to be a bevy of colorfully dressed women as well as several men with rifles who walked with a cadence appropriate to the solemnity of the "Streets of Laredo."

As they verged upon entering the great circle, about them appeared little figures who threw flowers in the path of the approaching entourage. The white-clad figure followed the path of the flowers toward the platform. In a short while, he stood before it while the torchbearer placed his fire stick in a kind of holder on the platform. Immediately, eight other torchbearers came forth and lit the entire area around the black-robed figure. The white-clad figure then stood before it and looked at the white man who then stepped to his side. The man turned with military precision and walked toward an assemblage of women who stood in a clump on the side opposite from where the white-clad Jomo had just entered.

As he approached the clump of women, the singing intensified and several women began to pull from their midst the most reluctant of brides. They brought her toward Crane, who sympathetically offered her the kindest smile he could muster and his arm. Realizing that further resistance was futile, she stood erect, took his arm, and turned stoically toward her fate, consoling herself with the old woman's words: "He will not harm you." With the tempo of a gallows processional, she and Crane stepped toward the makeshift altar on which Father Matteo Ricci stood before the towering figure of Jomo Raphael.

In the distance, Grant and his men watched the spectacle unfolding, realizing that here was the woman they were sent to rescue, the man who led the American Special Forces team, and the man they were to kill. They were in one place in front of over a thousand people.

Perhaps the others, thought Grant, *are still alive somewhere in the military-style tents or in one of the traditional huts.*

Gazing upon the spectacle, Grant asked himself one question: *How can I leave no trace when the entire village is before us, encircling those we are to rescue?* His reverie was short-lived.

Two men were brought forth and forced to kneel at a short distance from the center of the circle: the two Kenyan soldiers. The bride-to-be now stood next to her future husband, her escort having stepped to the side after bringing her to her lord and master. She trembled.

She and Jomo stood before Father Ricci.

Ricci declaimed, "Dearly beloved, we are assembled here this evening…" He enveloped both the bride and the groom with a trembling voice of one who felt as if the ceremony were the final instrument of his affliction. He felt completely defrocked. Not even the order of Melchisadek could save him. He was a sham.

The ceremony was fleeting, and through it all, Jomo smiled upon his bride with the magnanimity of one who loved the world, and this piece of the world in particular.

When Ricci came to that part of the ceremony that asks, "Do you, Jomo, take this woman ..." Jomo pronounced, "Yes, of course; that is why we are all here."

Moments later, Melissa whispered, "Yes," almost passing out as she did so.

Then Jomo turned not to face his bride but to the two kneeling figures. He raised his right hand to signify that everyone must be silent.

"This is a great day. A great day requires a great sacrifice. And like the great prophet Abraham who sacrificed the lamb to God, I today offer to him the most precious of all gifts: human life. These were delivered to me this day as a special gift so that I might honor God. This sacrifice to God will bless this marriage. It is a great gift for a great day. It will please God to see evil brought to his righteous punishment!"

The crowd cheered and began to move in closer. As it did so, the two Kenyans began to cry.

However, Jomo's last words were all that was needed to signal their end. Two men wielding machetes walked up behind them and swiftly cut off their heads, which they held up before the multitude. The bride turned away as did the American soldier. Father Ricci stood silently with his head down, uttering a prayer on behalf of the slaughtered men as well as for himself. Jomo smiled with satisfaction while the crowd took up the chant of "Jomo, Jomo, Jomo."

Jomo then held up his hands to signal for silence.

"Long ago, God blessed Abraham. In return, Abraham was going to sacrifice his son to God. Then an angel came down from heaven and saved his son. Today, like Abraham, I wished to show my gratitude to God for his blessing me and making me the leader of you, my people. Like Abraham, I too was prepared to make a sacrifice, a sacrifice of the intruders. God did not stop my hand. I waited for his voice. I asked him to stop the blades of the machete if he wanted me to spare the lives of these men. He sent no angels. And so I sacrificed these men on this holy day of my wedding. Their blood will bless our wedding, our marriage."

Jomo then turned to his bride, who had a pained look on her face. Crane stood uncomfortably, gazing at the forlorn priest. Jomo smiled benignly and offered his arm to his new wife. As Jomo turned his back on the altar and began to walk away, she limped at his side, dreading thoughts of that night's consummation. She limped as if she were dragging her soul behind her. Still, she had no idea that the consummation was, like the ceremony of marriage itself, to be a public display.

Crane and Father Ricci looked at one another helplessly. The crowd again took up the chant of "Jomo, Jomo, Jomo."

Suddenly, Jomo held up his hands again. Everyone was stunned as the silence was broken by a *whomph, whomph, whomph*. Seconds later, machine gun fire raked the compound. Jomo ran toward his tent and his guns. The crowd of villagers scattered in all directions. The source of the gunfire lowered itself over the village: a Chinook helicopter with a rope dangling from its side. Immediately, Kenyan combat troops dropped to the ground, shooting in all directions as they landed. Twelve men in all hit the ground. At first, they shot at the crowd with impunity. Gradually, as the crowd recovered from the shock of the unexpected intrusion, they attacked. The outnumbered and outgunned troopers began to fall in a hail of rifle fire and RPGs. The helicopter continued to fire, but then the gunship began to falter as rifle fire pierced the canopy. The pilot was seen crumbling over the controls.

Taking advantage of what might have looked to an uninformed observer like a well-executed diversion, Grant and company moved out in the darkness. Within minutes, they were on the periphery of the camp, trying desperately to stay concealed. Grant spoke in a voice that could hardly be heard amidst the gunfire and screaming of Jomo's villagers, "Our job is to save the lives of the Americans. We go for Jomo's tent and for the one hut in the woman's compound. Kill anyone who opposes you. Stay out of sight of that chopper. Now, ignite and fight."

With that, all four men simultaneously ignited their rocket packs and moved straight up above the camp. At about one hundred feet elevation, Grant and the Norwegian headed toward Jomo's tent, staying to the periphery and out of the line of fire between the chopper and Jomo's people. The Brit and Thomas headed toward the women's compound.

As they flew, the chopper suddenly turned in their direction. The pilot, though badly wounded, attempted to lift off and out of harm's way. As he turned the chopper, he could see something dark moving against the night sky. He could not make it out. Blinking several times, he wondered if the solid black shapes against the inky blue night sky were demons coming for his soul. In a panic, he turned the chopper around again and headed out as fast as he could, abandoning his men on the ground. But as he scurried out, yet another helicopter approached, whirling directly into his path of retreat.

Confused by the chaos on the ground and by his own excruciating wounds as well as his inability to make radio contact with his counterpart in the other chopper, who was coming directly at him, he banked right as yet more ground fire riddled the bottom of the craft.

The activity on the ground was everything Grant and his men did not want. Jomo's men were spread all over and alert. As he and the Norwegian approached Jomo's tent, four pairs of eyes were already looking skyward at the choppers. They could not help but notice the black shadows above them. They raised their guns to fire when two machine guns suddenly fired upon them like the wrath of Jehovah from on high or some demon indeed scouring the earth for victims. All four men dropped to the earth as their torsos momentarily jerked with bullet holes that relieved them of breath and ripped bloody seams from their chests to their groins. As they hit the earth, their blood flowed, turning the dust into gruesome muck.

Grant and the Norwegian dropped down and hovered above the tent and then, with the slice of razor-sharp knives, they cut directly through and dropped into a dimly lit room, Jomo's library. In the corner, sitting dazed and confused in her wedding garb, was the American girl.

The hissing sound of the rocket packs was terrifying, and she whimpered in fear at the black-faced men who put their fingers to their lips to signify silence. As Grant dropped to the ground, she looked at him in terror and disbelief. As he reached out to touch her arm reassuringly, he whispered, "We're here to get you out. Don't be afraid."

Suddenly, she put her hands to her ears and began to scream hysterically. Even amidst the gunfire, her screams rose above the compound. An old woman in the next room rushed in.

"No, no," she yelled. "Don't hurt her. Don't hurt her."

Grant brought his gun up as did the Norwegian. The old woman walked right up to them, fearlessly. Not knowing who they were, she attempted to protect the girl by uttering words that would have forced any of the villagers to give her a wide berth.

"I am Jomo's mother, and I say you will not harm her."

Grant reacted by smacking her hard alongside the head, forcing her to crumble to the floor. Millinson was still screaming hysterically and now wailing as well. Grant smacked her hard across the face to shut her up. She then went limp as she fell unconscious to the floor. Her mind had shut down in terror even before she felt the impact of Grant's hand.

Grant got on his headset, which was built into his helmet.

"Thomas, Thomas, we have the girl. We have the girl. Where are you?"

"We're at the women's compound. Nothing. It's empty."

"Get out," responded Grant

Before Grant could finish his statement, two more figures rushed in, an old priest and a U.S. soldier in camouflage. Neither was armed.

Immediately Grant and the Norwegian lowered their rifles, and Grant greeted Crane by rank.

"Major, come with us." The priest stopped in his tracks.

"Where are the others?" asked Grant.

"Who?" asked the priest before Crane could reply.

"CINC crew?"

"Dead," responded the major.

"And your men?"

"Dead, they're all dead. It's just me and the girl."

"Who's the man in black?"

"A priest. He may want to come with us."

Before they could act, Jomo reappeared behind Crane and Ricci in camouflage and holding two men by the scruff of the neck. It was two of the CINC team, emaciated and earless. Two other gunmen were right behind him. The major was stunned and looked again at Ricci.

"I thought you said, 'dead,'" uttered Crane. Ricci merely cried and held up his arms as if to surrender to an unseen foe.

"Welcome, my friends. Look what I have brought you. I ask for a van and I get helicopters instead. These two belong to you. Of course, you cannot have them."

Before he could say another word, four more of his gunmen entered. Then more shots. Jomo turned to see his men falling. Thomas entered from the doorway as Grant grabbed the reawakening Melissa Millinson. Still holding the two figures in front of him, Jomo slipped into the next room. In the darkness, he threw aside his hostages.

No one fired for fear of killing these two men. Grant and his men ran out the doorway of the tent and right into six or seven more of Jomo's men. They stopped to consider the situation when they heard Jomo's voice.

"Kill them."

Thomas lobbed a grenade in their direction. Jomo's men scattered even as they fired their weapons. Two fell dead from the explosion. Grant's men dropped to the ground, pulling Crane, Ricci, and the girl with them. All four opened fire. Within seconds, Jomo's men were likewise on the ground dead or wounded. The firing had others racing in their direction. But before they could close with Grant and company, the chopper returned and dropped down right in the middle of the compound's open area.

Grant thought that the pilot was crazy or very, very brave. But the chopper hit the ground hard and before most of the men could dismount, an enfilade of fire had disabled the tail rotor, forcing the chopper to stay grounded. Men ran from the chopper, attempting to get to cover. Again, they were cut down. The firing had so completely encircled them that several of Jomo's men fell from their own comrades' fire.

Grant gave the order to go back inside and grab the two hostages who lay on the ground where Jomo had cast them. They were dazed, confused, disoriented, of little help in their rescue, and entirely naked. The priest was still with them, an unexpected burden.

Grant looked above him and saw the first chopper returning in some poor measure of support for the beleaguered Kenyans. The pilot, who was still hurt badly, seemed to have recovered his nerve. Perhaps thinking that the avalanche of gunfire at Jomo's tent was incited by his fellow Kenyans' attempt to defend themselves, he hovered directly above them. He fired his guns in several spurts of lead toward the advancing rebels.

Grant realized that the rocket packs' limited thrust would prohibit their moving out of the area as planned. The entire strategy was predicated on surprise and stealth. All of that was now gone.

But Grant told Thomas to hold their positions and to move everyone back toward several other tents on the periphery of the compound, which was even then the subject of a rear and flanking movement led by Jomo himself.

Grant said to Thomas, "Keep them occupied and cover me; I'm going up."

Before Thomas could protest, Grant hit his ignition and zoomed right up to the now twice shocked pilot, who looked at him in wide-eyed disbelief. He attempted to veer the chopper away when Grant veered with him and right into the side opening of the platform. Realizing now the futility of "leave no trace," he pulled his Glock and pointed it at the pilot's head. He then spoke English to him with a Russian accent in one final attempt to misdirect the pilot's perception that his adventure somehow or another involved the Americans.

"You down. You down. Take to my friends or you die." He felt silly at his attempt at deceit and winced at the effort.

The Kenyan pilot, still in excruciating pain and feeling light-headed from loss of blood, lowered the chopper compliantly as he continued to fire at Jomo's men.

The chopper hit the ground. Thomas and the others threw several more grenades. They all climbed or were pushed aboard when gunfire started coming from behind them. Jomo and a handful of his men were at their rear. As quickly as the chopper had descended, it now spun straight up.

In the chopper itself, the pilot, despite a momentary glimpse of courage, was fading. His vision was blurred. The loss of blood was causing him to shake. Without ceremony, Grant pulled the young man from his seat and pushed Thomas into it.

"It's a Chinook. Fly it."

He had lost his Russian accent, but the pilot was losing consciousness too quickly to notice. "Get us back to our first planned stop."

Thomas, whose flying experience was limited, nonetheless handled the chopper with aplomb and used his own GPS to take all of them in the direction of their pack of rockets left behind. As they approached the first stop point, they hovered about one hundred fifty feet above it and Chisolm and the Norwegian launched over the side to retrieve the packs. They lifted them back into the chopper. For the next several miles, they repeated the process.

At first, Grant entertained the idea of flying the entire way to their rendezvous point with the helicopter and then relying on their hunting guides to get them inconspicuously out of the country.

However, the fuel supply was rapidly declining. The chopper's tanks had suffered significant damage. Despite their best attempts, they could not make it past the last stop to pick up the remaining rocket packs. Thomas set the chopper down in a clearing as the blades began to stall and stutter. He was running the bird on fumes. The blades stopped of their own accord.

Grant immediately jumped, the others following in quick succession. Thomas examined the pilot. There was no pulse. Thomas then attempted to rouse the others. The girl was groggy but responsive. Ricci had remained calm and alert, as had the major. The other two men, members of the CINC crew, had looked more dead than alive when they were first thrust before them. They too were now quiet and completely unresponsive.

Ricci volunteered, "Jomo would not let you take them. They were poisoned before they were shown to you."

Thomas confirmed. "Dead," was all he said.

They all knelt down and pulled up their GPS wrist devices but then stopped suddenly at a sound in the bushes a ways off. They raised their rifles and pointed them in the direction of the sound. It stopped. Then they heard, "Don't shoot. Don't shoot. We're American. We're American!"

"Come out," ordered Grant. Seconds later, two disheveled but coherent men in uniform stumbled forward.

"We're American," one of them repeated.

"Shit if they ain't," replied Crane. He stood up and said, "These are my men."

Grant's men lowered their rifles. Then Crane said to the two newcomers, "It's me, Major Crane."

"Oh my God," replied the other.

"Sgt. Jones, obviously you've survived the snake bite."

"Yes, sir, but not without some long-term effects I'm afraid. But hell, right now, I couldn't be happier to see you, sir."

"Me, too, sir," said Sgt. Maxwell Maldoon.

"But where are the others, sir?" asked Jones.

"They're dead, boys."

Stunned, they were silent. Then Maldoon said, "Sir, we didn't know if we should try to get back to Nairobi or not. We were afraid that we had been left behind. But we didn't want the mission revealed. We thought the Kenyans …" He stopped, "Sir, who're these people?"

"I'll explain later," replied the major. "For now, we have to get out of here."

Grant looked at the two dead men and said, "We can't take them with us. Too much weight. A quick burial is all we can spare. We have to move on. Major, give me some light; hold this up."

He held a flashlight pointed toward the ground, and Grant and the others began to dig a shallow grave. Within minutes, they had fashioned a foot-deep hole. They placed the two men side by side and covered it over with sand and dirt and then some brush.

Ricci looked at the site and muttered a prayer, which no one heard save God and himself. Grant mentally noted the GPS calculated position for a possible recovery of the bodies on another day.

Then Thomas held up a flexible keypad and equally flexible computer screen, which he laid on the ground. He connected with a special satellite through an encrypted site, revealing their exact location to some unseen computer in an undisclosed location. There, only one person knew the password to the coded site. Within a minute, the screen flickered and the text message appeared.

"Proceed to rendezvous C. Be there in eight hours. KK."

Grant did not know who KK was but he did not need to. He then called his crew over to one side and spoke in a low voice.

"Our job is to rescue the hostages while at the same time not revealing the technology we've used to do it. We have eight hours to cross forty miles of rugged terrain. We can only do that with rocket packs. The civilians will have to be drugged." They all agreed, and Thomas then reached into his sleeved and cushioned arm pack. With their backs to Ricci and the others, he took out a disposable syringe, as did the Brit; each extracted a dark liquid from a small vial. Nonchalantly, they walked back to the others. Ricci hardly noticed as Thomas and the Giles walked around behind them and Grant began to speak.

"We want to leave this area behind. The sooner the better."

Ricci and the Millinson collapsed and would have hit the ground, but Thomas and the Brit had anticipated their fall and caught them in their arms as the syringes pricked their backs.

Grant looked squarely at Crane, soldier to soldier. "You will be privy to top secret technology, which you may not reveal to anyone at anytime. UCMJ (Uniform Code of Military Justice) applies. You are now a member of the lightest cavalry that the world has ever seen. Help us upload our horses. Inform your men."

Without asking questions, the two sergeants and the major walked over to the silent helicopter and began to pull out the rocket packs.

Within thirty minutes, all of them had been given a crash course in how to maneuver with the devices strapped to their backs. Grant and Thomas would follow up the rear and would each take on one of the sleeping hostages. Ricci was tethered to Grant's front side, while Millinson was similarly tethered to Thomas. The added weight would curtail their range and speed. The others carried another rocket pack, which they would employ as soon as Grant and Thomas ran out of fuel. Within several more minutes, each had been given geocoordinates and UTM measurements that constantly recalibrated when they swerved off course.

The packs in total lasted them long enough to get over the most rugged terrain and into low bush country. The flight time had given them enough distance between themselves and any of Jomo's men that they could make it to rendezvous C with little prospect of interference. As they stopped with Grant and Thomas's first set of tanks depleted, they dug a shallow hole into which they placed the packs and set an automatic timing device that caused a small explosion to detonate, thereby destroying the chip boards as well as the tanks themselves. As they finally emptied the last of their tanks, they opened up the tank side holes and then threw them into a river by which they had stopped. The tanks filled with water and sank. A minute later, the tanks were detonated. A small blast of white water and spray emerged from the river as the packs were destroyed.

Over the next four hours, the physical fitness of Grant's men was put to the test. They all took turns carrying Ricci and Millinson. The two sergeants were too weak from malnutrition and the major from his wounds to do anything more than carry themselves.

Dawn broke. The blinding sun revealed a military-style Hummer partially concealed in the brush, along with an attached trailer. On its side it said "Big Game Outfitters, the Pride of Africa." Standing alongside the vehicle were two smiling and surly characters, Jeremy McMahon and Hunter Flloyd, nickname Sparky.

"Hello, gentlemen," said Hunter as they approached. Seeing their drivers, the pace of all the men quickened, even that of the Brit and Norwegian, who were then carrying Ricci and the girl. As Crane limped into their camp, Jeremy said, "Aren't you guys some beauts? You look like something one of our big cats might have dragged in. And is this sleeping beauty? She seems mighty oblivious. Maybe someone should kiss her."

"Shut up, Sparky. They're ours now for safekeeping. Help them."

Within two minutes, everyone was in the trailer, covered with tarps, and provided with cool beverages of lemonade or an energy drink.

Ricci and Millinson had started to come around, but Grant had spiked their lemonade with knockout drops and they were soon again fast asleep.

They proceeded over rugged dirt roads until they approached the outskirts of a village of thirty or so huts. Nearby was the big game lodge of the Pride of Africa, also known as the Lions' Den. When they all got out of their vehicles, Grant asked, "Where now?"

"Into the house. I've given the boys the day off. No one else is around. Sparky will drive you back to Nairobi after you change. Your hunting trip with us, you'll say, wasn't all that successful. The woman and the priest stay with us until they come to. We'll tell them how they were found lying face down in the desert. We came upon them while scouting for a hunting party. They seem so drugged up, they'll never know what's true or what isn't. On the way back, you'll be leaving your equipment at the U.S. Embassy. Sparky will handle everything."

Within an hour, Sparky and Thomas were seated in the front of the Hummer while Grant, the major, and the two sergeants all slept in back. Jomo's camp now seemed like a distant memory.

CHAPTER 36

THE SCOLDING AND
THE BLESSING

*Without an understanding of the nature of the universe, a
man cannot know where he is; without an understanding of its
purpose, he cannot know what he is.*

—Marcus Aurelius, *Meditations*

—MACARTHUR'S ESTATE

"THE GREAT DESIGNERS IN LIFE ARE THOSE WHO REALIZE THAT
everything must have a purpose and every purpose must have a reason.
You, sir, have not yet realized your own. But I trust that you will."

The sternness of MacArthur's words was surprising. Grant had
expected congratulations. Instead, he was getting a scolding during a
debriefing that was sharp, disconcerting, and narrow in its focus. Twice
MacArthur had used the expression "a new age." Twice he had followed
it up with a remark about Grant's failure "to leave no trace."

"Evidence of your work is too prominently displayed. Better if you
had rescued the hostages without firing a shot. The Kenyans found out
about things through their own devious means. Their unexpected and
unwelcome intervention represents a slipup of sorts that we will be hard
pressed to explain to ourselves or to them. Deniability is crucial in our
work. However, I want to complement you and Thomas and the others
for quick thinking. Drugging Ricci and the girl was appropriate. Our
sources tell us that she is still disoriented but supposedly telling her
CINC bosses about a rescue operation in which she flew through the
skies. Ricci has disappeared into the nether regions of the Jesuit order to

escape Jomo and his henchmen. At this point, the girl is thought to have lost her mind, the effects of the trauma she endured and all that.

"What's particularly interesting though is that, for once, Jomo was not tipped off about a raid perpetrated by the Kenyans. Every significant move against him in the past has been thwarted, compromised, by leaks within its own government."

MacArthur paused. "But you, I believe, will bring him down. And when you do, it will be a red night. He will not go easily. But for the first time, we may actually be on the verge of connecting him to the illicit diamond trade that shores up the empire of one none-too-likeable Dutchman who tarnishes the Highlands."

Finally, Grant had an opportunity to ask a question. "What was the point of providing us with weaponry and super technology if we were not to use it?" There was an edge in Grant's voice that MacArthur had not heard before. His frustration was coming through.

"Grant, you were indeed to use the technology and the weaponry while doing your best to separate the bodies you leave behind from yourself. You are a very good soldier. You need to be better. Your work is not yet done. Oz will soon contact you."

"I have another question. Why am I the only one to whom you are now speaking? What about Thomas and the others? Don't they deserve to know of your displeasure with the results?"

"I want this to be clear to everyone. You are in charge. Now I think you have some archaeological work to do. My men have secured the facility. It is for you some well-deserved leisure. I also believe that you have some friends who would like to explore the facility with you. Don't worry. There should be no repeats of your previous surprises. But I'd still like to know what else you discover—especially about the diamonds. If you find more, you'll let me know. This could be important."

"Another thing," said Grant. "Your men?"

"I alone among all the earls of the British Isles may maintain a private army. I do so. All my men are handpicked and devoted. It is a brotherhood of warriors. They are warriors who can keep a secret, which makes them doubly valuable. Even the queen recognizes that."

For a moment, Grant thought that MacArthur may have been letting on that there were unseen forces following and authorizing his movements not only in America, but even in the deepest regions of British royalty.

So much, he thought, *for the divesture of the royal family's real power and its having supposedly been surrendered to Parliament.*

As Grant stood to leave, MacArthur smiled and said, "I have a message from Dennis. He wanted me to give it to you personally." He handed Grant a small envelope. A puzzled look crossed Grant's face as he silently read the note inside. It said, "You are the sword and have therefore not fallen upon it. You are therefore David and not Saul. You will dance before God while your enemies shall crawl before the devil. Dennis."

CHAPTER 37

THE PATH LESS TRAVELLED

When his heart had taken its fill of wondering, he entered the great cave.

—Homer, *The Odyssey*

—*THE CAVE*

BLANCHE SAT BACK IN THE LIGHTWEIGHT FOLDABLE CANVAS CHAIR she had brought with her from Glasgow. She had drawn a map of the interior of the first two rooms while Rex Carruthers, Margaret, and her husband, Mermac, took pictures of the entire cavern. However, they had thus far explored only the left prong of what appeared to be a three-pronged pathway leading from the entrance to several possibilities.

On this occasion, Blanche had virtually prostrated herself in thankfulness before Rex Carruthers, Margaret, and Mermac. She knew that Regis MacArthur had actually secured the area to make their work possible. But keeping it all a secret for a prolonged period of time would prove more and more difficult. The hillside was visible from the Heather Inn for anyone with binoculars, and even MacArthur's most trusted guards might inadvertently reveal something about the site. Moreover, someone else already knew quite well of this location, and that someone would go to great lengths to gain access to it again without the intrusive presence of some archaeologists.

But that day, Blanche was asimmer with delight. That day, she and the others were to begin in earnest the exploration of at least one of the other two prongs.

271

"Rex, how shall we proceed? I've my video camera, and we should record the actual moments of discovery."

"I'm in agreement. But let's all decide."

"I agree. Who knows what we may find here—the diamonds, the evil intruder who tried to kill us all, a Nazi flag, and a mystery flow of water. What's not to marvel at? What could be next? The tomb of some Saxon king? Maybe even Tut's younger brother?" added Margaret.

"I wish the boys could be here," remarked Mermac, "But school's also important, and we wanted to make certain things were really safe this time."

"Yes, I'm glad to have our guards outside even if they don't look like real guards in their walking togs and backpacks."

"Well, shall we?" asked Blanche.

They stepped through the darkness, lit with their flashlights, into a cylindrical hole that was at least seven feet in diameter. Surprisingly, the floor of the cylinder was smooth and had obviously been fashioned by hand, perhaps over a period of hundreds of years, maybe even thousands.

Rex, Margaret, and then Blanche and Mermac stepped carefully and with almost quivering anticipation into the darkness. Occasionally, they braced themselves against one of the walls. The sound of their footsteps ricocheted off the walls—not enough to create echoes but enough to give each sound a distinction and precision, unlike in the greater world outside. In the darkness and the utter quiet, even one's breath seemed measured and precise. The sound of clothing rustling against other fibers was now noticed. Even a drip of sweat seemed to create a slight sound.

After several minutes of slow progress, the cavern narrowed and the air grew slightly stale. Then Rex stopped. The others did the same, Margaret almost bumping into him. He then kicked several small stones directly in front of him. They disappeared into silence instead of hitting against the rock on which they had been walking. Then there was a slight sound way below—rocks falling on rocks. They shined the flashlights directly in front, revealing a solid rock wall fifty feet ahead and a deep chasm at their feet. They were at a dead end.

Rex stepped to the very edge of the chasm and flashed his light to the bottom of a seventy-foot drop. There, he could discern the grayish color of the rock as well as an indiscriminate shape seemingly growing out from the chasm floor. But the light was too dissipated to make out details. Each of the others in turn cast their luminescence across to the other side and down to the bottom of a depravity whose full purpose could not be fathomed. Only an eventual descent into the pit with appropriate equipment of ropes and pulleys would enable them to understand the nature of this manmade tunnel leading into this mystery drop off.

CHAPTER 38

ABDUCTION

He makes no friend who never made a foe.

—Lord Tennyson, "Lancelot and Elaine"

—THE HEATHER INN

LATE IN THE AFTERNOON, BLANCHE ARRIVED BACK AT THE INN WITH the others. After a leisurely but exciting meal in which they discussed the potential of their find, they agreed that they would go back to the site the next day. Then on the weekend, one of them would return to Glasgow to get the equipment necessary for the descent into the chasm of the second prong.

But after the others had turned in, she remained in the lobby, continuing to study her notes, particularly those on the significance of the glyphs that marked the walls in the left prong chamber. As she did so, four men walked to the front desk and asked the innkeeper for a couple of rooms. Instead of going to bed upon getting the keys to their rooms, two of the men lingered at the bar where they ordered beers that they did not drink. Both men were broad-shouldered, dark-complexioned, bearded, and dressed in sweats and running shoes.

The other two sat themselves in easy chairs in the lobby directly opposite Blanche. These two men were smaller in stature, equally dark, clean-shaven, and dressed in dark suits with white, open-collared dress shirts. They each fumbled through an array of travel brochures concerning the sites of Scotland and England. Then they eyed each other behind a couple of magazines and got up, one of them smiling at Blanche as he walked by. Despite the brevity of the encounter, Blanche felt uneasy. Still, there was nothing to do but finish the examination of her notes. She then left the lobby for her room, where she received a call from Grant.

Although happy at his call after several weeks of silence, she seemed more relieved to know that her protector might once again be at hand rather than merely a companion.

When Grant arrived at the inn in the morning, he was relieved to see Blanche's car parked outside. Once inside the inn, which was still quiet with only an occasional sound from the kitchen where activities were just beginning, he sat himself down in the lobby in the very same chair in which Blanche had sat the evening before. He pulled out a packet of flash cards from a vest pocket of his motorcycle togs and reviewed Russian vocabulary. He enjoyed the learning and relaxed from the cycle ride through the distraction language studies provided. He waited for the others to awaken for breakfast and another day of exploring.

An hour later, Rex Carruthers walked into the lobby in jeans and a long-sleeved shirt with several zippered pockets. Grant looked up at his approach.

"Well, finally," said Grant, "someone gets up to do the work."

"Ah, Grant, we didn't know you were back from wherever. It's great to see you."

They shook hands and walked into the dining area, where they seated themselves at the table. The innkeeper walked in, smiling, having gotten over the strange behavior of these same guests from several weeks earlier. They had each ordered a traditional English breakfast of eggs, ham, and fried tomatoes when Margaret and Mermac walked in. On seeing Grant, Margaret immediately gave a look of mock shock and threw her arms around him. "What a surprise. We didn't know you were back. Where have you been?"

Grant ignored the question as she kissed him on the cheek. Mermac then reached out to shake his hand, saying, "When did you get in?"

"Just a little while ago. I didn't want to wake anyone."

Rex added, "Grant is an early, early riser."

"Well, I was hoping to see Blanche. She must be sleeping in. I talked with her late last night. I told her I'd be here early."

"If I were you, I'd go wake her. She's in room 12," said Margaret.

Moments later, Grant returned.

"I knocked at her door, but there was no answer. I looked inside; the door was unlocked, but she wasn't there. Did she go out early?"

"Excuse me," interrupted the innkeeper. "Here's your breakfast." He laid down the meal along with some coffee.

Rex looked up.

"Did our colleague, Blanche DeNegris, say anything about going out particularly early this morning?"

"No, no, not at all. I assume she's still in her room. I think she was up late."

Blanche's unease of the night before began to press down on Grant with alarm. He got up and walked to the window looking out toward Ben Nevis.

"She couldn't have gone far without her car," added Grant.

Then he asked the innkeeper, who was taking Mermac's order, "Was there anyone else who checked in last night?"

"Last night, only one group of four gentlemen. They arrived late." Then he glanced out the window toward the parking spaced and added, "They must have left early. Their car is gone. Quite a nice one, too. A Mercedes. I saw it last night when I took Gunnard, our dog, out for a walk. Well, they paid in advance so how can I complain?"

"What did they look like?"

The innkeeper paused and said, "Which one?"

When he had given a description of each, Grant got up and walked out to the lobby and got on his cell phone. Alarm bells were ringing in his head. Rex and the others looked on in silence. They agreed to go to the mountain in search of her, still hoping she had simply gotten an early start on the day's digs. It seemed in keeping with her excitement over the project. Grant called her cell phone. There was no answer. Still, she might be inside the mountain. But a feeling of foreboding enveloped him—something confirmed a short time later when he received a call from Oz.

"Grant, we've been in touch with Dennis. They've contacted him about Blanche. They've got her. Meet me at the Welsley Inn. We need to talk."

Later, after Grant indicated that he had to leave but that he couldn't explain more, the others went off to the mountain while Grant got on his bike and burned rubber on his way to Welsley Inn, only about eight miles down the road. He saw Oz waiting for him in the parking area.

"Grant, we don't know where she is but know with whom. Dennis received a call early this morning, reminding him of what had happened to Colonel Holloway. They want the package in return for her. Do you have it?"

"I do, but not on me."

"I've asked you this before: what's in it?"

"Nothing I can make sense of."

"But they think there's something there. They may also be the same people who you said followed you earlier on your first trip north. Whatever the case may be, they want it and seem to think it has some link to something very important. Dennis listened to their accents. Arabs. Tell me, Grant, is the package worth anything or might it all be a red herring? Because if it's not worth anything, we can probably make the trade."

"What does Dennis want done?"

"Everything possible. But he's afraid that turning over the package may backfire. He says that if they see the actual contents of the package, they will only feel as if they've been tricked. But it may also be, as I mentioned before, a kind of red herring in all of this."

"How do we get her back?" asked Grant.

"We'll have to work below the radar to find the car and then wait to hear from Dennis."

*   *   *   *   *

Unfortunately, Blanche had been conscious during her entire ordeal. When Grant had called the evening before, she was sitting on the edge of her bed, excited about the dig and tired from working in the dark and cool atmosphere of the mountain, sketching and trying to make sense of the glyphs upon the walls. Still fully clothed, she was debating whether or not to take a shower. After she hung up, she turned off her cell phone as she customarily did when she wanted no further calls. It was a habit she practiced unthinkingly. She then put the phone into her multi-pocketed fisherman's vest that she wore when digging. While she debated whether or not to take that shower, she drifted off to sleep on the bed. Lights on, covers torn back, and shoes still on. She curled up thinking about tomorrow.

When she awoke, it was to a large hand cupped tightly over her mouth. Something sticky and binding was pressed down beneath it to prevent her scream. Someone then put tape over her eyes so she couldn't see. Then another binding was wound around her mouth, forcing it shut even more tightly. At first she could barely breathe. Screaming was out of the question.

Then the two men in athletic gear lifted her while a man in a suit wrapped duct tape around her wrists and ankles. She could squirm but not run. Within a minute, they had vacated the premises and pressed her into the trunk of their car and were off. They eventually headed south on the A-1, careful to observe the speed limit. Several hours later, they were in a suburb of London.

While Dennis waited in London for more word, MacArthur used his back channels contacts to track down the four vaguely described Middle-Eastern-looking men. At every gas station from Scotland to London, MacArthur's men checked to see if anyone matching the description of the four men had stopped there. Every gas station was dry until one of the MacArthur's men arrived at a serving station outside Birmingham. They had been there. Yes, two had come in to buy some soft drinks and snacks.

Grant decided that in the absence of any clues, he would enlist Thomas, who was on a similarly long leash regarding military conventions. He asked him to meet him at the Union Jack. The location was sufficiently public that anyone wishing to make contact with him or Dennis would be able to find them.

On the way back, he stopped at RAF Mildenhall and, without fanfare, he asked if he could use the hobby shop facilities. He walked into the shop, still in his motorcycle gear and carrying a small box. The shop was empty except for one civilian employee, who seemed completely disinterested in what anyone might do. Grant opened the small box and took out three thin sheets of plastic the exact size of a credit card and put them down next to an electric rotating knife sharpener. He fastened one card in a small vice just next to the electric whetstone and turned it on. In about two minutes, he had honed one side of the plastic to a razor sharpness and then did the same to one of the adjoining edges. Then he took the card to the hole punch press and stuck the card in after setting it to a three-quarter-inch hole. He inserted his index finger into the hole and then slid the blade across a light cardboard container. Satisfied, he repeated the process with two other pieces of plastic. He then shoved them into his wallet, picked up his box, and walked out. He was now adroitly armed.

Late that evening, he sat in the lounge area of the Union Jack, waiting, hoping. Thomas called, "I'm on my way. I should be there in a bit. Had some explaining to do to some higher ups. Someone called and cleaned my slate for the entire week. I'm free and equipped for duty. Giles is already off to an undisclosed location to assist others in training. What about Tellef?"

"I hear he's off to hot spot number one."

"Well, it's up to us. See you."

An hour later, Thomas walked in dressed in jeans, and a dark blue Ban-Lon summer shirt along with a duffle bag full of clothing. As he and Grant sat in the lounge area talking quietly, Grant's phone rang. He looked at the number. Blanche was calling!

"God, help me. I need you. I'm locked in a room somewhere. It's padded and seems like someone's basement. It's completely dark. They didn't know I had the cell phone with me. Find me!"

"Where do you think you are? Stay on the line."

"I'm afraid they'll hear me or come back into the room."

"Stay on the line. We'll trace the call."

He pulled out his encoded cell phone. Within two rings, Oz answered.

While Grant attempted to reassure Blanche and to keep her on the line, Oz ordered his local contacts to trace the call. A van parked on the north side of London near the Finsbury Mosque, where it had been doing clandestine eavesdropping ever since September 11, acted on the number and spun the information through the link to a satellite and a mainframe computer. Another van near Waterloo Station picked up an encrypted relay and called Oz.

As they did so, Blanche, in a loud whisper, said, "My battery is low. My God, they're coming." The line went dead. As it did, Grant turned around.

"Mr. Grant. It is so good to see you."

Standing on the far side of the room near the entrance wall to the lounge area stood Ali. He was wearing a dark suit with a white open-collared dress shirt.

"Hello, Ali. Nice to see you." Grant's antennae went up. "Do you work here?"

"No, no, I'm here to see an old friend."

"Oh, I thought ..."

"Yes, I know, we dark-skinned people are always working for someone else," he responded facetiously.

Ali's smile vanished. "Mr. Grant, who is your friend?"

"Ali, do you know something I should know about?" he asked, ignoring Ali's question.

"Perhaps you would like to negotiate. Your options are few." Then in a move both arrogant and brazen, Ali made a boxing shuffle and gently pushed his right fist against Grant's midsection. Grant remained relaxed but his face darkened.

Grant responded, "You are not worthy of your namesake. What do you want?"

"The package and everything that's in it."

"What if I were to tell you that there is little to nothing of value in it?"

"That would be foolish. Certain others have already attempted to get it. They knew its value and now so do we. Bring it to me at the Marriott. The girl will be released when I have the package. I'll be waiting." He walked away and out into warm London air.

CHAPTER 39
UNINVITED VISITORS

Like all strangers, they divide by sex.

—Kingsley Amis, "A Bookshop Idyll"

As GRANT AND THOMAS PREPARED TO LEAVE THE UNION JACK, another unexpected visitor arrived. Pamela Credo entered the lobby in a svelte blue dress that hugged her womanly form. She paused to identify herself to the doorman, who asked if she were military or a guest of someone who was. Grant stopped abruptly. Thomas did the same, although only in concert with Grant. Pamela smiled at the doorman and said with a hauteur that Grant had never before seen in her, "Do I look military?"

"I don't know about that, miss, but the Union Jack is for military personnel and their guests. Simple enough."

"I'm here to see someone: Grant Chisolm."

"I'm here," responded Grant at hearing her utter his name.

She turned with her frozen smile and said, "Grant, oh, and a friend. I'm so glad to see you."

"I bet you are. Or at least that is more than I might have known from your last good-bye, if I can call it that."

Thomas felt distinctly uncomfortable at Grant's chilly response as though he had entered into a lover's squabble, something he very much wished to avoid.

The doorman, having observed his duties of screening for unwanted and unattended guests, momentarily looked away out of embarrassment but then looked back in voyeuristic pleasure.

281

"Why do I have the feeling that this is more than merely a friendly visit by someone who just happened to be in the neighborhood?"

"I'm on vacation. Doing some touring. Look, I'm sorry about the way I acted."

Grant then walked up next to her, took her by the elbow, and quietly but firmly escorted her over to a quiet corner of the foyer. "How did you know I was here?"

"I didn't, but you mentioned it to me once in conversation."

"No, I had mentioned staying at the Marriott, not here."

She blushed at her own predicament. "I'm here. Oh, I'm shy about this. Grant, I just had to see you again."

Grant remained aloof. She took his silence as an invitation to say more.

"Grant, can't we try again?"

Quietly, almost in a whisper, Grant asked, "Try what?"

"Please. Let's sit down. I need to talk." As she sat, he momentarily relented and did likewise.

"You still haven't told me how you knew I was here. I never mentioned this place."

She tensed and then relaxed. "I'm resourceful when I see a man who … Grant, I'm here because I'm in love with you."

Most men would have melted at a gesture of affection from such a beautiful woman, but Grant trusted his gut, and her presence on this day so immediately after Ali's visit struck him as too coincidental not to be above suspicion.

Instead of responding, and against his usually gentlemanly impulses, he stood up abruptly and said, "I've things to do. I've got to go."

Pamela was not so accustomed to such treatment from men. She remained seated, looking up at Grant as if doing so would force him to sit back down and hear her out. But he just stood there looking down at her and said, "Time to go."

As he started to turn toward the exit, she said, "Grant, I'm going to Amsterdam. I have work there. I hope to see you again."

Grant was uncertain if she were sincere or not. He walked away and thought, *Why Amsterdam? Of course, she's of Boars ancestry.*

He and Thomas walked hurriedly down the stairs of the Union Jack onto Sandell Street. They approached the corner of Sandell and

Waterloo Road and stopped as Grant pulled out his encrypted cell phone and dialed. Within five minutes, a white van pulled up. Thomas opened the side door and he and Grant stepped inside.

An hour and a half later, in the humid evening air, they pulled into a British Petroleum station to get gas. As the van's driver stood aside the vehicle pumping gas, Grant and Thomas opened the side door and disappeared into the evening. The driver then pulled off about a mile down the road, where he drove into the Grey Goose Inn. Wearing dark glasses, a full beard, and a skull cap, he stopped for evening fare. He ordered a dinner of lamb chops and a glass of water. They honored his request to prepare it with the mint green jelly and in accordance with halal dietary laws. He ate in silence and waited. A phone call would come. If not soon, he would take a room for the night.

*　　*　　*　　*　　*

A mini-mall stood only a block away from the service station. In it were several boutiques and salons, along with a haberdashery in which various hats, including an array of baseball caps with logos of various athletic teams from the New York Yankees to Manchester United as well as Rugby teams from around the globe. Even the logos of various cricket teams adorned the caps.

Thomas and Grant walked in and picked out caps that offered fashion and a small element of cover. Grant went with the Cleveland Indians and Thomas with Manchester United. They paid and turned right as they left, walking by several more stores and toward a row of three-story townhouses.

In the evening, children with black hair and brown complexions played soccer in the streets while their mothers, in traditional robes and veils, sat on the benches and their own portable lawn chairs, drinking tea. Thomas could have passed through unnoticed any day of the year.

"Achmed, Achmed, be careful," scolded one young mother. Her son's soccer career would be cut short if he again sent the ball sailing into the covey of women draped from head to toe in traditional black abayas.

The next ball ricocheted off a parked car and bounced to Thomas, who gently kicked it back with sufficient deftness to suggest he had played this game before. Grant smiled and said, "Soccer, a game for those who aren't tough enough to play American football."

"Oh, that hurts, my friend. But perhaps we will learn to play it when each of our soccer players puts on about one hundred extra pounds of fat."

"Touché," responded Grant.

After passing several blocks of row houses, they slipped down an alley and came up behind the residences where a lane allowed private parking for those who could afford to pay for it. Thomas and Grant walked through the dimly lit area until they came upon a blue-gray Mercedes. They walked by it, slowly taking note of the license plates. Walking on another two hundred or so feet, Grant pulled out his encrypted phone and dialed. Within ten minutes, a white van pulled up in front of the row of townhouses, slowly maneuvering through the world or would-be soccer greats wearing shirts that said, "Beckham," "Judek," and "Neville," among others. It circled the entire neighborhood slowly until finding a parking place two blocks past the alley into which Thomas and Grant turned.

Continuing to stand in the dark, they watched and confirmed the plates by phone to Oz. He consulted and relayed back.

"Omar Abu Abdul, here legally, unemployed, but always prosperous. Frequents Finsbury Mosque. Repeated trips from England back to Saudi Arabia. Lately, flights to Pakistan have raised suspicions. Although unemployed, also owns a home in Birmingham. Has degree in engineering from the University of Pennsylvania. Now is U.K. citizen. No run-ins with the law. Works out at a local health club. Thirty-five years old. Not married. Suspected of money laundering and small arms trafficking. Possible links to Nigerian and Central African illegal diamond ring."

Grant could not help but think that someone he cared about had been kidnapped. It was time to round up the usual and the unusual suspects. A moment later, Grant dialed Blanche's number.

She felt the vibration in the darkness and spoke in a whisper. "Please get me out. My legs are bounded but my hands are free. Battery is low."

"We're confirming your location. Stay on the line. We're right outside." As he was speaking, two men in sweat pants and running shoes came out the back door and sat on the steps, smoking cigarettes. The windows on either side and below them obviously led to a basement-level apartment. They fit the description the innkeeper gave of the men. Grant continued speaking to Blanche in a whisper. Then he felt a vibration in the other pocket.

"I'm two blocks away. When you're ready."

Grant responded, "Ready now, go," and he hung up.

Thomas then walked directly to the Mercedes and began kicking the front tires of the car.

"What the hell are you doing in my space? Get your own," he yelled.

Immediately, the two men jumped up, and one of them held up his hands beseechingly.

"Hey, hey, what do you think you are doing? That's my car."

"Then what's it doing in my space?"

"It's not your lot. It's ours. Now get out of here."

"What do you think? That you can steal another man's parking space because there are two of you?"

One of them put his hand against Thomas's chest. Instead of backing off, Thomas leaned into the man and said, "My friend, look at the number of the slot. Number 11 is the spot sold to me for one hundred pounds per month."

While Thomas argued with the two men, Grant slipped past them and slid into the now open back door. As he did so, the front doorbell rang. Immediately, a man in the front room got up and walked toward the door with his back to Grant, who lingered in a long hallway. The man opened the door to find a pizza delivery man standing before him. It was the van driver. Grant walked softly down the carpeted hall and silently opened a door. It led to a darkened stairway. Outside, he could hear the increasingly loud voices of Thomas and the two men. He then stepped down to the first two steps while the pizza delivery man insisted that he was at the right house and that he expected to be paid.

"No! No! No! Get out. Go! Go or I'll call the police."

The delivery man slammed the pizza down on the floor and yelled something in Arabic. The other responded in kind. Then the front door shut with a loud thump. In the darkness, Grant descended the steps, taking them two at a time, walking on the edge of the steps to prevent creaking. At the bottom, he turned immediately to his right. In the darkness, he could barely make out the windows. The panes were haphazardly painted over with a grayish paint that allowed a modicum of the illumination from the parking lot lights.

He walked softly to a wooden paneling that covered an entire wall. He ran his fingers down the groves, looking for indentations or a cut that indicated a doorway. The entire wall was deceptive. He ran his fingers across the wall horizontally and vertically and found nothing. He got back on his cell phone.

"Blanche," he whispered. "I'm inside but can't find the doorway. Help me. Can you get to it and press or knock gently against it so that they don't hear?"

"I can't," she said. "It's all padded."

However, a few seconds later he heard a muffled thump at the far end of the wall nearest the front of the building. He felt along the wall, trying to find the door. Then he realized that the door must have recessed hinges covered by the panel and possibly a pull string sticking out along one side. He felt along the paneling where it converged at a right angle with the basement wall at the front of the building. He then felt something soft. It was a two-inch-wide strap tucked into a virtually impossible to see crevice. He pulled at it until it came out. He tugged on it firmly but gently. In a slow, controlled movement, he opened a four-foot strip of paneling. He saw nothing but blackness before him. He put out his hand. Another wall. But this one was recessed a full six inches from the paneled door. Feeling along the edge, he found the hinges, door knob, and dead bolt locks. He again felt for a possible opening. Nothing. He knocked gently. The door was sold oak. A second later, another *whomph, whomph*. He bent down to the floor and whispered, "Can you hear me?" Nothing. Then, moments later, his phone vibrated again.

"Get me out of here before—" Her battery went dead.

Before he could respond, he heard someone walking upstairs. The basement door opened, and the lights flicked on. Grant saw the light switch right outside the door and immediately hit it. The lights went out. Someone upstairs hit the light switch again. Grant hit his again. The man upstairs responded with a curse and walked downstairs in the darkness, thinking either a fuse had blown or that the wiring was frayed somewhere.

He came to the bottom of the stairs and turned right, away from Grant, whose dark clothing kept him concealed. Grant's eyes were already accustomed while the other man's were not. Grant could make out the man's form as he moved to the fuse box along the back wall. The metal lid made a rusty creaking sound as he opened it. He depressed each of the fuse knobs, attempting to figure out which he might have blown.

As he did so, the sound of the backdoor slamming grabbed Grant's attention. He heard footsteps in the hallway as the two men who had been arguing with Thomas reentered. They stopped at the open door to the basement, which blocked their passage through the hallway. Seconds later, one of them, having first closed the door to get by it, peered into the darkness of the stairwell and attempted to flick the basement lights back on. Grant hit the switch next to him again.

"It's no use, Omar, the fuses must be blown," came the voice from down in the basement.

"Shit," was all that Omar said.

The man kept his back to Grant, who listened to the footsteps of the other two men who walked to the front room and sat down to watch a soccer game on the television. They both wondered at the television working while the basement lights did not.

The man kept working at the fuse box. Suddenly, he felt a hand over his mouth and a sharp pain on the left side of his neck. Something sharp was cutting into his jugular. The hand remained pressed against his neck along with a cutting instrument.

"Open the door to let the girl out or I'll slice your throat clean through," whispered Grant. The man braced for the slicing.

"Reach into your pocket and get the key out or I'll start cutting. We'll walk over to the door slowly. If you move too quickly, both jugulars will be cut. What you feel on your chest right now is a small flow of blood I've already created by cutting through your left jugular. You can live if you get treatment within the next hour. But I'll cut it and the other clean through if you make the wrong move."

The man moved compliantly toward the other door. Grant hadn't known whether or not the man had the key but assumed that a threat suggesting that he knew that he did was the fastest way to get at the truth. It seemed to be working. Omar reached into his pants pocket. Just then, the light went on.

"Omar, why'd you get the pizza? We just ate. You want some? We'll eat again if you make us," he laughed.

All of a sudden, there was a loud bang at the back door. Then came another, and this time the door window shattered. Both men pulled themselves back from the steps of the stairwell. Grant reached across the man's neck and sliced. He withdrew the bloody credit card, reached into the man's pocket, and pulled out the keys as the man collapsed to the floor, dead.

With the other two responding to the noise outside, he flicked the lights back on and inserted one of the two keys into the lock. He heard and felt the tumbler click. Then he inserted the other key into the other tumbler. Another click and a turn of the two knobs and the door opened inwardly, forcing Blanche to move away from it. Her legs were taped at the ankles, but she could still stand. Grant reached down with his improvised plastic knife and cut through the tape. Blanche immediately hugged Grant around the neck with her eyes glistening with fear, relief, self-pity, bewilderment, and thanks. But Grant pulled himself away and pulled her by one hand over Omar's body. They ran for the steps.

As they reached the top of the steps, Grant looked down the hallway. The backdoor was wide open, with glass shards from the window littering the hallway. Outside, he heard the two men shouting at someone. He then heard, "Move out."

Over his right shoulder, he saw the pizza delivery man, his driver, who now stood in the living room. Grant and Blanche followed. They went out the front door and to the white van, which was double parked, with another man at the wheel—hairy, dark, and wearing a skull cap.

The side door opened automatically. Grant pushed Blanche in and followed. The pizza delivery man ran around to the front passenger side as the side door shut. As they pulled away, a soccer ball bounced off the back of the van, and three twelve-year-old boys chased after it.

The back of the van was dark, with only a small overhead light, but had enough illumination for Blanche to see the blood on her hands. She looked at Grant, who sat directly opposite her on the floor of the van. The blood on his hands and the memory of the body on the floor of the basement caused her to tear and gently weep. She shuddered at the sight of the man who had just saved her life. He had killed someone. At that moment, she was both repulsed by him and yet felt an irresistible urge for him to hold her. Through moist eyes, she smiled at Grant. He stared back.

He seemed miles away. Crawling over to him, she leaned against him, resting her head on this shoulder and grabbing his arm with both hands. He reached over with his other hand, intending to caress her hair. As he did, he saw his own bloody hand. The plastic card was still there. He slid it into his pants pocket and reached into his jacket. He pulled out his encrypted cell phone and called Thomas.

Realizing that even encryption devices could be broken by advanced cryptographic eavesdropping devices, such as those known to be used by MI-6 or other government agencies, he was prepared to speak casually.

Thomas answered in a whisper. "They're looking for me. I'm behind them in an alley. If they stay with their backs to me, I can move out. Can you pick me up? Here's my GPS read at—"

"Enough," said Grant. "Yes, we'll pick you up, but you'll have to pay for dinner."

However, within minutes, the van was a couple of miles away. The driver's decision was to go on. Thomas was on his own. Grant protested but relented as the driver spoke.

"I have my orders just like you, sir."

But Thomas replied, "No problem. I know where I am. I'll call later." He hung up.

Frustrated at leaving one of his men behind, Grant saw the vulnerability of his situation. He had intended to let his driver know in no uncertain terms what he thought of him. Grant had always heard that the U.S. military never knowingly left a man behind.

An hour later, the van came to a complete halt. The engine stopped, and the driver opened the side door. Blanche and Grant stepped out into a large underground enclosure that looked like a bomb shelter left over from the Cold War. As they stepped out into the dull gray concrete structure, Grant and Blanche heard the door of the van shut. The driver pulled away into a long, dark tunnel. Grant hadn't had the opportunity to express his disgust at leaving a man behind.

"Hello, I'm so glad you're all right." Both turned around at the sound of the voice. It was Dennis.

"Oh, Grant, I should be eternally grateful. My dear ..." He hugged

Blanche. He then embraced Grant, as well. However, Grant was uncomfortable. He was concerned about Thomas.

"Dennis, I need to go back."

"Yes, I know that, but Thomas is safe. He's resourceful. For now, we have some debriefing to do." Grant felt lost. He was talking to a man who had showed up unexpectedly and now wanted a debriefing. Dennis, Oz, and MacArthur. This cast was a triumvirate that mystified him. Still, his gut said that this was a good man whom he could trust.

Dennis turned again to his niece and said, "Deborah, my friend, will assist you. You'll not be going back home just yet. Please. Let her help you."

Later, while sitting in a grimy office with a number of metal filing cabinets and two safes, Grant found himself with more questions than answers. After fifty minutes, Grant left the office with his questions remaining. The van had reappeared. At first, Grant reached for the front passenger's side door, but it was locked. The driver motioned him to the side door, which he opened with the press of button. Grant stepped in, and a moment later, the van moved through a passageway to a freight elevator. Grant felt the upward motion. He heard a garage door open and the sounds of nighttime London.

An hour later, Grant stepped out in front of the Union Jack as the van sped away.

He headed up the steps, through the door, past the doorman, and into the lobby. Instinctively, he walked through it to a door on the far side that led to the T. E. Lawrence Reading Room. There, sitting in the corner of the back cubicle of this room with his feet up on a chair, was Thomas. He was reading the *Guardian* newspaper, or actually he was looking at a full-page picture of a scantily clad display of British prosperity, a carefully coifed buoyancy of beauty with a smile as big as her fleshy and entirely womanly accoutrements.

Thomas ignored Grant, eyes remaining on the paper. "Well, we did it. What took you so long?"

Before Grant could respond, Thomas put down the paper, stood up, and grabbed Grant's hand.

"Yes, we did, Thomas. Yes, we did."

CHAPTER 40

DUTCH TREAT

Never allow a nervous female to have access to a pistol, no matter what you're wearing.

—James Thurber,
"The Lion Who Wanted to Zoom"

BYRON VANDERKIN SAT IN HIS WHEELCHAIR AS HE SPOKE.

"I consider them the bane of my existence, Mr. Williams. People think it is absolutely nothing these days for me to make last-minute arrangement for a charter plane any place their heart desires. But I must admit that it is their thoughtlessness that makes me a happy man. 'Forget the cost,' they say. It's nothing to them. The sheer extravagance. It's nothing at all. It's the government's money or it's corporate money; what do I care? You know, other people's money, not their own. Still, I relish the money such carelessness brings to our coffers."

The Dutch Embassy was situated near a number of others at Hyde Park Gate in the heart of London. The entire area had an international air about it—a cosmopolitanism as well as the sophistication that is part of the aura of people who customarily speak at least one foreign language and who move deftly from one subject to another. These are the dignitaries of schmooze and the grease monkeys of the world's political and economic engine.

Here on this particular evening, the Dutch Embassy functioned as a coming out for the new breed of dignitary. The Dutch themselves were forever tolerant of every foible and even the most egregious of etiquette indiscretions as a small nation with international interests must be.

Into this world of seeming insouciance and fetid diplomacy walked Grant Chisholm in his navy dress whites. His invitation came through official channels of the Defense Attaché's Office in London. Still, since he had never worked for the DAO, he assumed that the fingerprints of Oz or MacArthur were somewhere on the invitation. But why? When he questioned Oz, he responded with a pedagogical certitude.

"Of course, you're our man and you need to be savvy to the workings of the world. Some of the people there are just good people you'll enjoy meeting. Others are the unwholesome sort you even more want to meet. It's the dirty ones from whom you learn the most. But it's the good ones who you want to be like. Remember that."

Thomas, however, could not be accorded the same princely treatment. He would be Grant's driver, but also his eyes and ears outside the Dutch Embassy.

"Good evening, Mr. Chisolm or, should I recall my military insignias, lieutenant commander."

"Right you are, Mr. Ambassador."

"Did you bring a guest with you?"

"Not tonight, sir."

"Well, no matter; there's a lovely young lady here this evening. She came with an old friend. I hope to introduce you to her later tonight."

"Thank you, Mr. Ambassador. I appreciate this evening's invitation."

A short while after standing by himself looking about helplessly for someone with whom he might engage in conversation, he heard a familiar voice behind him. The British ambassador to the Netherlands, Mr. Neville Williams, was engaged in a conversation with a man in a wheelchair, with his back to Grant. Even so, he recognized the man immediately: Byron Vanderkin.

He listened as Vanderkin explained how his charter airline business, one of several enterprises he had, kept him awake at night. "Always someone needing to make an unexpected trip to an uncommon destination at a truly inconvenient time."

While Grant stood listening, the British ambassador looked up from Vanderkin and saw Grant standing alone. Although he did not know who Grant was, he showed the gracious smile and welcoming expression of one who could empathize with anyone standing by himself and disengaged from any conversation. After all, this was a fun function known as the debutante ball for new staff at various embassies. He motioned for Grant to come over and join him.

Reluctantly, Grant walked over to the ambassador and stood between him and the wheelchair. Vanderkin looked up. At first, his face changed to a frown. But then he composed himself and forced a smile. The ambassador extended his hand to Grant as he introduced himself. Then the ambassador looked down at Vanderkin, who smiled again and said, "This young man and I have already met." Neither offered his hand to the other.

After several minutes of strained conversation, the ambassador excused himself. A momentary silence ensued; then Vanderkin said, "Mr. Chisolm, your presence is, as before, an unwelcome one. In a less public place, you would not be so cavalier and arrogant as to dare appear. You are a fool. You have something I want, and I shall get it one way or the other."

"It'll have to be the other."

Grant looked around the room for more desirable companionship. Seeing two other men in white dress uniforms from the British Navy, he left Vanderkin without another word or even a nodding by-your-leave. As he approached his British counterparts, each of whom were holding an hors d'oeuvre in one hand while reaching for champagne with the other, a young lady crossed his path. She had a smile that lingered and promised adventure if he were quick enough to recognize the opportunity. But as she eyed him, he eyed another who stood several feet from the British sailors. She saw him as well and looked at him at first with a blank expression and then with a wry smile. He remained where he was, unaware that at his back yet another acquaintance approached.

Moments later, now standing before him was Vanderkin's nephew. "It's a surprise and uncommon of you to be here among your betters, is it not, Mr. Chisolm?"

"I'm in uniform; you may address me as lieutenant commander."

"Lieutenant commander it is. Small concession for the price you shall soon pay. A greater reward will soon befall me and a lesser one shall befall you."

"Small concession, as you say, but no reward."

"How much money do you want?"

"For what?"

"The real package and for you and the others to forget about a certain archaeological site?"

"Our interest is keen. Almost as keen as yours. Besides, I don't like others telling me or my friends what to do. Our disagreements are not yet legion, but I suspect that they shall soon be, Dutchie. However, in this moment of cordiality, perhaps you can tell me, have you any friends in the Middle East?"

"Why do you ask, commander? I have many friends all over the world."

"And many enemies as well, I dare say."

Most people were intimidated by Vanderkin's nephew. He found it particularly annoying that Grant had thus far proven unflappable.

"Remind me again, if you don't mind, Dutchie, exactly what is your business?"

"I thought you would know that, lieutenant commander. Why, we are among the primary charter services in all Europe. We can fly anyone anywhere."

"I bet you do, too. But perhaps you've branched out."

"Perhaps, but not something I wish to talk about. After all, you are the one who has been trespassing on foreign turf."

"Strange to hear a Dutchman living in England say such a thing. But then, having seen Amsterdam, the child porn capital of Europe, it seems appropriate that it claims you. Met any young boys lately?"

Seething, Vanderkin's nephew hissed, "You pig."

"Nice talking with you, Porky." Never having seen certain cartoons, Vanderkin didn't detect the allusion but assumed it was something insulting.

Before more could be said, Grant walked away, leaving yet another man stewing in his own juices.

But unlike his uncle, Vanderkin's nephew was not confined to a wheelchair. After about a half minute, he followed Grant and once again put his hand on his shoulder, coming down hard on his epaulet. Grant turned slowly and smiled.

"You seem attracted to male flesh, but I'm not your type, really."

"Look you ...you ... your days are numbered unless we get what we want. Besides, what we have in mind surely exceeds your military pay—"

"Tell me, have you been to Haiti, lately?"

"Why, what has this to do with anything?"

"Well, they have a conference there this week. It's entitled 'Boys for Men.' I'm surprised you're not there. And, by the way, I don't like certain kinds of people touching me. And I never threaten ... I only do. And now, why don't you pull a Henry Hudson? If I am not mistaken, he too was a Dutchman, only he had the good grace to mysteriously disappear. Why don't you? The mystery's not necessary, just the disappearance."

Again Grant turned and walked away.

Outside, Thomas stood dutifully alongside the limousine lent to him this evening by a friend of MacArthur's. As he did so, he noticed the comings and goings in the early evening, including a Mercedes that passed by the embassy three different times. It looked familiar, but the plates were different and the driver was someone new to Thomas, not one he had seen when they rescued Blanche.

CHAPTER 41
SIRENS AND SHOALS

Give pearls away and rubies,
But keep your fancy free.

—A. E. Houseman,
"When I Was One and Twenty"

PAMELA WATCHED AT A DISTANCE. GRANT SEEMED GENUINELY interested in the talk of his British counterparts, and she was hesitant to barge in on the men's conversation. He hadn't even looked in her direction once in the past twenty minutes.

Politely but without enthusiasm, she entertained and conversed with others, seldom extending a conversation beyond the dutiful requirements of a guest at any such function. Her silence and a refusal to ask conversation starters or any other questions were enough to leave her in semi-solitude, watching the man she hoped would be watching her. Finally, she decided that playing hard to get wouldn't work. She would once again have to extend herself.

So, as nonchalantly as she could but with a most deliberate goal, she walked toward him. She stopped at his side, and when he was forced to acknowledge her presence, he looked down at her and smiled. She then whispered playfully and said, "You, sir, are a pirate."

Realizing that he was falling for bait most obviously set, he relented and said, "And why am I a pirate?"

"Because you've been a thief. You stole my heart. What's a girl to do?" she asked with a playful pout.

296

"I don't understand how you are accustomed to showing affection. Maybe you do it differently in South Africa."

She grimaced and said, "I'm sorry. But I had to leave."

"I don't understand. Amsterdam. I see the connection, the Dutch Embassy and all," he said to remind her of one of her last statements to him when she sought him out at the Union Jack. "Still, this is not Amsterdam. You've a faulty reckoning of geography. You're difficult to believe, much less trust."

"And you are as bewildering as a crossword puzzle," she responded.

"How so?" asked Grant.

"You're mysterious, you're good with words, and right now you're cross. Can't we make up?"

Ignoring her appeal, Grant asked, "Why are you here? Why are you even in the same room with Vanderkin and his nephew? And you've not told me how you knew I was at the Union Jack."

"I really do have a job in Amsterdam. I have contacts there. Vanderkin helped me get it. I'll be working at a travel agency with an international clientele. Jet setters from the world of diplomacy. Please try to understand. Byron Vanderkin gave me a scholarship when I was in high school. I was one of the first TUDOR recipients. Without him, I wouldn't have made it past high school. My family wouldn't have had the money. Besides, the package ..."

For a moment Grant felt the enticement that fills men with the promise of delight while leaving them senseless in the face of an aesthetic composition. Like Ulysses, he wanted to stuff his ears with wax to deafen himself to the mellifluous quality of her voice, chimes that jangled with the subtle hints and insinuations of untold mystery. Her voice was pleasant with a touch of shrillness. At the moment, he heard only the voice of the siren without its peril. Yet while being swayed to an imaginative elopement with the beauty before him, the rocks appeared. Vanderkin and his nephew rolled and walked by, respectively, just within ear shot of Grant and Pamela. They seemed a little too interested. The voices of well-intentioned and sometime wise elders of his youth manned the oars and the rudder, steering Grant away from the siren song.

"You know, I think I'll be seeing you again, maybe in Amsterdam." And just when Pamela began to think he was softening, his face grew stern and he walked away. There was something about her he did not trust. Perhaps it was the perilous rocks about her or the mischief her womanly opulence suggested. Teased and tempted, he nonetheless shook off her allure and remembered Blanche.

CHAPTER 42

WHEELS WITHIN WHEELS

And, in his bed, lean hungry longings taunt him,
Pinprick and bite him.

—Burns Singer, "Marcus Antonius"

Hence, vain, deluding Joys,
The brood of Folly without father bred!

—John Milton, "Il Penseroso"

—NORTHERN UGANDA

JOMO SAT ON A PORTABLE CANVAS DIRECTOR'S CHAIR. IT SAID ON the front and back, "Jomo, Our Leader." It had been a gift from secret admirers in Nairobi who hoped to ingratiate themselves when he came to rule their entire country as well as the surrounding nations. As he sat there watching his underling, Jomo took out a Churchill cigar. He unwrapped it and put it in his mouth, but he did not light it. In fact, he never lit his cigars. When asked why, he explained that they lasted longer that way. His admirers missed the humor and thought this comment to be yet another indication of his wisdom.

Jomo sat on the tarmac of a former British air base in northern Uganda. Next to him was a young man, very dark-skinned, wearing a large crucifix and a white shirt with tan short pants. He catered to every one of Jomo's needs, real and perceived. He darted about apprehensively like a squirrel. His tongue flicked out, repeatedly licking his lips, which twitched nervously as he attended to his lord's needs.

As Jomo sat there, he pulled out a rosary made of amethyst and glass. Without hesitation, he began to say the Our Father aloud. No one was at the air field except Jomo and his underling. He said it while keeping his cigar tucked to one side. Then, in a gesture that confused the young man who now sat quietly and respectfully at a distance on the crumbling tarmac, he knelt down on the cement and faced north, not toward Mecca, but toward Rome. The gesture's significance was not communicated to his companion, who wondered if he should immediately begin to do the same thing. But then Jomo arose and sat back down in his chair as he stuffed his rosary into a shirt pocket.

In a parody of biblical significance, he turned to his underling and asked, "Who do you say that I am?"

"You?" he asked confusedly as if he had not heard Jomo correctly.

"Yes, who do you say that I am?"

"You, you are Jomo, our lord and leader, our commander."

"Do you think I am Elijah?"

"No, no, you are Jomo. Who is Elijah?"

Jomo smiled at the man's ignorance and said, "You will leave now. In four days, you will be back at our camp. You will tell them I am going to see my father and I will be taken there in a fiery chariot with wheels within wheels. Do you understand?"

The underling blinked in consternation. Jomo smiled again and said, "Go, for you are Abraham Willie. Upon you I can build nothing."

Jomo picked up Willie's backpack and his water filter and handed it to him. He then pointed to a pathway in the jungle and said, "Go. I must be about my father's business."

As the young man nervously walked away, he glanced back over his shoulder several times, and Jomo, acting as narrator of his own life, whispered, "Like Abraham before him, he went." He continued to chew on his unlit cigar.

Within an hour, a small commercial jet landed on the rugged and cracked runway. An electric walkway descended from an open doorway, and Jomo climbed into the plane. The pilot gave Jomo a knowing look and then turned the plane around and began his takeoff. As Jomo ascended, he thought to himself, *After all the years of struggle, after the crucifixion of his people, Jomo flew.* He smiled contentedly as he soared through the heavens on the way to his father. For three days and nights, he would fly across the vastness that is Africa, over the Mediterranean and into northern Europe, stopping several times for fuel. He would speak little to the pilot as he contentedly basked in the knowledge that he was Jomo, lord of men, lord of his people, who would now plot the overthrow of those who opposed him with the help of his father.

As he contemplated how he would orchestrate the actual overthrow, he spit out a diamond, which he had kept concealed behind one of his molars. This particularly precious blue diamond would be a gift to his benefactor. He would give it even before they began their bargaining. He would need more guns, more munitions, and, of course, some mercenaries from South Africa or Angola—or, for that matter, from anywhere, as long as they were good.

*   *   *   *   *

In Dar es Salaam, the capital of Tanzania, Jomo's admirers were secretly meeting with Marx St. George. He explained that Jomo had departed, perhaps even fled. "Maybe," he told them, "he will not even return."

Their meeting place was the newly constructed United States Embassy, where diplomatic conferences were routine and where Marx could come and go with little likelihood of being recognized. As he sat in the room conferring with these men, he thought of Jomo's awful presence and remembered a painting he had once seen in Jomo's large illustrated Bible. It was a painting by Leonardo da Vinci entitled *The Last Supper*. He did not imagine himself as one who should be depicted in the painting or at least not as one who should be seated next to Jesus.

*   *   *   *   *

Over a thousand miles away, Jomo flew, a solitary passenger aboard a solitary aircraft that zoomed swiftly and surely across the zones of internecine conflict. Yet from the grandeur of the heavens, any notion of conflict seemed an anomaly from the soft hush that Jomo heard from the jet engines as he traversed the cloudless skies. As he looked out the window, Jomo saw a world beneath him that seemed as tranquil as it was distant. He felt conflicted as he gazed upon it. A peaceful world was boring; he needed war to prove his manliness and his godliness. Where, he wondered, would Napoleon be in history if he had not engaged in war? What of Caesar? What of Mohammed? War made men. All others were as women.

Women have their purpose, he thought. They were to be breeders of men, convenient containers for the seeds of greatness. Then he thought of the man who had stolen the woman who was to have been his wife. As he did so, he glowered and his fingers tensed as they formed into fists. He hoped that God would someday bring him face-to-face with the man who had stolen his bride. He would avenge the loss of his prize. He imagined how he would subdue his opponent and then scalp him. He would then force the man to watch as he placed his scalp upon his own nearly shaven head to wear as a trophy. Then he would cut off the man's eyelids so that he could not close his eyes. The man's face would be cut behind each ear, and he would peel the skin from his head. Then he would feed upon the flesh and force the man to watch. And last he would hold up a mirror so the thief could see the horror of his face. Only then would he let the man go. He would let him live the rest of his life as a man without a face. Satisfied with his plan, Jomo drifted off to sleep.

As he fell deeply into the world of dreams, Jomo saw before him a pure red room in which he was surrounded by first a hissing sound and then his own voice coming out of the walls. "Lord, lord …" the voice was aspirated, very breathy, almost seductive. He felt fear as he tried to lift himself but his legs were constricted by an invisible force. Before him, the black head of a serpent appeared at eye level. It moved back and forth like that of a cobra.

"Sing to me," said the snake.

"No!" screamed Jomo.

At that, the entire body of the snake appeared to rise up from the ground, but the body and head were disconnected and were actually in the wall, embedded within its red transparent world.

"Sing to me," again said the serpent.

"No!"

"If you will sing to me, I will give you back your woman."

"No!"

"Turn my head into stone and kiss me."

"No!" shouted Jomo. " I am the Black Mamba, kneel before me, and I will suck the poison from your breast, o woman."

"No! No! No!" she screamed back. "It is *I* who draws the poison from *you*."

Jomo struggled to rise. As he did so, he spoke again. "I am the Black Mamba, and I alone shall you worship."

"I am your mouth," replied the snake as it extended itself to Jomo's full height. Its eyes were those of a woman. Still, it rose menacingly, striking at him as it shattered the red world. It missed even though Jomo was again paralyzed. It struck again, and this time Jomo grabbed it with his left hand. As he did so, the snake coiled its body mightily around his left leg. Jomo squeezed the snake right behind the head with both hands. Even so, the snake spoke. "Love me. I give you my poison as a blessing. Kiss me."

Jomo continued squeezing until finally the snake went limp. The eyes of the snake turned from those of a woman back to those of a snake, and then its head turned white and fell to the ground. The coils writhed convulsively about his leg and likewise fell to the ground. The head was now a stone and then a loaf of bread. The coils on the ground turned yellow, then silver, and then black and disappeared. The room lost its red glow as it quickly turned a brilliant blue like that in an aquarium. Into this aquarium swam a naked black woman. It was Jomo's mother. But she was much younger, and she rubbed herself against the blue wall until finally her head fell off and floated away. Jomo stood watching as the headless body grew a new one, only the head was that of a white woman with brown hair. It was the head of Melissa, and then it transformed into his own. Jomo watched as his mother's naked body rubbed against the wall even as the head of Melissa reappeared next to his own and then fell to the floor of the blue aquariumlike room

He gazed in horror at the she-man before him and shook until he awoke with a start. The plane was coming to a landing zone in a private airfield in the Hebrides off the coast of Scotland.

CHAPTER 43

THE LION'S DEN

Thus slowly, one by one,
its quaint events were hammered out.

—Lewis Carroll, *Alice in Wonderland*

—LONDON

THE CHAMBER WAS AN ANTEROOM OF CHURCHILL'S WORLD WAR II bunker about which even the current curator of the famous museum was unaware. The room adjoined the Churchill bunker and was therefore ideally suited to provide access to Parliament and other government buildings—that is, if anyone knew of its location. The room itself, however, could not be entered except through the basement of a townhouse that was privately owned and had at one point been Randall Churchill's and then later Margaret Thatcher's private house when the press of a public life made the escape from the media and parliamentarians necessary for sanity. Provisions in the unusual bill of sale indicated that the townhouse could only be sold to certain distinguished individuals whose names were known only to the few selectees on the list. In the event that none of these wished to purchase the townhouse, it would pass back into the hands of one Regis MacArthur.

The room was gray concrete with no sign of access to the world at large. No plumbing, no kitchen facilities, no electrical wires. Special battery-operated fixtures and cranks to generate the glow of light bulbs cast a dim but sufficient light. The furnishings were old but comfortable. A long, soft couch suitable for reclining and four great-backed chairs with plush cushions offered firm but very comfortable seating.

On each of the four walls was an original oil painting. Each was a rectangular canvas, in a simple pine frame, depicting a landscape; whether real or imagined was anybody's guess. In the right-hand corner was a white swirl of a signature that read "W. Churchill."

All the pictures had a crank light above them that enabled any admirer to turn the handle several times in order to light the oil painting and gaze upon the handiwork of a political giant whose artistic genius was dwarfed and stunted not by lack of talent but by an even greater talent in politics and rhetoric.

The pictures were situated squarely behind each of the four great-back chairs, thereby imitating the symmetrical perfection and perfidy of the eighteenth-century English garden. The four chairs surrounded a four-foot round table at which now sat Oz, Dennis, MacArthur, and Grant.

Several minutes into a conversation that ran the gamut from the America's Cup winner to who would hold the next summer's Olympic Games, MacArthur leaned back and said, "Our time is short. I fear the momentum may shift if we do not act quickly. We have ample evidence to suggest that our friends from the Middle East, as well as our Dutch friends in Scotland, may be aspiring to obtain a certain package. Moreover, we have heard from Thomas, who tells us that one Father Ricci has been found. He is the closest thing to a father confessor that Jomo Raphael has. He can make the link between Vanderkin and Jomo and the illegal diamond trade and who knows what else? Thomas has a meeting scheduled tomorrow. Maybe we can soon provide a certain Dutchman with a very special treat." Grant smiled at the obvious play on words. For over an hour, they speculated as to the whys and wherefores of Vanderkin's operations and asked themselves what they might do to break them. At first, Grant was tempted to offer to go back to Kenya for one more try against Jomo. But then Oz spoke.

"Why not let the Kenyan come to us?"

"How so?" asked MacArthur.

"If he is the conduit who moves the diamonds out of central south Africa, then we can count on one thing. If he senses disenchantment in his benefactors, maybe this will force him to solicit a meeting."

"But how to force him to second guess his relationship with Vanderkin, if indeed Vanderkin is his benefactor?" asked Dennis.

"Please, gentlemen, consider that Jomo is to Vanderkin as Hitler once was to Mussolini." The significance of the allusion was lost on Grant, but Dennis and MacArthur nodded in agreement. "The child must come to the father seeking forgiveness or at least approval. It's human nature," stated Oz.

Oz's instincts when it came to discerning motivation were exceptional. He knew what made people click better than they knew themselves. His analytical skills were well honed in years of underworld dealings and in his capacity as an interrogator in the aftermath of the U.S. invasion of Panama and later in the 1992 Gulf War.

Though the youngest of the lot, even Grant had come to appreciate that Oz knew not only what made a man risk his life for a cause but also the difficulties for which a man sought compensation. It was a skill that was bestowed, not one that was learned. If Oz said it was so, it was so.

As they concluded their discussion, MacArthur looked right at Grant, who was seated directly across from him. He seemed to detect the nature of Grant's ruminations. He answered Grant's tacit question with a cryptic, "Because, Mr. Chisolm, you have the will, the strength, the intellect, the character, and the pedigree."

Grant nodded and smiled at the obvious acumen of MacArthur. Oz looked at Grant and slapped him good-naturedly on the back. Dennis pulled out a cigar and handed it to Grant.

"Sometime, as Freud said, a cigar is just a cigar. Smoke it at your leisure and realize this is from my finest collection."

"I didn't realize that you smoked," said Grant as he accepted the cigar.

"I seldom do, except on special occasions and with special people. Be warned, however; the gesture is in earnest. Smoke that cigar and you truly are one of us. Leave it wrapped and unsmoked, you'll wonder all your life at the opportunity you might have had. Moreover, my young friend, this gesture has been observed only five times in this room in the last sixty years. Heed it."

"But you said, 'pedigree.'"

"Yes, and if you'll be patient, you'll understand."

"I'm beginning to feel like the karate kid. I feel as though I'm being tested even when I am not *apparently* being tested."

"You are," replied Oz, looking straight at Grant.

MacArthur looked on indulgently and smiled. Then he offered his hand, as did Oz. They shook, and Grant put the cigar in his left hand. As he did so, MacArthur looked at Oz and said, "Bubble, bubble, toil and trouble; not for us, I hope, but for Jomo and Vanderkin."

Oz responded with, "When shall we four meet again?"

"Tomorrow evening," said Dennis. "Thomas will inform us of the degree of cooperation we can expect from Ricci."

They then stood up and walked down the concrete tunnel with MacArthur in the lead, followed by Dennis, Grant, and Oz. They emerged through the backroom wall after MacArthur checked through a peep hole to make certain that no curious parliamentarians or dutiful custodians were using the facilities. But a man was just entering the bathroom, an old man who seemed to be on the verge of cleaning the room when he realized that the room had hardly been used and therefore didn't really require much, if any, cleaning.

Nonetheless, MacArthur cautioned the others that there was no point in unnecessarily risking the inadvertent exposure of their hiding place. So they continued down the tunnel. Two minutes later, they slipped into the townhouse. One by one, they left it in five-minute intervals to avoid being too conspicuous.

Grant walked out into the coolness of the late afternoon and sauntered toward a bus stand near St. James Park. There, he sat down, pulled out the cigar, took off its wrapper, and put it in his mouth. The end had already been cut. He then strolled down the street until he came to a small convenience shop and bought himself a lighter for two pounds. He walked over to a small park that had one bench and sat there by himself, puffing on a most aromatic leaf of tobacco, watching as the smoke rose slowly, almost beautifully, into the air. It was a sort of initiation for Grant. It was the first cigar he had smoked in his life.

CHAPTER 44
CONFESSION

Bless me, Father, for I have sinned.

—Confessional solicitation

—OXFORD UNIVERSITY

THOMAS PEERED UP AT THE EXTERIOR OF THE TWO-STORY BUILDING that was Campion Hall, the Jesuit residency at Oxford University, and walked up the stone stairway to the heavy oak door. Opening it, he entered an empty foyer and climbed the stairs to the second floor. Thomas was uncertain how anything in his military training suited him for what he must do on this occasion. He had fought in Afghanistan and later in Iraq. Fighting he understood. But since when did soldiers conduct interviews?

*   *   *   *   *

"Today," Ricci said, "I have nothing spiritual to offer any man. I have technical skills, perhaps, and a linguistic virtuosity that has given me access to people and institutions where I could quickly feel at ease. However, I fear that I talk too much, my son. It is good to see you again. But tell me, how did you find me here? I am teaching no classes. I am taking no classes, only doing linguistic research." Thomas sat and listened attentively.

"Well, Father, I too have connections, although I doubt that they are as extensive as yours."

"Please, I am curious. How did you find me? If you can do it, so can others. That could include people who are not as kind as you are."

"Well, I am a product of Jesuit education. I attended Mount Saint Mary's as a boy and then Stonyhurst College thereafter. Over the years, I've attempted to stay in touch with those who gave me so much. I admired them for their dedication."

"Ah, so you are a soldier, a true soldier of Christ," he said with a smile. "You must have taken your confirmation seriously. What is your confirmation name?"

"Well, it's Jerome."

"Oh, I see, a man of learning. A scholar. Did you admire him? Did you see yourself in him?"

"Well, perhaps. If he had been an athlete, I might have admired him even more," he added with a slight self-deprecating laugh. "But in my family there is nonetheless a great reverence for books."

"Few were as bookish as St. Jerome. You know, there are stories that he was not only a great scholar and a true father of the Church, but also a man of action. He did things. He led people to Christ."

"You mean, he was a priest like you."

"No, not like me. He was good man who saw the world as it was—he saw it with real eyes. I cannot say the same. I came to change the world. I fear that the world has changed me."

Thomas listened. He was hoping to change the subject. He wanted to ask a few questions that were of deep concern to himself and the others who had imperiled their own lives to rescue Jomo's hostages. But it was Ricci who wanted to talk, albeit not quite about the things as Thomas might have hoped.

Ricci looked at Thomas at first sorrowfully and then almost tearfully. "I was an idealist once. So I became a priest. Yes, I would change the world. The poor would at last have a place in it. But I became infected with my own idealism. Unlike you, I am not a man of action. I continue to run because I do little and think too much."

Thomas sat looking at Ricci, feeling awkward, embarrassed at having entered a man's inner most sanctuary. These were thoughts he was sure Ricci would soon regret having shared with him. He felt as though he were sitting in a cauldron of emotional turbulence that must be given vent or it would destroy itself.

"I yearn to be as you are, a man of action. But no, I ... I am what?" asked Ricci almost angrily. "I am the preacher of false hope. I am Beelzebub's son."

Thomas felt even greater embarrassment but then checked his own sense of consternation as he listened to Ricci go on about his own corruption.

"Father, I am a believer. I believe in redemption."

Ricci stopped and looked peculiarly at Thomas as if he were something unreal, something fantastic not be believed. Then he smiled and said, "I'm sorry. Forgive me."

"Father, you know more about Jomo and his connections perhaps than anyone. What are they and who finances him? Where do the diamonds go? You could help us."

Ricci gazed imploringly at Thomas. "Please do not ask this. Jomo is my creation. I cannot betray him. I cannot destroy him. He is ... he is like me, an idealist who is frustrated by man's ignorance."

"Another intellectual? Another frustrated man of action?" asked Thomas.

Ricci wanted to protest but sensed that neither Thomas nor anyone else could believe him, for he could not even believe himself.

"Please, Father. We are all capable of doing good. Jomo does no one any good. He is not as you trained him to be. He is cruel and power hungry."

"I cannot. He was once like a son to me. He alone has the potential to lead a great nation among today's African leaders. He is blessed with immense talent. He is a genius!"

"An evil genius," responded Thomas.

"He knows so little of true evil. He is a child in so many ways. Cruel at times, yes, but not so much more than other men. He intends to do good. He—" Ricci broke off his remarks abruptly and gasped. Then he lowered his head and brought his hands to his face. His shoulders shook, and he let out a sob and he ran his hands through his hair.

"He is ... he hates ... no man should be as cruel. God cannot forgive me."

Thomas remained quiet while Ricci sobbed amidst repeated attempts to speak. Finally, after a couple of minutes, Ricci knelt down and placed a hand on Thomas's knee.

"Stop him. His cruelty ... he bathes in it."

"Father, we need to know who his contacts are."

Ricci paused and then said, "I am foremost among them. I ... I am the one who transported so many diamonds. I am a priest. It is the best cover in the world. No one checks me. I travel freely. Who better?"

"But you must have delivered them to someone."

"Yes, but they are powerful men in Amsterdam and London—diplomats, business men. Men who I deceived myself into believing were committed to the revolution ... liberation of Africa from its poverty, from its ignorance."

"Who are they?"

Ricci paused, regaining his composure and wiping away the tears from his eyes. He patted Thomas on the knee and slowly stood up as if burdened by a great load.

"My friend, don't you see? I am a coward and an intellectual. I have no principles left. I am forsaken. Even goodness itself cannot save me."

"No, Father. I can't believe that. There is hope. I am a soldier. You, you are a soldier too. Of Christ. You must know that. Ignatius Loyola would tell you. Please help us."

Thomas felt extremely uncomfortable uttering words that reminded him of his high school and college theology classes, but he did not know how else to respond to Ricci.

Ricci looked sorrowfully into Thomas's eyes and said, "You forget yourself. It is I who should be counseling you."

"Father, we all help one another."

"Yes, I suppose. You know, I think you must be a very good soldier."

"So, will you help us?"

"Yes," he responded softly, almost imperceptibly.

"I need details," insisted Thomas.

Looking at him in a sidelong way, Ricci asked, "Do you have children?"

"No, I'm not married."

Ricci paused. "You remind me of a young idealist of a long while ago."

"What was his name?"

"Hmm. Matteo, Matteo, I think." Ricci smiled and then said,

"Can you come again tomorrow? I will prepare lunch. I will reconcile everything. It will be my last will and testament, so to speak."

"Yes," smiled Thomas, feeling satisfied. Then almost wistfully, he added, "And perhaps you can hear my confession."

"Rather, it is you who should hear mine."

As Thomas stood to leave, Ricci asked him, "Do you know of Seneca?"

"Seneca? You mean the ancient Roman writer?"

"I'm impressed; the Jesuits taught you well. Tell me, what do you recall?"

"Only that he was a great writer of letters and that he was Nero's teacher."

"Even more impressive. So do you remember how he died?"

"No, I don't recall. Perhaps I never even knew."

"His pupil turned on him. Emperor Nero disliked being scolded by his former mentor. So he let him know that if he wished for his family to be able to inherit his property, then Seneca would have to kill himself. The pupil had become the master, teaching his teacher the hard ways of the real world. But enough; go along. Thank you again. Tomorrow at noon. We will discuss everything."

"Tomorrow," said Thomas.

Within an hour, Thomas was at a nearby inn, where he sat through dinner and dessert while writing down specific questions for tomorrow's meeting.

As he did, a priest wearing a long black cassock walked toward Ricci's apartment and knocked on his door.

CHAPTER 45

THE SINS OF THE FATHER

My soul looks for the Lord more than sentinels for daybreak.

— Psalms 130: 6

In wardly trust
Vile self gets in
But Thou remembers we are dust
Defiled with sin.

—Robert Burns, "Holy Willie's Prayer"

—CAMPION HALL, JESUIT RESIDENCE

THOMAS KNOCKED ON THE DOOR. HE WAITED. AFTER ABOUT TWENTY seconds, he knocked again. Still no answer. He tried one more time. Still no answer. Thomas then looked down the hallway hoping to see Ricci walking toward him. The hallways were empty. Down below on the first floor and outside, he heard the sounds of various conversations drifting through the open windows. As he lingered, a feeling of foreboding crept up his spine and then a pang came across his chest. He tried the door knob. It was unlocked. He opened it slowly. The interior was dark. The windows were closed and the drapes as well. There was no movement. He called out.

"Father Ricci, Father Ricci, I'm here." Stillness.

Thomas walked over to the windows and drew back the curtains. The light fell upon Ricci's desk, on which sat a single rose in a glass of water. Next to it was a rosary made from black glass beads, a gift from

313

his mother at his first communion more than sixty years ago. The beads were laid out perfectly in an oval with the crucifix lying upon a single tissue in which it had been wrapped for decades. In the middle of the oval was a small white box on top of two hardbound books.

Thomas picked up the box and took off the lid. Inside was a small black and white photograph of a boy standing next to a woman in a long white dress. The mother had one arm on the boy's shoulder as she pressed him next to her. The boy wore a suit and held in his hand a black beaded rosary while his mother held at her waist a picture of some long-dead saint holding a lily in one hand. At the boy's feet was a large picture of a less discernible male figure in a wooden frame, perhaps that of a dead relative asked to bless the day with his spiritual presence.

He put the box aside and picked up the first volume. It was C. S. Lewis's philosophical discourse, *The Problem of Pain*. Thomas flipped through it rapidly, noting the frequent underlinings as well as the handwritten marginalia. As he paged to the end, he noticed, in one-inch-high letters and in English, the word *Coward*. Beneath that was a line which Thomas recognized from Shakespeare's *Julius Caesar*.

"Cowards die many times before their deaths; the valiant never taste of death but once."

Beneath that were the words *Morti jucti sunt* (The dead are cast).

He closed the book and set it gently on the desk to one side. The book beneath had a red cover, one that he recognized, that of the Loeb Classics Latin Collection. The books were legendary among high school as well as college students of the classical works of ancient Greece and Rome. The Greek works, however, always had green covers. Thomas lifted the text. As he did so, he noticed an envelope beneath it. Feeling that he might be prying, he set the envelope down without opening it. Then he opened the red-covered book. Inside the front cover was the ink-stamped emblem of Blackwells, the world-renowned printing house and book publisher affiliated with Oxford University. The inside cover revealed the name of the author, the Roman historian Tacitus. He flipped through the pages to the bookmarker. He paused and read the Latin text on the left side of the page.

"Sit huius tam fortis exitus Constantia penes utrosque par, claritudinis plus in tuo fine." Post quae eodem ictu brachia ferro

exsolvunt. Seneca, quoniam senile corpus et parco victu tenuatum lenta effugia sanguini (Tacitus, *Annals*, Book XV, LXIII.—LXIV.)

Though a good student in high school, Thomas looked to the right page for the English translation.

> "May the courage of this brave ending be divided equally between us both, but many more of fame attend your own departure!" After this, they made the incision in their arms with a single cut. Seneca, since his aged body, emaciated further by frugal living, gave slow escape to the blood, severed as well the arteries in the leg and behind the knee.

The foreboding that Thomas first felt now strengthened its grip around his heart as he looked down at the desk chair where Ricci's Roman collar was set neatly. Thomas reached for it. Grasping one end of the collar, he lifted only half of it. It had been neatly cut in two and placed on the chair with great care to make the two halves adjoin. Thomas read the gesture intuitively. He threw it down and rushed into first Ricci's bedroom and then the bathroom.

The steamy bathroom smelt of heat and a sweet scent that Thomas recognized all too well. He gasped, "Oh, no!" Ricci lay in the blood red water of a bathtub. Ricci's veins at the wrists, legs, and behind the knees had all been slashed. Ricci himself lay under the water, only his forehead and nose emerging slightly above the blood. At first, Thomas wanted to reach in and pull him out. But he could see the man was already dead and he did not need to leave any more indications of his having been there. Next to the tub sat a small three-legged stool. Atop it was an eight-inch-tall bronze statue. Thomas squatted down to look at it. At its base it read "St. Jude." Recognizing the saint's significance, Thomas whispered, "Patron saint of the hopeless." Thomas paused and pressed two fingers to his lips and then touched them to Ricci's forehead and uttered, "May God forgive you. *Dominus Vobiscum.*"

As if suddenly forced back into a soldierly attention, Thomas tensed and reached into his back pocket for a handkerchief. He used it to wipe down the doorknob of the room and the cut Roman collar as well as the books. He then wiped down the knob of the exterior door and was about to leave when he turned around and walked back to the desk and picked up the envelope. He reached inside and pulled out a photograph of a much younger Matteo Ricci. Standing next to him was a strapping, broad-shouldered black youth wearing the clean white shirt and starched blue pants of a Catholic school boy. Printed in black ink at the bottom of the photograph were the words *Jomo, age fourteen*. He put the photograph back into the envelope, slid it into the cover of the Tacitus book, and grabbed it, along with the work by C. S. Lewis. Walking down the hallway casually so as to not invite questions or arouse suspicions from anyone who saw him, he pondered what happened to change Ricci's mind from one day to the next.

CHAPTER 46
THE MORTAL REMAINS

I lay waiting
between turf-face and demesne wall

—Seamus Heaney, "Bog Queen"

—THE HEATHER INN

THAT EVENING, THOMAS RELAYED THE NEWS ABOUT RICCI TO GRANT, and Grant to Dennis and Oz. With their prize witness now dead, their immediate hopes of exposing the link between Vanderkin and Jomo were gone. But unlike the others, Oz seemed unperturbed.

"Hope springs eternal," was all that he had to say to Grant. Still, it was a simple enough protestation of hope in the face of dire news that Grant could not help but be buoyed. MacArthur had indicated that he would be in touch with Grant shortly. Grant made it clear that if there were no objections, he would soon be on his way to the north of England and then to Scotland. He asked if it were safe to once again explore the caves at the archaeological site.

MacArthur had said that he could not guarantee their safety as he had only one man guarding the place by day and another by night. Still, Vanderkin was unlikely to try anything more, as "He knows that we know."

Three hours later, Grant had contacted Carruthers and Margaret and Mermac Collins, who had agreed to converge once again upon the cavern. They would stay at another inn, a little farther from the site, due to Blanche's recent experience there. Within three days, Grant had arrived. He was soon joined by Carruthers and then Blanche, who attended over the objections of her uncle.

However, after only one night at the inn, Grant decided that the Heather Inn still offered a better location, a better view of the hillside, and certainly easier access. At first the innkeeper seemed surprised to see Grant again. He also seemed cautiously pleased that he had returned to his establishment.

*   *   *   *   *

Early on the first day of their investigation of the site, MacArthur's man, who was known to them only as Kenneth, assured them that no one other than himself and Travis, another of MacArthur's men, had entered the cavern. They had seen no one in the immediate vicinity and had limited their own exposure to prying eyes by spending much of the day concealed in the cavern.

On the first morning, Grant rose early and went for a five-mile run through the summer beauty of the Highlands. As he ran with the sun at his back, he watched his own shadow move before him and felt himself oddly delighted in it, not as a mere phenomenon of a moving absence of light but as a playfulness between the powers of light and darkness itself. His shadow seemed, in some mysterious way, a companion who came along this morning as a messenger who tried to warn him that the brightest days cast the darkest and deepest shadows.

At the halfway mark, Grant dropped to the ground and did fifty pushups. Here, along the side of the road, he sweated his way to maintaining the conditioning that had served him so well in high school and college sports and now in the most demanding regimes of military training. He rose up off the ground with his arms as pumped as his legs, somewhat red-faced at the exertion, and began his way back with his shadow trailing behind like a rear guard. It reminded him of the need to have the dark side of humanity ever tethered to the beauty of the sunlit world if one expected to survive in it. Grant was ready for risks and unexplored opportunities. At breakfast, after his run and shower, Grant found the innkeeper to be unusually ingratiating.

"How long will you be staying?"

Grant reminded him again, as he had the night before, that his stay was a day to day affair.

"Why have you returned so soon?"

"The Highlands could win any man's soul. I'm Scottish myself," Grant reminded him.

He wondered at the inn keeper's seeming need to be reminded of everything Grant had previously told him. Every question the innkeeper asked was an echo of one he had asked during Grant's first visit.

After breakfast, Grant arrived at the entrance to the cavern. Not far away and on the far side of the wall sat Kenneth, who kept himself concealed until he was sure that it was indeed Grant. He helped Grant lift the entrance opening. Grant dropped to his hands and knees and entered the passageway into the dark, womblike cavern, which he thought must conceal mysteries of life and humanity not yet tapped by modern man.

Upon entering, Grant switched on his flashlight. Kenneth remained outside. Grant and the others had not yet investigated any of the pathways in the caves thoroughly. But on this day, they would video record what they imagined would be another Carterlike moment. When Carter opened Tut's tomb, he did so with sufficient reverence and awe to suggest that he was indeed the right person to unveil a mystery that had concealed itself from the avarice of robbers and the violence of plunderers for thousands of years.

As Grant contemplated the world and all its secrets, his reverie was interrupted by a sound near the entrance. There, he saw the silhouette of Margaret Collins entering. The daylight from the outside world was partially obscured by three sets of legs behind her: Carruthers', her husband's, and Kenneth's. Carruthers and her husband followed her, and finally Blanche, while Kenneth remained without.

Carruthers carried the largest of the three backpacks, as well as a separate coil of heavy nylon rope and belaying equipment. Margaret furnished an array of snacks along with two canteens and a water filter. Mermac carried the video equipment along with two high-powered flashlights to help illuminate the darkness. Grant's pack contained two blank hardback notebooks and plenty of writing utensils, along with Jeremy Ong's work on Celtic symbology.

Upon entering the cave, they immediately and with wordless understanding moved to the entrance of the middle passage. Carruthers led with one flashlight, followed by Margaret, Mermac, and then Grant, who now held his own small flashlight while Blanche held the second. They rapidly navigated their way through the now familiar entranceway and came quickly and with anticipation to the abyss. There, they brought their flashlights to the edge and explored all the contours. Then, with some trepidation, Grant volunteered to descend. Since Carruthers was the most experienced climber among them, he orchestrated the descent. He pulled out the climbing harness and hooked up Grant. He then handed him a cap lantern with an elastic belt, which he placed upon his head and turned on with a flick of the switch.

Carruthers and the others twisted the nylon rope around themselves as Grant braced his legs against the cavern and leaned backwards and into the darkness. Using his feet like springs, he bounced off the hard rock surface, looking over one shoulder and then the other, moving with the airless slow-motion dance of an astronaut. Halfway down, a protrusion caught the rope and twisted him, causing him to bump hard against the wall with his left shoulder and bang his head against the wall with just enough force to scrape his forehead and ear against the granite.

"You all right?" asked Carruthers.

"No problem," replied Grant.

"We've got you," said Mermac. "We've a good grip." He grunted from the exertion of holding the ropes.

Grant regained his balance. He slowed his descent as the surface wall increased in roughness and unpredictability. Now he scraped his way toward the bottom and heard rocks hitting it with increasing volume. Only four feet from the bottom, Grant looked down between his legs with his head lamp and dropped to the abyss's floor. His face almost met the wall as he stood up straight.

"I made it," he said.

"Hooray!" cried Margaret as she loosened her grip on the rope. Carruthers kept the rope wound about himself even as the others stepped out of it. He had been positioned farthest from the edge. Now he approached it cautiously and inadvertently knocked down some small pebbles onto Grant's head.

"Hey! Watch what you're doing!" protested Grant.

"Sorry, it was me," replied Carruthers. "An unintentional gift."

"Do it again and I'll kiss you when I get up there."

"Is that a threat?" asked Carruthers.

And with that Blanche threw a small pebble of her own across to the other side and said, "Sorry, Grant, that was me. Does your threat still hold?"

Grant laughed as he detached himself from the harness and shouted up, "My threat holds regardless of what you do."

Blanche blushed.

Grant's head lamp cast a light in any direction that he looked while the powerful flashlight penetrated all around him. He slowly surveyed the entire bottom by turning in all directions.

"What do you see?" asked Mermac.

"Nothing that you don't," replied Grant.

The wall down which Grant had just climbed was about ninety feet wide, while the other opposite wall was of approximately the same dimensions. The wall to Grant's left as he stood with his back to his companions was approximately sixty or seventy feet across, while the wall to his right was about ninety or one hundred feet, giving the entire space trapezoidal dimensions.

Grant took his first step forward on the hard surface. The cavern bottom seemed to be nothing more than a boring, dried-up well—deep but uninteresting. But as Grant turned around several feet from the wall down which he had just lowered himself, he noticed its sheen. When he flashed his light on it, it seemed almost opalescent, almost beautiful. What caught his eye next, however, was stunning.

Near the bottom of the wall appeared a sort of ledge, shoulder width across. One step above it was another ledge that was clearly manmade: flat and the exact length as the other. He looked above it and saw yet another and then another. From the bottom of the pit to the very top was a chiseled ladder. It ended immediately to the right of where Carruthers was standing near the ledge. But neither he nor the others had yet seen it. However, as Grant's light flashed up and down the steps, the others came to realize his discovery.

Alongside each of the steps was an iron handgrip—old, no doubt, but still intact. They ran parallel to one another all the way up the side of the ladder.

"Looks like someone else was looking to make the climb a little easier," said Carruthers as he followed the movement of Grant's light.

Grant moved off to his right and noticed that his footing changed.

Instead of the rock and gravely bottom that he had been standing on, the terrain now seemed soft and at times brittle. He stooped down and touched it. It felt like dried grass or some desiccated weed. He rubbed it between his fingers and it flaked to dust. He reached down again and stuck his hand deeper into it. Dry, brittle, broken, and mysterious.

Man must have placed it here. Nothing could grow in this darkness, he thought, *not even mushrooms.*

Grant stood up and slowly walked the perimeter. As he did so, he sank six or seven inches down into the brittle depths with each step.

"What do you see?" called out Blanche.

"I don't know, some sort of vegetation."

"Bring me a sample," replied Margaret.

Grant didn't answer; instead he measured each step as he moved almost delicately around the periphery, for fear the vegetation might give way entirely beneath his feet. It took him a full ten minutes to step around the perimeter of the first three walls. As he approached the last section of the trapezoidal abyss, the perimeter grew tough. There was still the soft, dry vegetation beneath his feet as well as rocky protrusions the popped through it.

The last side was a mixture of rocks that made walking ungainly. The soft vegetation that sank with disquieting ease made Grant's awkward movement almost comical. Sometimes one foot was on a protruding rock while the other was on the brittle vegetation. Fortunately, the entire area was very, very dry. Not even a hint of moisture was in the air. There might be stumbling here but certainly no sliding on wet surfaces.

As he stepped toward the point of convergence of the two walls, he flashed his light ahead. There was something odd. He couldn't entirely make out what was lying in the corner. He approached it even as the others above tried to put their beams in the same area. Grant's spine tingled as he struggled toward the shape in front of him.

He stood right next to it and looked down at it in surprise and disbelief. On one of the rocks, protruding through the dried vegetation, lay a leg wrapped in some kind of cloth, pointed upward at an awkward angle. On the foot was a kind of canvassy looking tennis shoe with high tops, the kind he had seen in old photographs of people of a bygone generation. He reached out and touched the foot and followed it down the ankle, where a pant leg had a woolen cuff through which a string passed, apparently to close the cuff tightly against the elements. He followed the pant leg up. It was a kind of cottony material.

The other leg was pinned beneath it while the torso seemed twisted with the face looking down. Before he could gather his thoughts and explain the entire discovery to himself, Carruthers yelled down, "What is it?"

"I think it's a body, a person."

"Did you say a body?"

"Yes, body."

They were silent even as Grant moved his hand up the back of a dark leather jacket. He felt for the neck. His hand touched hair and the withered but still intact leathery skin and a piece of chalky skull. He then pulled back the collar and saw something. It looked like stenciled lettering. He pulled the collar back and flashed the light right next to the print. From his position the letters were upside down. Still he read them to himself. *Chisolm.* His hairs stood on end, and he gasped and almost choked. What were the chances? He steadied himself by placing both hands against the wall.

Just a coincidence, just a coincidence, he said to himself.

Still, he felt as if he had just been hit in the stomach with an iron fist. He knew more than he wanted to understand. Stories and fantasies and unanswered questions cried out from the corners of his mind. He found himself shaking.

"Coincidence," he now said aloud. "Coincidence."

"Hey, Grant, you all right?" It was Blanche.

Grant whispered, more to himself than to the others, "Yes, yes, it's just a coincidence."

Grant turned back again to the body. Overcoming his own disorientation, Grant reached down with both hands and attempted to pry the body from the floor. The head was wedged into a slight depression abutting the wall while the legs and torso were elevated, lying higher on the rock. The body lifted with surprising ease. The scalp was still connected to the leathery bits of flesh that adhered to the skeleton.

Grant held the torso with both hands and placed the body on an area of relatively flat ground. The skull looked back at Grant with an air of indifference. It was only then that Grant noticed the tarnished chain hanging around the skeleton's neck.

"Oh God," he whispered, afraid at the confirmation of the skeleton's identity that might be before him. With a palpitation of his heart and shaking hand, he reached for the chain. He lifted it and the metal dog tag from under the jacket. The dog tag was embossed with the words, "LT. Mark Chisolm, U.S. Army."

Damn, he even wore his old military tag for the return trip, thought Grant.

With a gentleness that sprang from the deepest well of his being and a reverence for the past as well as for his part in the present, he lifted the chain from around the neck and placed it around his own. He sat down next to the remains and looked up to the others, who peeped down from above. They were respectfully silent, waiting for Grant to speak. They sensed the moment and whispered to themselves as though they were in church.

Then Grant stirred and brought a focus to their observations as he put hands in each of the pant pockets, searching for more evidence of these being his grandfather's remains. He lifted up the skeleton again and felt the pockets of the jacket. As he did so, he noticed four distinct holes in the back of the jacket itself. He fingered each hole. As he did so, something heavy fell to the floor. He flashed the light at the sound and then lifted the form again. There beneath it was the source of the sound: a bullet with a flattened point. At least the source of one of the holes in the back of his ancestor was now apparent. Instinctively, he covered the spent bullet with his handkerchief and pocketed it. Then, as he reached around the back inside of the jacket, he felt the distinctive hard leather of a shoulder holster. The gun was still in it.

He pulled the gun gently from the holster and flashed the light directly upon it. The gun still had the braided tether attached to it, and as he fingered the revolver itself, he felt the touch of grease and oil. The lubricants had done their job after all these years. He checked the action and then spun it. The chambers were full. No doubt if he pulled the trigger, the hammer would come down and the bullet would fire. Grant stuck the revolver into his belt at the small of his back, looked up, and said, "Get ready. I'm coming up. But keep the slack for the moment and move over to the ledges. I'm going to see if the ancient smithies made something we can still use."

With that, Grant grabbed first one then the other of the iron grips embedded on either side of the ledge. Warily, he ascended, and the ancient iron held.

Carruthers reached down to extend a hand as Grant's head came up over the ledge.

Blanche looked at Grant and said, "You look different, like you've seen a ghost or something."

"I have. The man down there ... he is someone I think I know. He's my grandfather."

No one reacted. They all stared at him with a blank expression.

Without saying another word, he walked past them. He felt dizzy. The others followed, incredulous. Not knowing his family's personal history, Carruthers wondered at the statement and considered that perhaps there were undetected gases in the caverns that may have affected his thinking. He asked himself if he should buy a canary to use as a gauge of the air quality before he came to this place again. Grant went immediately to the opening and got down on his hands and knees and began to crawl out. The exit was still partially opened.

As he emerged, Grant was suddenly filled with nausea and vomited. He wondered if it could really be true. If so, how would he tell his grandmother? Grant sat down and took off the dog tags and looked at them in the daylight, unaware that his helmet light was still on. After about a minute, Carruthers came over and put his hand on Grant's shoulder. Grant's dizziness reflected the whirlwind of emotions he felt. Grant then reached up and held open his hand with the dog tag in it and the chain hanging down. Carruthers took the tag and looked at the name, then handed it to Margaret, Mermac, and finally Blanche, who read it and gave it back to Carruthers.

Carruthers offered, "I'm sorry, Grant. It must be quite a shock."

Blanche added, "My remark about seeing a ghost ... I'm sorry."

Grant smiled and asked, "Do you all believe in destiny?"

Blanche looked at him and answered, "Yes."

Grant reached out, and Carruthers gave him back the tag.

Before anyone could offer more condolences, Grant asked, "Where's Kenneth?"

At first no one answered. After a long pause, Carruthers spoke. "We have things to consider. And I don't like being up here unarmed in light of our last little mishap. Kenneth's absence bothers me. At least he or someone should be protecting our rear. I say we call this a day, however short, and consider what we do next. We can't just ignore the body."

"No, we won't ignore it," said Grant flatly, "but we can't let it change our plans about keeping this a secret."

"I don't know, Grant," said Carruthers. "He is your grandfather, but to discover a body and not report it ..."

"We will, but I suggest in due time. Not now. If this becomes a police matter, we might find ourselves permanently barred from this site for a number of violations of Scottish laws. Even a lawless American like me knows that. I think our best course of action may be to share this with MacArthur and no one else. He'll know what to do."

As they descended from the ruined church, Grant glanced around once more, looking for Kenneth. Understanding his shock at the discovery of his grandfather's body, Blanche touched his hand gently several times as they walked down to the road to their cars. Grant went with them back to the Welsley Inn rather than back to the Heather.

*   *   *   *   *

Several hours later, they reconverged upon the site. They once again pried open the site and entered into the world of darkness. But as Carruthers entered, he caught the scent of sulfur. Who, he wondered, would be so careless as to once again risk a conflagration? Or was it merely his imagination? Sulfur and matches were nearly synonymous with fire. The others smelled it, too. They turned their flashlights on and headed away from the location of the morning's discovery. They had decided to give MacArthur time to think about an appropriate course of action. MacArthur would try to reach Kenneth as well as Travis, the other guard who shared the responsibility of watching over the site and of guarding its explorers.

As they arrived at the mouth of the third entryway, they were filled with trepidation, anticipation, and the excitement of finding an undiscovered country. The morning's find haunted them all, and the whiff of sulfur tugged at them, warning of the need for caution.

The top and base of the entryway were almost seven feet across, while the vertical dimensions were slightly greater. Here the flooring was again chiseled and at times made of polished stone with striations running length-wise along the floor. These too appeared to be manmade.

Chiseled motifs decorated the walls on both sides with occasional large, circular engravings tinted with silver at the top, bottom, and on both sides. Each of them speculated in turn at the mystery unfolding before them.

Over the next fifteen minutes, they meandered down the low grade, encountering different motifs in a blend of Celtic swirls and decorations alongside scenes of war carved into the walls. Men on horseback appeared to be running down their enemy as if in some prequel to the sewing of the Bayeaux Tapestry. The motifs included a kind of detailed filigree surrounding stylized faces of dragons that had the looks of familiar gargoyles. But these seemed much older, with their unfamiliar designs and almost Easter Island consistency—dragons with fire that looked nearly identical, with only the circular filigree of their fiery breath to distinguish one from another.

But as they went deeper and farther, the motifs extended themselves to much more familiar figures. Crosses of Celtic design were carved deep into the walls. Not merely reliefs, these represented hundreds of hours of human endeavor. After a long and gradual decline, the reliefs gave way to polished walls with bowl-shaped depressions that one might imagine being used for water or oils for fires. No sooner had they shuffled through a half an hour of hand-crafted smoothness, than the pathway leveled off and the walls gave way on either side to an expansive darkness.

The darkness momentarily seized and distorted the light, causing it to reflect off of the cloud-colored rock that was partially transparent and turned the beam of the flashlight into something only vaguely luminescent, twisting the light into a mysterious, self-reflected glow. The beauty of it struck them all. Blanche wondered at the idea that such beauty might not have been seen for centuries. Margaret wondered if the beauty disappeared when their eyes were closed or when the caverns were forgotten. Grant was in the awe of the labor that had polished such rock into light-absorbent as well as light-reflecting material. Here and there, even at a distance, Runic-looking glyphs were painted and carved into the walls on either side. The span of the chamber eluded their shafts of light and dissolved into more mystery.

Grant cast his light behind him in a wary recognition of the fact that they all had nearly fallen victims to an intruder once before. Even he, however, was drawn inexorably forward to the intrigue of the unknown and the spirited recognition that they might be on the verge of a major archaeological find.

In the pitch darkness, their lights peered like miraculous eyes that cast their own sources of luminescence. They seemed like miracles of existence intruding into the realm of Vulcan or some ancient god whom they might awaken from its slumber. Here, Thor might have hidden an arsenal undisclosed to all but the few. Here, Woton might have hidden the souls of the great warriors until the Judgment Day, the Day of Doom.

Or else here might have been hidden the most precious of human artifacts. Here might have been the secret place of ancient wisdom. Here, the darkness, the quiet, the stillness caused them to hold their breaths at the mystique of unknown places. Here might have been the beauty of the sacred mixed with the silent wisdom and knowledge of the ancients. Here, modernity in the form of flashlights, mountaineering gear, and cameras met the awe-inspiring skill, craftsmanship, and monumental constructs of a long-dead people.

As they walked out into the full darkness, they shone their flashlights straight up. The ceiling was strangely vaulted as if it too had been touched by human hands. Leading toward the apex of approximately fifty feet, an array of straight lines converged. They met like the spokes of a wheel while touching the expansive perimeter all around, each spoke equidistant from the other. The entire room was no less than two hundred feet across, an almost perfect circle with anterooms situated throughout. And all along the walls, the glyphs and various motifs continued, ancient and Christian.

But it was what lay in front of them that drew them forward in awe. A long stone bench was carved directly into the wall, extending from a kind of central point, and a thronelike seat lay directly opposite the opening through which they had entered. They remained silent as they converged. Their lights revealed a monolithic rectangular stone that stood at a right angle to the end of the bench, to the right of the thronelike seat. Carruthers and Grant moved to the rectangular stone and saw protruding from it three sword handles.

Carruthers reached out with his right hand and gently touched the first of the three. It was an engraved handle that fit into an indentation of about two inches. Beneath was a slender opening into which a sword or dagger blade might have fit quite neatly.

"Look," said Rex. "How could anyone sculpt these openings?"

"Maybe ... wait, look here," said Grant. "It's as though they carved a large cylinder out of the rock and then, see, they dropped a new cylinder of two halves into the slot," added Grant.

"Here," said Blanche. "It's an image of a sword."

"It's more than that, I'd say," responded Grant. "This looks like something to fold hot steel into the shape of a sword."

"You'd say this is a black smith's den?" asked Margaret.

"Perhaps," said Grant.

"But a most unusual one."

"Look at the size and the shape of this image. If this was part of a mold to form a sword, it must have been an unusually large sword, for an unusually large man."

Rex then lifted the other two handles. Both were encrusted with ornate filigree and had a bulbous knob at the end.

"My God," gasped Margaret. "What a find!" For the first time, one of them spoke in a normal tone of voice.

"Three swords," said Rex. Then he squinted as he looked at the side of the stone. Along the top edge of the stone were three inscriptions chiseled into the rock. As Rex leaned over, Grant stood next to him. Rex traced his finger with one hand while holding the flashlight in the other. His finger traced the lettering. As he did so, Grant whispered the word, "Naegling."

"What?" said Carruthers.

"Naegling," again said Grant.

"Naegling?"

"Yes, it's Old English."

"You mean like ... you mean as in Anglo-Saxon."

"Yes, at least that old."

Blanche squinted to see the writing. "My God, it can't be."

"What's so phenomenal, other than the fact that we've stumbled upon something truly remote, obscure, ancient, wonderful, intriguing, and strange?" asked Mermac.

Grant turned to Blanche and asked in the way of confirmation, "Does it sound familiar?"

"It does, but it can't be. It has to be a hoax, doesn't it? How could it be?"

"Be what?" asked Carruthers.

"Beowulf," responded Grant.

"Beowulf?" asked Margaret. "You mean like in the poem? I read it as a student at the university."

"And I studied it in Old English, but what does it mean?" asked Rex.

"It's the name of Beowulf's sword. It's essentially our modern English word for *nail*. It's like calling your sword Spike," replied Grant.

"When was he supposed to have lived?" asked Mermac.

"About 450–600 AD, something like that."

"It can't be," repeated Blanche.

"Was he real?" asked Mermac.

No one answered; they only looked at the engraving.

Then Grant began to recite from memory, "*Da com of more under mist-hleopum Grendel gongan, Godes yrre baer.*"

"It sounds quite German," responded Margaret.

"It is. Old English and German are virtually the same."

"Maybe it's better to say that it's Anglo-Saxon," said Blanche.

"Then I assume this can't be real either," said Grant. He had moved to the next slot and picked up the hilt of the sword. This one was inlaid with jewels and in part wrapped in pearl and ivory or bone. Two dragon heads rounded out the engravings. Grant shone the light at the top edge, two feet from the handle, its slot, and the cylinder in which both were housed. There in clearly chiseled Latin script were the letters *Caledfwlch*. As Grant spoke the letters aloud, Blanche turned abruptly in realization of its significance.

"No!" she pronounced. "No, this is too much. Don't touch it. Only the chosen."

"What? The chosen?" asked Grant. "It's a sword hilt."

"My God," she exclaimed and then whispered it aloud six or seven times, trying to convince herself that this whole experience was real.

"Tell me," said Grant. By this time, the others had also gathered around silently.

"I think I understand," said Mermac.

"I don't," said Grant.

Blanche now spoke with a trembling in her throat. Her voice seemed to be on the verge of vanishing any second. Tears welled up in her eyes and wetted her cheeks. Hoarsely, she whispered, "Caledfwlch. It's Welsh." Then she stopped, the emotion causing her throat to swell with the word she dare not speak. "Don't … touch. It means 'battle hard' in Welsh."

Before Grant could bring himself to ask again of its meaning, Blanche's hand reached to almost touch the hilt. Then she froze and whispered, "Arthur's sword." The tears continued, and she reflexively bowed her head.

But Grant had to be certain. "You mean Arthur? King Arthur?"

Understanding his question before it was asked, Blanche said, "Excalibur was the French or Latinized form of the sword's name. Before the French adopted the Arthurian stories, Arthur was very much a king whose stories were preserved by the Welsh." She caught her breath. "He may have been one of them. His sword was Caledfwlch before it was known as Excalibur." Then feeling like a seer who was drained of all her energy by the strain and gifts of insight and prophecy, Blanche leaned against Grant, totally relaxed, totally relieved, spiritually uplifted, and nearly overcome with fatigue.

Grant felt almost compelled to kneel. Blanche looked again and said, "It can't be. It must be a hoax."

"It is the third that I cannot imagine," interrupted Carruthers, breaking the reverie.

The third handle was larger than the others. Rex held it at his chest and looked at it closely. Unlike the others, this one was plain, no filigree, but the knob was actually an engraving of a bearded head. Immediately, all of them looked to the top edge to see if a clue would be provided. "De Wallace du York." Unlike the others, this writing was more discernible.

"This seems modern," said Blanche.

"But who would name a sword?" asked Mermac.

Carruthers, who thought as an archaeologist, believed he had indeed died and gone to heaven. Then, as Carruthers looked more closely, he shook his head in disbelief.

"What is it?" asked Grant.

"This," he said as he pointed to a small skull and crossbones surrounding the engraved letters. Each of the four skulls and crossbones were equidistant from one another about the name Wallace.

Almost greedily, Grant and the others looked to the next slot where a sword had once been. To the edges their eyes moved and again there was a name: Salvation.

"I know now," said Blanche.

"No, I don't know," said Carruthers.

"What?" asked Grant.

"The skull and crossbones," she said. "It was emblematic of the Knight Templars, long, long before it became the symbol of Caribbean pirates. At the Battle of Bannockburn, the Scots were outnumbered three to one, and they should have lost the battle. Wallace, that great war chief, had already been captured and killed. "However," she added with raised eyebrows, "the Knight Templars, who had been banned in much of Europe, were mad monks who fought with Spartan ferocity. They showed up at the battle at the critical moment and turned the tide. The Scots won. Wallace must have been one of them."

"Look again," added Carruthers. "Here, another slot with another missing hilt. But there is no name."

"The slot of the unknown soldier," added Grant.

As they regaled themselves with speculation concerning all that they were seeing a soft white light appeared in the entrance way and gradually grew in intensity. On reflex, Grant and Carruthers turned off their flashlights so that they could see without being seen. As Mermac and Margaret turned toward the opening, she turned off her flashlight as well and stood silently awaiting the intruder.

CHAPTER 47
SHADOWS AND RIDDLES

Only men's minds could ever have unmapped
Into abstractions such a territory.

—Norman Maccaig, "Celtic Cross"

—THE CAVE

THE RADIANCE OF THE WHITE LIGHT GREW TO ILLUMINATE THE entire rectangular opening. At last, a figure stood at the very periphery of the great vaulted interior. The figure remained indistinguishable from the darkness itself and only at the figure's momentary movement to illuminate the ceiling did a flicker of light catch the spark of his two eyes. But as the figure lowered the light once more, the eyes became invisible and the slight glimpse of a human form dissipated into the darkness. Mermac, Margaret, Blanche, Carruthers, and Grant watched as the figure, with the nonchalance of a night watchman making his rounds, turned and trekked the long grade back up the passageway.

As the figure departed, the light silhouetted him against the passageway walls. A tall man with broad shoulder and a form that Grant recognized disappeared. Then, in what appeared an almost playful gesture, the figure stopped and turned the flashlight backwards, held it at arm's length, and stood midway in the tunnel to create an enormous black figure on the wall.

Beyond a shadow of a doubt, thought Grant. As the sound of the steps turned to memory and as the light completely disappeared, they all sighed in relief.

Grant whispered, "We must be careful. I recognize the man. He's dangerous and someone all of you should recognize, too. Only I've had the pleasure of more than one encounter with the guy. We'll wait. We must be assured he is gone, and we must find out about Kenneth. His disappearance and this man's arrival strike me as more than coincidence."

"Too bad there is no other way out," said Carruthers.

"Perhaps there is," replied Grant.

"Why do you say that?" he asked.

"Look again at the stone. It's more than merely a series of slots for holding weaponry. At this end, we see a large pit with vents on either side as well as other pits that're also deep and more than likely manmade. And here, feel this part. It's metal."

"So?" asked Margaret.

"It's a blacksmith's shop, or a smithy. This was set up to make the weapons here. Yet to burn a fire to heat and forge the metals would be near impossible without proper ventilation."

Blanche asked, "How do you know this?"

Grant smiled and said, "I'm an America. That makes me a cowboy. Cowboys ride horses. Horses need shoes. We know a blacksmith's shop when we see one. There is another way out."

Carruthers turned his flashlight upward again, looking for an opening. As he scanned the ceiling immediately above them, he noticed a squarish outline that looked as though it had been cemented shut. The surface of the domed ceiling was rough here and pockmarked where some of the ancient firmament had given way.

But as he scanned what they thought to be a onetime opening, Carruthers and the others shone their lights upon an oddity of circular forms about a foot in diameter. All of the circles had holes in their center along with a small and indecipherable protrusion underneath.

As Grant gazed at it, his training in celestial navigation suddenly took hold. "My God," he said, "look at this."

"I'm afraid to ask," said Carruthers. "My ignorance may be showing, but I see nothing unusual except the whole structure itself. Am I missing the obvious?"

"That's right. It's not unusual for man to look heavenward." And then as if to confirm his first intuitive grasp of the ceiling's significance, he shone the light all about the dome.

"This is heaven," remarked Grant again. "Look at the figures, the circles. They're constellations that are entirely common for anyone in the northern hemisphere. See there," he pointed. "It's the Big Dipper, and there is the Little Dipper. That must be Polaris, the North Star."

"It's a planetarium," added Blanche. "But why? Why here? Here under the earth?"

"Maybe it's a map of some sort, one that no one but a select few were chosen to see," added Carruthers.

"Oh wonder of wonders!" exclaimed Margaret. "This is remarkable."

Then as they shone their lights about again, Blanche said, "Stop, Grant, stop. Keep the light there. Look. It's a large, very large column and several others, I'd say. Do you see? Look! It's a megastone structure. It's like Stonehenge underground." She laughed in disbelief at her own hypothesis.

"Now it's my turn," said Grant.

Then in a good natured parody of Blanche's eternal skepticism, he added, "It can't be." "What wonders we have seen," replied Margaret.

"Darling, who would have thought. I wish the boys were here," added Mermac.

"I don't understand," exclaimed Carruthers in a loud stage whisper. "How could something like this be hidden for so many years? How is it that men did not write of it? How did we not know it was here?"

Grant laughed and said, "Even when you know exactly where something's supposed to be, you can lose it—like weapons of mass destruction in a certain Middle Eastern country."

"Maybe they didn't want anyone to know," said Blanche.

Then, as Grant walked away in the direction of the thronelike seat, he noticed a large hemispherically shaped device. Almost two feet in diameter, it was a stone that appeared to be one half of a complete circle. Grant picked it up and eyed it curiously. It looked like something he had seen once before while visiting a museum.

Perhaps in the Oslo Maritime Museum, he thought.

Blanche touched his shoulder as if to say, "Show me." He held it out to her and she said, "Let me." The stone semi-circle was heavy, and she held it with both hands. "It's Viking. It's a sort of direction finder. Before the compass, these were used."

Carruthers came closer to examine it as well. "Mega builders,

Vikings, Angles, Saxons, and who else? The sword handles. Still, how could they keep it a secret for so long?"

"No television," responded Margaret.

Grant then shined his light on the smoothed wall above the throne. There, in a kind of squarish lettering from what may have been a medieval hand, were the following words clearly engraved into the smoothed stone:

Foot to Foot
Head to Head
Rise Ye Up
From the Dead
Man and Wyf
Beneath the Ground
A New World Blest
A Cart There Found

"Hmm, I wonder what it means," asked Blanche.

Carruthers added, "We need more equipment. Even Carter would have canned his amazement long enough to get equipment."

Grant smiled and asked, "How big a find is this?"

"Same as my rank in the army," replied Carruthers.

"Very good, major," replied Grant.

"Yes, let's go back. We need to make plans. This may be more than anyone could imagine."

They moved toward the opening through which the intruder had entered the periphery of the dome only fifteen or so minutes earlier. As they walked slowly up the gradually graded granite, they moved with excitement as well as a vague uneasiness, the residue of the unannounced silhouette. Their steps were fairly quiet but heard.

After several minutes of mild exertion, they trudged into the area in which the three passageways converged near the exit to the outside. Carruthers led, followed by Margaret, Mermac, Blanche, and Grant.

As they moved toward the entrance, a voice rang out, "Stop or I'll shoot." All of them were startled and did as they were told. Grant turned around first to look upon the speaker.

"Put that flashlight down or that will be the last thing you do," said the disembodied voice. "Turn your flashlights off." He turned his on so that he could see them but they could not so easily see him.

Grant, having first recognized the silhouette and now the voice, spoke while looking downward so as to not be blinded by the light. "I was about to say, 'Nice to see you again,' but given your featureless presence, I'll merely say, 'Good evening, Father Wirtz.'"

"No need for clerical reverence, Mr. Chisolm, or should I say, commander. After all, what profits a man to save a soul long dead when he can gain the whole world? You'll forgive my parody of biblical lessons. My life as a spiritual guide was always a kind of farce, one that my father never approved of, but one which was inspired by one that you saved only so that he could later take his own life." He paused as though to give himself time to once again focus where he thought his attention should be.

"It's men like you, Mr. Chisolm, who cause other men to hate."

"How?" replied Grant. "It's you who have forced this encounter. You seem unduly attracted to confrontation."

"Shut up. Now you will listen. You and your friends have intruded for the last time. You seem incapable of taking hints to stay away from this place. You are equally indiscrete in the choice of your female companionship. No offense to you, miss," he said as he pointed the flashlight directly toward Blanche. "Your friend apparently has an appetite for more feminine company than is good for him. However, you, Mr. Chisolm, have something that I desire, a certain package that you seem most reluctant to part with. My friends and I are out of patience."

"I thought that might have been the case a while ago. We couldn't help but notice the hot reception we received at your cousin's hands a few weeks ago."

"Cousin? You're more perceptive than I thought. How did you know?"

"You and Martin Vanderkin have identical body types and even some facial and coloring similarities."

"Very good. I'm impressed. However, you and your friends received a most deserved retribution for your intrusion upon our property."

"Your property?" interrupted Carruthers. "This belongs to the Trust of Scotland. And much of this area is actually owned by the Ministry of Defense. You can hardly call it yours."

"I will continue to call it mine as it most assuredly is."

At Carruther's intrusion, Grant moved slightly away from Blanche so as to distance himself from the direct beam of light that still shined on her face. He had heeded the intruder's threat since discretion is indeed the better part of valor. However, he had not actually seen the supposed gun. Wirtz could be bluffing.

Then Margaret asked fearfully, "What do you intend to do to us?"

"Whatever I please. But as to whether you shall live or die, that depends upon Mr. Chisolm."

Carruthers asked, "Where is the guard who was on duty earlier, as well as the other?"

"Guards?" He paused. "It is enough to say that they are engaged in trivial tasks."

"Have you killed them?" asked Carruthers matter-of-factly.

"Hardly. But again, we digress."

As he considered exactly what to do with his victims, he took several steps toward the group. He was now standing just several feet from Blanche, who lowered her head to avoid looking directly at the beam from the flashlight. After another pause to collect his thoughts, he remarked, "None of you carry much weight in the world, so I can hurt you with little concern over getting my comeuppance. Who even knows you're here except for your imaginary friends, the guards who no one has seen? As for you," he added, pointing his flashlight into the eyes of Margaret and Mermac, "I am particularly disgusted with people like you. I know you have two children. Aren't you smart enough to realize that you have no business being here and that your children will soon be orphans unless you do exactly as I say? So, Mr. Chisolm, we are back to you." He shined the flashlight again in Grant's direction, but there was no one there. He hurriedly flashed it about him when he heard a voice from the passageway utter, "Put the gun down or I'll be the one shooting."

"Ha! You may imagine me a fool, Mr. Chisolm, but it is unlikely that you came to an archaeological dig with a weapon. On the other hand, archaeology has no interest to me. And, since I came intending to do you and your colleagues harm, I am indeed armed. So come out of hiding. I've called your bluff." His remarks were followed by silence.

"Mr. Chisolm." Again there was silence but for the slight sound of their breathing.

"Mr. Chisolm." A clicking sound like that of a gun being cocked. Father Wirtz froze.

"The hammer is cocked. Now either ..." He never finished the sentence. Wirtz dropped the flashlight and grabbed Blanche around the neck from behind.

"If you shoot now, you will kill your lovely friend. I doubt that you will do that. I intend to leave with her."

Grant realized that if Wirtz got to the entrance with Blanche, he could easily seal them in by pushing some stones onto the doorway. The others remained frozen while Grant again moved silently out of the passage and away from the light. The flashlights lay on the floor and cast enough light in Blanche's direction that he could see her feet as well as those of Wirtz. Stealthily and with small steps, he moved away and then across the space in the direction of where he surmised the doorway to be. As he did so, his mind flashed back to high school and collegiate days of wrestling blindfolded. He could feel his way across the room free of visuals, which most other men needed to keep their composure and their balance.

He approached the other side of the room near the exit tunnel. As he did so, the priest shouted, "I'll shoot," but his voice sounded uneasy. He did not know where Grant was. He moved back toward the flashlight, but as he did so, he heard the deafening sound of a gunshot and felt a stabbing pain in his back. His head buzzed with the explosion. He arched his back in agony but gripped Blanche even more tightly about the neck. Then there was another explosion and a zinging sound as if something were slapping off the wall of the cavern, and then another and another. Wirtz screamed and fired wildly three times. Carruthers and the others bolted for the general area of the exit. There was another shot and a loud moan.

Blanche screamed. Wirtz's arm froze around her neck, and then she heard a deafening roar. Her head felt as if it were about to burst. The priest fell backwards, dragging Blanche down with him. Everyone's head was vibrating in the excruciating pain of sound induced pressure.

"You are a fool," he whispered as his back hit the wall. Then he was silent. Blanche began to sob and shake. Grant rushed to her but grabbed Wirtz's hand and pried the gun from it.

"Oh my God!" cried out Blanche.

"It's all right. It's all right," said Grant.

At the sound of Grant's voice, the others shook their heads almost in unison to restore their balance and their hearing, and then rushed back and picked up their flashlights and shined them upon the scene. Grant had pulled Wirtz's arm away from Blanche's neck. Carruthers and Margaret and Mermac knelt next to Blanche, whom Grant was now helping to sit up. She was still crying.

Grant retrieved the flashlight that Wirtz had attempted to pick up. He knelt down at Wirtz's side and shined the light on his face.

"Shit!" cursed Wirtz.

Grant looked closely and realized that one of his shots had hit Wirtz's head, the frontal lobe having been grazed but not punctured. The other three shots from Grant's gun, however, must have hit their mark. Wirtz could not move. He was still fully conscious.

"Where'd you get the gun?" asked Carruthers.

"From my grandfather."

"Aaaah," said Carruthers. "How did you know it would still work?"

"I didn't."

The priest looked up helplessly.

"We need to report this to the police," said Margaret.

"Why?" asked Carruthers. "He tried to kill at least one of us."

"But the man's hurt. We have to get help."

"And how will we explain all of this?"

Blanche remained on the floor, quietly sobbing. Grant shined the light near Wirtz's face. His eyes were wet with tears, and he grimaced in pain and humiliation.

Grant leaned forward and asked, "Where are our guards?"

Wirtz smiled ruefully and tried to spit. Then, in a whisper, he said, "I'll die." And he did.

Blanche leaned against Grant. As he attempted to help her up, she slapped him.

"You could have killed me!" she screamed.

"Never," he said. "Never. I knew what I was doing. I moved to the side to see if I could catch his silhouette. The light from the flashlight was enough. I shot him in the side. Then he pulled you to that same side, so I ricocheted the second one off the back wall so that hit him on an angle. I did the same with the third."

She screamed, "Do you think I want a ballistics report!" and began to cry once more. Grant attempted to hug her, but she pushed him away as if to slap at him again. Instead, she abruptly pushed her head into his chest. He stroked her hair.

Carruthers looked at Wirtz. "Dead is dead. There's no need to report this now."

"Maybe we should," said Grant.

Carruthers interrupted. "This is the U.K. Here, a man's home may be his coffin but it is no longer his castle. He may not defend himself, only cry out to his assailant for mercy. I'm afraid that our present group of legislators care more for pets than people and more for the cruel than the kind. With such people as these, we'd have bowed to the Spanish Armada and Sieg Heiled our way into oblivion." Then he paused and, with a smirk, added, "Never have so few done so much damage to so many." Carruthers looked at Grant.

"I get your point."

"I thought you would, cowboy."

"Perhaps Rex is right. We could all end up in jail," added Mermac.

"For now, we'll leave him here. I'm still concerned about Kenneth and Travis."

Two minutes later, they were outside the caverns. Grant tried to call the two men again. Still no answer.

"I'm afraid our one source for immediate protection isn't available. There's not even a ring."

Blanche turned to Grant and said, "I don't think he was a very good priest."

Margaret and Mermac looked bewildered. "Who was he?" Margaret asked.

"Someone who left the priestly order permanently," Grant said sardonically.

Blanche clung to Grant's arm despite herself. She was still angry with him but indebted and grateful all at the same time.

Carruthers asked, "Grant, this isn't the same man we confronted before, and yet you seemed to think you knew him."

"Look again at his physique. Even the face, the cheek bones, the eyes, the coloring. If you look again, you'll see that in many ways he has the same features as the man you described who in fact did try to kill you the first time."

Then, without saying another word, Grant picked up one of the flashlights and went back into the cavern. He came out a minute later, holding the firearm that Father Wirtz had attempted to kill him with only minutes ago. He tucked it into his belt, underneath his windbreaker.

As they began to descend the hill, Grant considered his predicament. His thoughts on anything else were clouded by the realization that here he was, an American sailor on active duty in England who shot and killed a priest and then broke into a part of the Scottish National Trust that may well be the archaeological find of the century, with due respect to King Tut.

Only a few hundred feet down the hill, they heard a familiar voice behind them. "Please, I did not see you go in."

They all turned to look at the man who had emerged from a hillock near them. It was Kenneth.

"Kenneth, where have you been?" asked Grant. "You had us worried."

"You're not the only one. I've not been able to use my phone for over twelve hours. Something's going on. Travis and I decided to leave for a while to see about getting the phones fixed. Turns out they're fine. But something or someone has been jamming our signal. I don't even know how it could be done. Someone would have to have had a direct beam on us to intercept our transmission."

"I'm afraid that that possibility is all too real. Someone could have. Look, you're still needed here. What about Travis?"

"He went into town to get some provisions. He'll be back in a while."

"Well, look after the place. They're some surprises inside. I'll explain." added Grant.

"Regis told us about him."

"Regis?" asked Grant.

"He tells us everything."

Grant had a slightly quizzical look on his face as if to ask, "Why would he do that?"

"Oh, you didn't know? Well, we're both adopted. Looking at us, no one would expect us to be related. And by blood, of course, we're not. But he's our father."

"This day is full of surprises," offered Carruthers.

"We were both quite young. We're both from South Africa. But we were living in Angola with our family. They were killed in the civil war, and we were evacuated to an orphanage in South Africa. Regis came looking for us. He knew our parents."

"Things get curioser and curioser," said Blanche.

"My, this is all a surprise," added Margaret. With motherly delight, she thought of her own sons.

In the late summer sun that keeps Scotland lit even at ten o'clock at night, they continued their descent and moved on toward their distant vehicles. Blanche, Margaret, Mermac, and Carruthers went to one. Grant sauntered toward the Heather Inn. Kenneth stared up at the stars and then gradually drifted off to sleep on the hillside near the old church.

CHAPTER 48
ANAGNORISIS

Oh who has done this ill deed
This ill deed done to me?

> —Traditional Scottish ballad,
> "Sir Patrick Spens"

He was upset
By Germans and boats; affection was miles away.

> —W.H. Auden, "Edward Lear"

—VANDERKIN ESTATE

MACARTHUR SAT SILENTLY AND WITH A GLUM EXPRESSION ON HIS face. Never before had Grant seen him in such a temper. His usual conviviality and his "hail to thee good fellow" handshake, while still firm when Grant had met him earlier in the day, was somewhat perfunctory. When he had asked him questions about the nature of their return visit to Teutonic Nights Estate, MacArthur's response seemed almost cursory. Grant drove while MacArthur gazed forlornly out of the side window from the back seat.

Grant tried several times to bring up the matter of their findings at the site. Earlier in the day, Regis had been keenly interested. He had asked a number of questions. Now, as Grant tried to bring such matters up again, Regis replied with feigned interest, asking several of the same questions he had previously. After several attempts to carry on a conversation about the whys and wherefores of this trip, Grant relented, content to drive on in silence.

Three hours later, they approached Teutonic Nights Estate in the early evening. Up the long and winding road, Grant drove the black Rolls Royce. As the estate itself came into view, MacArthur told Grant that no matter what happened, Grant was to understand that he was there with him on this occasion by design. "There are no accidents," he told him. "The die will be cast. Be careful." He had reminded Grant that only a day ago he had been confronted by the prospect of death. Once again, he had been protected and had emerged victorious.

"We will do so again today."

The black Rolls Royce pulled into the curved stone driveway. The evening light illuminated the house, soft glowing balls that cast a lurid whiteness into the evening fog.

Grant got out of the car, and MacArthur did the same. MacArthur was dressed in a black suit and a blue striped tie. His days as an athlete and perennial mountain climber were indelibly stamped on his tall, thin frame. His carriage and general deportment were indicative of a life of intellectual, physical, and moral vigor. Still, as with any monument to human significance, the gods had attempted here and there to inflict their own rigor in the form of a general calcification of the frame. The bones and joints had hardened, causing an occasional limp in his left knee.

Grant was dressed in a suit borrowed from MacArthur. The sleeves were a tad too long, and the pants had to be cuffed and pinned in order to fit with any semblance of fashion. The suit was navy blue. His cream white and blue striped tie was of silk and entirely fashionable. Grant, having driven MacArthur to the location in his metallic *destrier*, felt like a squire, but a squire who knew the price of spurs and knighthood.

As Grant and MacArthur approached the front door of the Vanderkin estate, two men emerged through the doors, standing on either side to allow Grant and MacArthur to enter.

"Please allow me, sir," said one of them, holding out his right hand.

"We will move your car out of the way, sir. We are expecting others."

Grant hesitated. MacArthur looked at him and nodded approvingly. Grant handed the keys to the young man. They then followed the other man past the array of art and artifacts from around the world. They walked through the foyer, into the great hall, and eventually to Vanderkin's office. As they came to the door, another young African stepped in front of the door to stop their entry.

"Mr. Vanderkin is expecting us," responded MacArthur even before he was asked. The young man politely stepped aside and knocked on the door three times.

"Come in, come in," replied a firm and almost cheerful voice.

The young man opened the door. MacArthur had expected to find Martin Vanderkin alone or, at worst, with his nephew. Instead, Vanderkin was seated in his wheelchair, which was alongside an enormous high-backed armchair in which sat Miss South Africa, Pamela Credo.

Grant felt a pang surge across his chest. Until this moment, he was not aware of the effect Pamela still had on him. Her eyes were red with swollen eye lids and her cheeks were puffy, as if she had been crying.

While MacArthur and Grant waited for an invitation to sit, the door closed behind them. Grant turned and saw that the servants were still there. Despite their unease at the circumstances, MacArthur sensed that his own planning for certain unforeseen eventualities might even now be unfolding.

While they remained standing, another man came in. He was dressed casually and was black and very muscular. He also carried a gun, which he handed to Vanderkin's servant who had opened the door. He now searched MacArthur for a weapon. MacArthur raised his hands in an exaggerated gesture of surrender and stared indignantly at his smiling host.

"Come now, Regis, it's not all that bad."

This was the first time Vanderkin had ever called him by his first name.

"I did not know that we were intimates."

"More than you might ever like, and certainly more than you ever imagined, my good friend."

The man finished searching MacArthur and then moved onto Grant, who stood stoically with his hands at his side and tensed reflexively. The man, whom Vanderkin had addressed as James, patted down Grant and felt the undeniable hard metal of a gun tucked into his waistband. He reached beneath Grant's suit coat and jerked hard on the pistol to pull it out from the tight band of Grant's belt. He inspected it approvingly and then handed it to Vanderkin.

"A Glock. A most admirable design. But really, Mr. Chisolm, why would you bring such a weapon into my house? My kindness and generosity are well-known. Now please sit down."

As they did so, Grant noticed a chain on Vanderkin's large mahogany desk. The chain had a clasp at one end for a dog leash. Vanderkin noticed Grant's glance and reached over and picked it up.

"You'll recognize this, I hope. It's a symbol, one that I thought that you would successfully interpret. Unfortunately, you did not."

"I suppose now you will interpret it for us," said MacArthur.

"Of course; it would be inhospitable of me not to do so. You see, my symbolism is quite subtle. It's a dog's leash to remind two soldiers that they will soon surrender their own dog tags if they continue to interfere with my endeavors. It's also a gentle reminder that hounding me is ill advised. It can lead to accidents. And such interference may soon result in your being wrapped around someone's axel, or this chain could even be wrapped around you."

Grant was increasingly annoyed. However, Vanderkin eyed him steelily as he continued looking at the pistol. Then he put it down on his desk.

"I've called you to talk. You and I, Regis, have had some unfortunate discord. I think it is time that you be forced to face the indiscretions that have been so long hidden. And this day, the cloak that has hidden and kept us apart will be lifted. Your none-too-subtle contempt for me will be lessened if not replaced with appreciation of my largesse. You shall this day call me friend."

"Ah, friend. We are certainly acquaintances. But friend, now that would be most interesting."

"Not nearly as interesting as what I am about to reveal."

Martin Vanderkin then entered from the door behind the desk. As he did so, his uncle broke off and said, "I believe you already know my nephew."

Grant remained silent but watched Vanderkin's nephew with silent contempt as he went to the desk and sat down. His nephew's height, features, and shape seemed more familiar, more similar to that of another than Grant had at first realized. As Martin sat at the desk, he reached over and examined the Glock and smiled; then he put it back down.

"Well, now, I've waited a lifetime for this meeting. Still, in some ways, I hoped it would not be necessary. For a failure to negotiate a resolution to our differences today will mean the direst of outcomes for you two. You have, Regis, treated me like a poor, poor, long-lost, and unwelcome relative. And I must admit, long-lost, perhaps, and relative, well, more of a brother than you know. Of course, these days my personal assets are vast. Poor no more."

"As you say," replied MacArthur, "your holdings are vast. Inasmuch as I do know of the source of this vastness, I must also say that I find it vulgar."

"Ah, yes, of course; spoken with your usual contempt, and your usual impression, for you know next to nothing of the good that I have done. A goodness, I might add, perpetrated on your behalf. But you and I are old, and in our youth we were soldiers, much like Mr. Chisolm here. Tell me, before I proceed—after World War II, you purchased some land, land that added to the considerable wealth that you already possessed. It was, as far as I know, the last major purchase you made to add to the already considerable holdings of your family estate. From whom did you purchase that land?"

"You mean the Highlands Estate? Why, I purchased it quite legitimately, as you should know, if you know as much about me as you presume."

"I presume nothing. You purchased the land directly from the Crown. The government sold you land that did not belong to it. The land was not theirs to sell."

"Are you saying the Crown sold me stolen property? Hardly!"

"That is exactly what I am saying. For our younger friends who do not know the sordid details of your acquisition, I will tell what you and I already know. In 1939, the Crown began to purchase land in Scotland on the chance that it might be needed for training troops in the event of war with Germany. Some people did not wish to sell—my family in particular. Our land had been in the family for over two hundred years. Still, you know what happened. Your government took that land, and at a price that was hardly fair."

"Surely, you cannot overlook the fact that the purchase was necessary. World War II was upon us. Your country was at war."

"Yes, so were we told. But we were fighting an enemy who meant only to do what we ourselves would have done. Britain had the largest empire the world had ever seen. Greed and empire-building go hand in hand. So you took our land. Now I want you to look at me closely, Regis. Do you recognize this face?"

"It is the face of one scarred by unnecessary bitterness," replied MacArthur.

"I swore to reacquire that land if it took me the rest of my life. And today—"

"What has any of this to do with whether or not I recognize your face?"

"A good commander recognizes the face of each and every one of his own men."

A long pause followed. Everyone in the room looked at MacArthur, anticipating the glimmer of recognition. MacArthur and Vanderkin stared at one another. After more than a minute amidst the hush, MacArthur's eyebrows raised as a distant memory came into focus. He cleared his throat and whispered, "Your face ... your name is not Vanderkin."

"No, it's a bit of a play on words in recognition of my destitute status after our land was taken. I became a 'wander kid.'

"You were our commanding officer in a mission that should never have been. We left after weeks of training while you sent twenty-six men into North Africa to capture Field Marshal Rommel. We were discovered. There were three separate teams that went in. One man from each team escaped. No man knew the men of the other teams. So in this way, none of us could betray the others. But one man knew everyone on each team: our commander."

MacArthur then interrupted with, "Wirtz, Wirtz, that's who you are. Scottish mother, South African father. Good soldier, wicked temper."

"You didn't wait."

"Yes, I had orders to wait. But after two days and no word of your whereabouts, we could not wait any longer without imperiling the lives of those who brought you in and who were to bring you out. We had to assume that the mission had failed and that you and the others had been killed or captured. In this we were right."

"The others? History records that all twenty-three men were captured or killed. But in truth, there were twenty-six of us. Three escaped. And when I arrived at the beach, no rescue. I waited. Two others had escaped, and I have surmised over the years who they might have been. Of course, your friendship with one of them makes it clear who that person is."

"You utterly and completely disappeared. I personally perused German prison records and even interviewed survivors; no one knew what had become of you, not even the Germans. It was a war."

"Well, now you shall learn. Because I spoke German, my captors viewed me with less contempt than most others who they captured. Hitler had ordered that all special forces be executed, but Rommel intervened, thinking he could use me. For this reason, he kept my imprisonment— even from Hitler. His death only secured my anonymity. And while you did your good works, I did mine. I was able to make a small contribution now and then to the efforts of one Jomo Kenyatta and his Mau Mau's. Even the most idealistic of men cannot win a war without the instruments of death. To kill British troops, to fight the unbeatable foe, he needed to trade diamonds for guns. I was able to assist him in that endeavor.

"And you, you were a most energetic business man, hoping to tap the wealth of a vast continent and maintain the fortune of an empire that was already disappearing. While you were away, your wife died. You were still a relatively young man. She died in childbirth. But you could count; you knew that the child could not be yours. You had not been home for eleven months. Still, keeping up a good front, stiff upper lip and all that, you returned for the funeral of a dead wife and a dead child, one you knew was not yours.

"But you had a way of doing work that your own government could later disassociate itself from. Still, you were the British government. You could not deny yourself. And today, you will deny nothing.

"For you wandered the jungles and the savannahs and the cities of Africa to do the work of your government. But you did your own, as well. Perhaps in sorrow and in grief, you abandoned your own moral compunctions and used your wealth and your good looks to seduce whatever woman came your way. Then in 1984, a date in your life when your own philandering should have burned itself out, you found yourself once again at the call of your government. You were sent to Rwanda to gather information on tribal conflicts that would affect the politics of the region and which would culminate in the bloodlust between the Tutsi and the Hutu.

"You were in love with a young Catholic lay missionary whose husband was one of the victims of that war. She must have looked to you for consolation. You had long been a benefactor of her and her husband's missionary efforts. Her husband was beheaded by a Tutsi machete man for his efforts. You came to her aid—the aid of a woman thirty years your junior. She died shortly thereafter from complications upon returning too soon to her efforts in Rwanda. She died there, like the fool that she was, having brought her only child with her.

"But, fortunately, I too had done work for my people in Kenya and Tanzania, and in parts of Europe. We needed to keep the flow of diamonds going. As the years passed, Father Ricci proved to be an invaluable pack animal. And I offered my assistance to the good nuns who had taken your child into their care—an orphaned white child in the wilds of Rwanda. What would your friends have said, if they had known?"

"How could they know when even I did not know and even now am not at all certain that you are telling the truth?"

"Then, father Regis, allow me to make it all very clear. Daddy, meet your daughter, Pamela Credo *Stuart*. She is yours, and you owe me your deepest gratitude."

Everyone was silent. MacArthur looked directly at the face of his child. She looked up at him imploringly and then burst into tears. She stood and, without ceremony, attempted to leave the room by the door through which Regis and Grant had entered. The door was locked, and she merely stood there with her face pressed against it. MacArthur rose, walked to her, and touched her right shoulder. She turned and buried her head in his chest. Hesitantly, as if fearful of her rejection, he hugged her gently.

"You, sir, are a philandering bum. But your child is a great beauty—a beauty who would not have survived but for me. Will you trade her beauty for a price?"

MacArthur was silent.

"I want my land back."

"But it is no longer mine. I sold it years ago. It belongs again to the Crown."

"Exactly, and yet your colleagues, including Mr. Chisolm, have trespassed illegally several times within the past few weeks."

"What is it you want done?"

"I want the caverns abandoned and I want you to stay away."

Before he could finish his thoughts, his nephew suddenly picked up the pistol. He noticed the initials on the bottom of the grip for the first time: R. G. W., Robert Guy Wirtz. His menacing gaze went from the gun to Grant. His withering stare would have flustered other men, but Grant had faced more than stares and looked back almost nonchalantly. But as he did so, he examined the contour of Vanderkin's nephew's face. The angles of the cheek bones, the furrows of the brow, and the hairline on either temple, as well as the penetrating eyes, were enough to convince him of the kinship between Vanderkin's nephew and the man he had killed in the cavern. The form of the shoulders and the El Grecolike contours of the physique squared with those of the dead man.

Martin Vanderkin picked up the pistol and looked at his great uncle. "We've not heard from him for two days." He then aimed the pistol at Grant. "Where is he?"

"Stop! Stop!" cried Pamela. "You don't know what you're doing."

Vanderkin's nephew said, "Answer the question."

Grant responded, "You sent him to kill me."

"Not just you," said Martin Vanderkin.

"I don't like pimps who pick on my friends."

"Where is he?" cried Byron Vanderkin, wheeling his chair closer.

Grant's silence evoked a response that startled everyone. "Your grandfather's death … it was I who killed him, and I will do the same to you, you punky American. He returned to the U.K. two years after the war for a reunion, a reunion of his former comrades in arms. Even though my own family had moved to South Africa after our land was taken from us, I returned to help the motherland. I was, of course, betrayed again, this time by a commander who did not wait. But I waited. I waited for two more days with a bullet in my back, near my spine, and one in my hip. German doctors were able to remove the one in my hip while the one in my spine still remains and rubs against the nerves to this day. The

Germans took care of me, unlike my countrymen. I sit in a wheelchair today, complements of a country that knows no deceit but leaves its soldiers to perish on the sands of North Africa.

"Unfortunately for you, young man, your grandfather returned to the caverns he had found, as I knew he must. I could not let him again take from me what I knew was mine."

As though he had just heard nothing that Vanderkin had just said, Grant simply uttered, "I killed him." The admission was as surprising as it was truthful.

Vanderkin felt like a man who had pushed against a locked door only to find it suddenly opened. He almost fell from his wheelchair.

"No," he gasped as he reflexively tensed and almost walked out of his chair to get closer to Grant. "You fool. You might have bargained for your life, but now you have none left to bargain with. You are already dead."

"Your fight is with me, not with him," interrupted MacArthur. "My life for his."

"Why?" asked Byron Vanderkin. "It seems we can have both. We hold all the cards. There's no need to bargain. The ghosts of the dead do not haunt me."

"But what of the package?" asked Grant.

"You cannot give what I will now so willingly take," scowled Vanderkin, his lips positively drooling with contempt. "I had anticipated your resistance and so I have made plans for your demise and departure. And I can take from you, Regis, the son you wish you had as you have taken mine from me." He turned to his nephew and said, "Take him to the chamber." Vanderkin's nephew pointed the Glock directly at Grant's chest gleefully.

One of the servants opened the door through which Vanderkin's nephew had entered only a short while earlier. He waved the pistol at Grant, MacArthur, and even Pamela to enter. The servant led the way while Vanderkin's nephew followed along with Vanderkin himself.

They went across a carpeted hallway to a doorway through which Grant had entered stealthily only a few weeks earlier at Vanderkin's TUDOR Scholarship extravaganza. They descended slowly and deliberately into the nether regions of Teutonic Nights and deeper and deeper into the bowels of the ancient Celtic fortress upon which it rested.

They finally entered a great hollowed-out chamber dimly lit with blue lights. As their eyes adjusted to the vision of the soft blue lights, a huge dark figure emerged from behind an equally huge straight-back chair.

The chair had a reading light on either side. As the figure rose, he placed a copy of Caesar's *Gallic War Commentaries* down on his right. The figure, barely discernible at first, almost preened with delight at the sight of Grant. Then a menacing hiss emerged through his mouth from deep inside his huge chest.

"Look what I have brought you, my son. A true gift."

"One so precious is a true blessing from God and must be accepted." Jomo reached into his pants pocket and pulled out a vial of water. He uncorked it and then began casting droplets upon Grant in the sign of the cross.

"You are the Lamb of God, and so you must be sacrificed. I am God's instrument of mercy. Fear not, for upon your death, you will rise into the heavens in an SUV sent by Elijah himself."

Then, as the others watched, Jomo moved toward Grant, who threw off his jacket and quickly removed his tie.

Jomo reached out as Grant attempted to fend off his menacingly large hands. But before Grant could move away, Vanderkin's nephew stuck the pistol into Grant's spine and shouted, "Fight now, fight now, you shit!" He then pushed Grant into Jomo, who grasped him by his shirt collar and attempted to twist it around Grant's neck, only to find the buttons popping. Grant reached into Jomo's eyes with his full strength to gouge his eyeballs, digging his thumbs into Jomo's eye sockets. Jomo loosened his grip to push the hands away. As he did, Grant reached down into Jomo's crotch and squeezed. Jomo only laughed, pulled Grant's hand loose, and punched Grant across the face, knocking him to the floor.

As he fell, Grant reached almost imperceptibly toward his sock and then drew his hand back. Jomo reached down with both hands and began to lift Grant up by the neck. As he did so, he seethed, "Isaac, you disobeyed your father and you must feel God's wrath. No ram shall save you. *Agnus Dei, Agnus Dei.*" Slowly and with an ever increasing strength, he began to squeeze the life from Grant while he hissed and squinted like some great python. The tighter he squeezed, the closer he pulled Grant to his chest, until they appeared as one in a death embrace.

Then Grant squeezed out one last choking breath as he slashed at Jomo's jugular with a sharpened credit card. At first, it seemed futile. Jomo continued to squeeze even as Grant slashed again at the jugular and then at his wrists. Then blood began to spurt from Jomo's wounds. He felt the pain and relented, startled and in disbelief. He let go as Grant cut the card across Jomo's left eye. Jomo cried out and then attempted to open it. The eyeball was sliced and Jomo looked like a model for a Bunel experimental film, a figure of *film noire* without the benefit of trick photography.

"That's for Isaac," shouted a recovered Grant.

Jomo staggered toward Vanderkin.

"Father, Father, it hurts."

Vanderkin reached up and grabbed the pistol from his nephew and pointed it at Grant. "You will beg me …" Before he could finish the sentence, Grant dropped his slashing card, reached behind him into his belt, slid out the Webley revolver, and pulled the trigger. The blast in the confinement was deafening as Vanderkin slumped over in his wheelchair. Jomo, like some great monument from the ancient world, toppled over as his eyes rolled up into his skull and knocked over Vanderkin and his wheelchair, blood spraying out from his neck and wrists like molten lava from some great mountain

Vanderkin's nephew howled in anger, grabbed Pamela by her hair, and pointed his own gun at her temple. But as he did so, he turned at the sound of rapid clicking sounds behind him. Recognizing the sound, he threw the girl down and ran through the winding corridor. Converging from two pathways were three white wolves on one side and four on the other. Starved for five days to incite their feasting on Grant and company, the wolves tore into Vanderkin's nephew. They ripped at his neck and bit into each appendage and dragged him down as they might some sick four-legged prey. As the wolves bit into his neck, the servant turned and ran by Grant. Fearful that he would lock them in the chamber, Grant whacked him across the head from behind, sending him bleeding and staggering to the floor.

Grant grabbed the Glock that had fallen from the wheelchair and then Pamela. He led MacArthur back out, sealing the door and the servant's fate behind them. Within moments, the growls were at the door, the wolves scratching to get out. The faint sounds of the servant's anguish were overcome by the snapping and choking sounds of the predators.

They all raced through the office and into the foyer. To their surprise, three more menacing figures now appeared. One of them Grant recognized. He and the other two approached the startled Grant and company.

"Good evening, Mr. Chisolm. I am, as always, so glad to see you.

"Mr. Vanderkin and I have formed an agreement to work with one another to overcome the obstacles that have kept us apart. You look as though you've already had an encounter. Please, where is he? His servants are running about and seem upset. Do you have anything to do with this?"

The bulge under the jackets of both Ali's cohorts telegraphed their intentions. With a snap of the fingers, Ali ordered his men to finish Grant. But as they moved, Grant snapped the Glock from his belt and shot directly into Ali's heart. The shock froze both of his cohorts as Ali fell face down with not so much as even a look of dismay.

Grant pointed the pistol at one of the men, then the other. Both moved back and raised their hands. As Grant, MacArthur, and Pamela moved toward the doorway, two black men entered with pistols in hand. Grant raised his gun at them as each of them fired. He hit the floor with a slight wound in his right shoulder and an empty pistol. The two men, upon hearing the clicking of his trigger, moved forward, when four shots rang out in rapid succession. Both men fell to the floor. Gunfire erupted from behind Grant and the others. Thomas had emerged from behind and exchanged fire with Ali's men. One shot winged Thomas in his gun arm but not before he brought one down, causing the other to flee.

"Turn back!" shouted Thomas. "The outside is blocked. Others are waiting." MacArthur and Pamela followed Thomas while Grant picked up the revolver from one of Ali's dead companions. They followed Thomas down a familiar hallway into a corridor that led to a door. Thomas opened it and motioned for them to follow. Running through the dimly lit concrete hallway, Grant asked, "Where to?"

"The car."

"But we don't have the key."

"Stop! Stop!" huffed MacArthur. "I can't keep up. But, I have the key. Always … always carry … spare. Whew!"

Grant and Thomas slowed to a walk, and then Grant took Pamela by the arm. She was visibly shaking and Grant said, "Come on."

She surrendered MacArthur's arm and took Grant's, which she clung to viciously, her nails cutting through his skin. MacArthur braced himself against a wall.

"We can't stay long," said Thomas. "I've released the wolves to create confusion and …"

"You've done all right," replied Grant. "A little messy with the Glock-a-mole you've left about, but still all right."

MacArthur recovered enough for them to make their way to the underground garage where the Rolls was parked. Thomas jumped in front as MacArthur tossed him the keys. Grant jumped in alongside Thomas while MacArthur's daughter slid quietly into the back seat. There were six other cars parked on either side of them, with the only visible exit immediately behind them. Thomas started the engine, hit reverse, and slammed the gas pedal, sending the tires spinning and smoking into a violent assault on a garage door, shattering it on impact.

"Leave no trace," said MacArthur wistfully to himself.

As they sped through the door, two men jogging down the driveway toward the garage were startled by the sight of the rear moving vehicle. They jumped to either side, one of them getting his feet and shins smacked painfully and powerfully while the other rolled out of the way. The driveway gradually rose from the underground entrance to the leveled-off area in the rear of the mansion. When they reached the crest of the driveway, Thomas switched to drive and kicked up gravel. He sped toward the front, only to find his way blocked by another Kenyan standing there with a shotgun pointed directly at Thomas.

Thomas ducked as the glass shattered. He directed the Rolls right at and over the shooter, who bumped along the roof of the Rolls and smacked the ground in a graceless flight, the shotgun cartwheeling along the gravel road into a stone wall where the barrel cracked and bent.

As they rounded the first turn, three wolves appeared, fast on the heels of two dark-complexioned men wearing sweat pants and running shoes. Thomas hit the brakes, and they all watched as the wolves drove the men over an embankment into the void that led to the rocky chasm over a hundred feet below.

Thomas spun the car toward the front of the house, turning left hard and then hitting the gas just as another car appeared, heading toward them, its high beams temporarily blinding Thomas. As he swerved right, the other car swerved to its right as well and right into a two-foot-high retaining wall that enclosed part of Vanderkin's front yard. Its front right tire blew on impact, and the driver popped through the sun roof and fired two shots at the rear of the Rolls. Turning slightly to his left, Thomas exposed the side of the car to more of the gunfire while Grant fired off three rounds from one of the revolvers of Ali's buddies. The figure who had popped up to fire at them rose even higher as his head exploded and then disappeared back into the car, the engine still running.

Thomas straightened the Rolls and sped down hill when yet another car appeared around a curve, speeding toward them through the mist on the single-lane road. With no shoulder on which to merge, Thomas gripped the steering wheel in a dramatic game of chicken. The other car stopped and flashed its lights. Hitting the brakes, Thomas guided the car to a side-winding stop on the gravel road, the rear end of the Rolls perched perilously close to a steep drop-off of fifty feet.

Before any of them could get out of the car, Oz jumped out with his hands in the air. "It's me!" he shouted. "It's me!"

Grant and Thomas jumped out and then MacArthur followed, telling Pamela, "Wait."

Oz spoke first.

"I had the transmitter on, knew exactly where you were. Thought you might need help."

"We do," said MacArthur.

Grant looked at Thomas and said, "Where'd you come from?"

"From behind," replied Thomas. "Part of the rear guard. I was in the trunk."

"Why wasn't I told?"

"You can't reveal what you don't know," replied MacArthur.

Oz then turned to the van and waved. Three men dressed entirely in black and wearing ski masks slid out from the rear of the vehicle. Grant thought the gait and physique of at least one of the figures looked familiar.

As the three men stood silently behind Oz, he smiled.

"These are the Furies," Oz said. "They devour the dead and clean up debris. We have a lot of work to do before dawn."

They returned to their vehicles. Thomas slowly backed up, maneuvering the Rolls onto the road and backing it slowly up the road to the source of the tumult as Grant peered out the side window for more triggers and wolves.

"The falcon ..." said Grant in a low, almost imperceptible voice.

"Cannot hear the falconer," finished Thomas.

"And why is that?" Grant asked.

"Because the wolves are dead, mostly, and so is the alpha male."

Grant remained silent while MacArthur wondered at the barely discernible conversation in front. Pamela sat stoically, exhausted of tears, and depleted of either joy or sorrow.

As they cautiously stopped in the front of the mansion, three pairs of eyes peered out from behind the torso of one of the Kenyans whom Grant had wounded.

"Leave no trace," MacArthur said to Grant. "We'll show you how it's done."

Grant exited the car on one side and Thomas on the other. As they approached the grotesquely contorted and partially disemboweled corpse, one of the wolves moved toward Grant with its ears back. It let out a menacing growl while the two others tore at an unidentifiable organ of the body.

Grant fired one brain shot at the farthest wolf and then two heart shots at the other while Thomas shot the other twice in the chest. Dead. The Furies descended and threw each of the corpses into the back of the van and then pulled out black rubber body bags and packaged the dismembered.

The Furies and Grant and Thomas, as well as MacArthur and Oz, worked at a steady and professional pace to secure the bodies and remove any evidence of their presence. By dawn, all the bodies had been bagged and stacked in the van. Several hours later, a private plane from Vanderkin's own stable of airlines landed at a military facility near Aberdeen and took on the cadaverous cargo. Within an hour, everyone had been accorded a sailor's burial in weighted bags that hurled through the violence of the North Sea.

CHAPTER 49

A DOUBTING THOMAS

"I doubt that it ever happened," interposed Parzival.
"I will remove your doubts," his host replied.

—Wolfram Von Eschenbach, *Parzival*

"THIS CAN'T BE," INSISTED BLANCHE.

"Of course it can. A brotherhood of the sword. Among certain warrior societies, weapons of great value were given, on behalf of a society, to a warrior, a very special warrior who attained the highest ideals of that society. The sword itself was crafted with great care. It was a symbol of a people and their aspirations," said MacArthur. "They hoped that crafting the sword of great value would bring forth the warrior. So each of the hilts to the swords you've discovered were kept in waiting for the next perfectly forged blade that would bring about the great warrior."

On this occasion, while in London to make last-minute arrangements concerning a most important matter with Dennis and Oz, MacArthur had asked Dennis to make plans for the three of them to meet with Blanche to ascertain what she had deduced about the findings in the cavern and to determine her level of comfort in keeping the whole thing a secret indefinitely.

"But it just can't be," protested Blanche.

"Given your protestations of doubt, it is you who should be named Thomas."

Blanche blushed at her own skepticism.

"My dear, the Hebrews passed on the stories of Abraham for how long before those stories were even written down, before the scriptures were ever fulfilled?"

Then MacArthur paused as Blanche considered what he had just said. Dennis and Oz looked on quietly and sipped on their glasses of wine as they waited for their meals to arrive.

Finally, MacArthur said, "It can't be, as you say, and yet it is. You have a right to be skeptical, as well you should be. It can't be, just as there can be no oil in Scotland and certainly not in the North Sea, and yet there is. There can be no palm trees in Scotland, and yet there are. There can be no grand pianos sitting on top of mountains in Scotland, and yet there are. And the Scots could never go to Nepal and win the world title in elephant polo, and yet they have."

Blanche blinked in disbelief but knew that everything he had just said was true despite its being unlikely if not downright impossible. The rest of the meal was filled with good food and the sense that Blanche's skepticism remained despite her own experience in the cavern. They knew she could be trusted not to reveal what she knew was true but couldn't possibly be.

CHAPTER 50

THE INDUCTION

Question me: I am a warrior.

—Celtic mythology

—*MACARTHUR ESTATE, ONE WEEK LATER*

GRANT SAT OPPOSITE MACARTHUR'S DESK, MUCH AS HE HAD SEVERAL months earlier. They reviewed everything that had transpired in the recent past, trying to piece it all together. They had crushed an international diamond- and drug-trafficking cartel that even dabbled in high-end prostitution.

After half an hour of official business, MacArthur asked Grant what he would like to drink.

"It's England," he smiled in response.

"Black or green?"

"Green."

"I thought as much. I also hoped that you and I might take it in the next room. I have one of those new plasma giant screens, more for company than for myself. But I thought you might indulge me, as well as Dennis and Oz. They're already here."

"They're here?"

"Yes, they're watching one of our favorite films."

"What's that?"

"*Miracle.* Do you know it?"

"You mean the one about the American and Russian hockey game?"

"That's the one. They're well into it. But I thought we could watch a bit of it."

"Sure. But why do I think it strange that you'd want me to watch a hockey movie with you?"

"Sometimes you don't ask enough questions and sometimes you ask too many. Just watch and learn."

As Grant and Regis entered the room, Oz and Dennis stood and shook hands with Grant. They were already sipping on tea and immediately sat back down. Grant could tell they really were watching the movie. They didn't talk until well into the film. Then Regis looked at Grant and said, "This is my favorite part."

Grant watched as the film portrayed the American hockey coach berating his players after tying Norway in a build up to the Olympics. After the game, their coach made them do repeat sprints on the ice to build up their stamina and to drive home that they were not playing like a team that knew what was necessary to win the Olympic Gold medal. Then, at the moment of near complete exhaustion, their coach asked the same question he asked repeatedly throughout their training: "Who do you play for?" In the past, each member was apt to respond with "University of Boston," "University of Michigan," or some other cold-weather school. In this instance, Mike Eruzione, on the verge of physical collapse, uttered, "The United States of America."

At that point, MacArthur picked up the remote and hit Stop.

Grant, who was by now drinking the last of his tea, put it down and looked at MacArthur. "I like the question. But when one is doing more than playing a game, the answer will be different." Grant was then quiet but sensed that a critical moment in his career and his life had arrived. MacArthur turned to Dennis and then to Oz, both of whom rose from their chairs with MacArthur. For the first time, Grant noticed that each of them had on his respective end table a leather-bound book that looked as though it had seen the ages.

"I thought you'd be interested to know the fallout from your efforts in Kenya."

"I would."

"Yesterday, I was informed by my sources that the Kenyan government intends to release a communiqué thanking the United States for its cooperation in working with the Kenyan military in attacking and destroying the organization known as Christ's Army of Liberation. They will also state that the bodies of your American colleagues will be repatriated. Jomo Raphael's death will be confirmed through DNA testing that is even now being conducted at an undisclosed location."

"How can they conduct the DNA testing without a body?"

"The miracle of modern politics and of the benign effects of full cooperation of the peace-loving Kenyans, the brave Americans, the most resourceful British."

Grant smiled and said, "I think I understand."

Suddenly, MacArthur looked squarely at Grant. Oz and Dennis did the same. Then MacArthur walked over to a doorway and motioned for all of them to enter. They moved into a small elevator and slowly descended into a brightly lit corridor. Oz and Dennis pulled back on the grated accordion door and stepped out. Grant followed. Then they walked into a small, darkened room. MacArthur turned on the lights.

The room itself was made entirely of hand-polished granite, not unlike that on the interior of the cavern. The four walls were covered in ornate designs, an array of Celtic crosses and even stylized dragon heads. Grant was struck by the similarity between the various motifs here and those of the caverns. The room itself had no place to sit. In the middle rose a kind of altar about three and half feet high with a two-foot-by-four-foot rectangular tablet of pure white marble. On top of it lay a six-foot-long sword with a five-foot blade with a hilt made of ivory and polished steel. Grant sensed but did not know that his life was about to be touched by a most unusual, if not sacred, event. MacArthur and the others were still carrying the leather-bound books. MacArthur asked Grant to stand next to the hilt and to place his right hand on it. MacArthur stood directly opposite it. Oz and Dennis stood on either side of the altar.

MacArthur looked at Grant as he spoke.

"You have, over the past several months in particular and throughout your military career, confirmed that you are who we thought you were. Like your grandfather, you are a great warrior, and like your father, you have been loyal to that legacy. Over two thousand years ago, a select group of Romans began a secret society, a brotherhood of the sword. It was one founded by good men who sought not glory but an opportunity to serve. The society's members began a tradition whereby the youngest member of the group was given the responsibility of keeping the sword that symbolized service to others, service to country, and service to self. These warriors persisted not only in keeping their brotherhood secret but also in keeping the talisman of their spiritual kinship with one another and their devotion to just causes equally well hidden.

"Each generation of devotees to this secret guild bequeathed to the greatest warrior among them a special sword, a sword to be used in combat against their common foe. The first of these swords was made of iron and was of the finest metallurgy. The agreement was that there would always be two such swords: one to be used in battle and the other, the one on whose hilt the warrior held his hand as he was inducted, to be kept in an undisclosed place. It would be kept and treasured much as the crown jewels are kept and treasured. Upon the death of this warrior, whether in battle or of old age, the original sword would be broken and melted down. However, a piece of the metal itself would be retained when all were in agreement that the warrior who wielded it was truly a man of uncommon valor.

"A piece of the metal from these few swords would then be embedded into the hilt of the sword made for the new warrior. This sword was kept in a secret chamber beneath the old Roman Senate building. One of the men to join this society was one of the finest rulers Rome has ever seen, Constantine the Great.

"When Constantine traveled north to England, he took the valued swords with him and brought them to the north of England, where he was stationed. In his time here, perhaps reflecting his own cosmopolitanism, he expanded the membership to include not just Roman warriors, but any great warrior regardless of his nationality. Then, at the barracks that is now the site of the city of York, he built a chamber for the housing of these swords. In 306 AD, he was crowned emperor of the Roman world in York itself. He then left for Rome, but the swords stayed here.

"But in the fifth century, the last of the Roman legions withdrew and the various Germanic tribes invaded. But before Constantine left, he bequeathed the legacy of the sword to another warrior, a Celt and king who then moved the treasure of sacred swords farther north for safekeeping. Over the years, great warriors who were also good men yearned for the recognition of this by then not entirely secret society

"In the 1830s, the father of modern geology, William Smith, was asked to design one last project whereby he would connect the waters of the North Sea with those of the Irish Sea. In the process, he and his construction team stumbled upon the opening to the cavern. Members of my ancestors had been entrusted to oversee this sacred mausoleum for swords. Smith's men explored the entranceway and then abandoned the effort in the name of completing the canal on schedule. The entrance way was simply covered over with debris from the canal construction, forgotten about, and then submerged.

"But then, even before the canal closed off the entranceway, a warrior stepped forward. He was a mystery man. His name was Pedro Francisco. It is with some reluctance that I speak of one who is your countryman but whose great endeavors were at the request of George Washington against a most resourceful adversary, my countrymen, the British.

"So, as I was saying, this mystery man simply appeared as a child, apparently abandoned on the shores of some American eastern port. He was adopted by a kind fellow who reared him as his own. He grew to manhood and enlisted to fight with George Washington's troops and—now for the somewhat painful part—he distinguished himself in battle against my countrymen. For that, George Washington eventually awarded him a specially made sword suitable for a man who stood six foot six inches tall. Later, in yet another battle, this great warrior slew eleven British soldiers with his sword. He may well be your country's greatest warrior of the War of Rebellion.

"Years later, his sword disappeared from its place of safekeeping quite mysteriously. Your hand now rests on that sword. It too would have been among the hilts that you found in the cavern. But, of course, after William Smith's canal work, my ancestors could no longer access the cavern. We did not know of the alternative entrance. So, from George Washington to Pedro Francisco to Grant Chisolm. Now we begin."

Each of the men opened their leather bound volumes. MacArthur began in Latin:

Arma virumque cano (*Aeneid*, Book I, line 1)
(Of arms and the man I sing)

We still call him brother, he who turned the sword from rust to burnished steel to protect his people. This you too shall do for yours and know that we are your brothers.

Dennis responded, "*Naegling forbearst.*"

Then all three answered, "But not so you, for steel can break but be reformed, and in your soul the sword is reborn."

Although Grant heard all the words, it was not so much their sound as the otherwise unearthly quiet of the place of their recitation that struck him. The silence in between the words was transformative. And to the silence as well as the sound, Grant submitted. The words continued as Dennis recited the names of great warriors who had fought for great causes from antiquity to the present. With the completion of each stanza of names came again the utterance by Dennis in Old English, "*Naegling forbearst.*" The reference to the breaking of Beowulf's sword was immediately followed by the reminder that great swords may break but not great warriors: "But not so you."

The litany of warriors and their virtues continued for several minutes as Dennis, MacArthur and Oz blended their voices in a recitation as old as England. Incantatory and antiphonal, the voices melded and the words reverberated in the chamber, and then in the mind, the body, and the soul of Grant. Finally, their voices stopped as MacArthur handed Grant a sheet of paper. Grant read:

I, Grant Chisolm, a son of man, man of earth.
The sword I touch shall prove my worth
And among brothers whose lives touch mine
Mine touches theirs in a bond divine.

I rise now, a man of steel
Who gives to goodness
What God does will.

To you and thine, I now pledge all

My life, my liberty, and my sacred honor.

The goodness of men
Now long gone
And still in the living
Who do no wrong
In me their virtue
Their legacy lives on.

Then MacArthur reached across and touched Grant's hand. Dennis and Oz in turn placed theirs upon MacArthur's as Dennis again spoke, "*Naeling forbearst.*"

Grant read, "But not so me."

The recitation continued three more times before MacArthur again intervened and they all removed their hands. Grant recited:

I touch this sword with my right hand
Adroit not sinister
And thus I say
I wield this sword for all good men.

Then Oz spoke:

You stand before us a brother in arms
A man of virtue with much to give
A man of virtue of whom it may be said
Long after you live.

Then MacArthur spoke again in Old English:

*Cwaedon paet he waere wyruld-cyning
Mannum mildest on mon- waerst
Leodum li ost.*
He was the kindest, most gentle, most just to his people.

In unison then they all intoned, "*Arma virumque cano.*"

MacArthur, Dennis, and then Oz said, "Welcome brother," as they took Grant's hand.

MacArthur, ever the pragmatist, added, "On a perfectly mundane note, remember also, 'Leave no trace.'"

Grant laughed and felt an invisible mantle of responsibility fall upon his shoulders.

They took the elevator back upstairs and walked again into the room with their books and sat in their respective seats as a servant walked in with four glasses of wine.

MacArthur raised his glass and said, "Aeneas," and each drank.

Dennis raised his glass and said, "Arthur," and each drank.

Oz raised his glass and said, "Beowulf," and each drank.

Then they all raised their glasses and said, "To Grant," and each drank.

CHAPTER 51
RIDDLING RHYME

Though none know whence ...
Some secret Hook, hid in what bait

—I. A. Richards, "Anglers"

"FOOT TO FOOT, HEAD TO HEAD, RISE YE UP, FROM THE DEAD." ALL of a sudden it struck Grant. He looked at the half wheel Blanche had identified as a Viking direction finder. For days, the idea of this direction finder being in an ancient Celtic cavern had pricked the back of his mind. Why was only half of it here? Was it just a bit of debris, a broken artifact? But even so, why was a nautical instrument here, so far inland? Why would it not be some place near a harbor or at least in some Viking burial mound with a Sutton Hoo ship?

Then suddenly, as if his brain snapped into gear, everything seemed perfectly clear: the less than chance encounter with a Norwegian-trained archaeologist to explain the artifact's use, the finding of the cavern site itself, and the fishing guide consenting to take him for a private tour of an ancient Viking site that he had not known even existed until the gillie told him of it. Invisible hands, it seemed, were opening doors and inviting him in.

The lines chiseled into the granite walls kept spinning over and over in his mind as he sped north to Gairloch.

Foot to Foot
Head to Head

Rise Ye Up
From the Dead.

He arrived at the Loch Maree Inn to find it open but seemingly deserted. When he entered, he found a skeleton staff of employees, none of whom he recognized from his previous visits. He was able to obtain a room for the evening. Indicating that he would also like to do some fishing later in the day, Grant made arrangements for a boat and some tackle. He explained to the proprietor that he would be fishing late as he needed some solitude. A gillie would not be necessary.

Now he stood alone on the island at the site of the Viking graveyard in complete darkness, only feet from where St. Colomba, over a thousand years ago, stopped to begin his preaching of the Gospels to the Scots, those Celts who left Ireland rather than save civilization through their monasteries, asceticism, and Keelian copies of sacred texts. As he contemplated what he was about to do, Grant thought of all those stories he had heard about the little people and their treasures. For a moment, he fancied himself a simple fool on an improbable errand from a mysterious crone who advised him to go north for adventure. He realized he couldn't go much farther north than Scotland. He also knew that in most such stories, the fool usually ends up with untold treasure that he can acquire only because his innocence itself causes some spiritual force to reveal it to him. The spontaneity of the fool's action springs from an intuition that connects with forces of the past that speak to the present. Already Grant felt like a fool for being here and for even thinking that he could be the fool who actually gets the treasure. Perhaps, he thought, he should just buy a lotto ticket and thereby join a real fool's club.

Grant placed two lanterns at the foot of the graves of the Viking lord and his lady. He began to dig. Within an hour, he had dug down a full two feet. Then his shovel hit something hard. He reached down with a trowel to dig around the object. In another fifteen minutes he cleared all the soil away from the object. Lifting with gentle but firm force, he brought up a half circle of stone. Even before he held it up to the light, he knew.

As he sat upon the ground, he looked at the other half of the Viking direction finder. In his imagination, he pressed the half from the cavern into the crevices of the half he now held in his hands. They matched perfectly, and the ancient runic inscriptions blended with the modern desire to solve a riddle and measure directions to a site somewhere. The ancients must have thought it worth their while to remember this site's location and to conceal it from others.

Grant then dug down another six inches to make certain that he left no other important stones unturned. Satisfied, he filled in the hole, stomped the earth down with his hands and then his feet, turned out the lamps, picked up the stone, and headed toward his boat. Quietly, keeping the outboard motor on or near drift speed, he slowly inched his way back to shore near the inn.

∗   ∗   ∗   ∗   ∗

As his boat scraped the sand and pebbles of the shore near the inn, a flashlight turned on from underneath a tree. Grant tensed and made ready to fight or, if need be, to put the motor in reverse and push on the oars to disengage his boat from the sand. As the flashlight came closer, he heard, "Grant, I was hoping I'd find you. It's me, Regis. Mind if we ride out together? I brought my own tackle. I'd like to talk and to do a bit of fishing. Perhaps you can listen once more to an old man and even console."

Though surprised at Regis's driving to see him and even more at his invitation to console, Grant steadied the boat as MacArthur stepped in. Then Grant got out, shoved the boat out, leaped in, and pushed the reverse lever on the motor, backing up the boat. MacArthur pointed north and looked back at Grant to say, "I fished here as a boy. Go north for about a mile. I'll show you my favorite spot."

Several minutes later, Grant eased up on the gas as Regis extended his arm and made a patting motion with his hand as if to say, "Slow, slow, slow." He then immediately threw out a daredevil lure connected to a six-pound test line from his Abu Garcia pole that wrapped around a Shakespeare spinning rod.

Grant cut the motor, and the boat slowly drifted north as he hooked a night crawler to his own rented tackle, the same he had used months earlier with the gillie who first took him out on Loch Maree.

"Here, I used to catch the finest of fish: trout." MacArthur then sat quietly as he cast his line several times. Grant said nothing. He was waiting for Regis to say something more, something about the real reason for his unexpected visit. Then MacArthur began.

"I am old. My time has come and gone. Of course, I would like to think that Tennyson was right: 'Old age hath yet its honor and its glory.' And I have a purpose even if it is to do no more than what I am doing now: fishing and explaining certain things to you. In this I will preserve my honor and my glory.

"Grant, there is more to your archaeological site than first meets the eye. You have, however, unwittingly answered a riddle that has plagued me for some time." He then paused and took a deep breath.

"What I am about to tell you is something that I've never shared with any man—not even Oz, not even Dennis—for fear that they might not believe my own denials of such matters. However, neither of them has seen the Nazi paraphernalia inside the caverns. You have, and therefore you must have questions. I alone can answer them."

"I do have questions," replied Grant, "but I thought it better not to ask them."

"Truly, I wish you had so that I could unburden myself to someone. I now come to you as a supplicant and I ask that you listen. Tell me, Grant, do you know the name Rudolph Hess?"

"Rudolph Hess? You mean the German advisor to Adolph Hitler? The one who parachuted into Scotland to try to talk the U.K. out of fighting the Germans?"

"Exactly; that's the one. Tell me, doesn't the whole story seem bizarre to you?"

"Yes, but then again, the entire Nazi movement seems bizarre to me."

"During the war, he, as you say, parachuted into Scotland. But why? Why here?"

"I have heard stories," replied Grant.

"The story of Rudolph Hess relates to my family. My own father had spent some time on diplomatic missions in Germany, especially Berlin. While there, he met a number of prominent Nazi figures. Several years later, one of them supposedly decided to parachute into Scotland in hopes of meeting with my own father, whom he had met three years earlier. At least that is the story.

"However, this is not the real story. You see, we, my family, think that Rudolph Hess came here because he had reason to think that a certain family would hide him as he planned for the German invasion. Vanderkin's father was the contact. This is the rumor that has persisted to this day. Your finding of the Nazi paraphernalia and the radio confirms one suspicion: the diamond trafficking had already begun. The Germans were using their South African and Tanzanian connections to buy the services of the disaffected—Scots, Irish, and ultra right-wingers—Quislings in infancy.

"Vanderkin would have you and me believe that it was the injustice of having their land forcibly sold to the Crown and their righteous indignation and bitterness that fomented their betrayal of their countrymen. Of course, this feeling of betrayal was only exacerbated by my supposedly leaving Vanderkin behind in North Africa after the failed attempt to get Rommel. Vanderkin and his family were working for the Nazis even before my supposed act of betrayal. His family had already shed their Scottish loyalties when they left for South Africa. The swastika replaced the tartan long before I came into their lives."

"But what about the diamonds themselves?"

"After the war, the real Vanderkin, Guy Wirtz, reemerged. He had a new name, a new passport, and a wish to exact revenge. Travis and Kenneth examined letters found at the site. Wirtz, Vanderkin, whatever we call him, continued his contacts, not with the Nazis but with the criminal elements of the Irish Republic Army. The site itself became their Fort Knox, the location known only to Wirtz and his none-too-priestly son. It seems even his son's Catholicism was part of an elaborate ruse to cement his good standing with the IRA. Wirtz was actually reared as a Calvinist, Church of Scotland. Still, his son was a product of Catholic upbringing and pernicious familial exploitation by a vengeful man. The diamonds, by the way, have been removed. Oddly, one of Wirtz's unintentional good works, the TUDOR scholarship program, will continue under new management, funded by his own substantial supply of blood diamonds already paid for."

Grant considered all that MacArthur had revealed and then asked, "Does your daughter, Pamela, know any of this?"

"She has not forgiven me. I tried to talk with her, but she left for South Africa. She has nothing but contempt for me. And you know, after all these years, I have suffered battle wounds from guns, rifles, explosions, and even machetes, as well as the fists of thugs and other criminals. I have healed from all those wounds. But this wound, knowing that I forsook my principles for the love of a woman; this wound, that of a father who forsook his daughter; the wound of ignorance, vanity, and sheer sorrow—I am broken. This wound … it will not heal."

Grant suddenly jerked up on his line as a trout hooked itself on his dappling fly. The fighting fish's onslaught relieved the tension, and Grant reeled in his catch to the side of the boat. As Grant pulled his line taut, MacArthur reached into the water and grabbed the sixteen-inch fish with both hands and pulled it in. He tore the hook from its mouth. Regis uttered, "This is breakfast," and smacked the fish's head against the gunnels. Dead. He tossed the fish into the side mounted fish tank. They fished for two more hours, reeling in two more of twelve and fifteen inches.

Finally, Regis asked to go back. Grant sensed that the old warrior was bleeding emotionally and that his time would not be long. He wanted to tell Regis of his find, and he wanted to ask him more about his life. But he somehow felt it disrespectful. Instead, he listened as MacArthur continued.

"It is not good to be so alone; it makes men weird. I suspect that you will find that of many who are angry at the world and God. They are alone. I think that may have been the case with many of those with whom we have recently dealt."

Then, as they walked ashore, MacArthur's reminiscing and advising came to an end and he changed again into the more familiar and seemingly more sanguine figure with the stern exterior that Grant had known. It was as though he was telling Grant, "Now you are on your own and the contents of the satchel are for you to decipher."

The next day, as MacArthur shook Grant's hand, he looked at him with a certain sadness and remarked, "Like my cousin from Wisconsin, Douglas, once said, 'Old warriors never die; they just fade away.'" He got into his car most stiffly, and, for the first time in Grant's eyes, he looked frail. He slumped behind the wheel and then drove off, not in a Rolls but in a Cooper S.

A little while later, Grant headed south in the minivan he had rented for the occasion. In Glasgow, he would share his find from the burial site with Carruthers.

EPILOGUE
ARCHIVAL DUST AND SMOKES

Slowly, beautifully, the search for knowledge continues.

—Salman Rushdie, "Darwin in Kansas"

—RAF ALCONBURY

GRANT SAT IN A CHAIR WITH HIS LEGS PROPPED UP. ON HIS BED LAY the Viking direction finder, both parts. What his imagination had at first envisioned joining together, his hands now joined together in fact. The two halves fit one another like the present and the past.

Also spread out on his bed were the various sheets of paper and parchment from the satchel. Much of it was indecipherable to Grant, either because of the obscurity of the texts' features, the ink's fading, or the paper or parchment's material degradation. The most intriguing and immediately inviting of the material was a translation of what was entitled *The Zeno Narrative*, a fifteenth-century Italian manuscript of sea captains from an illustrious family that once traveled to Scotland.

To fully decode the significance of all that lay before him, he would need the assistance of Carruthers, Blanche, and perhaps others. He sat staring at the intriguing but beguiling materials, wondering what to do next. Also on his bed lay an object that had acquired more than merely sentimental value in his short relationship with it: a .455 Webley and Scott Mark VI Service Revolver. This gun had done for him what it had apparently not done for his grandfather. It had saved his life. Technically, he was not allowed to have a gun of any sort on base unless it had first been duly registered with base authorities, and even then it could not be kept in his room. However, registering a British weapon distributed to

British officers during World War II without explaining how he came to acquire it, or, if he lied, trying to explain how he brought it with him into the country, seemed worse than trying to hide it in his room indefinitely. He thought that he could send it back to the United States in his sea bag at some future date when he might return to the United States on a military transport. Besides, it was merely part of an even more convoluted and perplexing problem.

While staring at the puzzle on his bed, his phone rang. The watch at the front gate said, "Lieutenant Commander Chisolm, a Miss Blanche DeNegris is awaiting you at the front gate. You must vouch for her personally and escort her to any place on the base."

"I'll be right there."

Grant walked to the front gate and identified Blanche to the guards. Her blue-gray Toyota was pulled off to the side near the MOD facility outside the gate. She stood next to her car, talking to an MOD policeman who was obviously intrigued by her smile and the sharpness of her wit. He was laughing as if they had known one another for years. As Grant approached in civilian attire but with an unmistakable demeanor, the uniformed policeman smiled resignedly at Blanche and backed off with a furtive glance at Grant. They both got into the car and drove it past the gate and into the parking lot of Hotel Britannia.

Once inside Grant's room, he showed her the various documents and admitted his frustration at his inability to decipher any of it. Blanche seemed similarly perplexed but more optimistic, mentioning that Carruthers was examining the pictures taken and the sketches made of the cavern walls. The glyphs and the runic writing he found intriguing and the excuse to continue his own studies in the ancient writings of northern Europe. The *Icelandic Sagas* held Carruther's attention as few works of history had.

Meanwhile, Margaret and Mermac Collins had agreed to meet with Carruthers to assist in the exploration of the cavern to help catalogue the findings. Their boys were to assist so long as they could keep everything a secret. Strangely, the innkeeper, who may or may not have been the man who informed Ali and his cohorts or even Vanderkin of Grant and Blanche's stay there, disappeared one day. Without its owner and proprietor, the inn was closed.

*　　*　　*　　*　　*

Several hours later, in the early evening, Grant and Blanche arrived at Glastonbury Tor, the reputed site of the legendary Camelot. And then the next day, they stood on a cliff in the southwest of Wales, overlooking the Atlantic Ocean at Tintangel, another ancient site of untold glory and long ago lore inextricably mixed with the name of valor. As they stood on the coast with the fall in the air, Grant's cell phone rang.

"My friend, I am here. I'm behind you in the coffee shop, overlooking the terrain. I spoke with Oz yesterday. He has plans. May I speak with you and intrude upon your reverie with that beautiful woman?"

"You already have," replied Grant. He turned around to see the coffee shop at a distance, where Thomas stood on its outdoor veranda, binoculars trained on Grant. Grant waved, and Thomas responded. Blanche blessed the moment with a smile and again looked out to sea. And for all three, there was the realization that the delight in investigating the past filled the present and promised a future of untold and unexpected intrigues, adventures, and crucibles in which the strongest steel would be forged or broken.

*　　*　　*　　*　　*

Two weeks later, Beth Chisolm, Grant's grandmother, opened the letter from Dennis Bernard, who offered that the search for her beloved had at last come to an end. Explaining the details as well as he could without revealing the exact location of his remains when they were found, he also sent her a small urn.

"Herein," he wrote, "are the remains of a friend, a companion": her husband. That evening, Beth Chisolm finished her knitting and took care of the dog, then lay down in her bed, the same one in which she had passed her first night as a bride, as she held the urn with both hands before lifting off the lid. Squeezing some of the ashes between her right thumb and two of her fingers, she touched the ashes to her eyelids, then to her ears, to her nostrils, and then to her lips and her tongue. She rested, feeling again his touch, sensing his musky smell, and seeing his face once more. She felt the weight of his embrace, which caused her to tremble as she heard him call her name. She had fended off the suitors who could not know of his presence. She had waited a generation, and she again tasted the sorrow of mortality and felt the yearning to be held by a man who belonged to his nation as well as to her. That night, she held the urn tightly against her and then, as the sun came up, secure in the knowledge that her beloved had at last come home to rest, she turned her back on it and embraced the remnants of the night with a vitality that stilled her heart. She breathed him in one last time, turning her own flesh into kindred dust and mixing the mysterious elements of being into its quintessence and into the majesty of a quiet leaving. She was grace.

*　　*　　*　　*　　*

High on a Munro overlooking Loch Maree stood a solitary shepherd gazing off into the distance at the quiet and strangely forlorn-looking Vanderkin estate. Telly Cromarty wondered at the recent lack of activity in the surrounding area: no cars, no unexpected demise of his sheep, and no talk of mysterious beasts wandering the Highlands in the late of night. Braced against a sudden wind off the north Atlantic, he looked again at his sheep perched like small white clouds on the mountainside. The cool air caused him to thrust both hands into his jacket, where the fingers of his right hand touched a cigarette butt. Not a smoker himself, he wondered at it and then remembered having picked it up some time ago, intending to use it as a clue to determine who might be responsible for the death of his sheep. He held the cigarette in his hand, examined it for a moment, and then said, "Nasty habit," and flicked it into the wind.

*　　*　　*　　*　　*

In the forgotten space of a Crusader castle in Bodrum, Turkey, silent blood, now dry and embedded in the rough-hewn stone of a cellar cut off from life, from light, and from the memory of all but the few, memorialized the body of a saint who sanctified its surroundings. The spirit of a good and holy man continued to linger, consoled by the grief of those whom he knew to be anxious at his disappearance and by the hoped-for redemption of those who assailed him in the pursuit of knowledge. This was a knowledge that he had retained amidst the most horrible of travail.

Tortured beyond human endurance, he had remained silent as he fled to the consoling breast of his creator and redeemer. The secret that others sought remained as deep in his psyche, as deep in the penetrating world of time, and as far removed from the unenlightened who sought to force him to speak, as the world of the dead was from the world of the living. The cup before him had not passed, and even his enemies were blessed at the blood he had spilt at their malice. No Saul could pass by without wanting to change his name.

Printed in the United States
215048BV00001B/7/P